DARK HORSE

NATE TEMPLE SERIES BOOK 16

SHAYNE SILVERS

ARGENTO PUBLISHING

CONTENTS

The Nate Temple Series—A warning	1
Prologue	3
Chapter 1	17
Chapter 2	22
Chapter 3	28
Chapter 4	35
Chapter 5	43
Chapter 6	48
Chapter 7	53
Chapter 8	58
Chapter 9	63
Chapter 10	68
Chapter 11	74
Chapter 12	80
Chapter 13	86
Chapter 14	92
Chapter 15	98
Chapter 16	105
Chapter 17	111
Chapter 18	116
Chapter 19	120
Chapter 20	127
Chapter 21	134
Chapter 22	139
Chapter 23	145
Chapter 24	149
Chapter 25	155
Chapter 26	160
Chapter 27	166
Chapter 28	172
Chapter 29	176
Chapter 30	181
Chapter 31	185
Chapter 32	190
Chapter 33	196
Chapter 34	202

Chapter 35   207
Chapter 36   211
Chapter 37   218
Chapter 38   223
Chapter 39   229
Chapter 40   233
Chapter 41   239
Chapter 42   245
Chapter 43   251
Chapter 44   258
Chapter 45   265
Chapter 46   269
Chapter 47   274
Chapter 48   279
Chapter 49   284
Chapter 50   290
Chapter 51   296
Chapter 52   301
TRY: UNCHAINED (FEATHERS AND FIRE #1)   307
TRY: WHISKEY GINGER (PHANTOM QUEEN DIARIES # 1)   313

MAKE A DIFFERENCE   317
ACKNOWLEDGMENTS   319
ABOUT SHAYNE SILVERS   321
BOOKS BY SHAYNE SILVERS   323

Shayne Silvers

Dark Horse

Nate Temple Series Book 16

A TempleVerse Series

ISBN: 978-1-947709-88-1

© 2022, Shayne Silvers / Argento Publishing, LLC

info@shaynesilvers.com

THE NATE TEMPLE SERIES—A WARNING

Nate Temple starts out with everything most people could ever wish for—money, magic, and notoriety. He's a local celebrity in St. Louis, Missouri—even if the fact that he's a wizard is still a secret to the world at large.

Nate is also a bit of a...well, let's call a spade a spade. He can be a mouthy, smart-assed jerk. Like the infamous Sherlock Holmes, I specifically chose to give Nate glaring character flaws to overcome rather than making him a chivalrous Good Samaritan. He's a black hat wizard, an anti-hero—and you are now his partner in crime. He is going to make a *ton* of mistakes. And like a buddy cop movie, you are more than welcome to yell, laugh and curse at your new partner as you ride along together through the deadly streets of St. Louis.

Despite Nate's flaws, there's also something *endearing* about him...You soon catch whispers of a firm moral code buried deep under all his snark and arrogance. A diamond waiting to be polished. And you, the esteemed reader, will soon find yourself laughing at things you really shouldn't be laughing at. It's part of Nate's charm. Call it his magic...

So don't take yourself, or any of the characters in my world, too seriously. Life is too short for that nonsense.

Get ready to cringe, cackle, cry, curse, and—ultimately—*cheer* on this snarky wizard as he battles or befriends angels, demons, myths, gods, shifters, vampires and many other flavors of dangerous supernatural beings.

DON'T FORGET!

DON'T FORGET! VIP's get early access to all sorts of Temple-Verse goodies, including signed copies, private giveaways, and advance notice of future projects. AND A FREE NOVELLA! Click the image or join here: www.shaynesilvers.com/l/219800

FOLLOW AND **LIKE:**

Shayne's FACEBOOK PAGE:

www.shaynesilvers.com/l/38602

I try to respond to all messages, so don't hesitate to drop me a line. Not interacting with readers is the biggest travesty that most authors can make. Let me fix that.

PROLOGUE

Bellefontaine Cemetery was dark and cold and eerily silent. Nadia and her daughter, Asha, seemed to have the place to themselves. Fat snowflakes drifted down from the night sky, dusting the cemetery in a patchy layer of white death—much like how the first shovelful of brown dirt thumped and skittered over the top of a shiny new coffin after a loved one was lowered into the ground.

The sound of that hollow *thump* striking her husband's coffin one month ago still haunted her dreams, mockingly reminding her of the time he'd knocked on her apartment door for their first date.

Then that same hollow *thump* had hit her son's coffin in the adjacent grave, reminding Nadia of the first time he'd kicked inside her womb, giving his mommy a thump of his own. His first hello.

The terrorist attack at the St. Louis Arch last month had taken her boys from her, leaving Nadia and Asha all alone in a world seemingly gone mad. Two simple headstones were all that was left of her boys, now.

Henry Pickwick. Loving husband and father.

Thomas Pickwick. Loving son and brother.

Nadia brushed her dark graying hair out of her face and tucked it behind her ear. The cemetery was peacefully silent as Nadia watched Asha kneeling before the two fresh tombstones in the withered grass. Although fifteen years old, she looked so much younger and smaller on her knees before the silent stones. Her dark hair fanned down her back, and her fingers trembled as she reached out to touch the words etched into the rock. They hadn't been able to afford anything special, and that harsh reality only added to Nadia's anguish. A cheap bouquet of flowers rested on each headstone. Nadia winced to see the price tag still nestled into the wilting daisies, a hurtful reminder of their financial woes.

Two bouquets for $5!

And that had almost been too much money for her to spend. It was almost Christmas, after all. Their first holiday as a broken family. She realized she was absently rubbing her belly and she hurriedly lowered her hand, relieved that Asha hadn't noticed. Every dollar counted. Diapers were going to be expensive. She hadn't told her daughter the big news yet. Nadia was determined to make the most out of the holiday, knowing it would be remembered for years to come as their first victory over trauma.

What better way to celebrate the tragedy than to tell Asha she would again get to be a big sister? That they would have the opportunity to fill the gaping holes in their lives with a new bundle of life to love and cherish? It was a small hope. A tiny yet powerful hope. A candle flame in the darkness.

Why did you leave us, Henry? Nadia thought to the stone marking the final resting place of the love of her life with a silent sob, swiftly wiping away a lone tear before her daughter happened to turn and see it. Henry hadn't known she was pregnant either. She had intended the news to be his Christmas gift. He'd always said he didn't want presents for himself, but she knew the greatest gifts she had ever given her husband had been their children, Asha and Thomas.

He had loved them fiercely and passionately. Their births were the only times she had ever seen Henry cry.

She had wanted to see him cry again...

Henry had been her childhood sweetheart. The first boy she'd danced with. First boy she'd kissed. Her whole life of firsts had been shared with Henry.

And now...

She had new terrifying, debilitating firsts to face, and she would have to do so without her husband.

Asha stared at the headstones for her father and brother with a faraway look in her eyes. She lowered her fingers and dipped her chin in silent prayer. Her shoulders trembled faintly but she made not a sound.

That silence was dangerous, and Nadia didn't know what to do about it.

Before the fateful event, the lithe teenaged girl had been the first to whip her long ebony hair back into a ponytail to get into a fight with a perceived bully, the first to get into mischief, and the first to take unreasonable risks—often roping her younger, impressionable brother Thomas into her shenanigans. Each scrape, bruise, and bandage was taken as a badge of honor to the spitfire girl. She simply did not know fear.

Or she chose to reject the premise on the principle of pure, stubborn foolishness, her mother thought with conflicting emotions of pride and concern.

In essence, Asha had been a firebrand.

Impossible for her mother and father and brother to control.

Or, as Henry had often claimed with a glint of fatherly pride in his eyes, *my girl is full of grit. It will serve her well.*

Nadia studied the strangely foreign, nymphlike creature that was her adolescent daughter, wondering whether she should be concerned or overjoyed. Asha...had changed dramatically. She no longer rebelled or took risks. She had become a ray of sunshine in every way imaginable. Nadia could tell that it was forced but it was no less genuine for it. Asha had applied her grit to turning her grief into gratitude, her agony into appreciation, her horror into happiness, and her loss into love.

It was remarkable.

As long as it was healthy. Denial was a very real concern. Therapy was too expensive with a baby on the way—everything was too expensive with a baby on the way and Henry's income abruptly halted. There were no life insurance payouts for acts of war, she'd been informed earlier today. She didn't have the money to pay a lawyer to fight the heartless claim.

Asha gasped, making Nadia jump and shift her attention to her daughter as her pulse skyrocketed. Asha lurched to her feet and pointed up at the sky, her bright green eyes as wide as could be. "An angel!" she blurted with a look of awe on her face, her ebony black hair whipping back in a sudden gust of wind.

Nadia blinked rapidly and followed her daughter's finger to see...

She sucked in a breath, clutching at her stomach. A mighty angel wearing gleaming golden armor with strange metallic wings was flying away from the front of the Temple Mausoleum, sweeping her gaze across the cemetery as if searching for evil. As if hearing Asha's declaration, the angel halted in mid-air less than a hundred feet away, flapping her wings in a steady rhythm as she turned to look directly down at them.

The angel looked nothing like any stories Nadia had ever heard. She was a stunningly beautiful woman. Her blonde hair seemed to glow, backlit by the moon's luminescence. She wore gleaming armor that looked like it was designed for a queen of old, except it had a crimson hue to it like it was spattered with blood. Her wings were not feathers, but looked more like two fans of golden swords. Her face was stark and beautiful.

And deadly.

But her eyes...

One was blue and one was green, and they seemed to contain living fire within.

The angel pointed a shining trident directly at Nadia and Asha, and a commanding voice struck their ears in an urgent whisper, even though she was too far away for such a thing to be possible. The hair on the back of Nadia's neck stuck straight up as the angel seemed to speak directly into her ears. The look on Asha's face told Nadia she was experiencing the same thing.

"Get your children out of here, woman! HIDE!" the angel commanded. Nadia jerked her hand away from her belly like it was a hot potato. The angel had said *children*, plural. She'd somehow recognized the idle action of a pregnant woman fondly rubbing her belly. Or the angel had looked into her heart and soul and seen the truth.

Asha grasped her mother's hand, squeezing it tightly as she stared, slack-jawed at the angel. Nadia was too startled to react, staring up at the impossibility like a deer in headlights.

The angel let out a string of violent curses seemingly directed at Nadia and Asha. Angels couldn't curse, could they? And was her golden armor covered in blood, or was that some trick of the moonlight? The mesmerizing angel swiveled in the air as if deciding to approach them, but she halted as a ball of fire as big as a man abruptly screamed through the air towards her, coming from somewhere behind the Mausoleum—the same place she'd fled moments before. Nadia heard men shouting from that direction, but she was too transfixed with the fireball to look for them. The flames were yellow and blue, and its passage illuminated the cemetery in a blinding glow. Somehow, Nadia knew it was a deadly projectile rather than some kind of firework or flare shot into the sky. The fire looked...alive. Hungry. The angel dodged it with a sweep of her wings, and her face contorted into a look of despair and outrage, torn between two difficult decisions. A second and third fireball came screaming towards her, making the decision for her. With a frustrated snarl, she took off in the opposite direction from Nadia and Asha, racing across the night sky like a shooting star. She abruptly winked out of existence between one moment and the next, leaving Nadia and Asha physically shaking.

The two fireballs arced downward from their missed target and struck a stand of trees near the entrance to the cemetery. The trees instantly ignited into towering pillars of flame like the Gates of Hell.

Nadia swept her gaze across the cemetery, taking the angel's words to heart. They needed to hide. Right now. This part of the cemetery was wide open and making a run for the cemetery's exit would put them in full view of the fighting men. Nadia knew they wouldn't want witnesses to their battle, so she couldn't risk anyone seeing them. The surrounding tomb-stones were too small to hide behind and would only hide them from one angle. If anyone scouted the area, they would be caught out in the open.

She wished she hadn't left her phone in the car. She didn't see the men who had launched the fire into the air, but she could now hear plenty of screams and shouts, roaring of fire, beastly growls, and the sound of metal striking metal. The fact that she couldn't see the source of the noises only made the scene more terrifying. Every shadow looked sinister and threatening.

There was only one hope for safety. She turned to face the Temple Mausoleum.

The large gothic building loomed over the cemetery, looking like it had been plucked out of medieval Europe and settled here. The building was massive, sporting tall statues of fantastical creatures and gods from various religions. She recognized only a few of the more iconic figures—like Zeus, Thor, and Anubis—but the others were only vaguely familiar.

The Temple Mausoleum must have cost a fortune to build.

The late Calvin and Makayla Temple had been industrial tycoons of some sort. All Nadia knew was that the name was considered nobility in St. Louis, and the heir was a degenerate playboy named Nate Temple.

Well, she didn't know anything about him, but that's what all her friends at church claimed. Greta supposedly knew him, but Greta seemed to despise everyone who didn't attend church on a regular basis. She hadn't seen Greta in what felt like years. The cantankerous old woman had supposedly moved to Kansas City to work at a Catholic Church of some kind. Maybe her grandson had moved there and she'd chosen to follow him. He'd often come to visit her over the summers. What had his name been? Yahn? Something foreign. She dismissed the line of thought, knowing time was not a luxury to waste.

The statues lining the sides of the building were large and Nadia spotted plenty of hiding places behind them where they would be hidden from multiple angles. "Let's go," she urged her daughter. And then the two were running towards the building, pounding through the snow like they were fleeing a pack of wolves. The statue of the jackal-headed Anubis was the largest and closest, granting them the biggest space to hide behind. Unfortunately, it was also closest to the front corner of the Mausoleum, but it was safer than the risk of being quickly discovered behind a smaller statue.

They ducked behind the jackal-headed god in a little space between the wall of the building and the base of the statue. They tucked their legs close so as not to be spotted if any of the dangerous men circled the building. Nadia clutched her daughter in a tight hug, holding her close and whispering reassuring prayers into her daughter's raven-black hair.

Shouts now filled the air, along with screams. So many screams. *Slice. Scream. Cut. Scream. Slash. Scream...*

She could have sworn she heard beastly growls and roars intermixed with men shouting, but that was impossible. St. Louis didn't have animal predators. Especially nothing large enough to make sounds like that.

Nadia knew, beyond a shadow of a doubt, that the men around the corner were not common men brawling—no one brawled in a cemetery because the only times large groups of people visited were for funerals. There was a taste of madness in the air. The whiff of death. This wasn't just a fistfight; this was a battle. Men were dying. A lot of men. And they seemed to be drawing closer to their hiding spot, spilling out around the front of the building.

She felt a wave of panic threaten to overwhelm her, reminding her of the chaos in the aftermath of the explosion at the Arch. Everyone running and screaming, the fiery debris falling from the sky, the cloying smoke, and the hundreds of impossibly large feathers raining down from the sky that no one had ever bothered to explain in the news. The National Guard now openly patrolled the streets in military vehicles and St. Louis was under curfew. Nadia and Asha had broken curfew to come to the cemetery tonight because her double-shifts at work had given them no other option.

Unfortunately, these men had done the same.

Lightning cracked down from the sky in rapid succession and she heard more screaming, fireballs tearing through men and beast alike, judging by the feral screams. She...was losing her mind. Was she in shock?

She clutched her daughter protectively in the shadows behind Anubis' statue. "They won't find us—"

The world abruptly flashed white and Nadia's ears popped from a deafening explosion.

Nadia let out a whimpering groan as pain rippled through her body and the world spun crazily. She realized she was now lying on a cold floor, her cheek pressed against polished marble, but she couldn't remember how she'd gotten here. She blinked in confusion. Dust filled the air and she coughed into her elbow, blinking away warm liquid dripping into her eyes. She wiped the back of her hand across her face and looked down to see it covered in blood. She gasped in horror, immediately clutching at her belly. She found no wounds and let out a cough of relief to find no injury that put her baby at risk.

"Mom," Asha whispered groggily from a few feet away. The dust and debris made it impossible to see her daughter and she no longer felt the cold winter wind on her cheeks. The air was oddly warm, in fact.

"I'm here, Asha," Nadia whispered, reaching out blindly with her bloody hand. Her ears rang and everything sounded oddly muted and muffled. She saw several small fires through the dusty air and she could even feel their heat. "Are you okay?"

"A little banged up but I'm okay," Asha whispered back as she grasped

Nadia's hand and then came into view, emerging from the dust like a specter. "The wall exploded. I think we're inside the Mausoleum."

Nadia bit back a sob to feel her daughter's fingers clutching hers. It didn't matter how they had gotten inside the building, but they were definitely still in danger. The men had blown up the building.

She saw a motionless silhouette towering over them through the smoke—another statue of some kind, although much smaller than the one outside—and she promptly tugged her daughter towards it, scrambling over chunks of stone and other unknown debris. "Let's hide back here, Asha," she whispered, shoving Asha ahead of her.

It was some kind of tomb with a statue looming behind it. Asha tucked herself back against the wall behind the statue, making room for her mother. They clutched each other in the smoke and shadows as the sounds of pitched battle continued in the near distance.

Suddenly, Asha flinched and let out a hiss of pain, followed by the sound of metal scraping across stone.

"What is it?" Nadia whispered, her pulse thundering in her ears.

"I cut my finger on some hot metal," Asha whispered, shoving a finger in her mouth. "I thought it was a person. A body," she amended with a shudder. "I'm okay. Just startled me."

"Let me see," she breathed, reaching past her daughter with a trembling hand into the darkness. Fire flickered on the ground behind Asha, so the metal must have absorbed the heat. Her fingers touched cold metal and she instinctively recoiled. It was not hot in the slightest, but she said nothing. Everyone made mistakes when fear gripped them. The object hadn't responded to her touch, so she doubted it was a person. She held her breath as she reached out again. This time, her fingers touched the cold metal and she swiftly trailed them over the surface, trying to determine what it was. "It...feels like a...helmet," she murmured with a frown, suddenly understanding why Asha had thought it was a body. Had it fallen from one of the tombs? The Temples were an old family and she could easily imagine sets of armor lying around their Mausoleum. It must have tumbled over in the explosion and fallen too close to the fire—

"I hear little mice scheming and plotting," a man's voice snarled from directly in front of them, and a face suddenly broke through the smoke, hovering before Nadia and her daughter. He had long, black, greasy hair, and his blue eyes were cold and heartless. His features were gaunt and angular, emphasized by a deep cleft in his chin. "What have we here? A sorceress and her apprentice?"

Nadia squealed, snatching the helmet on instinct and lifting it up between her and the threat as she leaned away from those cruel eyes. "Please don't hurt us! We are innocent women, not...what you just called us!" she pleaded. "We were paying our respects in the cemetery when—"

"Silence, you filthy old hag," the man snapped, and then a ball of angry-looking blue and yellow flame crackled into life above his palm, illuminating the area just enough to reveal two men standing behind him but not enough for Nadia to make out their faces. Nadia recoiled, recognizing the flame as the same that had been thrown at the angel in the sky. She didn't know how he was making it, but she knew how dangerous it was.

Was this the infamous Nate Temple? He looked manic and murderous and...*excited*, all at the same time. His eyes locked onto the helmet in her hands and he grinned wolfishly as he grabbed for it. "She has a suit! I claim it as mine!" Nadia reflexively pulled away, instinctively wanting to protect the baby in her belly.

The man took it as her attempting to steal his prize.

She never saw a knife in his hand—in fact, he never took his hand off the helmet—but she felt something long and sharp tear into her belly. Something invisible. She gasped, feeling as if someone had sucked the air right out from her lungs. Agony rippled outwards from her belly and she struggled to breathe against the sudden fiery, wet pain. The man snatched the helmet from her hands and climbed to his feet with a deep, triumphant chuckle.

Nadia could hardly think straight and she heard Asha screaming wildly, clutching at her shoulders and face, incoherent with fear. Nadia glanced down and saw a bloody, sucking wound in her belly. She gasped, clasping her hands over the wound, swearing to any god who would have her to keep her unborn baby safe.

"What a hero, Martin," one of the other men said in a dismissive tone, sounding as if he was walking away. "She's a Regular, not a sorceress. Leave her be, brother."

"And what about the filthy little urchin behind her?" the first man—Martin—snarled.

"L-leave...us...alone," Asha whispered in a hollow, terrified whisper. "P-please..."

"Oh, no!" the second man scoffed, sounding farther away. "Beware of the deadly tweenager!"

Another man chuckled his agreement, but his voice faded as he departed deeper into the Mausoleum. "You got your suit, so it's time to fucking run before Temple shows up. Follow the plan."

Martin muttered a curse as he stomped out of view. He let out a hungry chuckle and there was a strange whispering sound. He let out a triumphant *huff* and then laughed. "See you on the other side. If you're lucky. Arete, brothers," he added with a malicious laugh.

Silence answered Martin, his two supposed friends apparently off to hunt for their own treasures from the Mausoleum.

Nadia sucked in a breath, struggling to dampen the pain tearing through her abdomen. She reached out a shaking hand to squeeze Asha's leg reassuringly. "We need to leave, Asha," she whispered, biting back a sob of pain. Blood seeped out from between her fingers as she tried to maintain pressure on her belly with her other hand.

Asha grabbed onto her shoulders and wrapped her up in a tight hug. "Are you okay, mommy?" she sobbed, burying her face into Nadia's neck. "Did he punch your belly?" she asked, sounding more alarmed than such an injury would warrant. Had Asha...known she was pregnant? She obviously hadn't seen a knife either. The man truly hadn't moved, so Nadia had no idea how she'd been stabbed. By what?

It didn't matter at the moment, so Nadia nodded stiffly. "Don't worry about me, honey. We need to find a new hiding spot," she whispered, struggling to disguise the agony tearing through her mind, body, and soul. *The baby! I need to go to the hospital!*

But she knew she was in no shape to shamble through a war zone to their car. Not with men like Martin out there. Strangely, she felt a wash of heat rip through her, almost as if she was feverish. She glanced down at her stomach and saw the wound was black at the edges. And the black poison seemed to be spreading across her skin, radiating outward right before her eyes as if it was sentient.

In that moment, Nadia was certain that she would not leave this Mausoleum alive.

Another figure abruptly materialized out of the smoke, their face looming only inches away from Nadia's nose, but their head was hooded, shrouding their face in shadow. Nadia immediately panicked, pressing Asha behind her. The person gently but firmly clamped a hand over Nadia's mouth and held a finger over where their lips would be, shaking their head. "It isn't safe here. Follow me," a calm voice said from within the hood, and Nadia could not tell if it was male or female, but they did seem to have an accent of some kind.

"Who are you?" Asha demanded in a threatening tone.

Instead of answering, the stranger wrapped an arm beneath Nadia's shoulder and around her back and pulled her to her feet. Nadia bit her cheek to keep from crying out as she felt blood ooze out of her wound. She tugged her coat tighter to conceal the severity of the wound from Asha, not wanting to alarm her further until they knew they were safe. Thankfully, the dust in the air helped her conceal it. The hooded figure glanced down at Nadia's bloody hand, definitely noticing the wound. But the stranger said nothing.

Nadia stubbornly straightened her shoulders and detached herself from the person to stand on her own two feet without assistance. Asha clutched her mother's hand and they both faced the black hooded stranger with no face. "Thank you," Nadia whispered, gritting her teeth. She knew dangerous men still prowled the Mausoleum so she gestured for the figure to lead on.

The hooded stranger nodded and turned to creep deeper into the mausoleum. Nadia ignored the numerous statues hugging the walls, squeezing Asha's hand reassuringly when her daughter noticed them with a sharp intake of breath.

Nadia heard men shouting and whispering throughout the mausoleum, which apparently sported several different hallways. The place was much bigger on the inside than it had appeared from the exterior.

Thankfully, none of the voices noticed their passing as the stranger came to a halt before a short-walled pool of water in what seemed like the center of the mausoleum. The back wall of the fountain was decorated with a large tree, except the roots of the tree seemed even more prominent and extensive than the branches. Asha gasped, pointing at what appeared to be rubies and sapphires marking each root. Nadia squinted and noticed names etched into the stone beside each gem. She frowned. An inverted family tree? She had never heard of such a thing.

The Temple family was exceedingly, maddeningly queer.

The stranger pointed into the pool, motioning for them to hurry. Nadia frowned, noticing the shallow pool had only a few inches of water. Then her eyes widened to see that the base of the pool opened downward into a waterslide. The water spilled down the slide yet the pool did not drain away, obviously recirculating the water somehow. Nadia thought she recognized a staircase running parallel to the slide, but it was too dark to tell. It looked like some kind of secret exit rather than an established feature of the mausoleum. There were no ornate decorations or stone carvings like the rest of the Mausoleum.

"You'll be safer down there," the stranger said, pointing at the slide. Voices from the mausoleum drew closer and Nadia heard a steady metallic pounding sound like running feet fast approaching. "Hurry up! You've only got a few seconds before they arrive!"

Asha squeezed her mother's hand and nodded. "We have no other choice, mom."

They approached the slide and clutched hands as they sat down in the shallow warm water, hanging their feet over the lip of the slide that led down into nothingness. Nadia bit her lip, biting back a cry of pain as the movement wrenched at her stomach. Her eyes watered at the effort.

"I've got no idea what you'll find down there," the stranger said from behind them, "but whatever it is, try not to make any noise. That'll only bring trouble. Just keep quiet and stay hidden."

"Are you sure—" Nadia began.

"I'm sure. Your job is to protect your daughter, so focus on that. Trust me, she'll need it."

"What?" Nadia whispered. "Why would you say that?"

"There's no time," the stranger replied, faintly exasperated. "Just know that she's been marked, and that only the Dark Horse can save her, now."

"The Dark Horse?" Nadia whispered.

"What can I say? Destiny can be a real bitch sometimes?"

The stranger cursed and waved a hand over them as though bestowing some sort of blessing, at which point Nadia felt a soothing warmth settle over her and her daughter. Asha shuddered at the sensation, a faint smile tugging at one corner of her mouth.

The footsteps were getting louder and she could hear voices rapidly approaching. Many voices. The stranger stepped into a shadow and abruptly disappeared. Nadia pursed her lips and squeezed her daughter's hand with false reassurance. "Don't make a peep, Asha," she whispered. Then, in utter silence, they pushed themselves down into the darkness.

The abyss swallowed them and Nadia silently prayed that whatever or whoever this so-called Dark Horse was would keep Asha safe after she died.

1

I surveyed the dystopian landscape of dust, blackened trees, and sun scorched rock. Embers and sparks danced through the black sky of the Elder realm, looking like we stood in the heart of a raging wild-fire—but there was no fire. The crimson moon hung pregnant in the sky, thrice as large as the moon in St. Louis. Maybe it looked bigger because we stood near the top of a mountain that overlooked the infamous wizard-lizards' home. A turbulent stream of water—emanating from the Temple catacombs behind us—roared past my boots, coalescing into a colossal waterfall that tumbled down several hundred feet to crash into a pool far, far below.

I clenched my jaw in frustration, not seeing anyone to fight or pursue. No evil wizard Knightmares prancing about. No Talon. No Carl. I ran a hand through my hair and growled at Grimm, who was standing beside me, "Where do we even start?"

Grimm had arrived minutes before, trotting down the stairs that ran parallel to the waterslide from the Mausoleum as if it was not the strangest thing in the world. He'd complained about not being able to travel here via magic, even though his magic had informed him that I had entered the Elder realm.

His eyes blazed with an infernal hunger as he considered my question. "Well, I'm going to start with fucking that unicorn," he growled in a tone that made his first stab at romance—at least to my recollection—sound more like a lethal threat in a boss fight as opposed to a heartwarming quote from *The Notebook*.

His tone and choice of words hit me like a Gibbs' slap to the back of the head, and I flinched, frowned, and then glanced over at him with a judgmental stare. "Dude," I said, shaking my head. "Who are you even *talking* about?"

For the record, unicorns were nothing like the majestic, noble creatures depicted in childhood bedtime stories and cartoons. Real unicorns were NC-17-rated, homicidal deviants only found in the unabridged, raw manuscript of the Brothers Grimm journals.

Foul, wicked, remorseless, murderous beasts. But I still loved Grimm. He just had some starkly rough edges that desperately needed to be domesticated.

Grimm flared his wings out in a restless gesture, causing the red orbs at the tips of his long, black, peacock-like feathers to spatter me with blood because, well, for some strange reason, the red orbs on his feathers were constantly damp with actual blood. My unicorn was painted in the aesthetic palette of violence incarnate—the midnight-black and virgin-blood-red of an unrepentant murderer.

His eyes burned with a fiery glow and, when he was angry enough, strips of fire occasionally danced across his flesh like cracks in stone, revealing molten lava within. I didn't ask unnecessary questions of my unicorn.

His long gnarly horn was actually a fairly new prosthetic I had made out of crystallized rainbow after some asshole had broken off his original horn and stabbed him in the chest with it. Said asshole was later impaled by a spear through the heart and left dangling on Camelot's castle wall. Since Grimm had wings, he was technically an alicorn, but he used the terms interchangeably. I was fairly certain that he saw wingless unicorns as unfortunate cripples doomed for extinction.

Empathic, Grimm was not.

He tucked his wings back close to his body and shook his mane in agitation, spattering me with *more* blood. I frowned, comparing his colors to the black sky with the red moon silhouetted behind him. I'd first met Grimm in the dark lands beyond the Dueling Grounds, an inky abyss of darkness and terror that seemed to at least share the same weather patterns with the Elder realm. Were the two places connected in some way?

Grimm still hadn't answered my question, so I followed his gaze, squinting as I scanned the desolate plains far below us. Then I blinked in surprise and rubbed my eyes to make sure I wasn't imagining things. A white unicorn ambled across the unforgiving landscape, passing by a thicket of bushy, thorny shrubbery, unfazed by the ever-present embers and sparks dancing on the warm breeze. I cocked my head curiously, noting the wild unicorn's pristine white wings. The creature looked too...*pretty* to be here. Other than the wild unicorn, I saw no other signs of life below us. Last time I'd been here there had been numerous Elders peppering the landscape and staring up at the new waterfall spilling down the mountainside—because the water had been damned up inside my family's catacombs until I opened the door to the Mausoleum.

So...where was everyone? Had Aiden's Knightmares already killed them all? Were they in hiding?

As we watched the lone unicorn, it suddenly galloped forward in a burst of speed, and a massive wolf-like creature howled as it leapt out of the thicket and fled on all fours. It looked to be twice the size of the unicorn and had long spikes all over its back like a porcupine.

Grimm stopped breathing and his nostrils flared with excitement.

The unicorn screamed a horrifying shriek and then impaled the spine-wolf with a single blow. At least I was guessing it had impaled the spine-wolf with its horn, because all I saw after contact was an explosion of blue mist like a grenade had gone off in the center of the creature. I realized I was leaning dangerously far out over the cliff, transfixed by the violent confrontation. "What the fuck is the blue stuff?"

"Blood," Grimm whispered in a strange tone.

The cloud of blue blood faded away and I saw the two distinct, spiky black halves of the spine-wolf splattered on the ground. The unicorn's elegant white coat was now painted in blue blood, and it was calmly chomping on one half of the black carcass much as a normal horse would clip the grass.

I slowly turned to look at Grimm with a stupefied expression. "Well. You sure know how to pick 'em."

He neighed loudly and his whole body shuddered. "I am in love," he whispered dreamily. "Is this what it feels like when you see Kára bury her axes into an enemy or impale them with her trident?" he asked absently. Before I could respond that, no, as a matter of fact that was never my first reaction to Kara's violent actions, Grimm continued. "I am *definitely* going to fuck that beast of a mare. Even if it kills me."

I sighed. "Priorities, man."

Gunnar stepped up beside me, no longer in his Horseman form. Thankfully, he hadn't been paying attention to our conversation or he would have had to wash Grimm's mouth out with soap.

He wore jeans and a tank top that he'd found in my bottomless satchel. His other clothes had been shredded and covered in blood and guts, and I always carried spare clothes for the shifters in my crew. He only had one eye, which was inconvenient for me whenever I wanted to get his attention.

I'd resorted to snapping my fingers, which he'd quickly learned to ignore. I'd called him inconsiderate. He'd ignored that too, the jerk.

Where his other eye used to be was now a stone eyepatch that was fused to his skin—whether a consequence of our bond as friends or as Horsemen, I wasn't entirely sure. The quartz-like eyepatch matched my Horseman armor whenever I put on the Mask of Hope. Sometimes he put a normal eyepatch over it so he could avoid the topic of explaining how stone was fused to his flesh. I'd informed him that he could switch it to his good eye and it would double as a sleeping mask.

He'd punched me in the stomach and then walked away, leaving me wheezing on the floor. For a man with one eye, his ability to target the solar plexus was alarmingly accurate.

"The entrance is blocked," he said, snapping me out of my thoughts. "We are officially trapped here." He sounded livid.

"You sure?" I asked him, clenching my fists at my sides. We had only been here ten minutes, but a few seconds after Grimm's arrival, the secret hatch leading back up to the Mausoleum had slammed shut. I'd felt only a brief pulse of power, too quick to do anything about, before the door sealed, trapping us in the Elder realm. Yet the water continued flowing from above, even though it wasn't possible for water to flow through solid stone.

"Fucking half-brothers, am I right?" Grimm muttered.

2

I clenched my jaw, agreeing with his allegation. Who else could have trapped us down here? But it also made no sense whatsoever. The Mausoleum had been secure, and we had sensed six Knightmares enter the Elder realm, so how the fuck could he have trapped us here? Some kind of timed spell over the entrance?

Had Grimm triggered it somehow?

Knowing it was a trap, I hadn't wanted to try making a Gateway or Shadow Walking back up to the Mausoleum. Aiden would have anticipated that. He wouldn't have wasted the effort of locking the door if the solution was as simple as me using my magic to get back out. And Grimm had also complained about not being able to travel directly here.

The more I thought about it, I had a gut feeling that making a Gateway or Shadow Walking was a terrible idea. I didn't even want to risk using a Tiny Ball until I reunited with Carl to ask him some specific questions on the Elder realm.

I saw Kára out of the corner of my eye, pacing back and forth inside the catacombs. She looked agitated about something—probably the door.

Gunnar nodded, bringing my attention back to the scene before me. "I huffed and I puffed and everything. The door back up to the Mausoleum is secure. Our Knights agree that Aiden and his five Knightmares are still out there," Gunnar said, scowling at the wasteland before us. "As are Talon and Carl." I let out a sigh of relief. At least we had confirmation through their strange GPS tracking ability. "At least no one can sneak up behind us," Gunnar said with a resigned sigh. I nodded, relieved to know that no more wizards or Fae or Einharjar would be able to flank us while we were hunting down Aiden's new Knightmares. Fresh on the heels of our fight in Fae and then at Bellefontaine Cemetery, we'd entered the catacombs beneath the Mausoleum ready for round three—an immediate fight against Aiden's Knightmare wizards. Unfortunately, we had quickly realized that there were no immediate threats waiting for us. The cowards had run away, deeper into the Elder realm. I noticed Grinder standing on the other side of Gunnar.

"It's a great plan," Grinder said, standing beside Gunnar. I hadn't noticed him in the giant man's shadow. "Burn the longboats behind us. Straight up Viking vengeance! Thor would have totally loved it." The murder goat surveyed the landscape far below with an almost excited smile.

"Except we didn't burn the boats. We fell right into an obvious trap," I muttered.

He shrugged dismissively, not looking remotely concerned. In a way, he wasn't wrong. This didn't change what we had come here to do. We were here to hunt, and it seemed that the Knightmares wanted to make sure we hunted them. I would oblige, but I didn't want our passion for vengeance to get us snared in one of Aiden's likely traps.

Grinder leaned over the edge with a mischievous grin, assessing the waterfall beside us as it crashed into a wide pool hundreds of feet below us. A wide black river stretched out from the pool, slithering out into the Elder realm like a giant serpent. That was new—a result of me bringing back the waterfall the last time I was here. "How many bones do you think I would break by jumping?" Grinder asked, licking his lips eagerly.

"Don't," I said. "I don't want our food to get soggy."

"And who knows what kind of parasites might live in that water," Gunnar added, frowning at the water running from the cavern behind us.

"Somebody dare me. Please," Grinder begged, checking each of our faces for approval. Thankfully, everyone ignored him and he let out a long-suffering grunt. I studied him sidelong, prepared to grab him with a tendril of magic if he tried to jump anyway. Thankfully, he chose to remain in place, but he did have a dreamy look in his eyes that made me twitchy.

He was probably fantasizing about the numerous different ways he could be brutally murdered here, because he and his brother were like the mythical phoenix—they came back to life the day after they were killed. And they absolutely *loved* getting killed. It was pretty much their most favorite thing ever.

I frowned at a new thought. "Is your brother going to be able to make it past the locked door?" I asked the sadomasochist goat, knowing Snarler would be reborn sometime soon.

Grimm's ears swiveled towards the conversation but he kept his fiery eyes on the feasting unicorn.

"Oh, sure," Grinder said. "We show up wherever our boss is."

"I wasn't able to do it," Grimm said, not breaking eye contact with his romantic conquest.

Gunnar frowned and turned to look down at the goat. "Really? How?"

Grinder opened his mouth to respond and then bleated. "Hold on. Gotta pinch one off really quick."

I pursed my lips. "That's just gross."

"Noted. The wizard is not into butt stuff," Grinder said. He flicked up his tail and made a straining sound deep in his throat, heralding the arrival of a stream of noxious pebbles.

We stepped away from him with an assortment of muttered curses. Grinder hopped up and down excitedly for a few moments and then looked back up at me. "Much better! To answer your question, I don't know how we get back here. Magic? Some kind of bond to Mjolnir? All I know is that the Bifrost sends us back to our boss."

I glanced at Mjolnir, which was hanging from a thick leather belt at Gunnar's waist. Gunnar caressed it with his thumb, studying it pensively. He looked up at me and I shrugged, not having any further explanation for him. It was curious that Grinder mentioned the Bifrost as his traveling option. Grimm had broken the Bifrost back when we fought Thor, and then Odin had later demanded that we repair it again. Thankfully, we had.

Odin had warned me that he would not be able to dismiss such a crime, and that it would bring grave consequences unless I fixed it. Had he known I would later need the goats back then? Or that Gunnar would?

Maybe he hadn't been threatening me. Maybe he'd been warning me the only way he knew how.

With another fucking secret.

I needed a damned godly decoder ring to keep up with the various pantheons' gods and their allegedly altruistic schemes that always seemed to ruin my day.

Maybe we could ride the Bifrost out of here when it was time to leave. Barring that, I had no idea how we were going to get back home without Gateways or Tiny Balls. There was also the chance that when Snarler tried to come back, he wouldn't be able to make it through whatever ward seemed to be shutting off the Elder realm. Like Grimm's failed attempt.

"Why didn't you try riding the rainbow bridge, Grimm?" Gunnar asked, smirking at the word rainbow, knowing it would piss off the unicorn.

"Suck a micropenis, Lassie," Grimm snapped. The harsh rebuke was more than Gunnar had anticipated, and his expectant smile shifted to a moody glare. Then Grimm lifted his front hoof and pointed his horn towards his expected conquest, like a hunting dog en pointe. "I'm going to fuck that unicorn," he said before stamping his hoof into the stone cliff, sending up a small cloud of dust. I'd already counted a dozen bones littered like dead twigs all around us, so we were definitely inhaling bone particles of...something.

Gunnar flinched upon hearing the bizarre claim. I let out a resigned sigh, shrugging. "Yeah. That."

Grinder giggled merrily. "Sweet. Now you guys get dinner *and* a show!" He stretched out one of his back legs and proclaimed, "I bring the meats!"

Gunnar pursed his lips and shook his head at the kamikaze goat before following Grimm's intense look to spot the wild unicorn. He only had one eye, so he had to try twice as hard. He stiffened in surprise and then glanced at me as if to make sure he wasn't imagining the unicorn. I nodded and shrugged again. Gunnar puffed out his chest and waved a fatherly finger at my unicorn—

Alicorn. Whatever.

"You can't do that," the werewolf chided the unicorn.

Grimm snickered dismissively. "I'm a uni-can, not a uni-can't."

Gunnar shook his head. "No. That's not how romance *works*."

Grimm snorted and stamped his hoof. "Does this look like a movie on the Hallmark channel? Who said anything about romance? This is literally how unicorns handle these situations. Dominance wins. You humans wouldn't understand."

I studied the unicorn feasting on the disemboweled spine-wolf and cocked my head pensively. "Hey, Grimm? What if it's a *guy* unicorn?"

Grimm was silent for a few moments, considering my question. Gunnar gave me a fist bump and nodded. Finally, Grimm responded with a wicked chuckle. "Well, then he is going to be *very* surprised when he makes my acquaintance."

Gunnar's eye widened in surprise. "Wait. You don't care if it's a dude?"

"It's called a joke, Gunnar," my unicorn replied drily.

Everyone was silent for a few moments, and then Gunnar fired back. "Well...what if they like *rainbows*?" he asked, smirking at the chance to turn the tide back on the horny unicorn.

Grimm's humor immediately evaporated and his eyes blazed with utter disdain as he lowered his head, looking like he was about to charge down the mountain right here and now. "Then I will impale them with my other horn," he said, and then he somehow made his glittering horn twinkle at the tip—and only the tip.

I sighed.

"Neigh means neigh," Grinder chuckled.

Someone tapped me on the shoulder and I turned to see Calvin looking up at me. His new white armor was pristine and unblemished, and it looked like a whole lot of...well, responsibility—which I was allergic to. "Whatcha talking about?" His voice cracked in the middle of his question, transforming his words into the equivalent of a drive-by trumpet blast.

Grimm snickered.

Gunnar frowned down at his son with a critical glare and Calvin practically flinched, even though he immediately pretended to act suave and in control, as if his voice hadn't just jumped three octaves.

"Spare the rod, spoil the child," Grimm said sadistically. "When a daddy unicorn is very horny—"

I cleared my throat loudly, cutting him off. Then I shook my head at him in warning. "Drop it, Grimm."

I turned back to Calvin and pretended not to notice him pointedly ignoring his father's judgmental glare. Boys needed to learn to stand up on their own two feet, especially under the scrutiny of their idols. For a teenager, Calvin looked freaking *tough*, as if he'd done hard time in gen pop at a maximum-security prison and had been sent back out to the civilian community as a stronger man with lucrative connections to the most dangerous people in town. His eyes were alert and cold, ready to make difficult decisions. Even if his voice had started cracking non-stop since our descent into the catacombs. I hoped that was a coincidence and not some kind of warning that he was about to make another drastic jump in age like when they'd been transformed from their original wolf forms into human kids for the first time.

I shrugged. "We're talking about impulse control and an utter lack of it—"

"NATE!" Kára yelled from within the cavern. Everyone spun, drawing weapons at the sense of urgency in her tone—Gunnar drew Mjolnir with a growl and Calvin suddenly sprouted foot-length claws from his white gauntlets. I held a ball of fire in my palm and I was already running.

Gunnar and Calvin were right behind me. I shouted back at the four-legged degenerates from over my shoulder. "Stay here and keep watch!" After a brief thought, I added, "No cliff jumping and no unicorn fucking!"

"I'll dare you if you dare me," Grinder said to Grimm. I clenched my jaw and hoped for the best as I ran into the cavern.

3

In my head, I'd taken to referring to the bizarre cavern as my family's catacombs, even though there were no bodies buried down here. The stairs and slide descending from the Mausoleum above had somehow slipped through an unseen portal between St. Louis and the Elder realm.

The Temple Mausoleum in the Bellefontaine Cemetery featured statues and sarcophagi of my ancestors in noble, academic, majestic, peaceful poses. The building had been crafted and constructed with respect and appreciation for order and glamor, and then my parents had put an insane amount of money into securing it from assault. Unfortunately, it had not been enough to protect against Aiden Maxon, my alleged half-brother.

In contrast to the statues in the Mausoleum, the cavern below was lined on either side with statues of those same ancestors in wild, primal, savage depictions of war and chaos.

Ordo ab Chao, I thought to myself. *From order to chaos.*

Or, as Hermes had once said, *as above, so below*.

Blue-flamed torches crackled between the statues, casting a cool blue glow over the cavern. At the back of the cavern, at the base of the slide and stairs, was a deep pool of dark water. That water spilled out to form a wide, and surprisingly turbulent, black stream that gurgled down the length of the cavern before spilling into the waterfall where Grimm and Grinder stood watch over the Elder realm.

Before my first visit here, that stream had been dry. Only the pool at the back of the cavern had existed, but my mere presence unlocked some sort of mechanical dam that birthed the stream and waterfall, shocking the locals from what I'd gathered.

We skidded to a halt at the mouth of the cavern.

Despite the urgency I'd heard in Kára's tone, a quick scan of my gathered allies told me they were more warily concerned than immediately homicidal. Everyone seemed to be sweeping the cavern as if they were searching for a set of lost keys or something. And their angry scowls told me they were having no luck.

Well, Yahn was actively searching for the lost keys, checking behind statues, one-by-one.

Kára and Ashley were sweeping their gazes about the cavern, using women's intuition or something. Kára looked at me and pointed at Mac, scowling.

Mac was crouched down beside a bloody smear on the ground next to the rushing stream.

"Motherfucker," I grumbled, clenching my jaw. "How did nobody notice the giant pool of blood earlier?"

"Because it appeared out of nowhere," Kára growled. Unlike everyone else, Kára still wore her golden armor, even though it was speckled with dried blood. She gripped her trident in a fist as her blue and green eyes scanned the cavern, searching for something to kabob.

Her lethal tone didn't seem to be directed at me. Then again, when it came to women blaming men for something, 'seem' was very, very thin ice for a man to rely upon for his wellbeing. Like a twisted version of the Salem Witch Trials, 'seem' was enough to get a man burned at the stake— if for no other reason than to punish the menfolk for their ancestors' crimes centuries ago.

Win-win. Either he was guilty of the current crime or guilty of his ancestors' crimes.

A very dangerous precedent indeed.

"Do you know you're talking out loud?" Calvin whispered from beside me.

I looked down to see his face was pale and he was pointedly not looking at the women. I glanced up to find every single one of the majestic females glaring daggers at me. I was reminded of the Eye of Sauron abruptly focusing directly on Frodo Baggins.

The ball of fire in my palm sputtered out like a starving candle.

"Heh-heh," I said nervously, brushing my hands together. "Jokes are... fun. Brings everyone together..."

The women looked at me like hungry leopards spotting an innocent lone monkey caught in the joyful act of sniffing butt-finger.

Calvin took a very pointed step to the side, letting the predators know he was not with me. Then he took another step, just to be abundantly clear. "Traitor," I muttered out the side of my mouth as I darted a quick glare over at him. The little punk refused to meet my eyes. Yahn was also studiously ignoring me, pretending he was engrossed with his search.

Gunnar sighed and muttered something to me that sounded like *degenerate* before making his way over to his wife, Ashley, who had her arms folded as she shifted her frown of disapproval from me to the stream. Mac smirked in amusement and flashed me a thumbs' up.

I winked back at her. Within moments, the women lost interest in deciding whether to burn me at the stake or drown me with a stone life-jacket, and I felt like a lead blanket had been lifted from my shoulders.

I eyed the bloody smear. "Magic," I mused, rubbing my jaw between my thumb and first knuckle.

Calvin grunted and I turned to see him squinting at me with a dubious frown.

"I'm a wizard. I know things," I said mysteriously.

One of his eyebrows arched up and then started to twitch. "Yeah. I think they're already well past that part of the investigation, Godfather." His adolescent voice squeaked halfway through, and he flushed deep red as he cleared his throat in an attempt to cover it.

I instantly went on the defensive and decided to attack his vulnerabilities—the young werewolf's hilarious Odyssey through puberty. "Yeah, well, your voice cracks every other sentence, Pube-wolf," I said, and then I turned my back on him.

"Pube-wolf?" he blurted in a horrified tone. "That...that makes it sound like...something completely disgusting."

I grinned to myself, calling it a victory either way—although I hadn't given the made-up term enough thought before saying it. Either way, pube-wolf was now a thing.

Mac sniffed at the air. "The blood is human and...fresh." I frowned. Human. That...was impossible. She lifted her gaze to study the various statues with a pensive frown. "Almost as if it's still flowing from the wound," she added, wrinkling her nose with a confused look on her face.

At this news, an aura of violence seemed to come to life like visible heatwaves around Kára. My girlfriend looked like she was ready to start dropping bodies.

I swept my eyes from statue to statue, frowning at the violent depictions of my ancestors. Many were forever cast in stone in the throes of extreme fury and chaos, all wearing visages of violence as they balanced atop piles of skulls and bodies, or actively fought vague depictions of numerous flavors of monster.

Some of those monsters I had no name for. Most of them, in fact.

But if Mac thought the blood was fresh, she would have also picked up on the physical scent of the actual wounded...human. But, how the hell had a human gotten down here in the first place? Since none of the werewolves were picking up the smell of an actual body, and there was no way a Regular had stumbled into the mausoleum during a deadly battle and then wandered down to the secret catacombs below, there had to be some other explanation.

Was this another of Aiden's little traps? A spell we had triggered? Or maybe it was some kind of message passed down to me through time? My ancestors were assholes like that, and my parents had been equally assholish. They would definitely set up a riddle like this. I crouched down and studied the bloody stone, eyeing the crimson stain with a thoughtful frown. "And you are absolutely certain you didn't accidentally overlook the blood?" I asked her, careful to keep my tone nonjudgmental. "It's kind of dark and the blue torches almost make it look black, the same as the water."

Mac looked up at me with a grim, determined scowl on her cute little face. "I watched it appear out of nowhere," she replied. "Like it was splattering to the ground in real time." She grabbed my wrist and slapped my palm down into the puddle before I could react.

My eyes widened. "It's warm!"

She nodded smugly and finally released my wrist.

I arched an eyebrow at her, and I saw Kára and Ashley nod in my peripheral vision, confirming her claim. I settled my elbows on my knees and pointedly swept my gaze over the cavern again, pondering what other methods to attempt. "Well, you werewolves sense nothing else here, right?" I asked. They shook their heads, looking uneasy and frustrated. "Maybe one of the Knightmares was wounded and tried to hide their tracks with a spell that faded over time," I said, shrugging.

The cavern was eerily silent for a few moments, and I realized everyone was staring at me, waiting for me to do something wizardly, heroic, or vaguely resemblant of a leader. I reached out with my magic, searching for any signs of power that might indicate Aiden's influence. I sensed nothing, so I focused my power on sniffing out any signs of life: a hushed breath, the pulse of a failing heart, a throb of power...anything.

I came up fruitless, but that only made me *more* suspicious. Blood didn't just appear—

Calvin abruptly shouted, and I looked up to see him pointing his claws at a bare patch of stone a few paces away from the edge of the stream. As I turned to look, I watched as a fresh, wet pool of blood slowly materialized over the previously bare section of stone.

I immediately rose to my feet and narrowed my eyes, preparing to incinerate anyone not wearing a Team Temple jersey.

"What is this, Nate?" Gunnar growled. Arcs of lightning abruptly crackled around his hammer.

I glared at the spot, hoping to pick up on some form of illusion or deceit, but I sensed no magic whatsoever. The ground leading from the stream showed a long smear of blood and...water? The stone was damp, and small wet boot prints led away from the stream, angling towards the back of a statue.

The statue that looked suspiciously like a work in process of...me. And someone had been working on it since I had last visited. Which meant Carl had not been the sculptor—as I had originally assumed. I didn't know any other Elders, though, so who the fuck was carving my likeness in a catacomb for dead Temples?

I wasn't fucking dead! Yet.

But the shadows behind the statue seemed empty. Felt empty. There was no sign of life behind it.

At least I had confirmed that my allies were not hallucinating. The blood truly had appeared out of nowhere with no apparent cause, and the werewolves still sensed no other signs of life in the cavern.

I frowned suspiciously and shot Kára a pensive look. She shrugged. "The blood and water just materialized out of nowhere," she reminded me, gripping her trident. "Like we told you."

"All right," I grumbled. "No need to womansplain it to me." Ashley snorted, obviously biting back a laugh. Kára rolled her eyes at me. Gunnar shook his head very discreetly, warning me against such flippancy.

Coward.

I reached out with my magic again, questing for any hidden threats whatsoever. After a few moments, I picked up absolutely nothing. For the second time, I let out a frustrated sigh. "Um..." I murmured in a wizardly tone, struggling to think of something helpful to say. "It seems that the blood is appearing out of nowhere..."

Kára gave me a frank stare, but it looked like she was biting back a smile. "You know, Nate, it's strangely endearing to see you trying to assure us when you obviously have no fucking idea what you're talking about."

Gunnar smirked faintly. "Even when Nate has no idea what's going on and is pulling answers out of his ass, I've learned to give his seemingly asinine warnings more credence than they merit. His instincts are often close enough to gamble on." I shot him a grateful nod, even though we would need to talk about his unflattering explanation of my esoteric wizardly processes.

His aggressive posture didn't change in the slightest as he gripped the legendary hammer of Thor. Mjolnir was an eternally hungry weapon, and I found myself debating whether it was changing qualities of my childhood friend or merely honing them into something new. Hopefully not something like its previous owner, Thor. That guy had been the poster child for anger management issues.

Then again, maybe fatherhood was the true explanation for Gunnar's shift towards a more aggressive temperament. Whatever the cause, Gunnar was less hesitant and careful than he had been in recent years. More committed and determined. Less likely to balk at the unintended consequences his actions might bring.

I realized that the change in my best friend was none of those things, actually.

What I saw in my friend was actually exceedingly simple: confidence.

Gunnar had drawn a figurative line in the sand and nowadays he straddled that line with a roguish curl of his lip, always a heartbeat away from flashing some fang and fucking up a threat before it had time to drink a morning cup of coffee. He trusted me, for better or worse. His morals hadn't evaporated; he had just clarified them.

He wasn't more *violent* than before...

He was less *conflicted*. His single bright blue eye was calm, assured, and prepared for the worst.

Gunnar was dangerously close to becoming a living hero. The only problem with heroes was that they always died. In fact, they didn't often become heroes until *after* they died. So...was this recognition a warning? Did I need to pay more attention? To make sure he didn't become overconfident? Did I need to keep...an *eye* on him? Heh.

Yes, a voice whispered in my mind. *You need to keep an eye on all of them here. Kára, Grimm, Gunnar, Ashley, Calvin, Makayla, Yahn, the little bloody girl hiding behind the statue...*

I noted she hadn't mentioned the kamikaze goat, Grinder, but that made perfect sense.

I started nodding to the voice, agreeing with my own inner Dr. Phil—

Wait.

Little bloody girl?

4

Calvin abruptly let out a shout that squeaked halfway through, instantly making me think of Beaker from *The Muppets*, but I was so distracted by his sense of urgency and my subconscious Sherlock Holmes that I didn't even consider teasing him for his cracking voice. Instead, I was staring at the shadows behind my unfinished statue, and I clearly saw as another bloody smear on the ground came to life like an invisible body was being dragged into the darkness.

With absolutely no sound, which made the hair on the back of my neck stand straight up.

The red smear was again accompanied by a pair of small bloody boot prints, as if a diminutive little monster had dragged a fresh carcass back into the shadows to feast on its meal in peace.

"Leprechaun," I breathed, saying the name of the first little monster that came to mind. "One of Summer Fae's leprechauns snuck down here, probably plastered on Guinness and Bailey's—"

"Do leprechauns wear Doc Martens?" Kára asked with a dubious frown. I blinked, realizing that I was seeing clearly portrayed boot prints with the familiar Dr. Martens logo.

I harrumphed, recalling Mac saying the blood was from a human. Even with the blood appearing out of nowhere, I still had sensed no magic.

What kind of power was this creature using for me not to recognize it? I opened my mouth to demand that the fashion-focused monster come out of hiding, but I felt a hand pull at my sleeve. I looked down to see Mac standing at my side, absently tugging at my arm. She was staring into the shadows with a curious look on her face, and then she took another step closer to the danger. Before I could protest, she squatted down on her heels again and held out her hand with the palm up. She smiled invitingly.

"A girl," she whispered, waving in a friendly manner. "Hello. I like your boots."

A pair of eyes abruptly materialized from within the shadow of my statue, reflecting the glow of the blue-flamed torches. Despite the eyes appearing out of nowhere like magic but with no discernible magic sensed, I didn't flinch. I stared stoically and absently acknowledged a faint chill in the air. She was spelled up somehow, and by something I didn't even know how to register. A concealment spell.

A shaky voice called out. "I...I'm not scared of you!" she said with false bravado. It was the sound of a doomed cause. A girl willing to do whatever it took—even knowing she would fail—to defend herself.

In my peripheral vision, Gunnar took a protective step forward. I glanced back in time to see Ashley promptly sweep his legs out from under him, sending him crashing to the ground as he let out a startled curse.

"This is women's business," Ashley said in a tone that threatened Gunnar with a swift introduction to involuntary celibacy as she glared down at her husband. He lifted his hands in surrender and slowly sat up. Then she casually leapt over the stream in a single bound, landed softly, and approached her daughter—which would bring her dangerously close to me. I lifted my hands and took a step back, letting Ashley know that I didn't need to be hip-tossed or emasculated in any manner whatsoever.

Kára smirked faintly and gave me a nod, approving of my wise decision, but she remained out of the girl's line of sight and did not approach with Ashley and Mac. Her golden armor was covered in blood, so it was probably a wise choice. Since I was a smart man, I didn't provide aid to my best friend, Gunnar, who was only now climbing back to his feet. Instead, I stepped up beside the traitor, Calvin, and decided to study the strange development in real time. Yahn leaned back against one of the statues with his arms folded across his chest. He'd been abnormally silent since we entered the catacombs.

None of his usual cheer and positive mental attitude were on display.

Ashley halted a few steps away from the statue and squatted down beside Mac, replicating her posture, close enough to let the feral child know they were confronting her but far enough away to let her know they meant no harm. I couldn't clearly see the girl, but I still saw her eyes glittering in the shadows behind my statue.

"My name is Mac," my goddaughter said in a soft, friendly voice. "I think we're the same age. What's your name?"

The girl leaned out of the shadows to get a closer look at Mac. I reached out with my magic on instinct, testing the young girl for hidden power. I was surprised to discover that she...really was a Regular. Her concealment spell hadn't been blocking me from sensing a hidden power of some kind, so how had my subconscious alerted me to the presence of the frightened bloody girl behind the statue even before Mac had seen her. Not even a *whisper* of power emanated from the girl.

What the hell was up with magic in the Elder realm? It seemed all topsy-turvy.

The girl had dried blood on her cheeks, and she had obviously been crying. "My name is...Asha," she whispered, meeting Mac's eyes. Yahn cocked his head curiously and stared at the girl. She had raven-black hair tied back with a long blue ribbon, bright green eyes, and sharp cheekbones. She wore dark jeans, a black hoodie, and a black jacket that matched her black Doc Martens. None of her clothes looked to be expensive or statement pieces. She was gaunt and gangly, in that awkward stage of adolescence where one couldn't determine what she might look like once she matured.

But there was something...captivating about her. From her crouch within the shadows, I couldn't determine what that particularly notable aspect was. Regardless, my bet was that Asha would soon become a beauty, though an otherworldly beauty—almost haunting in a fae-like way.

I glanced down at my Godson, Calvin, and realized that he had been sucker punched by his hormones and was now bewitched by the vexatious *twitterpated* curse. I watched as the pube-wolf fell hopelessly, futilely in love with the girl he'd only seen for the first time approximately 2.6 seconds ago. Foolish puppy. Romance was for losers.

I nudged him with my elbow, causing him to stumble. "Easy, Thumper."

Calvin blushed and then blinked rapidly before frowning over at me. "Who the heck is Thumper?"

The pup's ageist attack hit me like a blade to the heart, but I sucked in the pain, knowing it was not his fault. Still, *Bambi* was a classic. I would talk to Gunnar about it later. "You're not old enough to understand the Tao of Bambi," I said in a solemn tone. Then, with an amused smirk, I murmured an additional piece of helpful advice. A warning. "Keep an eye on our six, not *her* six."

Calvin blushed deeper and stammered for a moment before managing to rein in his emotions. He wisely clenched his jaw as he took the advice of his loving, devoted, determined Godfather. "Noted," he squeaked. I smiled smugly as his birdcall echoed through the cavern, causing the women to momentarily glance back at him with a scowl. Once they turned away, Calvin leaned closer to me and spoke in an entirely too innocent tone. "Unlike what you did with Indie?"

I swept my hand out to backhand the flippant pube-wolf, only to find that he'd already ducked and side-stepped out of reach. I glared over at him for a moment, hurt by my godson's bone-deep betrayal. "Your father lies. Never trust a man with one eye. They never see the whole picture."

He snorted. "My *Mom* told me about Indie," he said with a shit-eating grin. "Are you saying she is a liar, too, Godfather?" he asked with an amused grin.

I scowled. "She…" I trailed off, sensing Kára watching our exchange with an arched eyebrow. She was close enough to have possibly overheard some of our conversation. "Your mother is wise…but misinformed. I'll explain the situation to her. Pube-wolf," I added in an adolescent whisper.

Calvin snorted. "Your solution is to *mansplain* it to her?" he hissed with a grin. "Oh, man. I remember when dad tried that one time." He met my eyes. "One. Time."

I scowled at the disrespectful little dog. "Well, he must have done it wrong." Then I gave him the cold shoulder. "Women love having things explained to them," I said blithely over my shoulder. The cavern was strangely silent except for the echo of my last comment. I looked up to find everyone staring at me as my echo slowly faded away and died—a metaphorical depiction of my future, judging by Ashley's glare.

Kára folded her arms and sighed, a silent but deadly warning that I was well beyond thin ice.

"Maybe you could explain it to them," Calvin chuckled. "You know. To show me how it's done."

Kára bit back a laugh, and Ashley shook her head in resignation. Mac hadn't turned away from the girl, focused in like a hawk with a mouse, as if no one else existed. I realized she was speaking in soothing tones and nodding her head at Asha—which was strange enough by itself. Mac had gone from not ever talking to people to suddenly being a social worker. "We won't hurt you. We were just startled to find you back there. It looks like you are hurt."

The girl licked her lips nervously, glancing from face-to-face with a wary, feral gleam in her eyes. I took another step backwards and lifted my palms in an innocent gesture as I flashed her a reassuring smile. She watched me for a few moments and then turned back to Mac. "Are you the Dark Horse?"

Mac flinched as if struck. I stopped breathing. Then Mac slowly pointed a thumb over her shoulder, directly at me. "No. But he is." The girl let out a breath, looking strangely relieved. "Where did you hear that name?" Mac asked.

Asha hesitated but was finally won over by Mac's apparent sincerity. "The man said to hide down here. To wait for the Dark Horse. I...don't know why," she whispered.

"Man?" I rasped, fearing the worst.

The girl shrunk under my glare. "A man in a hood. At least, I think it was a man. I didn't see their face," Asha said in a nervous tone, not sounding remotely certain of her story. "There was smoke and fire and screaming and...monsters—I mean, animals. They sounded big, like big animals," she said, sniffling.

She'd been topside during a fight between Baldur's Einherjar, the Summer Queen's army, the Academy Justices, and various flavors of crazed shifters.

Yet...paranoia was a dear associate of mine. Some might even say a blood-brother. So, I put my empathy in a cute little box, tucked it on a shelf in my mind, and then I tried to assess the situation with a little more cynicism, because lives depended on it.

Aiden had been wearing a hood in the cemetery, and he knew everything about me. My weaknesses, especially. How I had a soft spot for wayward kids. He would most definitely try to use that against me, given the opportunity. So, I hated myself for considering it, but that was what leaders had to do.

And they had to accept the consequences either way.

What would Aiden do? I asked myself.

A stranger had sent Asha down here and told her to wait for me, using a moniker that Mac had only recently given me. Had I mentioned the nickname to Aiden in the last few days? A slip of the tongue? The whole situation started feeling a helluva lot more like a trap. Gunnar grumbled softly and started walking the perimeter on the other side of the stream, checking behind each statue. Calvin swiftly hopped over the water to join him and speed up the process.

I turned back to Asha. "How long have you been down here?"

"Maybe an hour?" she said after a few moments' thought. "It all happened so fast," she whispered.

That must have been right after the Mausoleum was blown open.

I felt a tingling sensation in my ear, almost like someone had whispered into it but no one was there. I turned and saw Gunnar pause and look at me from across the catacombs, almost like he had felt something similar. He pulled out his Horseman Mask with a curious frown and I realized I was doing the same. Something had just happened, but magic was acting so strangely that I couldn't place what it had been. My Horseman Mask felt no different than before, so why had I subconsciously checked it? We frowned at each other for a moment, but then I felt my attention pulled to a statue directly behind Gunnar. Oddly, he turned to look at it as well, cocking his head and sniffing at the air. The sensation seemed to radiate from the stone statue.

The statue was a beefy, grizzly ancestor of mine. I had no idea who he was, but he looked vaguely familiar to a statue I had seen above—a man with a big belly and a kindhearted smile. The statue above had made me think of Santa Clause—a man full of goodwill and cheer. But that was where the resemblance to this statue ended.

This statue's entire head was surrounded by a wild mess of hair—long hair tied back behind his head and a beard that knotted down his chest, tied together with trinkets and bones and what I presumed to be metallic rings, making me think of how Norsemen had often decorated their beards. The man, ironically, had only one eye—except it was a gaping wound, complete with blood still oozing from the gaping socket—and where his right arm should have been was only bone. No flesh or muscle or anything. The wizard held an eyeball between two bone fingers; he held it before him like it was a weapon. I shuddered at the grim depiction, deciding that all of my ancestors had been crazy bastards. My gaze shifted back to his bone arm and I realized that the surface was carved with symbols and runes. I saw four that stuck out to me, practically glowing. I had never seen the symbols before, but I somehow knew—beyond a shadow of a doubt—what they meant...

Hope. Despair. Justice. Absolution.

The symbols of the Dread Four—my Horsemen. I recognized their meaning, even though I had never seen them before.

Four more symbols seemed to mirror the Dread Four runes, placed directly below them and standing out to me like photo negatives, yet I could not decipher them or sense their meanings. One of them was marred by a black streak, as if cancelling it out. But none of the four symbols were what held my attention. It was something...larger than any of the individual symbols. It wasn't even the actual wizard depicted in the statue, and how closely he resembled Gunnar standing before it.

It almost felt like those optical illusion posters where you were required to let your eyes slip out of focus to see the hidden message within the hyper-detailed picture. I tried doing that now, wondering why my magic seemed so intently drawn to it rather than the girl behind the statue.

My gaze absently drifted to the hundreds of other runes of power carved into my ancestor's skeletal claw. I saw hieroglyphs, kanji, druidic runes, spell forms, Norse runes, words in English and many other languages. But there were others that I could not put my finger on. After a few seconds of scrutiny, it hit me.

An icy shiver went down my own right arm and I shuddered. Many of the runes were from the Omegabet, a dangerous language of mixed symbols that were incredibly powerful and dangerous. The mysterious runes called to me in a haunting, hypnotic, sing-song hymn, and I felt my rage burning hotter in my chest. The song of those bone runes was compelling me to fight, soaking me in a shower of wonton bloodlust. I was the last Temple heir.

I was an agent of death. That was my purpose.

A horseman of war, even though my title was Horseman of Hope.

And those in times of war often had to make tough decisions.

5

I slowly turned back to Asha, ignoring Gunnar's pensive look. Yahn wore a troubled expression, and he was scratching at his head. Mac was still speaking to her in soft tones. "This could be a trap," I interrupted, staring straight at the girl. "I'm not claiming she's in on it, but I find it highly suspicious that a Regular just happened to come down here, somehow escaping the insanely deadly battle up at the cemetery. We lost dozens of good men and women, experienced warriors all." I met the girl's eyes and cocked my head. "And here you are, girl, surrounded by monsters and yet you are unscathed."

The catacombs were silent for a few moments, and I could tell Asha was scared to answer my question. Then Mac cut through the tension like a scalpel. "If anyone tries to lay a hand on her, I will sever the offending limb," she said in an eerily sweet voice. Then she glanced over her shoulder with a fiery twinkle in her eyes, making sure we each saw the commitment in her gaze. "We will ask questions like civilized people." Then she turned her cool gaze back to Asha. "I hope you are not trying to deceive us. That...would be a very painful, dreadful, torturous poor life choice for you, Asha."

For some strange reason, the girl didn't flinch or cry. She nodded, obviously afraid and confused, but resolved. Determined.

I nodded my agreement. "We need to be alert," I said. "This sounds exactly like something Aiden would plant in our midst. The Elder realm isn't even safe for Freaks. Even the sun is fatal. So, how does a child arrive in my super-secret cave ahead of us? Who was the hooded stranger?" Everyone shifted their attention to the girl in the shadows. "Perhaps you could step into the light as a gesture of good will?"

Mac held out a hand and smiled warmly, even though she'd just threatened the girl a moment before. "We mean you no harm. You are only in danger if you mean us harm. We are very scary people, but only to those who mean to hurt the innocent. To everyone else, we're all fluffy teddy bears."

Asha studied Mac warily. "What are you doing down here? You look like you're expecting a fight."

Calvin puffed out his chest proudly. "We are hunting Knightmares."

The girl flinched. "Nightmares? Like...bad dreams?"

I shook my head. "Bad men who wish to hurt my friends. They wear black armor like...Knights of the Round Table, but they are perverse, evil versions," I said. "I need to know anything you can tell me about this stranger, Asha. Exactly what he said, word for word. Anything could help."

Asha studied me for a few moments, seeming to realize that none of us were likely to suddenly lunge forward and murder her. "He said to hide down here, be silent, and 'the Dark Horse is your destiny'," she finally said.

I managed not to flinch, but my gaze did flick upwards to read a passage carved into the stone wall of the cavern. *Dynasty is not destiny. Nobility is not class.* Even still, I let out a frustrated sigh, getting nothing useful from her answer.

The girl nodded uncertainly. "I saw men in black armor," she whispered, turning to stare deeper into the shadows behind her. "They hurt my mom. I...think she's dying," she croaked.

My eyes widened in surprise. "You're not alone? Why didn't you say anything earlier?" I whispered, trying to stare past her into the shadows. My heart skipped a beat, and my stomach did a strange flip-flop sensation. How had none of the shifters sensed that? Was her mother already dead? Was Asha in shock, unable to process the situation?

My suspicious, paranoid interrogation tactics suddenly felt disgusting to me. I opened my mouth, but I was unable to speak through my guilt.

Kára had been out of Asha's view, but the girl mentioning her injured mother drew the Valkyrie out with an anguished look on her face. She advanced, plastering on a sympathetic smile and held out her hand reassuringly. "We thought you were alone, Asha. Of course, we can check on your mother. Do you mind if—"

"It's *you!*" Asha gasped as Kára stepped into her field of view, scrabbling back against the wall and deeper into the shadow behind the statue. "The angel!" she croaked, sounding torn between awe and horror.

Kára stiffened in surprise. "I'm...no angel, Asha," she said very slowly, looking pensive. "My name is Kára."

"I saw you in the sky! You told us to hide!" Asha argued.

"What's this all about?" I asked, frowning.

Kára's eyes widened, and she took a step back as she sucked in a breath. Then she hung her head as if she were about to be sick. "That was you and your mother in the cemetery," Kára whispered, sounding heartbroken. "Oh, you poor girl," she whispered.

Asha nodded adamantly. "You warned us," she said. "But...then they threw fireballs at you, and you left," she added, not sounding judgmental or angry. Instead, she sounded heartbroken. Asha bit her lower lip. "There was nowhere for us to hide. We tried. But then you left..."

Kára blinked and a tear rolled down her cheek. Guilt racked her features. "I am so sorry, child," she whispered. Kára's eyes were misty, and she wouldn't meet Asha's eyes. "I'm sorry, Asha. I...had to get help," she said, and then she pointed directly at me. "This is Nate. He protects people." She opened her mouth as if to say more, and then she simply stood there, unable to formulate words. "He is the Dark Horse."

I clenched my jaw in frustration, not knowing why Mac had taken to calling me by the moniker, but I definitely didn't appreciate everyone else adopting it like it was an actual title. I sure as hell didn't know what it meant, or why Mac had used it, so I was annoyed that someone else—this unknown stranger—had heard about it and had told Asha to seek out the Dark Horse as some kind of savior.

Most of my attention was drawn to the agonized look on Kára's face. I knew guilt and shame were warring within her heart. She must have encountered the girl and her mother in the cemetery and tried to warn them, but was forced to abandon them in order to go to Fae and alert me to the fight. I knew it wasn't her fault. She had made a choice to warn me rather than to save the mother and daughter, and that realization was hurting her heart, even though she knew it had been the right call.

Unfortunately, the heart didn't care about logic, but it definitely recognized shame and guilt.

I knew Kára had done the right thing.

Kára knew she had done the right thing.

But guilt was a cruel taskmaster. There was always a cost to difficult decisions, and they always had unintended consequences. That lesson should have been a wizard's rule or something, judging by how many times I'd tripped over it. *Someone needs to write a book about wizard's rules*, I thought to myself.

Mac held out her hand. "Why don't you come with me for a minute while Kára and Nate check on your mother?" she asked Asha, smiling warmly. "Have you ever seen a unicorn before?"

Asha blinked in bewilderment. "Unicorn?" she asked incredulously. "Um. No. I...haven't," she said, rising to her feet. She stumbled forward out of the shadows, and I had to bite back a grimace at the state of her clothes. They were torn, filthy with dust, and covered with damp blood. Hers or her mothers, I wasn't sure. She met my eyes as she took a few tentative steps towards Mac. "Please...help her," she whispered. "She's all I have left."

I nodded stiffly, recalling the fact that they had been at the cemetery before all of the fighting started. The mother and daughter had lost someone very close to them. A father or sibling, for her to say she had no one else left. "We will do everything we can, Asha," I promised, choosing my words very carefully. I had no idea if her mother was even alive, so I didn't want to lie to her.

Rather than get involved, Yahn had turned his back on the exchange and seemed to be reading the writing on the wall. Weird.

I waited until Mac accepted Asha's hand and began pulling her towards the mouth of the cave before I rushed over to the back of the statue, mentally preparing myself for the horrors I might face. Kára skidded to the ground beside me with a grim look on her face.

"Magic was protecting these two," she whispered to me. "I haven't been able to sense Asha's pulse this whole time. Maybe that's why I haven't sensed her mother," she added, sounding like she was trying to convince herself.

I nodded grimly and lifted my palm. A ball of light winked into existence to reveal what looked like a scene from a horror film. The entire floor behind the statue was slick with blood. A woman sat leaning against the back wall, clutching her stomach. Her head hung to the side, and I instantly feared she was dead.

Then I saw her chest expand with the faintest of breaths.

I gasped in disbelief. "She's alive!" I whispered. I tapped her on the shoulder firmly, knowing we needed to wake her up. Unconsciousness was entirely too close to death, and I knew it was important to keep the wounded awake. At least, I thought that was a thing. EMTs were always telling the wounded to *stay with me*, and *don't fall asleep*.

The mother's eyes cracked open, and she sucked in a deep breath as her eyes bulged to see two strangers rather than her daughter. She gasped and clawed in terror, searching for her daughter. "Asha!" she croaked.

"It's okay," I reassured her, gently squeezing her shoulder. "Asha is safe. Right over there," I said, gesturing at the statue—only realizing after the fact that it made me look like a crazy person. The mother struggled to sit up and peer around the corner of the large pedestal, but she immediately gasped in pain, clutching at her stomach. Her fingers did not hold back a fresh wave of blood.

Thankfully, Asha's voice echoed into the cavern from outside, loud enough to be heard over the stream. "He's beautiful."

"I prefer regal and remorseless," Grimm replied in a haughty tone. "Are you a snack?"

"Hey!" Grinder grumbled. "I'm the snack."

Asha, surprisingly, laughed. "How is any of this possible? A talking goat, a unicorn, werewolves, wizards..." she trailed off, sounding like she was straddling the tightrope between hysteria and delight.

"Magic is pretty neat, eh?" Mac said. "It's mostly beautiful and harmless..."

I managed not to snort at the lie. Barely.

6

The mother's shoulders relaxed at the sound of her daughter's voice and laughter, and she let out a faint sigh of relief. Then she locked eyes with me. She furrowed her brow as if vaguely recognizing me, but then her eyes danced towards Kára and bulged all over again. "The angel!" she wheezed. "Oh, Lord! You sent me an angel!"

Kára smiled uneasily and shook her head. "My name is Kára. I'm not an angel, but I am here to help you and Asha," she said in a gentle tone, her dual-colored green and blue eyes glinting in the glow of the blue torches. "What's your name?"

The mother frowned, looking confused. "Nadia—" Her eyes abruptly widened again, and I saw terror take a grip on her thoughts. "We are in danger. Bad men are—"

"I know," I told her. "We are here to stop the bad men, Nadia." I glanced down at her wound. Despite bleeding freely, the edges of the wound were puckered and almost crispy. It was also black, and tendrils of darkness seemed to be radiating outwards from the wound. It was most definitely some kind of poison or magical malady. "Did one of them do this to you?"

She nodded, biting her lower lip. "Y-yes. But someone saved us. Took us to the family tree with all the gems..." She trailed off, frowning at me thoughtfully. "You're Nate Temple," she whispered.

I nodded guiltily. "Yes, Nadia."

She frowned pensively, eyeing me up and down. "You are nothing like Greta said you were," she murmured. My own eyes widened in surprise. This woman knew Greta, the cantankerous old Bible Thumper? Yahn's grandmother? Wasn't she in Kansas City now?

Yahn's sudden stoicism began making a lot more sense. He had recognized Asha and hadn't wanted her seeing his face. Maybe she'd crossed paths with Yahn during Bible camp or at their church and Asha had developed a crush on him that he'd had to shut down. He would have been in his mid-teens and she would have been ten, at most. Young love drama was going to be the death of me long before any wizard's fireball managed to do the job. I could imagine my tombstone now. *Here lies Nate Temple. He died from close proximity to tween angst.* My statue would be of me fleeing from a mob of Dawson's Creek fans.

I gave Nadia a roguish grin. "Greta does love her soapbox, but she means well. In all fairness, half of what she told you about me is probably true." Nadia smiled but it turned into a grimace of pain. I almost told her we needed to get her out of here, and then I remembered we were trapped down here.

Shit.

She squeezed my hand and I looked up at her. "It's okay. You don't need to lie to me. I know it's too late for me," she whispered sadly. "Just...take care of Asha," she sobbed, her lip trembling. "She has no one else. Her father and brother died in the explosion at the Arch last month."

Her words hit me like a punch to the heart. The explosion at the Arch... had been my fault. When I'd freed Prometheus, he'd ridden his feathered nemesis down from the skies and crashed into the Arch, causing a panic in St. Louis. The city was basically under Martial Law as a result.

My actions had literally killed nearly everyone in Asha's family. Kára sucked in her lower lip and shook her head discreetly, silently telling me it wasn't my fault. She was wrong, but I loved her for it.

I blinked at the fiery burning sensation in my eyes and nodded. "Okay, Nadia. I will."

I knew that strange asshole of a healer in Camelot if I dared to try opening a Gateway, despite my trepidations and gut feeling. And what if Aiden had sent this woman down here? He knew I would try to save them.

Maybe he wanted to force me into making a Gateway, triggering some other trap that would get some of my friends killed.

"I can't travel out of here either, Nate," Kára whispered to me with a nervous tremor in her voice. I can feel all my power, but there's something preventing me from traveling."

I opened my mouth to reassure her when I felt a flash of power ignite directly inside my temples. My eyes bulged and I gasped in shock, waiting for my brain to melt. But...no actual pain hit me. I panted hoarsely and then I felt a strange purring sensation in my mind, almost like a cat was nuzzling against my head, waking me from a deep sleep. A warm sensation rolled down my body from my head to my toes, making me shudder with pleasure. The sensation faded and I panted hoarsely, realizing Kára was shaking me with a panicked look on her face. "I'm all right," I mumbled. "I think my brain just climaxed."

"Nate!" Gunnar bellowed in a dazed tone. "I just felt something very, very strange." I looked up to see him gripping his hammer with a distant gleam in his eye.

"Good tingle or bad tingle?" I asked.

"I...don't know. Both?" he finally said.

"I felt it, too," I said, my mind instantly thinking of our Horseman Masks. No one but us two had felt it. "I'm sure we're fine. It felt good at the end, so we're probably okay—"

A powerful burst of magic struck the catacombs, feeling like the shock-wave from a grenade, and the air suddenly grew ten-times as dense. The blast sent me flying past Nadia and into the wall, where I heard and felt my shoulder pop out of the socket. I struck the ground on my knees, eliciting another flash of sharp pain because I had old man problems. Kára snarled from beside me and I looked up to see her crouching as she turned to face the stream in the center of the cavern. She'd lost her trident in the shock-wave. I clenched my jaw to fight back the fiery pain tearing through my shoulder as it hung limp at my side, dislocated.

I'd felt that strange type of magic before—the atmosphere of death. From the Underworld. Whatever power had hit Gunnar and me had been a dire warning of some kind, although I had no idea what that was.

The catacombs were eerily quiet for a moment, as if we'd imagined the whole thing. I glanced back to check on Nadia and was relieved to see she looked just as terrible as before, no worse. I turned back to the cavern and swept my gaze from left-to-right, not seeing any of my friends.

"What the fuck was that, Kára," I growled through clenched teeth. "You sense anything?"

Her eyes were faraway, as if she were staring through the fabric of reality or into other realms. "Some...thing is here," she whispered, drawing one of her gleaming hatchets. "Something bad. Something *dead*."

The black stream abruptly started bubbling like it was boiling oil, burping steam up into the air. Then the water started to rise up in an impossible manner like it was living quicksilver. As the tower of liquid rose, it started looking like a semi-humanoid figure trying to press through an embryonic sack. But...the stream was water, so the figure should have just risen out of it like anyone else coming up for air after an underwater swim.

The tower of water continued to rise in abrupt fits and jerks that made the column ripple, as if the figure within were fighting against the black water that was inhibiting its presence. As the figure strained, it started to take on a form, looking like a ten-foot-tall monster of a man. The black water pressing against him made it look like he wore a midnight black cloak, yet two tall, pointed ears rose from his head, the only distinguishing characteristic. I knew it sounded ridiculous, but it looked suspiciously like Batman.

The Dark Knight imposter radiated obscene levels of power, making the hair on the back of my neck stand on end. I rose to my feet, gritted my teeth, and slammed my shoulder into the nearest statue, popping it back into place with a sickening sound. My vision grew dizzy for a moment, but then the ass-kicking brain chemicals hit my bloodstream and the pain subsided to a dull throbbing.

I heard Asha scream in the near distance, somewhere outside the cavern. Had she seen the monster rising up from the dark stream?

Nadia let out a terrified gasp. "My baby! Please protect my baby!"

I shot Kára a grim look and she nodded. "Go, Nate. Protect Asha. I'll watch Nadia."

And then I was running towards Asha's scream, keeping the giant death baby and his embryonic sack of black water in my peripheral vision. Part of me wanted to take the fight directly to him, but there was no way in hell I was going to risk anything happening to Asha after her mother's plea. Once I knew the girl was safe, I would come back to end the threat of DC crossovers once and for all. The movies and shows had grown increasingly worse over the years, but this...

Was over the fucking line. They had to be stopped.

And that's when the strangest fucking thing happened.

Candy Skulls started winking into existence all over the place. Those black-cloaked Wardens from Hell with their creepy, overly decorated white skull masks. I spotted half-a-dozen outside the cavern, fighting Grimm, Grinder, and Yahn as Asha huddled behind a boulder. The Randulfs were just inside the cavern, fighting back-to-back against a mob of Candy Skulls who'd just winked into existence.

All four of them exploded into their upgraded werewolf forms, three Knights of the Round Table and the Horseman of fucking Justice. Gunnar let out a roar and bit the top half of a Candy Skull clean off, leaving his legs to stand there looking ridiculous. Ashley's claws tore through the enemy like hot knives through squishy insides, and Calvin and Mac blinked in and out of their mist forms, appearing in unexpected locations to slice, maim, and murder.

Gunnar bellowed a roar loud enough to make dust fall from the ceiling and cause a few of the Candy Skulls to trip over each other. Hilariously, the legs without the body remained standing upright.

As I made my way to join in their fight, about a dozen Candy Skulls appeared directly between us, popping up right out of thin air. I skidded to a halt, feeling my throbbing arm hanging by my side like a wet towel as I glared at their stupid painted skulls and their billowy black robes.

"Death to the fucking Pez dispensers!" I screamed.

7

I ran headlong into battle with one arm tucked close to my body, ignoring the deep aching joys of a recently relocated shoulder. "Grimm! Yahn!" I roared, my voice booming through the cavern. "One of you two winged wonders get Asha to safety right fucking now!"

A beam of power lanced into the cavern, sweeping from side-to-side, a prism of blacks, whites, and grays that disemboweled a vast chunk of the Candy Skulls with a steaming hiss. "Taste the Pain-bow!" Grimm screamed before the blast of power winked out, and then I heard a frightened squawk of alarm as I saw Asha flip up into the air and land on Grimm's back. My unicorn leapt off the fucking mountain with the terrified teen, shouting at her to grab onto his mane and to grip his back with her asscheeks.

Grimm was not the best flight attendant, but as I think Confucius once said, a drunk pilot was better than no pilot.

I let out a breath of relief to see Grimm escape the insanity with Asha, and I turned to face a trio of Candy Skulls standing between me and the inky specter rising up from the water. Judging by the arrival of the Candy Skulls and the specter's tall, pointed ears, I was putting my money on Anubis, God of the Underworld.

I summoned my Horseman's Mask and felt the velveteen fingers latch onto my face with a soothing purr. Quartz rolled over my flesh as if it were sentient and alive—which it kind of was—armoring me for the battle to come.

It also strengthened my arm enough to let me use it again.

Greetings, Hope, the familiar voice of my Horseman's Mask purred in my ears. So far, we hadn't talked much, but I decided it was past time we got better acquainted. *Do you want to see what we are capable of?*

I smiled through my black mask of liquid stone. "Yes, my dear. I think I do," I rasped out loud.

I grabbed the nearest Candy Skull by the chest and jerked him towards me hard enough to snap a mortal's neck. But he was not mortal, so my motion turned into an inter-dimensional headbutt. His skeletal mask exploded into a cloud of bone fragments as fine as dandelion puffs, and his headless body crumpled to the floor of the cave. I turned to the other two and grinned. "Want to play a game?" I asked in a deadly calm voice as I brushed my armored hands together, emitting a spray of sparks as stone ground against stone.

Several more Candy Skulls shimmered into existence alongside their two coworkers, apparently clocking in for their nightshift. The gang of eight Candy Skulls leapt for me with outstretched claws.

I let them.

We could use some warmth and light, I told my Mask. *They look cold.*

The mask snickered gleefully. *How about lava?*

I grinned my agreement as the Candy Skulls swarmed me, dog piling me to the ground. I felt a soothing shudder of warmth splash over my body like I'd just fallen into a hot tub.

Candy Skulls screamed in high-pitched whistles that seemed to rip the air to shreds, and the space around us filled with acrid, pungent smoke. I watched as liquid lava splashed all over my foes, practically liquifying them before my eyes. I calmly rose to my feet and flashed a thumbs up at a very bewildered looking Kára. She stared at the living lava rolling down my arms and dripping off my long claws to spatter and sizzle on the stone floor of the cave. I lifted one hand to scoop up a glob of the molten rock and held it up to my face with a growing grin. It felt only mildly warm to me.

Then I hurled the glob at a Candy Skull near the mouth of the cavern.

It struck his face and splashed everywhere, splattering over his body like a living parasite as he erupted in flames.

"Lavaball fight," I murmured to myself, and then I started scooping up more globs of molten stone as it continued to ooze from my very pores. Candy Skulls screamed as I started a lavaball fight in the Elder realm.

Howls filled the air as Gunnar and Ashley tore into the Candy Skulls on their side of the cavern, Gunnar in his Horseman's Mask and Ashley in her fancy new armor.

"I will floss my teeth with your spine!" Ashley snarled in a spitting coughing sound. In my peripheral vision, I saw she was in her Wulfra form, except now she was candy-coated in pristine white metal. The Lady Knight...well, she wasn't much of a *lady*.

She was a furious soccer mom on steroids after neighbor Karen swung by to comment on the excessive length of the grass in her front yard with a *tsk-tsk* sound. Ashley didn't have a lawnmower.

But her claws worked as an impromptu weedwhacker.

She lunged forward with those foot-long claws and tore through a Candy Skull's chest, ripping his spine out through his back before she hoisted him in the air hard enough to strike the ceiling of the cavern with a wet, splattering sound. Except...she still held his spine in her claw. And, true to her word, she flagrantly flossed her fangs with the grisly spinal column, introducing a clacking sound into the cavern that sounded eerily similar to when I had clothespinned a card to the spokes of my bicycle as a child.

As the lifeless body fell from the ceiling, Gunnar leap-frogged off Ashley's back and caught the carcass in midair, ripping it in two pieces with his fangs. He landed atop another Candy Skull, slamming the creature's face into the ground with one paw—pulverizing it with a spray of gore and bone fragments—as he simultaneously reached out to grab the throat of another standing nearby. He promptly pulled it close and bit the poor chap's head off.

He dropped the headless body and swallowed audibly as he turned his glowing eye to half-a-dozen more Candy Skulls. They hesitated, but then a dozen more winked into existence between them. Gunnar didn't even hesitate against the overwhelming odds.

The Horseman of Justice simply rolled up his figurative sleeves and went to work, leaping into the fray with spinning claws, ripping fangs, and howls of glee.

The twins were hardly seen, but the effects of their misty passages filled the cavern with screams, fonts of blood, and severed limbs, making it look like the work of ghosts. I saw one Candy Skull actually grab Calvin by the armored tail and yank him backwards. Before Calvin could get his balance, the Candy Skull punched him in the metal snout.

Calvin burst out laughing, entirely unfazed as the Candy Skull lifted a shattered hand to his face and made a sound like a teapot whistling. Calvin lunged forward and ripped his throat out before shifting back into mist and assisting his sister in her act of mass murder like any good brother should.

A sneaking suspicion hit me as I considered Calvin not being harmed by the punch to the face. That was either the armor protecting him or...

Because I had dipped him and Mac in the River Styx. Judging by Anubis' arrival, I was betting it had more to do with the latter, and that sent an icy shiver down my spine. He'd finally come to make them pay for that act—a decision I had made to keep them safe from Freya's enemies.

Shit.

Ashley continued her flurry of violence against a vast number of foes, because the Candy Skulls just kept appearing out of thin air as if summoned by a necromancer. Which was probably the case.

I shifted my attention to the inky-black form still struggling to break out of the water. "Anubis," I snarled, knowing it could only be him. He ruled the Underworld, as far as I could tell. The last time I'd encountered the Candy Skulls had resulted in a confrontation with the Egyptian Jackal-headed god. "I think it's time to take you out behind the shed for your last walk," I growled, sensing my Godkiller powers rise up beneath my Horseman's armor, turning my molten lava armor into liquid golden light, orders of magnitude hotter than the lava had been.

My golden lava balls struck him with explosions of steam, instantly solidifying into frozen rock. Anubis roared in outrage and started pounding on both the impossibly resistant black water and the casing of stone I was shellacking upon him. I realized I was screaming as I alternated between my left hand and right hand, throwing lava at him as fast as I possibly could.

I saw Mac and Calvin now standing back-to-back with their parents. Despite the ferocity of the Randulf clan, there were far too many foes to continue fighting. Even for them.

8

I started lobbing every other ball of lava their way, hoping to even the odds. I saw Kára zip through the air over my shoulder and I risked a glance up to see she was carrying the bloody Nadia to the Mausoleum entrance. *Good girl*, I thought to myself. Maybe whatever Anubis had done had affected the sealed entrance, giving us an opportunity to get Nadia out of harm's way so we could end this fight quickly. I needed to keep Anubis distracted so Kára would have a chance to sneak back and attack him from behind.

"What the fuck is this all about, Anubis?" I roared, shifting my attention back and forth between both threats. I saw a long, black paw with obsidian claws finally tear through the black water. Then a murderous, jackal-headed face tore through the same opening, looking like that scene with Jim Carrey and the rhinoceros in *Ace Ventura: When Nature Calls*.

"Horseman of Hope," Anubis snarled. "Kinkiller."

I glared at him, having no idea what he was talking about. Was he referring to my fight with Aiden? I felt the lava covering my body grow even hotter and brighter at the proximity of a god for me to kill. A screen of steam surrounded me as I lifted a clawed finger to point at him. "Stand down, or you will die, godling."

Anubis laughed. "Death is dead. Long live Death!" he howled, pounding his claw into his chest like he was hyping himself up for a competition.

"I have no quarrel with you, Anubis," I growled. "Call off your dogs, or you will all die here."

"Speaking of dogs," Anubis snarled, curling his lips as he glanced towards the Randulfs, who were now furiously battling an even larger contingent of Candy Skulls. "You never should have let the pups play in the River Styx!" the god of the Underworld yelled. "My waters are sacred. Now, the dogs of war are *mine!*"

I threw balls of lava directly at his face, feeling only the slightest flicker of satisfaction as they burned through his jowls, revealing massive fangs through his burning fur and melting flesh. One of his ears melted under the heat, and he roared in pain. Despite his torment, his inky black eyes were determined and focused like a laser as he flung his claw outward. A huge ring of Hellish light screamed into existence, slicing entirely through one of my ancestor's statues behind Gunnar. I stared in horror at the fiery Gateway, recognizing the realm beyond.

An infernal landscape of torment and anguish.

Hell.

The Underworld.

"Nate!" Kára screamed. "The exit is still sealed!" she shouted.

I ignored her as I opened my mouth to scream a warning to Gunnar, but I wasn't fast enough. As one, the Candy Skulls tackled the Randulfs through the Gateway, successfully sending all of them through the portal. I roared in outrage and leapt for Anubis with my claws outstretched. In my hand, a chain of blinding white light crackled into existence, and I was suddenly swinging my murderous Feather—a black blade connected to the end of the ephemeral white chain in my grasp.

My Horseman's blade.

It swung for Anubis' face, ripping the air with an otherworldly scream. Right before contact, Anubis slammed back into the black water of the cavern with a bubbling hiss. My Feather whistled through the space where his head had been and instead slammed into one of my ancestor's statues, decapitating the stone head of the bearded, one-eyed brute I had seen earlier.

Anubis' laughter echoed in the cavern as the Gateway started to shrink.

I hurled my wizard's magic at the edge of the Gateway, knowing I wouldn't be fast enough to leap through. Claws of lava, like extensions of my hands, gripped the edges of the Gateway, straining to hold it open. The lava started to cool and solidify, cracking against the strain of the Gateway trying to close. I poured more fire into it, hoping to hold it open long enough to pull myself through, but I found I could not move my feet. I glanced down to see the lava pooling around my legs, cooling and cracking as if to anchor me into the ground for leverage.

I realized the only way to hold it open was to keep my feet planted.

I heard Asha scream in a terrible shriek and I risked a quick glance to see...creatures of some kind fighting Grimm and Grinder near the waterfall. They looked like Big Bird's inbred cousins, and their long, knobby legs were covered with spikes. Long spines intermixed with their bright yellow feathers like they shared genes with porcupines. Yahn was hovering in the sky in his crystal dragon form, blasting fire at a flock of the winged creatures swarming the ledge. Some of those winged beasts had landed to avoid Yahn's fire, and Grimm and Grinder were doing everything they could to keep them away from the cavern. Those still in the air swept low to launch volleys of their spines down upon Grimm and Grinder, who were shielding Asha as she huddled behind a boulder.

The birds seemed intent upon the animals rather than the girl, but that could change at any moment. She was the easier prey. The birds must have chased Grimm and Asha from the sky, so they had returned for shelter and backup fire support from Grinder and Yahn.

Grinder had several bone spines piercing his body, but he swung his massive horns left and right, shattering bones and beaks, chomping down on anything that he could sink his teeth into. Grimm's Horseman armor seemed to be keeping him relatively protected.

Although I saw blood dripping from his chest and down his legs, and he looked exhausted.

I had to choose. My godchildren or Asha. I had vowed to protect my godchildren with my life. There was no question. I gritted my teeth, preparing to hurl myself into Hell after them. Then another thought hit me. I had made a promise to Nadia as well. That I would protect her daughter—because it was my fault her family had been destroyed in the first place. Her father and son were dead because of my actions. Now, her mother was dying, and I had no way to get her help. It was a foregone conclusion. Asha had no one, and no way to defend herself from the dangers of the Elder realm. She couldn't even leave without help.

On a tactical note, I couldn't hunt down Aiden's Knightmares without the help of the Randulfs. They were six powerful wizards protected by incredible armor. I needed the wolves.

But...Asha was not strong. She was utterly defenseless, in fact.

So, protect the innocent, defenseless, soon-to-be-orphan girl, or protect my investments—my warriors—for my fight against Aiden and the Masters.

I was damned either way.

Principles are armor against the poison of guilt, the voice in my Mask whispered. *If ever in doubt, always choose principles over anything else. Without those, everything else about you will crumble. You would be a false god.*

The words hit me like a physical blow, even though I had already considered her point.

Because Gunnar would never forgive me if I let an innocent girl die. Mac would be disgusted with me. Calvin would lose all respect for me. Ashley would never trust me again.

I clenched my jaw as the Gateway fought me like I was trying to hold up a mountain. I only had seconds before it would snap shut on me.

"Asha!" Nadia screamed, and I risked a glance back to see that Kára had set her down as the Valkyrie raced towards me, sweeping her glare left-to-right, recognizing the dilemma I faced. Nadia, although fatally wounded, was now crawling, dragging her body towards Asha's screams. Nadia left a sickening smear of blood in her wake, but her eyes were pure fire, even as her muscles began to betray her, shaking and trembling in protest.

Kára's face was pale and haunted as she met my eyes. She had picked up her trident, and she was shifting her gaze from Asha to the Gateway, where we could see and hear Gunnar's family battling what had to be hundreds of Candy Skulls.

"Protect Asha, Nate," she whispered. "I'll protect our godchildren. As a Valkyrie, I might have more power in the Underworld than you would."

I nodded in frustration, knowing she was right. I would figure out why the entrance back up to the Mausoleum was closed, get Asha to safety, and then find a way to Shadow Walk or make a Gateway to the Underworld.

To Hell.

But the words that had lit my heart like a fuse was when she'd said *our godchildren*.

Not mine. Ours.

"I love you, and I'll come for you as soon as I can!" I vowed.

She nodded with a macabre smile. "I know you do, and I know you will," she said, responding to both my claims.

Without another word, she set her jaw and leapt past me through the Gateway into Hell. The golden-armored Valkyrie hit the Candy Skulls like a bowling ball striking pins, and she screamed a Valkyrie scream, sounding like she was ripping the very fabric of creation as she tore into the enemy.

9

I wanted to feast on the vision of Kára slaughtering the Candy Skulls, so I held open Anubis' Gateway as long as I could. But spikes of agony were ripping through my mind, seeming to stab into the back of my eyes, so I finally released it. It snapped shut like a rubber band, sending a shower of sparks over the cold stone. The cavern was eerily silent as the remaining Candy Skulls abruptly faded away like smoke, apparently retreating after their master. I growled, wondering at the timing of it all. Why had Anubis chosen to challenge me at this exact moment? The timing was too perfect. Was he working with Aiden? Had this been a trap?

And what had he meant by saying death is dead? Was that some kind of catchphrase or something?

I saw Nadia lying on the floor, motionless, and I recalled Kára saying that the entrance to the Mausoleum was still sealed, even though Anubis had made a Gateway here. I released my grip on the lava and I instantly felt my armor cool and harden back to the normal black quartz. I rushed to her side and crouched down, lifting her head up enough to rest it in my lap. "Nadia!" I hissed, knowing she was mere moments from death. "I will get you help. Just hold on!" Grimm and Grinder were still fighting the mutant Big Birds at the mouth of the cave, and Yahn was still in an aerial battle, but their numbers seemed greatly diminished. "Keep them back, Grimm!" I shouted hoarsely. "I'm on my way!"

"Hurry!" my unicorn snarled between skewering a pair of monsters with his horn. "We can't hold much longer!" he shouted as he used his back hoof to kick a monster over the waterfall. "And I can't fuck that unicorn if I'm dead. You don't want to have cock-blocking a unicorn on your conscience!"

I grunted at his last comment as I flung my hand out and made a shield of air between Asha and danger. At this distance, it was far from perfect, but it would hold long enough to let my friends do their work.

Nadia moaned weakly and her eyes peeled open to look up at me. "I... am exhausted," she whispered, weakly clutching at my fingers. "I'm barely holding on."

"Well, hold on a little longer!" I growled, glancing up at the entrance to the Mausoleum, debating which was more urgent—Grimm's battle or getting Nadia out of the Elder realm. With my magic, I could get her to safety within moments. Maybe Alex was still up there and would be able to get Nadia to his strange healer—the grumpy man who had been a student —or something—of Pan.

I grimaced and sunk a claw of my armored hand into the stone of the cavern, pulverizing it to dust, as I recalled that same man healing Aiden.

Back when I thought he'd been a friend. An ally.

Because I'd fallen for his magician's parlor trick.

The Doppelgänger Golem.

I glanced down at my satchel and cringed, knowing the spell was tucked inside. If it came down to it, did I dare use it? What were the consequences? It was so secret that I didn't even have anyone to ask. I didn't know the consequences of the spell. There was always a price. I shook off the thought for later consideration.

Knowing time was of the essence, and going against my better judgment, I attempted to Shadow Walk us to Camelot. I instantly groaned, feeling like I'd head-butted an electric fence. I blinked dazedly, clutching at my forehead with my free hand. I was blocked, just like Kára had claimed. I'd had no problem using my magic in other ways, though.

With more caution, I tried opening a Gateway instead. It fizzled out with a puff of smoke, and I heard a deep, ominous chime that seemed to shake the whole cavern and make my vision ripple before the sound rang out into the Elder realm like a dinner bell. I instantly groaned as a warning flash of pain struck my temples, heralding an epic migraine.

The chime faded and I shuddered, wondering what kind of repercussion such a loud noise was going to cause. That sound was definitely going to draw attention to my cavern. The sound had been louder than the chime from when Anubis created his Gateway to the Underworld. I knew my magic wasn't failing, because the shield I had summoned to protect Asha had worked without issue.

Had those bird monsters arrived as a result of the first chime from Anubis' Gateway?

That...was concerning. Had I just summoned more of them?

Snapping me out of my thoughts, Nadia coughed roughly, spattering my leg with thick, phlegmy blood, and I realized I was hunched over her from the surprise pain that had just struck out at me. I backed off so I wasn't looming over her. I stared into her eyes, masking my own grief and frustration at my impotence to save her. The bird monsters shrieked, their cries often morphing into bloodcurdling screams. "Please..." Nadia croaked, looking up at me with dazed eyes, "protect Asha. Prove...Greta... wrong about you," she wheezed, her cheek falling into my lap as her strength finally gave out. "Be the man she needs to see existing in this world...and give...her...hope," Nadia murmured. "Asha means hope," she added with a weak smile.

"I will take care of her," I promised, ignoring her comment about Greta as I stroked the woman's hair back from her forehead. Asha's name meant hope. Of course it did. "Rest, Nadia," I said, smiling sadly.

"O...kay," she murmured. She let out a sigh of relief, and her chest did not rise again. Asha's mother died in my lap. My shoulders trembled with pent-up rage and disgust. I felt sick.

All sounds of battle and the stream's flowing water faded from my ears. I sat in a cocoon of guilt with a dead mother in my lap.

You did not do this, Hope, the Mask whispered to me, and I felt a massaging pressure on my shoulders, as if to comfort me. *This war will have many casualties, but it will have many more if you lose yourself to guilt. Maintain your humanity...*

I hadn't knowingly harmed this family. I had not intentionally done anything to them. But...I had indirectly ruined everything they held dear. I was responsible either way. My actions had resulted in consequences. Period. Me freeing Prometheus from his bonds had resulted in him crashing down to the Arch, resulting in the death of Asha's father and brother.

I didn't even know their names.

I continued brushing Nadia's temple with my thumb, blinking though blurry eyes. The cavern was still strangely silent, and I realized it was not just my perception tuning everything out.

I glanced up to the mouth of the cavern and saw Grimm squatted low on his front hooves, head down as an achromatic painbow spewed out from his horn. Except...the bar of light was frozen solid as it tore through three bird monsters who hovered motionless in mid-air. Feathers hung suspended in the air rather than falling to the ground. Grimm did not blink. His power blast did not move or wink out. It looked like a glowing icicle of gray shades.

His muscles did not move.

His feathers did not flutter.

Grinder hung skewered on a long, curved, bird-monster claw. He looked to be laughing, but he was also frozen still like I was viewing a picture. A snapshot.

From behind my shield of magic, Asha stared back at her mother resting her head on my lap. Pain filled her innocent eyes, as if she'd known the exact moment the last member of her family had died.

Nothing moved. Absolutely nothing.

Except me, the Horseman of Hope.

I had not caused time to freeze, which only meant one thing...

I continued caressing Nadia's temple with my thumb, and I felt a tear drop from my cheeks. I forced myself to look down at the dead woman, committing myself to endure all the pain the look would entail. Her face was frozen in a grim, haunting smile as she stared at Asha. I spotted a semi-long hair wrapped around the button of her jacket and I frowned. Nadia and Asha's hair was black, but this looked blonde or maybe light brown. It was hard to tell because it was coated with dried blood and dust, but I knew it definitely didn't belong to Nadia or Asha. Could it belong to the stranger? Aiden?

I plucked it free and shoved it into my pocket. I might be able to track him with it.

One of Nadia's fists weakly grasped my thigh, but her other hand was clenched in a white-knuckled fist at her side. I frowned, staring down at it. The corner of a piece of cardstock extended from her thumb and forefinger. I pursed my lips, seeing that it was a black and white picture of some kind.

I murmured a prayer, begging forgiveness as I carefully pulled it free from her death grip. I straightened the bloody paper and stared down at it. My heart thundered in my chest like a stampede of unicorns, and I struggled to breathe.

It was a sonogram.

Of...a little baby boy.

My eyes widened in horror, and I stared down at the mother's gaping stomach wound. "No," I rasped out loud, the pain of my voice echoing in the cavern. My Horseman's armor evaporated as I stared down at the picture of the little man.

He was smiling. At least, it looked like a smile. His tiny fists were clenched, and he was smiling.

More tears fell down my cheeks and splashed down onto Nadia's face.

My soul shattered.

I reached out with my power, not knowing what else to do. What if the little boy was still alive? What if he had a chance? How could I help? What could I do? I gripped Nadia's waist, sobbing and mumbling incoherently, begging for the boy to be alive and well so that I might—

"Nate," a familiar voice murmured in a sympathetic tone as a massive hand settled over my shoulder.

10

I did not flinch in surprise. When time had frozen, I had suspected his arrival. It was the party guest no one ever invited, who always showed up unannounced and unappreciated.

I slowly looked up to see the Boatman towering over me. The cord of knotted leather sewing Charon's lips shut had been torn partially free since the first time I'd met him—by him. There were now only two knots left, and this little mysterious tidbit had almost made Anubis shit his kennel once upon a time in the Underworld. Ironically, the dog God of the Dead did not want Charon unmuzzled. I did not know why. A broad, heavy hood covered his features, but I saw a reflective glint in the shadows of his cowl. His eyes. He thumped his long, iron paddle into the ground, using it as a cane to support his weight.

Anubis had also been very skittish around Charon's paddle. To me, it looked suspiciously like a tool for murder. Perhaps an old glaive of some kind—a long handled axe or spear. I could sense the power humming from the ancient paddle, even now.

"Damn it," I whispered.

Charon let out a soft sigh. He gave my shoulder an empathetic squeeze. "I am sorry, old friend," he said, his voice coming through my mind rather than out of his knotted lips. "I am here to collect *two* souls..."

Two...

Because one was an unborn baby boy, his tiny flame snuffed out before he could experience the magic of life. A Knightmare had killed a fucking baby. My vision flashed red with rage, imagining all the gruesome, terrible, horrible, over-the-line things I would do to this man once I got my hands on him.

As much as I wanted to rant and rave about how unfair their deaths were, I knew Charon was not responsible. He hadn't killed them. His job was to grant them peace. Everyone treated the Boatman like some nefarious fear merchant, but he was actually a hope dealer...for the newly departed.

"I don't even know if she knew about him," I said, risking a quick glance over my shoulder at Asha hiding behind my shield. Even though she was frozen still, those eyes staring at her mother felt like lasers and I quickly looked away. Like a coward.

Charon gripped his paddle blade and nodded as he cast Asha a look of compassionate sorrow. "Then you should tell her about him. She would want to know, despite the pain it will give her. She will become stronger for it if you help her."

I nodded woodenly, knowing he was right, even though saying those words would feel like rancid oil in my throat. The toughest choice was usually the correct choice.

Apparently, Charon was not in a rush to go back to work because I heard him crack open a beer. I rose to my feet and extended my hand, choosing not to look down at Nadia between us. He shoved a cold can of his microbrew into my palm and then cracked open one for himself. We clinked cans.

We drank in silence for a few moments, turning to stare out at the frozen panorama of violence that was Grimm and Grinder kicking the shit out of monster chickens. Yahn's glass dragon form hung in the air, letting loose a blast of crystalline, transparent fire upon a pair of Big Birds.

"So, you are here to face the Reverie, at last," Charon finally said, as if he were remarking on the weather.

I slowly turned to stare at him, feeling a sickening twist in my stomach —which was becoming a common occurrence over the last hour. "I came here to hunt down Knightmares," I told him, "and you think I'm here to enter a...daydream?" I asked, defining the word *reverie* out loud. "Not sure what the fuck you're talking about, Charon, but the coincidental irony is not lost on me—nightmares and daydreams. What the hell is the Reverie?"

Charon scowled pensively, only just now seeming to consider the irony I had pointed out. He also looked surprised to hear the actual reason for my presence here. "The Reverie is the heart of the Elder realm. Its purpose. The only way for a Temple to truly reach his full potential."

I blinked at him. "Well, that sounded like a high school counselor pitching me a welding degree. Speak clearly or we're done. I've got people to kill."

Charon did not appreciate my tone, but he understood my short temper, judging by how his eyes flicked towards Nadia's corpse. "The Reverie is the only true path out of the Elder realm for a Temple. The only way out is through. You are a dreamcatcher."

Dreamcatcher? I stared at him with a blank expression and finally shrugged my shoulders. "Right. Well, thanks for the beer and you can go fuck yourself, Charon. Great chat." I turned my back on him.

"Do you wield the scythe?" he asked from behind me.

I frowned at the unexpected question and reached into my satchel as I turned to look back at him. Charon was grimacing at the satchel, apparently concluding that wearing a satchel made of ancient Elder hide was in poor taste when backpacking through the Elder realm. "This?" I asked as I whipped out Cronus' scythe—the same blade I'd used to execute Zeus. "To me, it looks bigger than your canoe paddle," I added with a challenging sneer.

Charon frowned at the blade with a distasteful look but said nothing to my subtle challenge. Instead, he glared past me out at the Elder realm and let out a weary sigh. "I guess this is as good a place as any for a Horseman to die."

I narrowed my eyes threateningly and lowered my beer as I gripped the scythe tightly. "What is *that* supposed to mean?"

He shifted his gaze back to me and sighed, not remotely concerned by the weapon in my hand. "That this place is incredibly dangerous. Put that away before you hurt yourself," he muttered dismissively, and then he poured some more beer on his face—which was how he consumed beer. He was entirely unimpressed by my aura of hostility. I was a barking puppy to him. I could tell he wasn't even trying to offend me. I was literally that unthreatening to him, by his estimation.

I slipped the blade back into my satchel with a resigned scowl. "Let's suppose that I suddenly want to leave this place, but the door is locked behind me," I said, pointing my beer towards the stairs to the Mausoleum. "And I'm now responsible for a Regular who will spontaneously combust when the Elder sun hits her skin."

Charon looked over his shoulder at the stairs and didn't speak for a few moments. He finally turned back to me and this time he did look concerned, although he tried to hide it. His gaze shifted to Asha and then back to me. "She took a dip in the River Styx," he said, waving his can of beer at the stream beside us. "That will protect her from the sun." Then he poured some more beer on his face.

I stared at him, unable to speak as a faint ringing sound started in my ears. I took a healthy gulp of beer and then stared at the black stream. His battered canoe bumped against the bank of the river, remaining in place even though it didn't appear to be anchored. "That's the River Styx." I said flatly, unable to process such an outrageous concept.

Charon nodded. "You did not know this?"

I was officially about to lose my fucking shit. "Of course I did not fucking know this!" I shouted, mocking his tone.

He cocked his head, unfazed by my anger. "But you unleashed the waters of death from your family tree," he said calmly, gesturing with a claw towards the sealed Mausoleum as he took another sip of his beer. He lifted his can with a faint smile. "I make my beer in this cave. With this water. I thought I told you that."

He *had* told me he brewed his beer with water from the River Styx, but that had been when we were in the Underworld, and I had assumed he was talking about the River Styx in the land of the dead. There was absolutely no reality in which I should have taken his words to mean the strange water in my newly discovered Batcave, and he knew it.

I stared at him, feeling anger clashing with confusion in my mind. "Then why is she dead?" I snapped, pointing at Nadia's body with a fiery glare. "They both took a swim, and the Styx grants immortality, right?" That was what I had done with Calvin and Makayla, after all—how I had managed to piss off Anubis so much.

Charon shook his head calmly. "This is where the River Styx is birthed. Like a newborn baby, it is merely untapped potential right here," he said, and I was moved to see him pause and stare down at Nadia's belly with a look of sorrow, silently acknowledging the bitter similarity of his metaphor. "The Styx only gains the abilities to grant immortality once it progresses through the Elder realm, maturing, and then ultimately reaches the Underworld—a cynical irony, if you ask me." He gestured at the stream again. "But this should protect the girl from the sun. Your armor will protect you, much the same as your Knights." He frowned at Grinder. "The goat is a coin-flip."

Grinder was going to love to hear that. It looked like we didn't need to cook our dinner for the duration of our travels, since the sun might broil him alive. I shook my head, struggling to process everything he was telling me. "This whole time, the cute little water feature beneath my family tree was, what, the fountain of death?" I blurted, my mind instantly contrasting it to the legendary fountain of youth.

Charon nodded. "Clever, clever Temples," he said with an amused wink. "Hidden in plain sight. Pinch of Temple bone dust—death—and it reactivates the Elder realm. This place is full of Temple bone dust," he added. "It just keeps on accumulating, multiplying. Very strange," he said with a grin, obviously not intending to elaborate on why the Elder realm was full of my ancestors' bone dust.

Then again, if enough of them had died here, it made sense. I dismissed the thought.

I nodded absently, my mind racing. "The Elders first came to Chateau Falco when I raised that tree in my front yard," I mused. "The one bonded to the tree just outside this cave. But I only saw the Elders when I peered through Falco's glass windows. Enchanted glass."

Charon was already nodding. "Glass is made by heating sand. I wonder what would happen if the maker were to add in a pinch of bone dust to said sand?"

I grunted, having already assumed as much. It was entirely logical, in an insane way. I also caught the subtle term he'd used. Maker. A person who could do more than simple magic. They could accomplish things with a single thought, not needing to manipulate elements to their will. For a time, I had been one of them, courtesy of my parents' experimenting on me as a young child. Or maybe it had something to do with my upbringing in Fae. Or both. I had never gotten a clear, solid answer.

I ran a hand back through my hair and let out a frustrated breath before taking a big gulp of beer. "My parents could have saved me a lot of liver damage by writing this shit down in a journal or something. Assholes."

Charon grunted. "Your parents were but anal polyps compared to the assholery of their forbearers." My eyes widened at the horrifying visual, and then the claim itself. "Trust me, Nate. I knew them all."

I folded my arms, unsurprised to learn that he'd known my ancestors. "Then why the hell were you so buddy-buddy with them?"

He smirked, his lips tugging at the leather cord partially sewing his lips closed. "I did not say they were evil. I said they were assholes. You, too, are an asshole. Me," he said, thumping a bony thumb and his beer can into his chest, "also a giant asshole. You think a nice guy could do my job? Even I have to drink my sorrows away to cope with the stress."

I nodded, finding myself smiling faintly as I appraised the grim statues of my savage ancestors. "Other than them being assholes, what were my ancestors like?" I asked, gesturing all around. "They must have done a lot of good to make up for all the bad."

Charon smiled wistfully. "Glorious. Noble. Dangerous. Ruthless," he whispered nostalgically as his eyes shifted from statue to statue. Then he turned his attention back to me. "Not all maintained the balance of good and evil. In fact, many were truly terrible men and women. Or, at least, they did very little to counteract the evil feats they had accomplished. Despite that, they were all great. Every. Single. One." He saw my mouth opening to challenge him and he lifted a bony finger, waggling it in a lecturing gesture. "Greatness is not always moral or ethical, on the surface. Your inventor, Leonardo, did ghastly things in the name of science, and now all of humanity benefits from his learnings on human anatomy." He propped the spear against his shoulder and then shifted both hands up and down in a familiar gesture of balance. "The scales of justice are not always kind."

11

I grunted, knowing the argument very well. My father and I had hashed it out numerous times over my adolescence. Now, I found myself wondering if he had been preparing me for this conversation with Charon. "The argument to your claim is that the path to Hell is paved with good intentions. Believing the ends justifies the means is a very, very slippery slope into the paradise of tyranny."

Charon smiled approvingly. "Correct."

I glanced up at the sealed entrance and scowled in frustration. "I will show you fear in a handful of dust," I murmured, recalling my father's quote. Bone dust had opened the entrance to the Elder realm and unleashed the waters of the River Styx back into the Elder realm. Dust. Fear.

I turned to stare out at the inhospitable Elder realm. I saw the black river snaking through the desolate land and I shuddered. I'd made that happen.

"Fear..." Charon mused in a meaningful tone, picking up on my father's quote. "How does one defeat fear?"

"Face it," I said without hesitation.

Charon nodded approvingly, his eyes glinting sagely. Then he draped his arm around my shoulder and pointed his beer out at the Elder realm.

"One cannot run from fear and then claim it a victory. One cannot deny its existence, hide from it, or defend against it so strongly that one never has to face it," he said with a stern glare. "Fear must be faced *directly*—addressed and dominated or acknowledged and eradicated. Period."

He was giving me advice without saying it outright, for some reason. "This is a land of fear," I said, gauging his reaction. Charon winked but did not nod. He was being very careful right now. On the surface, this revelation sounded obvious to me. Everyone was terrified of the Elders. But there was a deeper significance to Charon's insinuation.

The Elder realm was quite literally a land of fear. And Aiden had intentionally lured me here. Why?

"With the entrance sealed, you must seek out the Reverie," Charon said as he removed his arm from my shoulder and took a step back. "I would advise against attempting any magical means of travel." He eyed my satchel pensively, harboring some inner thought. "It won't work, and it will attract the local predators like a dinner bell." He glanced at the chaos outside the cave. "But I'm guessing you already learned that," he said drily.

I took a drink of my beer. "No. That wasn't my fault. Anubis made a Gateway to the Underworld."

Charon dropped his beer. His can crashed to the ground, spilling the booze all over Nadia. He stared at me, his eyes like daggers. "What?"

I furrowed my brow, surprised to see such a reaction from the typically calm and collected Boatman. "Anubis poked his ugly mug up from that river," I said, pointing at it, "and then made a Gateway to abduct the Randulfs. He said my godchildren needed to pay for the crime of bathing in the River Styx—even though that was my choice—and then some crazy nonsense about death being dead. Long live death. Charon, I think he's lost his mind. He seemed unstable."

Charon studied me in stunned disbelief. "I had not known this," he finally murmured, sounding deeply concerned. "For Anubis to take such a risk...I would call you a liar if I didn't know you so well. He is terrified of you. It...makes no sense."

I gestured at the dead Candy Skulls in the cavern, a fact that Charon had not seemed to notice until now. "Exhibit A. I think he must have coordinated it with my brother, Aiden."

"Your fucking *what*?" Charon blurted, almost dropping his paddle this time. "Brother? You have proof?"

I decided that I liked seeing Charon shaken. It was a nice change of pace for me to be on the knowing side of the conversation; although, I really would have liked him to blatantly denounce the suggestion that I had a brother. Unfortunately, his reaction only served to fortify Aiden's claim.

I shrugged. "Allegedly, he's my half-brother—from my mom. No proof, but I came here to kill him. He stole suits of armor from Camelot and lured me here. The Knightmares I told you I'm hunting," I explained, "work for him."

Charon stared at me, blinking rapidly. "You must get to the Reverie. Kill this man. The Styx will lead you there," he said, pointing a bony claw at the black river stretching out toward the horizon.

"Weird. Sounds like the exact plan I just told you. Why are you so nervous?"

"If he knew enough to come here, he must know about the Reverie. You cannot let him take it. You—" His voice abruptly cut off and I saw him straining furiously, looking like he was holding his breath.

I frowned suspiciously. "You can't talk about it, can you?"

He shook his head and visibly relaxed, choosing his next words very carefully. "Not unless you've been there."

I studied him intently. "You've been there."

He hesitated for three whole seconds before nodding.

"You're an Elder, aren't you?" I asked.

He didn't look like Carl, but he didn't necessarily look human either. He looked like a hybrid of the two.

Charon clammed up and stared at me for about five tense seconds. I thought I saw his eyes flick towards my satchel, but I couldn't be certain. Then he continued on as if I had not asked the question. "As have your ancestors. *Almost* all of them," he said, bringing the conversation back to the Reverie. He then pointedly appraised a few of the statues behind me. Was he implying that those ancestors with statues had made it to the Reverie, or that those who had failed on the journey were made into statues as a warning for later descendants?

Also, how the hell would he know?

I opened my mouth to pester him, but he shook his head, cutting off the question before I could voice it. "All I will say is this..." he leaned close until he was mere inches from my face and smirked, causing his lips to pull at the coarse leather sewing his lips shut. I cringed internally but did not pull away. "Who the fuck do you think carved the statues? While I was waiting for my beer to finish brewing."

My eyes widened in surprise, and I slowly turned to sweep my gaze across the numerous statues that marked generations of my ancestors. Charon...had been squatting in my cave. For centuries. I slowly turned back to him, and he drew a finger across his throat, implying that any further discussion would result in my death.

I let out a frustrated breath and downed another gulp of his home-brew, forcing my brain to focus back on the priorities. My allies had been motionless for quite some time now, and it was weird to be hanging out with the Boatman while seeing them frozen in the act of terror and madness and murder.

I chose my next words very carefully. "But Aiden might not actually be related to me and, even if he is, he wouldn't be a Temple. My mom married into the family, so she technically isn't a Temple by blood either."

Charon grunted, looking wildly offended. He reached into his robes and pulled out a fresh can of beer. He cracked it open and splashed some over his sewn lips. Then he glared at me. "What an incredibly moronic thing to say."

I arched an eyebrow at the haughty rebuke. "Pardon? It's *science*. She literally has no bloodline to—"

"Science?! Bloodlines?!" he snapped, his voice booming in my ears like a ruler cracking over my knuckles in grade school. "We are talking *magic*, you midwit! There is more to family than blood. More to a dynasty than DNA!" He closed his eyes and took a deep breath, looking to be on the verge of murder. Then he opened his eyes and glared at me. "Which is more powerful, your fists or your magic noodles?"

I sputtered incredulously. "My magic fucking *what*?"

"The tentacle things you do with fire and ice," he said dismissively, flopping his arms about like one of those giant inflatable advertisement dummies at car dealerships.

"Whips!" I snapped, finally understanding what he was talking about.

"Not fucking *noodles*. Whips have been around forever. How the hell could you not know what a whip is? I'm pretty sure it's a commonly used torture device down in the Underworld," I muttered. "You really need to stop drinking so much, Charon," I chastised, pointing my own beer at the new one he had cracked open.

"I need to drink *more*, if anything." He snorted and splashed some more beer on his lips to prove his point. Then he held out a fist and used his other arm to mimic a whip. "Whips," he muttered with scorn. "Which is more powerful—your magic noodle or your fist?"

I rolled my eyes and pointed at the hand he was using to demonstrate my whip. "My magic noodle, obviously. All the girls agree."

"And where does the noodle get its magic? It's power? Do you have to sacrifice anything each time you use it? A bit of blood or bone or flesh? Is there paperwork you must submit to prove your bloodline prior to each use of your magic? A stamp of approval on your birth certificate?" I shook my head at the ridiculous questions, so he pressed on. "But if you punch someone with your fist, you *do* actually damage your flesh, blood, and bones—to various degrees, depending on the force used, correct?"

I frowned, surprised by his logic. It reminded me of debates I'd often had with my dad in his office over Macallan and cigars every Friday night during my college years. My dad had prepared me—conditioned me—for such esoteric arguments on magic. I shook off the wave of nostalgia and focused on the lessons my father had taught me—to utterly destroy the enemy's foundational structures, one-by-one. I zeroed in on Charon's arguments like an eagle on a rabbit.

"Yes. But using magic drains my power reserves, so your last point is not a sufficient argument—"

"Podsnappery!" he barked, and I spotted a mischievous twinkle in his eyes.

I took an involuntary step back, almost dropping my beer, feeling as if he'd sucker punched me in the gut. That single word confirmed his claim of knowing my ancestors. I no longer had any doubt whatsoever. Judging by the playful glint in his eyes, he knew *exactly* why I had stumbled back a step.

My father had often said the same nonsensical word—podsnappery— passing it along to me as his father had passed it on to him, which was whenever he decided I was making a fatal flaw in my arguments. My father would gesture emphatically with his Gurkha Black Dragon cigar in one hand, his glass of scotch in the other, and a judgmental scowl on his clean-shaven face as he barked, "Podsnappery! A willful determination to ignore the objectionable or inconvenient..." I whispered.

Charon nodded, and then continued the definition my father had shared with me, even mimicking his tone. "At the same time assuming airs of superior virtue and noble resignation." The Boatman's eyes took on a momentary flicker of compassion. "I told you. I knew him well. We often smothered a parrot together." I smiled absently at the bizarre idiom. It meant drinking absinthe straight. Charon gestured at the cavern. "Right here. He even started brewing beer with me," he added.

12

I smiled distantly, imagining my father pounding absinthe and brewing beer with the Boatman—right here where I now stood. Much like I had debated him over scotch, Charon had debated him over absinthe. I hung my head and let out a sigh, realizing I wore a sad smile at the memory of my father. "Fine, Charon. Elucidate your argument, good sir," I said, using the same phrasing my father had often used in our weekly debates.

Charon dipped his chin like we were gentlemen in a duel, respecting my courtesy—exactly as my father had taught me. "When you use magic, your reservoirs are not damaged, they are expended—much like your body needs to consume more nutrients to recover from physical exertion. That is your stomach's *function*. It is not harmed by this act. Your magical reservoirs are precisely the same. But," he held up a bony finger to herald his definitive final point, "punching something with your fist *does* damage your body—your skin, knuckles, bones, and ligaments."

Charon had a solid argument, but I wasn't yet convinced. I took a calming breath, drawing on one of my father's many lessons: *nothing is worth believing or adopting as fact that cannot withstand rigorous argument. A cloth cannot be called an umbrella until it can verifiably prove that it withstands rain.* "I recognize what you're saying, but without my bloodline, I wouldn't have any of that magic, so your point is incongruous. If my mother wasn't born into the bloodline, she's not part of the bloodline. Whether she has magic or not is irrelevant."

Charon narrowed his eyes, looking dangerously angry for some reason. "If you light a man on fire with a flamethrower versus using your magic, is he any less murdered? Either way, he dies by fire. The origination of the fire is not *relevant*," he said, turning my words against me—a common tactic of my father. "Being born a certain way means absolutely jack shit. Birthright does not entitle you to a crown and it does not demand you live in chains. Being born does not make you a victor or a victim. You're the same bawling brat of blood and excrement as every other babe kissing the air for the first time." The *you fucking moronic child* wasn't spoken, but it was implied.

My anger was rising in response to his tone. I had never liked being talked down to. I knew what he was saying, but that didn't make his words gospel. A master debater was not a reputable role model. "Fine. Semantics aside, what the fuck does this lively debate have to do with my mother being a Temple or not?"

Charon turned to look at me, and his eyes were practically aflame, as if his life depended on it. As if he were defending his own family name—like I was an interloper adopting the last name Temple without any right to do so. "Being a Temple is in your *soul*, boy. It's in your passion, your magic, your drive, your rage, your fear, and your *mastery* of such fear. Why the fuck do you think your family uses the term *Master* Temple?" His voice trailed off and I found myself smirking wolfishly. Pride filled me, dousing my anger. "Temples aren't born, son. Temples are fucking *made*."

In the ensuing silence, his statement echoed through the cavern like rumbling thunder. There were many layers to his claims that were only just now starting to seep into my thoughts.

Master my fear.

Master Temple.

The Masters threatening to send all the pantheons to a resounding conflict in the upcoming Omega War.

How Aiden had slaughtered G-Ma of the Academy, then claimed he was the new Grandmaster.

Temples—physical buildings of worship—were not *wished* into existence. They were constructed with painstaking effort by many: the passion and vision of the architect, the resources of the investors, and the time, blood, sweat, and tears of the laborers.

Also, my father's words rang a little more true to me now.

We tip our glass to ancestors' past. Dynasty is not destiny. Nobility is not class.

Dynasty and nobility were often used as terms of entitlement: birthrights.

But they had not always been so defined. Originally, they had been rewards earned through sacrifice. Deserved titles earned by the pain of the individual's quest through life.

Yet the other words in my familial quote—*destiny* and *class*— were the result of a steadfast dedication to an ideal. Striving to embody these ideals would ultimately *lead* to nobility and, later, a respectable dynasty.

If the heirs could live up to those standards, at any rate.

Finally, I nodded to Charon's words, sensing that my heart was now beating a little stronger. "You win."

He scoffed. "We were never fighting. I was educating you."

I dipped my chin with a smile. "Okay. You were right. Temples are made, not born. Masters must dominate the crucible of fear or die in the fire."

He studied me for a few moments, debating whether or not he would accept my defeat. Finally, he sniffed haughtily. "If I ever hear you say that Makayla was not a Temple, I'll slap the living shit out of you with my paddle," he muttered protectively, turning his back on me.

I let out a sigh, pondering his fiery reaction to our little debate. I knew he had nothing else to offer me at the moment because he was staring down at Nadia with a weary grimace.

"I will seek out the Reverie, old friend," I said, now feeling a deep sense of responsibility in the simple words.

He flinched as if the words had been physical blows. He slowly turned to look at me, and I could see sorrow in his eyes. Regret. Pride. "Like thine ancestors, thou willingly chooses to court fear. Be warned that this mistress is vicious and seductive. To persevere through the end of this romance, thou must remain steadfast at the beginning," he said in a formal tone, as if reciting an official initiation to an occult following.

The occult of the Masters. The Temples.

Silence ensued.

Charon watched me.

"Right now, I guess?" I asked.

He smirked, the movement tugging at his sewn lips again. "That was the intention, Nate. I thought I made that abundantly clear by my usage of the words *thine* and *thou*," he said dryly.

I felt my cheeks heat up and I nodded. "Of course. I do have one last question, though." He let out an annoyed sigh and gestured for me to proceed. "I still need to break my friends out of Hell, but I can't do that if I can't use my magic to travel." I eyed his boat with a roguish grin. "Unless you're up for perpetrating a heist, because that would make for a super cool story."

He narrowed his eyes and shook his head. "Nice try. I'll pass."

I drank the last of my beer and then tossed it behind a statue. "Fine. How else do I get to them?"

His eyes settled on Nadia, and then he poured the rest of his can of beer on his face. I watched it drip off his chin and onto her dead body. Finally, he looked back up at me. "You must steal a soul from the recently deceased. Hijack their ride to the Underworld."

I instinctively jumped back a step in horror at the abominable suggestion. I stared at Nadia and the unborn son in her womb. I almost gagged at the thought of such a selfish, evil act. The baby boy hadn't even experienced his first breath, and now I was expected to take away his afterlife as well? Or, what, take his mother's soul, leaving him to live on in the Underworld without a mother?

No. There was absolutely no way.

"Take their place on your boat?" I whispered, knowing it would damn my soul for eternity to even consider such a thing. "Wouldn't that trap them here forever?"

Charon met my eyes and gave me a single nod. "Yes. I imagine it would." He waited, giving me the opportunity to do so right here and now. To own my decision without his judgment.

I took another step back, shaking my head adamantly. "No. Not them," I whispered.

Charon leaned on his paddle and tossed his beer can beside my empty.

"If you want to get to Hell, this is the only way. Sooner or later," he said, his eyes flicking towards Asha, "you will have to choose."

I shook my head and clenched my jaw at the thought. "No way. I would save my friends only to have them damn me forever."

Charon nodded sadly. "True. Yet my response does not change. If the need is great enough, that is the price."

"Unless I can get to the Reverie first," I argued. "Once I'm out of the Elder realm, I will be able to find another way, right? Death once helped me enter the Underworld. He could do it again."

Charon studied me in silence for a few tense moments. "Can your friends survive Anubis' hospitality that long?" He then rapped his paddle on the ground three times, the sound booming through the cavern like a drum. I had never seen him do that before, and I was opening my mouth to ask him about it when his voice cut me off. "Souls get sticky when you leave them sitting for too long," he said with a grimace. "Have to get out the old spatula to scrape them out." I felt my mouth salivate—the precursor warning of violent vomiting—at his disgusting metaphor. Then I saw a flicker of movement in my peripheral vision.

I saw Nadia's soul now seated in Charon's battered canoe, and she was holding a beautiful, glowing baby boy in the crook of her elbow, smiling down at him adoringly. I sucked in a breath, feeling my eyes tear up with both joy and grief. She was holding her son for the first time in her...afterlife.

Nadia looked up at me, and her spirit glowed with a fiery unconditional love that was melded directly to her son as if they were only one soul. She smiled at me, and I felt like my heart skipped a beat at the level of gratitude in her eyes.

My knees wobbled precipitously, and I almost collapsed.

Nadia pointed at her daughter as she hoisted her baby boy up to take a gander. "That's your big sister, Asha. Isn't she lovely?" she asked, her voice no longer burdened with pain or despair. "Nate promised to take care of her until we can see her again."

The baby boy's soul let out a hiccupping giggle and I felt a tear roll down my cheek, her words hitting me like a blade to the heart. Asha would never know him, but he now knew her.

I vowed to honor her claim. I would keep Asha safe.

Charon had climbed back into the canoe without me noticing his departure. He dipped his paddle into the water and met my eyes. "Beware of the unicorns," he warned. "They are the greatest predators here, and they are very, very territorial."

I smiled at his obvious joke as I wiped the tears from my face. He was not smiling. My humor withered. "So, hypothetically," I said, censoring my words for the baby soul's benefit, "what if Grimm tried to...bang one of them?"

He blinked at me. "You would all be slaughtered. Period. It would be a cacophony of bloodshed."

I shuddered at the intensity of his voice. "But what if he managed to... seduce one? What if she really, really liked him or something?"

"That's not how unicorns..." he trailed off, remembering his underaged passenger. "That's not how they...court each other. Their union is a violent, bloody, gruesome affair. The males do not survive. Ever. The only living male unicorn is a virgin male unicorn."

Despite the deadly nature of the talk, I grinned. "Grimm...is a *virgin*?" I hooted. "Oh, man! That...that is rich!" I said, slapping my knee.

Charon rolled his eyes and turned his back on me. "The fate of the world hangs in the balance," he muttered in disapproval, "and Master Temple is joking about..." he let out a huff of frustration. "Unicorn porn."

A moment later, they winked out of view, leaving me all alone in my creepy cave as I started giggling uncontrollably about Charon's last words. Unicorn porn. I imagined anonymous submission letters sent to Hustler magazine from angsty, horny unicorns seeking romantic advice.

"Unicorn porn!" I crowed, my voice echoing throughout the cavern as I wiped the tears from my eyes, unable to stop giggling.

13

I managed to regain control of my adolescent demon and I let out a weary sigh.

I studied the statues of my relatives in a new light, considering the fact that Charon had sat up here like a hermit carving them for the last...however many years. Generations. He was the family historian. The archivist for the Temple dynasty.

But had he been immortalizing the failures or the heroes? My gaze settled on the statue of my parents, and I felt an uneasy ripple of anxiety rush through me. He'd called all my ancestors great, even the ones who had done terrible things, comparing them to Leonardo DaVinci's study of dead bodies.

I realized I was studying the statue of the one-eyed man I'd noticed earlier—the same one I'd accidentally decapitated while trying to kill Anubis. I was staring at the runes etched into his skeletal arm—especially the four that symbolized the Dread Four. I studied those four runes, linking each to their respective Horseman—Hope, Despair, Justice, and Absolution. Me, Callie, Gunnar, and Alucard.

Then I studied the four runes below ours, especially the rune that had been defaced with a black streak of charcoal or something similar. Had Charon done that? Why had the statue drawn my attention in the first place? Why had Gunnar felt drawn to it? Was it because of the Dread Four runes? How did I even recognize them when I had never seen them before—

"Shit or get off the pot, cock-block!" Grimm shouted, snapping me out of my thoughts. I heard the bird monsters scream and squawk as everything abruptly returned to normal speed. I spun on my heels and faced the invaders.

I felt a soothing purr tickle my mind, like a separate being massaging my shoulders. *Burn down the world...*

It wasn't my Mask.

Since this wasn't the most startling thing I'd experienced in the last twenty-four-hours, I obliged the creepy voice. Liquid fire blasted out from my hands, striking the birds all at once. They burst into flames and let out piercing agonized screams as I waved my hands from left to right, filling the air with fire and smoke. I accidentally hit Grinder, judging by the Mr. Kool Aid impersonation that instantly screamed *OH YEAH!* through scorched vocal cords.

I found myself cackling as I made us some fried chicken and goat for dinner.

Don't worry. I hadn't lost my shit yet. This was only chapter thirteen.

Still, I caught Asha staring back at me with terrified eyes and my laughter abruptly cut off. I released my magic and cleared my throat awkwardly. "All clear," I said sheepishly, realizing that all our enemies were now smoldering, charred husks. "And watch your mouth, Grimm. We have a lady present."

Grimm and Asha stared at me for a few moments, neither of them blinking. "You okay, boss?" Grimm finally asked. "Mac was just telling Asha here how beautiful magic was. She didn't mention crazy and erratic."

I nodded stiffly as I brushed my hands together. "Right as rain." I did not mention the strange voice I had heard because I was fairly certain it had not been a strange voice at all. I was pretty sure that had been all Nate Temple. Charon had indirectly warned me that the Elder realm was insidious, that fear was seductive here, and that I needed to be on guard against it. So, had the voice been my fear coming to life or had it been me successfully dominating fear? I had no answer.

I realized that navigating the Elder realm was going to be much more difficult than avoiding gangs of horny unicorns, mystical lizards, and power-drunk tin-pot-wizards. I also had to be on guard against myself. My emotions. My fears.

I felt Nadia's sonogram picture in my pocket, and I fought back the sick feeling in my stomach. I would wait to tell Asha about that. I made my way over to them, recalling Charon's warning about magical means of travel being like a dinner bell to the local predators. Was that the source of the strange chime I'd heard when I had tried to open a Gateway for Nadia?

I shuddered at the thought.

I saw Yahn flying away from the mountain, and I frowned. I looked up into the dark sky and saw him racing towards a flock of more bird monsters headed our way, already peppering them with long-range blasts of crystal spears rather than fire. Shit. The birds must have either heard the chaos over here and responded as backup or they had sensed me trying to open a Gateway like Charon had warned.

I walked towards them, assessing the situation.

"I thought you said magic was beautiful," Asha said to Grimm, slowly climbing to her feet.

Grimm was now staring down at a charred and smoldering body with a thoughtful frown. It was still moving, slowly crawling towards the unicorn in pitiful, jerking movements as it let out a pleading, whistling sound. "Looks like Grinder is still alive!" Then he unceremoniously stomped down on the pitiful, burning goat's head several times in rapid succession, pulverizing his skull and snapping off one of the horns. Grinder's leg twitched and then he was finally still.

Asha abruptly vomited.

Grimm looked over at her with a puzzled frown. "Oh, don't worry. He'll be back tomorrow morning. Every time he dies, he's reborn the next day," he said in a consoling voice. "See? Magic *is* beautiful."

I shook my head at him and then I crouched down beside Asha, holding her hair back as she continued emptying the contents of her stomach. Once she was finished, I reached into my satchel and pulled out a water bottle from its bottomless depths. I'd stocked it weeks ago when I had been exploring Chateau Falco with Kára. We'd loaded the satchel with everything we might possibly need, from the ridiculous to the Ragnarok.

We had wanted to see if there was any kind of limit to its ability to hold stuff.

After several hours of intense effort, we had grown bored and given up.

All I had to do was think of the item I wanted inside the satchel, and I could pull it out on my first attempt.

"Are you hurt?" I asked once she was finished rinsing her mouth out.

"No," she said, staring down at the ground.

She didn't need to tell me what was on her mind. I was surprised that she hadn't passed out in shock—either from fear of the monsters battling mere feet away or her mother dying. "Asha, we need to get out of here. More of those...things are on their way. Once we get somewhere safe, I'll answer all of your questions. I have a change of clothes from Mac that should fit you, and anything else you might need in my bag," I said, patting my satchel.

She nodded stiffly and wiped her mouth with the inside of her elbow. "Okay." She looked past my shoulder with red-rimmed eyes at her mother's corpse. "Do I have time to say goodbye—"

"YOU!" a deep, burly voice shouted from behind us.

I leapt to my feet and spun to face the threat. A knight in gleaming black armor stood near the cliff. The giant red moon hanging behind him like a bloody sun, and the free-floating embers and sparks made him look all the more ominous. The armor was dripping with muddy water, and I realized he must have climbed the goddamned mountain, which explained how he had appeared out of nowhere.

"Yes, me," I growled, preparing for the fight of my life. I shot Grimm a meaningful look for him to protect Asha. I spotted Yahn off in the distance fighting the flock of incoming Big Birds. There looked to be two dozen of them, but Yahn was holding his own, peppering them with blasts of dragon fire and glass spikes. So, that meant the Knightmare was on my to-do list.

It was fun being a hero.

I studied the Knightmare, analyzing him for weaknesses. He looked exhausted and pale, his cheeks windburned and dry, like he'd been here for a very long time. I frowned uneasily at the thought. He had long, oily, black hair and his blue eyes looked like chips of ice. He had one of those butt chins that was so pronounced that it looked fake.

"You know," I drawled, "if you got a small zodiac sign tattoo just above that ass-crack of a chin, it would literally look like a tramp stamp. A great way to show Aiden you're willing to...take one for the team, if you know what I mean," I said with a lewd wink.

He completely ignored me. I sensed he had magic, so he had obviously been a wizard when he put on the armor. In all honesty, I hadn't known whether or not that would be the case.

Aiden could have recruited a fucking god to put on the armor, judging by how badly Baldur and the Summer Queen had been angling for a suit.

But this guy...seemed decidedly unimpressive. I wasn't stupid enough to underestimate him—anyone in that armor was a deadly foe—but...this guy looked to be a junior varsity player at best.

"What took you so long?" I asked him with a frown, annoyed that I was not annoying him. "I've been waiting for one of Aiden's cucks to come wrestle with me," I teased, openly appraising him up and down to try and rile him up. Manipulating emotions was an excellent yet dangerous tactic, and I knew I was taking a gamble. An original Knightmare had easily dispatched Gunnar and Talon the last time I'd encountered one.

Alex had then proceeded to whoop the living shit out of him even though he had no armor. Granted, he'd tapped into the Hand of God to assume the power of King Arthur's soul but that was neither here nor there. If Alex could take one down, I definitely could. Especially with my Horseman's armor all ready and willing to play.

I realized that the man had not even acknowledged me. In fact, he hadn't even been talking to or pointing at me. He was focused on...Asha.

I frowned anxiously. What could she have possibly done to piss off the Knightmare more than his duty to murder me?

"Hey!" I said, snapping my fingers. "She's not a damsel in distress, and you're not a real Knight. You're just wearing your daddy's shoes and tie," I said with a condescending smirk.

Still, the Knightmare ignored me. He pointed at Asha with a level of hatred I hadn't seen in quite some time. "You!" he shouted, spittle flying from his lips. "This is all your fault! You're the reason it won't work! Why he abandoned us!"

Asha squeaked in terror, backing away. In that terrified gaze, I saw the spark of recognition. She knew him and he obviously knew her. "I didn't do anything!" she pleaded, shooting a terrified look my way. "He's the one who stabbed my mom!" she croaked, trembling with fear.

The gaunt man's armor started emitting a thick black vapor and I realized he was panting so heavily that he couldn't even speak. Judging by the look of unchecked rage in his eyes, I wasn't even sure if he'd heard her say anything to me.

I slowly started walking to the spot that would cut him off from his direct path to the helpless young woman. I lifted my Horseman's Mask to my face between steps. My armor rolled over my body like warm oil, and I shuddered involuntarily. "Time for you to pick on someone your own size, tin-man," I said, and I heard my voice come out as a demonic growl. Bone spines erupted out from my shoulders and slammed into the ground like diamond-tipped spider legs.

They were wings, but no one would have guessed that by looking at them.

They were simply the skeletal portion of what might have been bat wings, with none of the membrane between spines. Several long black feathers with red tips—matching Grimm's unicorn feathers—hung from parts of the spines, looking like the worst arts and crafts attempt ever.

A kid would have been permanently expelled from preschool—and the rest of his future in public education—for such a terrible depiction of wings.

But I loved them.

They scared my enemies.

And this made me deliriously happy, in the words of Sir Anthony Hopkins from *Meet Joe Black*.

14

"I'm not a fan of men who think it's okay to stab pregnant mothers. That's pretty much the most heinous individual crime I can think of," I rasped. "It looks like I'm going to have to send you to Hell, you son of a bitch."

He finally seemed to notice me, and he wore a slightly confused look on his face, but it immediately flickered away as he realized I was geared up to the max and staring directly at him.

"Temple," he said, his eyes dancing with sudden dark hunger. "Yes. Your severed head will grant me a place by his side. Then I will kill the feisty little bitch for weakening the armor. I will make it very slow and painful for her."

His helmet slammed down into place with a metallic clang that echoed off the rock walls around us.

Whips of black fire exploded from his hands and latched onto my upper arms. They were pleasantly warm through my armor, but I knew they would have incinerated my bare flesh. I smiled wolfishly at his surprised grunt. Before he could yank them away, I flung my hands forward and started twining the black whips around my forearms before grabbing each of them in a tight claw.

My armor was somehow preventing him from releasing his own magic.

He couldn't let go of the whips he had summoned. I watched as this sudden realization hit him on a subatomic level as he fitfully and frantically tried yanking his arms back, fighting desperately to tug the whips out of my grip.

I tugged back.

Much.

Much.

Harder.

He let out a shout of surprise as he flew towards me. I tucked my chin low against my chest as his black whips screamed and burned the very air, growing slack like coiled ropes between us. He flew into me so hard that when I head-butted him, part of the helmet over his eyes cracked with a shattering sound like a glacier calving. The air around us blew out in a concussive ring of force that sent up a cloud of dust and debris that made Grimm curse as his hooves scraped across the ground.

The Knightmare stared at me through the shattered hole in his helmet, which was only big enough to show me one very surprised, bloody eye. I gripped his chest and smiled. "What goes up must come down," I said.

And then I roped his own burning black whip around his throat like a noose and yanked it tight, choking him despite his armor's protection. Then I sprinted for the cliff's edge, holding the choking Knightmare before me like a riot shield. I leapt out into the open air, cackling wildly as we plummeted out over the waterfall. Embers and sparks whipped past my head with alarming speed, but I ignored them.

I knew how tough their armor was. I'd underestimated these Knightmares before.

I would not do it again.

And this sick bastard had murdered Nadia and her unborn son.

No mercy.

This would be retribution.

I let go of his chest and tucked my feet up to crouch on his breastplate. Then I leapt off him, using him as a launching pad while my bone wings flared out above me. The force of my jump crumpled part of his armor and, unfortunately, I had completely forgotten to let go of his whips.

The unnamed Knightmare wizard flew downward until his own magic noose of sizzling black fire jerked the whip tight, almost ripping his head off with the force of the abrupt halt. He choked as he dangled below me. His one eye stared up at me in stunned disbelief, wondering how this had happened to him if his fancy new armor made him so powerful.

He hadn't faced enough adversity in his life so hadn't learned the art of the street fight. He had used the old school mentality of war where everyone got lined up in front of each other and took turns shooting. I'd introduced him to guerrilla tactics.

He had figuratively walked up to me and slapped me with a leather glove and a disdainful sniff.

I'd lifted his shirt up over his head, kicked him in the nuts, and then slammed his face through the coffee table. He literally had no idea what to do when the setting wasn't exactly as he'd been taught in the Academy.

His wizard brain finally kicked in and he started hurling magic at me. And he was no chump with magic.

I laughed, using my wings to maneuver me from side-to-side as truly stunning blasts of power screamed past me. Some hammered into the face of the mountain behind me, sheering off massive sections of rock that then cascaded down the mountain. I swung the Knightmare directly into the path of a free-falling boulder and I bellowed out a laugh as it hammered into him, batting him to the side like a spinning pendulum and sending his next blasts of fire wild, making him resemble a cheap knock-off spinning firework. One of his balls of fire struck the actual waterfall and I almost shit myself as the water of the River Styx ignited in a *whoomph* that buffeted against me, sending me spinning as well.

I managed to regain control with my wings. I glanced back to see the waterfall erupt with flames, the fire racing upwards to the cavern above like a fuse on a firework. My eyes widened in horror to see Grimm leaning over the cliff, staring at the approaching firestorm with a stupefied look. Asha was on his back, and I saw her lean over his head. She let out a scream to see the waterfall of fire defying gravity to race towards her.

The flock of Big Birds had been reduced to a mere handful, but they were moments away from divebombing Grimm and Asha. Yahn had noticed the fire too, and the glass dragon was screaming at Grimm to get the hell out of there as he took his own advice and tucked his wings close to freefall out of the blast radius. Grimm finally took Yahn's advice and leapt out into the air. My unicorn sailed out into the dark sky of embers and sparks, clearing the fiery waterfall just as it rolled over the lip of the cliff.

In my mind, time slowed as Grimm screamed out into the air like a comet and the bird-like monsters seemed to only just realize they had missed their prey by seconds.

The cavern exploded, belching fire and molten rock that immediately incinerated the bird-monsters, shrouding them in smoke and fire so hot I couldn't even see them as the fire bubbled and expanded tenfold, reaching out into the night sky and seeming to blow the top off the mountain.

I caught sight of the strange tree just outside the cavern—the one connected to Chateau Falco where I had recently found Carl on my first visit here. He'd been beaten and battered and left for dead with his lips sewn shut by silver wire as he tried to claw his way through the bark to reach Chateau Falco.

The tree went up in flames like kindling, as if the sap within was made of napalm, and shot a streamer of lava up into the air like a geyser. If anyone was at Chateau Falco right now, they were going to be very, very startled when the weird giant tree out front spontaneously combusted with lava sap.

The blast of force sent Grimm and Asha spiraling out into the sky like a cannonball, and I prayed for dear life that she managed to hold on. Unfortunately, the rapidly expanding flame consumed them, swallowing them up in its hunger. I spotted Yahn sweeping his wings to hover in place as he searched for Grimm in the inferno. I opened my mouth to shout but then Grimm exploded out from the blob of fire like a shooting star. His wings were tucked close and wrapped around him and I heard the motherfucker laughing his head off.

He finally unfurled his wings and I saw a very pale, terrified Asha clutching onto his back for dear life.

I let out a gasp of relief and realized that I was grinning and laughing alongside my unicorn. "You crazy bastard!" I shouted at him. "FLY! FLY! FLY!" Yahn let out a roar of his own, cheering them on as well.

The blast shook the mountain, and I heard a loud crack followed by a rumbling roar. Lava exploded out from the edge of the cliff as if my cavern had been the opening of a volcano. Lava sprayed out, turning the waterfall into a raging shower of molten white and yellow rock.

I glared down at the wizard, who thankfully hadn't attacked me in the interim. It must have only been a few seconds, because he was staring at the result of his magic's consequences as if he was just as stunned as me. Before he could regain his focus and destroy the fucking world, I used his magic leash to swing him into the side of the mountain, slamming him into it like he was a rag doll.

I did it again, enjoying the crunching, clanging, screaming sound of each impact.

Then I swung him into the waterfall of lava for good measure. He screamed as the molten rock poured over him and into the hole in his helmet, but the bastard still didn't die. This fucking armor was insane.

I resumed slamming him into the cascading avalanche of rock as the mountain continued to suffer echoes of the original explosion. Each smack of Knightmare against rock left a wizard shaped splat from the fresh lava coating him.

I felt like I was painting in one of those high-brow art studios. Covering a soccer ball in paint and then kicking it at a canvas because I was oh-so-sophisticated.

When the lava paint started to run dry or cool off and harden, I swung the Knightmare back into the waterfall to refill my wizardly paintbrush. He continued to scream and curse and beg me to stop.

But an artist didn't stop painting halfway through a masterpiece.

Then I proceeded to slam him into the wall as I started to descend to the ground far below. I angled my flight from left-to-right, paying more attention to the wizard-shaped lava splats decorating the face of the mountain. They looked like those crossing pedestrian sign figures, except one where he was tumbling down an entire skyscraper of zig-zagging stairs.

He hung limp now, no longer fighting, possibly dead.

I realized I still had time before I reached the canyon floor, so I slammed his body back into the waterfall, only to realize that the lava was already hardening. I slammed his body harder into the waterfall and cracked the surface of the rapidly cooling lava, which sent up a geyser of steam to scald the Knightmare. Since he screamed in abject terror at this new and unexpected flavor of agony, I surmised my wonderful muse was still with me.

Freshly coated with more lava paint, I resumed slamming him into the rock wall as I continued my descent to the base of the mountain. Finally, I yanked the Knightmare up high above my head and then whipped him back down to the ground harder than any of the other times. His body hit the ground with an explosive splat of orange lava and the Knightmare twitched fitfully in the center of his Rorschach magma blot.

"Looks like a pretty sunset," I murmured to myself in a brief psychoanalysis. I released the whip and beat my wings so that I would land gently. I didn't want to sprain an ankle or stub a toe. I was getting older and parts of me were beginning to pop and crack and ache for no good reason.

I had a long journey through the Elder realm ahead of me and I hadn't packed any Icy Hot or Bengay.

15

I released my armor as Grimm and Asha landed beside me, staring at the already hardening black magma and the Knightmare lying in the center like a Christmas pig. Yahn circled the air above us, focusing on something beyond my view. A threat or was he just scouting for us? He took one look at the battered Knightmare, surmised he was no danger, and then he flew away to check out whatever had caught his attention.

"Communication and teamwork are not our greatest strengths," I complained.

"Nice," Grimm murmured, nodding his approval at my artwork decorating the mountain. He lifted his front leg and extended it towards me. His hoof hung down at the...bendy bit, but his meaning was clear. I reached out and bumped my fist against his ankle or whatever that part was called. Brother formalities completed, he lowered his leg back to the ground and gave me a wink.

I frowned, spotting a flash of blue near his mane. I leaned to the side to get a better look and I saw Asha blush. I met Grimm's curious gaze and pointed at his mane. "She tied a blue ribbon to your mane. You look like a girl."

Grimm cocked his head. "That's assault."

She squawked, offended. "What? It's a thank you for saving my life up there! I didn't have anything else to give you, so I wanted to show my appreciation," she said, folding her arms in a huff. "I thought it was appropriate," she said, her eyes flicking towards the Knightmare.

"How would making me look ridiculous be appropriate? Killers don't wear bows."

Asha smirked at me. "Maidens used to give honorable knights a favor. A ribbon or a flower to remember them by before battle. We are fighting knights, which makes you two knights."

He considered her words, no longer looking as offended. In fact, he looked rather proud. "Does it really make me look like a girl?" he asked me. "Tell me the truth, Nate."

I nodded, biting back a smile. "Like a big, black and beautiful diva. Especially with that rainbow horn."

His nostrils flared and his eyes narrowed dangerously.

"I think it makes you look dashing," Asha argued. Then her face lit up with a smile. "Oh! It has blood spatter on it, so it looks incredibly manly. A warning to all your foes!" She bit her lip hopefully, waiting for Grimm's response since she couldn't see his face.

Grimm's chest puffed out and he let out a proud neigh. "I accept this blood-soaked trophy."

I finally let out a laugh and shook my head. "I was just messing with you. Looks super cool, man." I turned back to Asha. That ribbon had obviously been special to her. It was the only colorful item she had. The only semi-girly thing she wore with her all black outfit. "That was very kind of you." Her hair was still pulled back, even though she'd removed her bow to give to Grimm.

"I always have extra hair ties," she said, showing me a few on her skinny wrist.

I nodded, silently wondering how I wanted to proceed with this mysterious girl and my current dilemma.

The Knightmare's last words came to my mind—his accusation against Nadia or Asha or both—and I forced myself to continue smiling. The Knightmare had claimed she weakened his armor and he had come back to the cavern specifically to kill her. At least, he'd wanted to kill her so badly that he had almost failed to notice my presence.

He'd also claimed that my head would grant him a place beside Aiden, yet he had sounded bitter about it. Was there trouble in paradise? Had Aiden screwed the man over like he had screwed over every other temporary ally? It was obvious that Aiden didn't have friends. He had pawns he used for a time and then sacrificed for a greater victory elsewhere. Everything was a means to an end for Aiden.

And his current end was tormenting me for as long as possible.

But...why let this wizard claim a suit if Aiden only intended to abandon him a few hours later? I frowned at another thought. How long had they been here? Maybe to Aiden and the Knightmares, it had been hours or days or weeks. To me, the battle at the cemetery had been only a few hours ago.

And, even worse, how was time flowing in Hell for Kára and the Randulfs?

This inter dimensional shit was for the birds. Everything needed to change to Central Standard Time. Every realm, every dimension. The world needed to conform to my version of reality so that I wouldn't be inconvenienced as much.

I focused back on the matter at hand. Asha had done something to infuriate the Knightmare and she hadn't told me anything about it. I would watch her closely over the next few minutes, seeing what kind of information she voluntarily provided.

Or what information she tried to hide.

It wasn't out of the realm of possibility that she had been planted in the cavern specifically to bait me into certain actions, whether she knew it or not—again, she could just be an unwitting pawn in one of his fucked-up schemes. Aiden knew me better than I seemed to know myself. He knew how I felt about kids, and he knew I was bringing Knights with me—Knights who devoted themselves to protecting the weak and innocent. A clever sociopath would know exactly how to exploit such characteristics.

That was how we had gotten to this point in the first place.

Aiden was not a clever sociopath. He was a genius sociopath.

As much as I empathized with Asha, I needed to find out more. I didn't think she was intentionally involved in anything, but an unwitting pawn on Aiden's game board was just as dangerous as a willing partner. I kept my face blank of these suspicions and fears as I smiled at Asha. She was staring at the twitching Knightmare in stunned disbelief.

"Is...he dead?" she asked nervously.

I squatted down to the ground and picked up a bone that looked suspiciously like a human femur and then I hurled it at the Knightmare. "Hey, Tramp Stamp!" I called out to him. The bone struck him in the head, and he whimpered faintly. I dusted my hands off and turned back to Asha. "Nope. Still kicking."

She shivered with fear, knowing that he should be dead several times over after falling off a mountain and being dipped in lava. I cleared my throat. "How about you?" I asked her. "At least your hair didn't burn off in the explosion. Then you would have looked scared and ridiculous," I quipped. She frowned at me, and I found myself wishing Mac were here to translate. "Silver lining."

She nodded woodenly, shifting her attention to the semi-living Knightmare. "Y-yeah. At least I'm not bald," she murmured. She gulped slowly, looking as if she were fighting back bile. "H-how is he still alive?" she asked, her eyes flicking up to my painting that marked the entire wall of the mountain. Unfortunately, my lava spatters now looked like black splotches, but that was simply part of the artistic process. No mere spectator could see the true beauty behind a masterpiece.

That was solely for the artist.

"It's the armor he wears," I explained, turning to keep the Knightmare in view. There was a possibility that he wasn't as injured as he let on. His leg spasmed awkwardly and I amended my prognosis. Nah. Dude was definitely in the throes of death. I told Asha about King Arthur and the Knights of the Round Table, how their armor had been stolen and was nigh impervious to typical harm as I continued to watch the broken, dented, scorched husk of a man for signs of subterfuge.

"King Arthur," Asha said flatly, blinking slowly.

"The last punk kid Nate adopted became the new King Arthur," Grimm piped in, "so I see bright things in your future."

I shrugged at the bewildered look on her face. "It's not the craziest thing you've seen today. You saw Anubis, the Candy Skulls, carnivorous Big Birds, and a Horseman," I said, thumping my chest.

She glanced over at me and flinched, only just now remembering my armor and how it had transformed me into a monster with bone wings.

She'd obviously been distracted by the chaos and had blocked my Horseman armor from her memory.

"It's just me, Asha," I assured her. "The armor doesn't change who I am."

She nodded stiffly and her mouth opened and closed several times, unable to form words.

Grimm shook his mane irritably. "And you saw a majestic unicorn. In fact, the noble creature saved you a few times in the last thirty minutes, valiantly fighting off Big Bird's inbred cousins and saving you from an exploding volcano. I know you didn't forget about that, right, Asha? I mean, Nate hardly did anything for you so far," he complained jealously.

She let out a nervous laugh and shook her head. Then she bent down to hug Grimm's mane. "Thank you, Grimm. You're a beautiful and majestic warrior. That's why you got the ribbon, not Nate."

She lifted her head and I winced to see bloody circles painting her cheeks. I subtly wiped a thumb on my cheek, discreetly encouraging her to wipe at her face. "Grimm's feathers bleed," I told her with a shrug.

Her eyes widened and she wiped at her face frantically. "Grimm! Are you okay? I had no idea you were hurt!" she said. "I thought the blood on the ribbon was from the bird monsters!"

Grimm chuckled. "I'm fine, toots. It's just—"

"I would never forgive myself if you were hurt while keeping me safe," she said, rubbing his neck soothingly.

Grimm suddenly realized his opportunity. "Well, I mean...I was hurt. Just a little, but it was all in the cause of protecting an innocent damsel in distress," he said in a stoic tone, scraping a hoof on the ground. "A true unicorn would gladly sacrifice his life to protect an innocent virgin like you."

Her face reddened and her eyes widened. "Oh. Um..." she said, shooting a panicked look my way. I swiftly turned my back, wanting no part of Grimm stepping into some shit. "That...was very personal," I heard her say. "But I'm not...*that*," she said, sounding flustered and embarrassed.

Grimm chuckled. "Toots..." he said in a dry tone, "you can't lie to a unicorn about that. Touching a few bases doesn't count. Only homeruns. We know. We *all* know."

"Hey, Grimm," I said, feeling uncomfortable for her as well as myself. "Maybe you should just drop it—"

He ignored me as he rambled on. "We form an instant kinship with virgins, Asha. Don't think of virginity like your horny teenager friends do. To unicorns, it means you're pure. Abstinence is A-OK," he said reassuringly. "It is the noble, virtuous, and honorable thing to do and be."

The air was dead silent for a few moments, and I felt my shoulders tensing. This was going to be bad. He'd just found a way to alienate her when she was already petrified and likely in shock. I really wished that I hadn't sent Kára away. This was definitely a conversation for a woman to resolve—likely by beating the feathers off Grimm until he ran away in shame—

Asha cleared her throat. "If being a virgin is so noble and honorable, then why were you so adamant about wanting to fuck that other unicorn?" Asha asked in a perfectly innocent tone that was actually pure deviance.

Grimm sputtered. "Well..."

"Since you are such a noble, majestic creature, and all," Asha continued, turning his words back on him.

"Look," Grimm argued, sounding flustered. "The thing is—"

"Because hypocrisy doesn't sound noble or majestic at all. I would know because I'm so virtuous and pure and whatever else you said. Do I need to take back my ribbon?"

I glanced over my shoulder, grinning at Asha. She shot me a wink and a smile, and I realized she looked older than I had initially thought. Not old enough for these kinds of conversations or anything, but maybe old enough to almost start driving. Old enough to snark back on a topic that was likely commonplace among her peers.

Grimm saw me smiling and narrowed his eyes. "Oh. I see. It's time to side with the humans. Gang up on the unicorn. Right after I saved your life. That's how it is, huh?" he grumped. "I thought we were going to be friends, Asha."

Asha patted his neck consolingly and let out an infectious laugh. "I'm just trying to wrap my head around everything, Grimm, and you embarrassed me. I get mouthy when I'm off balance."

Grimm's ears swiveled her way, but he looked content to give her the silent treatment.

"Forgive me, Grimm?" she asked, and then she started rubbing his ear with the palm of her hand. "Your...painbows, I think you called them, were very impressive. Burned away all those chickens like they were nothing."

I watched his eyes momentarily roll back in his head as he leaned into it, moaning with pleasure. "Yeah, okay," he replied dazedly. "I forgive you. Maybe you're just hungry."

She winked at me, and I realized she was much more devious than I had given her credit for. "A salad does sound great right about now, but I'm betting that's not an option."

Grimm snorted. "Are you kidding? We have roasted goat! Grinder made dinner for us!"

Asha blanched as her eyes settled on the haunch of semi-roasted goat leg sitting in the dust at Grimm's hooves. I hadn't even noticed him carrying. Had he held it in his teeth or had Asha carried it off the mountain for him? My frown matched Asha's, considering that it might have been in Grimm's mouth already and was now dry rubbed with Temple bone dust. "No, thank you," Asha murmured, looking a little green.

"What, are you a vegan or something?" Grimm guffawed at his obvious joke.

Asha was nodding. "Yes, actually. I am a vegan."

Grimm's humor evaporated. "Get off my back. Now." His tone was cold and harsh.

Asha lifted her leg and slid off, sensing the seriousness in his demeanor. "Grimm?" she asked softly, leaning forward to peer at his face with a half-smile, unable to tell if he was teasing her again.

"Vegans have no souls," Grimm said, and then he scooped up his leg of goat and trotted away from her. "Look at those beady eyes. She's probably going to kill us in our sleep."

"Hey!" I called out to him. "If you're going to pout, keep an eye out for Yahn. He obviously saw something interesting, and we might have to leave in a hurry." He didn't acknowledge me, but I saw Asha flinch in recognition of the name, although she tried to hide it. Then again, I wasn't sure if she'd seen him in human form yet, so she might not have made the connection that he was Greta's grandson.

16

A sha turned to look at me with a hurt frown at Grimm's words.

I waved a hand at her. "He's fine. Grimm is an asshole to everyone. He didn't mean anything by it. And he kept the ribbon," I whispered with a smirk, "so I'm sure he'll come around." I swept my gaze across the floor of the canyon, not seeing much vegetation other than succulents and bare, windblown bushes. "I don't see much in the way of produce," I said, "So we will have to make do with the snacks in my satchel," I said, patting the white leather satchel at my hip.

Asha nodded absently, looking to have already forgotten the food topic as her eyes took in her surroundings for the first time.

I studied the pool beneath the waterfall. For some unknown reason, that water hadn't ignited like the rest of the waterfall had strangely done. The pool was a deep, dark blue—almost black—and it broke off into a river leading deeper into the Elder realm towards the mysterious Reverie Charon had told me about. Where the new river flowed through the land, I saw faint hints at greenery growing along the banks. Nothing luscious but a faint tinge of green—very, very faint.

I definitely didn't want to eat anything grown with water from the River Styx, even if it was pure and innocent here like Charon had said. Berries along the bank of the Styx might accidentally give you superpowers or super curses. I had enough headaches.

I frowned, glancing up at the black smear of cooled magma where the waterfall had been. It stretched all the way up to the cavern high above. Great clouds of black smoke billowed out of the rupture in the mountain, but I realized that water was once again flowing over the frozen magma as if it had always been there. But...if the water had caught fire and exploded the cavern, where was the new water coming from?

Was the cradle of the River Styx eternal in some way? That would actually make a strange sort of sense. Regardless, the waterfall was rapidly growing larger and larger, back to its earlier size—except now it ran over a fresh cliff of hardened magma.

I shook my head, wondering what the hell the wizard had done to cause such a strange reaction. Had it been his armor's magic or had it been something to do with the River Styx reacting to his magic? I wasn't sure if I had touched it with my magic in the cavern above when we'd been fighting Candy Skulls and I'd taken a swing at Anubis. If that explosion would have happened while we were all trapped inside...

Well, this adventure would have turned into a short memoir.

I jumped as Asha tapped my shoulder. I hadn't noticed the virginal vegan sneaking up on me. Maybe they really didn't have souls—like gingers—and that was why no one had sensed her in the cavern. I met her eyes and waited. She averted hers to look at the Knightmare and I watched her wringing her hands nervously. "Is...he dead *now*?"

"We could throw another bone at him," I suggested. She smiled nervously but I hadn't been serious. I studied him thoughtfully. The lava had completely cooled and fresh blood was pooling around the motionless armor. Why hadn't the blood instantly dried from the heat? I tapped the black mound with my boot, expecting it to crack and reveal hot lava beneath the cooled shell of stone. It did not. In fact, it felt completely solid and not even remotely warm. I frowned as I squatted down and touched the black, smooth magma with my finger. It really was ice cold. What the hell? I'd assumed it might be warm, at least. It felt like the lava had cooled months ago. Centuries ago.

"This place doesn't make any sense," I murmured as I rose to my feet, considering the many contradictions to physics. The waterfall had caught fire but not the lake below. The ground around us was littered with bones like they were weeds and the giant red moon kept the nightscape bright enough for us to see as clearly as if it was daytime. And those damned embers drifting through the air like snow didn't seem to burn anything.

Asha bent down and repeated my action, tapping the black stone with a dirty finger. "That's way too fast for magma to cool," she said, glancing up at the dark sky. "The weather is almost hot enough to make me sweat." She reached out a finger and caught a pinch of sparkling ember between her fingers.

"No!" I snapped, grabbing her wrist and prying open her fingers. I frowned, staring down at her uninjured fingertips. They weren't burned at all, even though I'd seen her catch it.

She grinned at my stunned expression. "A few of the...fireflakes already touched me, so I knew they wouldn't hurt. I wanted to see if they remained solid upon contact since they can't melt in your hand like a snowflake would, being fire and all."

I stared at her. "Fireflakes," I repeated in a flat tone. "They're called embers and sparks and they are very dangerous—"

She opened her mouth and caught one on her tongue with a delighted laugh. She saw me scowling at her and she shrugged sheepishly. "Sorry. Very dangerous fireflakes," she said in a somber tone, and gave me an obedient nod. "Sir."

I scowled at her. "You are going to be trouble, Asha," I said, shaking my head. But I realized that I had failed to hide the smirk at the corner of my lips. I let out a sigh. "Just...be careful here. These things," I said, gesturing at the embers and sparks—

"Fireflakes," she offered, watching me with a dutiful, too-innocent expression.

I grunted. "These fireflakes could be more dangerous than we realize. Like that pretty little waterfall somehow being combustible and causing the mountain to explode," I said, pointing a finger upwards. "Water doesn't combust like that in Missouri," I continued, meeting her eyes and leaning forward to prop my hands on my knees so that I was only inches away, at eye level with her. "Asha, we're not in Missouri anymore."

Her eyes flicked to the Knightmare and her playfulness faded. She took a deep breath and nodded. "Okay."

I reached out and squeezed her shoulder reassuringly as I gave her a warm, genuine smile. She'd just lost her mother. If snark and insubordination—to some extent—were her coping mechanisms so that she wouldn't fall to pieces on me, then I had no problem giving her a loose leash.

But I wasn't about to give her so much compassion that I would let her coping mechanisms get her killed. Or the rest of us killed. It was a very fine line between making sure she had a healthy respect for the dangers here yet giving her the ability to figure out this scary new world without her mother.

I remembered the sonogram of her brother in my pocket and I almost flinched.

"Look, Asha. I'm not going to let anything happen to you. I promise. But I need to make sure you have a healthy respect for this place. It's not like home, so we need to think twice before making any assumptions on anything. Deal?"

"Of course. I wouldn't have done the fireflake thing if I hadn't seen it already touch my arms without hurting me. I accidentally caught one in my mouth when I was flying with Grimm, so that wasn't me being childish either," she said. Then a faint smile crept over her cheeks. "Flying," she breathed wondrously, her eyes glancing up at the sky. "I wish my brother could have seen this," she whispered. Then she glanced at me. "You would have liked him, Nate."

I squeezed her shoulder and nodded, managing not to flinch when she'd used the word brother, even though it felt like the picture in my pocket had just zapped me. "I'm sure you're right, kid."

I finally turned back to the Knightmare and took a deep breath. "You should stand back in case he's faking it," I told Asha. She wisely scurried back ten feet and watched me like a hawk as I approached his now motionless form. He remained completely still.

I studied the armor, scanning him from head to toe. I'd really done a number on him. Despite not wanting to damage the armor, I couldn't risk taking it easy on a Knightmare to salvage the treasured suit. That was a great way to pull my punches and get my friends killed.

Still, I'll admit that I felt a huge boost of confidence and pride at having beaten the Knightmare so handily.

Did that mean these weren't as strong as the original Knightmares—

the original twelve Knights turned bad—had been? It would make sense. Those guys had been legends.

Maybe their strength had been in themselves, not necessarily the armor.

I thought more wizardly thoughts as I studied the intricate black armor, wondering what to do with it after I finished the grisly task of removing the body.

Something that definitely would kill Asha's appetite—for meat or anything else.

I peered into the hole in his helmet and saw a blackened, charred skull staring at me. I clenched my jaw and glanced over my shoulder as an idea hit me.

A soul. Charon had said I could hijack a soul to get back to the Underworld. I waited for him to arrive, for time to freeze so I could use the bastard's soul to get the Boatman to take me to Hell and save my friends.

I waited some more, with a whole lot of nothing happening for my troubles. A scowl settled over my cheeks as I realized he was not going to show.

"What's wrong, Nate?" Asha asked, having seen me glancing back and forth anxiously. "Grimm is over there. Do you need him?"

I shook my head with an irritated sigh. "He's not coming," I mumbled under my breath. "It's nothing, Asha." I wasn't about to explain my old friend, the Boatman, to her right now. Not after he had just taken her mother. That would definitely kick me out of her circle of trust. Instead, I leaned over the body and tugged back the visor on the helmet.

I leapt back with a shout as the remains of the wizard disintegrated before my eyes, sending up a wispy cloud of black grit into the air. I scooted back farther as the dead wizard's ashes lifted away on the breeze. I wasn't interested in inhaling dead wizard, so I waited until I was absolutely sure it was all gone. I was about to approach the armor when it abruptly flashed with bright light, temporarily blinding me and sending me skidding back a few feet as a blast of hot air struck me.

I wiped sand and grit from my face, coughing violently as I realized I'd just inhaled a bunch of my ancestors and possibly dead wizard remains.

"Look!" Asha gasped from beside me as she tugged at my shoulder. "It's not black anymore!"

I wiped at my eyes and blinked rapidly to clear away the dust and hopefully regain my vision from the unexpected flare of light. Thankfully, I hadn't been permanently blinded, but I did still see purple after effects dancing in my peripheral vision like when you inadvertently stared at a camera flash.

Atop the black magma was now a perfectly pristine white suit of armor. My eyes widened and I grinned wolfishly as I leapt to my feet, pulling Asha along with me. "We did it!" I crowed. "Grimm! We fucking did it!"

"That's great, Nate," my unicorn muttered in a monotone. "But I don't talk to vegan enablers, so you're going to need to iron out that little wrinkle before we can resume our work relationship."

I rolled my eyes and shot Asha a reassuring smile. "He's a drama-queen."

Asha smirked and glanced back at Grimm with a mischievous look. "What if this vegan lures your ladyfriend over here so you can...bang her?" she asked him in a loud voice. "Virtuous virgin, remember?"

Grimm slowly turned to look at her with a very, very intense gaze. "That...would be very...virtuous of you, vegan." He studied her suspiciously.

"I could *try*," Asha said, shrugging her shoulders. "If you stop pouting and calling me vegan." She folded her arms smugly. "If you want to get lucky, I want to hear you say it. Say my name, unicorn!" she shouted. "Say it loudly and proudly!"

Grimm turned to face her, flaring out his wings. "Asha!" he snapped, scraping his hoof across the ground as if he was going to charge her. But he was grinning as his eyes lit with inner fire. "I accept your terms...Asha." Then he dipped his head in a faint bow and tucked his wings back. He stood still for a few moments, and then he started cackling as he pranced about excitedly and started singing to himself. "Grimm is gonna get some, Grimm is gonna get some!"

17

I shook my head and shot her a resigned grimace. "You didn't have to do that. He would have forgotten about it in an hour or so."

Asha shrugged. "If virgins attract them, and they won't harm virgins," she explained, studying my face to make sure she was getting the facts straight. I nodded. "Then why wouldn't I help? I get to see another unicorn. Grimm gets to...get some," she said with an eye roll, "and I get to be a help to the team. Win-win."

I studied this strange creature before me. I discreetly delved her again, wondering if I might have overlooked some magical trait or maybe a ward of some kind concealing her powers. There was nothing. She really was a Regular in every sense of the word. I smiled at her. "Thank you...vegan," I teased.

She flashed me a bright smile and nodded matter-of-factly. "I also made a friend."

I smiled warmly. "You made two, Asha." I glanced at Grimm who was still hopping about and cheering on his future conquest. "And you showed him you have a spine. Attagirl."

She beamed happily. "My mother used to say I had too much spine for my own good. I was kind of a troublemaker in my youth."

"Youth?" I sputtered, gesturing at her teenaged body. "You can't even drive yet, can you?"

She narrowed her eyes, and then I watched as her fire flickered and faded. "I guess I just feel a lot older than I look after...everything." She glanced up at the cavern high above. "Even older as of today."

I nodded, hating to see her in despair.

She visibly shook herself and forced a smile onto her filthy cheeks, banishing her darker thoughts. Her gaze shifted past me to the armor and she cocked her head quizzically. "So, what does that mean? Changing white like that. What did you do?"

"It means the armor is pure again. No longer tainted. We can use it for good. We took away a very dangerous weapon from the bad guys. I thought it might remain black, which would mean it would brain-wash anyone who tried to put it on, turning them bad."

Asha shook her head, struggling to take in her new reality and process everything. "And it did this all by itself? You didn't magic it?"

I shook my head, biting back a smile. "I did not magic it."

But there was one thing still bothering me. Charon had not shown up. Which meant these Knightmares would not grant me a free ride to Hell to save Kára and the Randulfs. I needed to resolve this Elder realm situation with Aiden before I could go save them. I needed to find the Reverie, which meant I needed to find Carl, since he was the only Elder I knew.

There was a good chance that Kára had already taken over Hell and they were currently having a tea party in her new domain, propping their feet up over Anubis' dead corpse.

The visual gave me a hopeful smile. I had no doubts in the strength and abilities of my friends, but Anubis wouldn't have abducted them unless he had been confident he could control them—which was another reason I had wanted to send Kára after them. Anubis had planned to take all the Randulfs. The only wrench I had been able to throw into his scheme was a Valkyrie.

And my wench was one hell of a wrench.

I couldn't focus on that right now. Charon had left me hanging, which meant my only option was to send Yahn out to find Talon and Carl, and for all of us to head to the Reverie. I realized I was staring at the suit of armor and I let out a troubled sigh, deciding I needed to address something here and now.

"How did you know this man, Asha?" I asked softly. "He definitely recognized you."

She nodded. "I told you. He stabbed my mother up in the...building," she said. "The crypt?" she asked with a frown.

"Mausoleum," I corrected her. "My family Mausoleum."

She glanced back up at the cavern, as if she could see the building from here. "All those statues and tombs were all Temples?" she asked incredulously.

I understood her innocent disbelief. Having a building set aside for your dead ancestors was not common. Most people got a shallow grave and a cold tombstone, surrounded by strangers. The Temple dynasty stretched on into the land of the dead. We remained united, even in death. I nodded. "Yes," I admitted. "Part of the burden of sharing a bloodline with rich assholes, I guess."

After a few moments of silence, I cleared my throat. "So, he stabbed your mother," I said as gently as I could. "But why was he so angry with you? He said you weakened the armor and he wanted to kill you for it. He wanted you dead so badly that he almost didn't even notice my presence, which makes no sense at all. I'm their biggest enemy. I'm the reason they came here." Her face paled and her shoulders slumped. "What was he talking about?"

She licked her lips, staring at the empty armor as if he were still wearing it. "I don't know. We ran into the Mausoleum after the explosion and hid behind a statue. I found a metal helmet and showed it to my mom. Then that man and two others showed up, stabbed her, and took the helmet." She shuddered and I saw the fire of anger in her eyes. "I will never forget his face. He killed my mom."

I pursed my lips, sympathizing with her. But part of her story was nagging at me. "That helmet?" I asked, glancing down at the empty suit. They had thought her mother was trying to take a suit of armor and had killed her for it.

She nodded. "It was dark, but it looks the same. When we were hiding behind the statue, I cut my finger on something sharp and found the helmet there." She held up her hand, showing me a cut on her finger. "I showed it to my mom. Then they showed up and took it from us." She stared down at where the dead man had been with a hateful look in her eyes. "*He* took it from us."

I stared at the cut on her finger, my blood running cold. She had cut her finger on the helmet. Something like that surely would have bonded her to the suit of armor. Especially after hearing the wizard say that the armor had been weakened. He'd been furious. Asha had unintentionally bonded with the armor. But...how had the armor then worked for the wizard if it had bonded to Asha? And why wasn't it bonded to her now?

"Did the armor do anything when you cut your finger? Did you feel anything?" I asked.

She frowned. "Well, it hurt," she said, frowning in confusion.

How did I explain magic to a Regular? I ran my fingers through my hair, furiously trying to think of a way to interrogate her without putting my own fears and suspicions into her head. Then she would just parrot them back to me. I needed her to tell me in her own words what she'd experienced. If I asked questions that were too specific, my words might fill in the empty gaps in her memory, making her agree to something that hadn't actually happened, or remember things that hadn't actually occurred.

"Other than cutting your finger, did you feel anything strange? Something...unnatural?" I asked.

She cocked her head, thinking intently. Finally, she shrugged. "The helmet felt hot, but there was fire everywhere. When I yanked my hand away, I cut my finger. It hurt really bad, but we were both scared out of our minds. Nothing made any sense. Monsters were running around and the building had just exploded and I thought I had just seen an angel in the sky before fireballs tried to take her down," she admitted with an apologetic shrug. "*Everything* felt strange and unnatural."

I nodded. "It was a scary night. Even for me," I assured her. I pointed my thumb over my shoulder at the armor. "Can you...feel anything right now? I don't know how to explain it, but does that feel like it's...yours?"

She blinked. "Mine?" she asked flatly. "It's a suit of armor. I know it's not mine."

I sighed, nodding. "I know. But..." I took a deep breath. "I have an idea."

Imagine that you are suddenly wearing the armor. Believe it as strongly as you can."

She stared at me as if I were daft. "Like...right *now*?" she asked, looking as if she thought I might be insane. I nodded encouragingly. She shifted her attention past me and stared at the armor with an intense frown. "Come to me, armor," she said in a lofty tone. Nothing happened and she let out a laugh of relief. "You almost had me going."

I frowned at the armor. "Fuck it," I muttered. I needed to keep her safe here, and this was the best way to do it. I reached over to the armor, picked up the helmet, and then I spun towards Asha, lobbing it at her. "Catch!"

18

Her eyes bulged in panic but she had no other choice than catching the helmet or letting it slam down onto her toes. She gasped as she caught it, staring down at it as if she feared it might explode at any moment. She took a few nervous breaths and then shot me a panicked look. "Now what?" she whispered.

I frowned. Was it broken like the wizard had claimed? "Think about the armor being yours. Protecting you. Try to picture it in your mind."

She scrunched up her nose and closed her eyes, looking like she was constipated. After a few moments, she opened them with a hesitant look my way. "Did it work?" she asked.

I shook my head and frowned pensively. What the hell? If it was bonded to her from the earlier cut on her finger, it should have done... something. Reformed their connection, solidifying it.

But even if the armor was now neutral and unclaimed—since it had turned white after I killed the wizard—it should have formed an entirely *new* bond with her here and now. Like when everyone else touched it with an inclination to wear it. "Maybe it doesn't work for Regulars," I mused, scratching the stubble on my chin thoughtfully. But if that was true, why had the wizard been so pissed off about it not working? "And you are absolutely certain that man was the one who stabbed your mother and took the helmet?" I pressed. "It wasn't someone else? There are six of these bad men with similar suits. You said you saw two other men."

She held the helmet gingerly but she nodded vehemently. "It was him. I would bet my life on it. He stabbed my mom. I didn't even see the other two faces, only him," she said. Then she grimaced at the helmet, as if remembering it had just been on his head. "Can I put this down?"

I walked up to her and took it. She let out a great breath of relief and brushed her hands together. I reached out to take her hand and then I inspected the cut on her finger. It was deep and had definitely bled, but it looked to be healing. I touched the helmet to the dried blood and waited for a reaction. Nothing happened. I let out my breath, not realizing I'd been holding it. "I don't understand," I murmured to myself. "Either way, it should have worked."

"I can't fight monsters," she said, sounding on the verge of bolting. "The armor would be wasted on me."

I smiled warmly. "No one is asking you to fight monsters, Asha. I just wanted it to keep you safe."

She licked her lips nervously. "Can you stop experimenting on me now?" she asked, sounding on the verge of panic. "You're scaring me."

I shot her an apologetic look and pulled the helmet away as I released her hand. "I'm sorry, Asha. I'm trying to figure out what made him so angry with you. You recognized him and he definitely recognized you. You see, the armor can...bond to people, so I thought that when you cut your finger on it that you might have paired with this suit of armor."

She stared at me with wide eyes. "You mean that the armor could be mine?" she whispered, not sounding the least bit excited about the prospect. Instead, she sounded horrified. "No. I do not want that. I could never walk around in that thing. It's way too big and heavy."

I smiled at her. "The armor changes with magic. It adapts to the user. If you're big, it molds to you. If you're a werewolf like Calvin and Makayla, it adapts to their form." I waggled my fingers mysteriously. "Magic is weird."

She let out a nervous laugh and took a step backwards, putting distance between herself and the armor. "I don't want any armor. Thank you."

"What if it could protect you from danger?" I asked thoughtfully. "It would keep you safe here."

She shook her head. "No. I don't fight anymore."

I arched an eyebrow. "You used to fight?"

She flushed with embarrassment and gave me a faint nod. "I wasn't a great kid. I wasn't bad, but I got into a lot of scrapes. I don't like bullies. I got into a few fights with them when I was younger. Got suspended and all of that."

"What changed?" I asked her, reminded of my own troublemaking days.

She shrugged. "My brother always followed the rules and kept me on the straight and narrow." Her eyes grew misty and she blinked a few times. "After he died, I thought long and hard about what kind of person I wanted to be. I didn't want him looking down on me and being disappointed."

I smiled warmly. "I don't think that's possible, Asha. I'm sure he's very, very proud of you. They all are, and now it's my job to keep you safe. Your mother asked me to take care of you, and I never break a promise. And, for the record, disagreeable people make the world go round. There is no virtue in being a meek sheep."

She smiled thoughtfully. "My father used to say something like that."

I dipped my chin. "He must have been a very wise man. I'm sure he would want you to be strong and brave right now."

She nodded, looking like her spirits were lifting. "He also said to be mercilessly kind. A rising tide lifts all ships. A laugh and a smile are often stronger than muscles." She flexed her sticklike arms and grinned. "So, I'll try to keep you grumps smiling. That's why I gave Grimm the ribbon."

I laughed. "That sounds great, Asha. Maybe you can go talk to Grimm? I need to collect this armor," I said, patting my satchel. She frowned dubiously and I smiled reassuringly. "It's magic."

"You have a magic purse? That sounds cool," she said, and then she turned away, calling out to Grimm.

I scowled at her back. "It's not a purse," I muttered under my breath. Then I set to shoving the armor into my satchel. Although it was bottomless, I still had to finagle the pieces into the opening. As I worked, I contemplated our current situation.

The Knightmare had been furious at Asha, claiming it was her fault the armor didn't work and that some unnamed *he* had abandoned them. Obviously, he was referring to Aiden. But...that made no sense at all.

Unless Aiden truly had escaped the Elder's realm, trapping me here in hopes that Anubis would do his dirty work. Had Aiden found the Reverie and then escaped? But he had only been here a few hours. Unless time moved very differently here. Since I was unable to contact my friends, I had no way of knowing how much time had actually passed since we'd descended from the Mausoleum.

As plausible as these fears sounded, they didn't jive with what I knew about Aiden. He wanted to play a great game with me, as he'd called it. He wouldn't want Anubis to steal his fun, and he wouldn't want our game to end just yet.

But why would he abandon his newly minted Knightmares after going to so much trouble to get the suits?

There was more to the story. I was missing something.

Which meant I needed to follow Charon's advice and get to the Reverie. Maybe Yahn could track down Carl and Talon. Carl would have to know something about the Reverie—at least how to get there.

I also wanted to use the hair I had found to give Aiden a nasty little surprise of my own, but I wanted to find a safe place to do it, not here at the foot of the volcano I'd inadvertently awoken. That was bound to have drawn the attention of the locals, and I wanted to be as far away as possible when they came to investigate.

I didn't know who to trust here.

But I knew fear was going to be infecting us the whole time, and the only way to beat it was to face it.

"Incoming!" Grimm shouted as I was shoving the last gauntlet into my satchel. I leapt to my feet and spun to face him. Asha hid behind him, peeking up over his back with big frightened eyes.

19

Before I could get too riled up, Talon and Carl trotted over the rise, led by Yahn, who was now in human form with his white armor. Talon and Carl also wore their fancy white armor, but their faces wore grim frowns. The pair looked like they'd seen better days. Their eyes were red-rimmed and they looked tired. Their armor was decorated with spatters of dried blood here and there. They had seen battle recently.

Yahn marched ahead of them with a scowl, not looking pleased about his victory. He'd found them! This was the best news I could have hoped for!

I let out a breath of relief and turned to Asha, who was on the verge of panic, hiding behind Grimm. "It's okay, Asha. They are friendly."

She looked over at me with a hesitant frown. "They don't look very friendly right now," she said. I saw her studying Yahn with a perplexed look, cocking her head in confusion. So, she hadn't gotten a good look at his human form until now, but she definitely seemed to recognize him.

Grimm chuckled. "It's okay, Asha. They are very good at being unfriendly, but only to our enemies."

Talon and Carl were both looking up at the smoke coming out of the cavern high above, frowning anxiously. Talon hissed at Yahn and the blonde folded his arms across his chest with a petulant frown. Then he leaned against a tree stump as Talon and Carl jogged over to me, their armor not making even a whisper of sound despite them looking like they were transformers. Well, Carl looked like a robot velociraptor, but Talon looked more or less human in silhouette. With the head of a feral mustached feline, of course. Carl's long tail was covered in metallic scales since the armor had adapted to his body style. They came to a halt in front of me and they were still gripping their weapons.

Talon held his spear with a murderous scowl as he noticed the blood coating the black rock behind me. He sniffed at the air and grimaced before his shoulders relaxed. Carl studied me from head-to-toe as if searching for wounds. When he found none, he smiled and nodded. "It is good you finally came, Master Temple. Sending the dragon into the sky was ill advised. He spooked a herd of arachno-deer, and now they are stampeding this way."

Talon glanced over his shoulder and hissed at Yahn again. "Who gave him armor?"

"Alex," I told him in a meaningful tone. Talon's anger wilted and he let out a resigned sigh. I ignored Carl's comment on my punctuality because he didn't mean to come across as an asshole. He just said what he was thinking with no filter or nuance. "What the hell are arachno-deer? Can't we just smoosh them? You know, like spiders."

Talon shuddered and Carl burst out laughing. "They are about to smoosh us!" He hooted, taking my comment as an attempt at a joke. When he saw I wasn't laughing, he flicked his tongue out at me. "They are as big as cars with eight legs made of bone that resemble their antlers. They are scavengers, but they are formidable."

I shuddered at the bizarre image. "We have three Knights."

"The herd is several thousand strong, and they are headed this way, searching for the sparkly dragon they saw flying about in the sky. Shiny things attract them." He glanced up at the cavern. "And fire. They like fire."

"What the hell?" I muttered. "This place sucks. It's like Australia on meth."

"You have no idea," Talon agreed.

Carl glanced over his shoulder and sniffed at the air as if gauging how much time we had. He turned back to us without giving an update, although his tail was twitching anxiously. "No more flying. They hate flying creatures. And no more sparkling. Or making fire. All bad bad," the Elder said.

"What about the bird monsters up there?" I asked, gesturing at the mountain. "They fly."

Carl looked at me as if I were a particularly moronic child sniffing glue sticks. "Which is why they live on the mountain, far away from everything. They are not fools."

I pursed my lips. "Fine. I'm sure we can get away from the herd without too much fuss. How long do we have until we're in danger?"

Talon looked dubious but he didn't say anything. Instead, he was watching Carl, deferring to his expertise on the local wildlife.

Carl sniffed at the air curiously. "Not very long. We need to get away from the mountain. The explosion will draw other attention we do not want. And if a herd that large is on the way, then the unicorns won't be far behind. They hunt the arachno-deer."

Talon actually flinched and his tail puffed out upon hearing about the unicorns. I wasn't sure why his tail wasn't armored, but my alarm quickly washed away the curiosity—because curiosity killed the cat.

Grimm's ears perked up and he trotted over with Asha on his back. "Oh? Maybe we should stick around for a little while, Nate—"

"No," I said, shaking my head as I recalled Charon's warning about unicorns. "We need to get out of here."

Carl's attention had locked onto Asha and he cocked his head, flicking his tongue out to taste the air. "What is that?" Carl asked, glancing back at Asha for the duration of a few blinks. Then he went back to eyeing our surroundings as if he anticipated an ambush. He would know better than anyone else what kind of dangers lived here. What threats lurked in the Elder realm.

"That's a vegan," Grimm offered with a snide snort.

Asha blindly swatted him with the back of her hand but she didn't say anything. She looked ready to bolt, nervously watching the two Knights.

Carl shrugged. "She won't bother us for very long. The sun will burn the flesh from her bones," he said absently, as if he was commenting on the weather—which, in fact he was.

Asha's eyes widened with fear but I waved my hand at her in a calming gesture. "She took a swim in the river water, and I have it on good authority that this will keep her safe from the sun's heat."

Carl swiveled his reptilian head and frowned at me. He looked surprised to hear such a thing, but he trusted my word. He shrugged and turned away again. "Then she will bother us until something else kills her. We should not get attached. Don't name her."

Fucking Carl. She wasn't a goldfish won at a carnival. "Her name is Asha, Carl, and we are going to protect her. You are Knights of the Round Table and she is a damsel in distress. She is important to me," I said, choosing my words very carefully. I needed to convince the others to see her as valuable, but I didn't want Asha to think I was treating her like an item on my checklist. A responsibility to be managed rather than a life to cherish. I focused on Carl. "And she is friends with Mac."

Carl stiffened abruptly and spun to face her. He stared at her intently, flicking his tongue out to taste her soul or whatever creepy shit his tongue told him. Finally, he nodded and dipped his snout. "I will keep you safe, pathetic human girl."

She arched a cool eyebrow at him, looking like she was preparing to tell him a few things he wouldn't like to hear. "Carl speaks very literally. He doesn't do nuance."

"I apologize if I offended you, pathetic human girl," Carl said in a sincere tone. Then he bared his black fangs at her, attempting to smile even though it looked more like a threat. "We will be friends and you will not die a horribly gruesome death in the Elder realm. Unless we *all* die, of course."

She stared at him in stunned disbelief, not sure whether to run away screaming or to get angrier. Finally, she glanced my way and then flung her hands up. "It's not like I have a vote or anything. Nice to meet you, Carl."

"Sir Carl," he corrected. "I am a Knight of the Circle Table." He tapped the armor over his chest with a proud grin.

"Round Table," Grimm muttered with a shake of his head. "Fucking Carl."

"Sir Fucking Carl!" The Elder hissed, glaring at Grimm.

The unicorn rolled his eyes and said it correctly for Carl's benefit.

I cleared my throat, drawing Talon's suspicious glare away from Asha.

Then I spoke softly so Asha couldn't hear me. "She was lured into the cavern by a hooded stranger," I told them. "Most likely Aiden. One of the Knightmares killed her mom. I killed him back," I said, pointing a thumb over my shoulder at the bloodstained rock.

Talon and Carl both nodded satisfactorily. Yahn clenched his jaw, looking shaken by her ordeal.

"We need to go to the Reverie," I said, pointing at the River Styx. "What do you know about it?" I finally asked Carl.

He stiffened and instantly averted his eyes.

"This is serious, Carl," I said. "It's our only way out of the Elder realm, and I think Aiden is trying to get there. I need to hear what you know."

Talon cleared his throat awkwardly. "Well, that's another thing we need to talk about. Aiden...isn't here anymore." My eyes almost popped out of my head. "He and three Knightmares left. We can no longer sense them." He swept his eyes across our party, frowning at Asha. "Much like we can no longer sense the other three Knights you entered with. They disappeared at the same time as Aiden and his three Knightmares."

My blood ran cold at the confirmation of Aiden not being here in the Elder realm. The only reason he would lure me here, lock the door, and then flee...was if he wanted me out of the way for something much bigger he was setting up. Like something in the Underworld with Anubis or back home in St. Louis.

Shit.

"We have to get to the Reverie, Carl," I growled, clenching my jaw. "Will the river lead us there?"

He hesitated and finally nodded. "I have never been to the Reverie, but I know someone who has." He turned to look at the scorched forest I had seen from on top of the mountain. "There is one person who may be able to help. If she doesn't eat us."

Talon cursed. "Well, eating us wouldn't be very *helpful* of her, Carl."

Yahn was walking over, feeling left out or sensing the tension in our conversation.

"Who is this delightful very hungry woman, Carl?" I asked, knowing I had no other options.

He shuddered and then let out a resigned sigh. "My Grandmama. Come."

In typical Carl fashion, he turned and started jogging away, motioning for us to follow. I turned to Talon who looked equally as shocked. "Carl's Grandmama?" he said, tugging at his whiskers.

I shrugged. "Maybe she bakes cookies. I'm starving," I said, motioning for everyone to follow me as I started jogging after Carl. "Yahn and Asha, you can stop pretending you don't recognize each other. Get reacquainted because I don't have the patience for any new bullshit to deal with. Yahn, you are her new knight in shining armor. Keep her alive. Asha, I don't know if you need to slap him or moon over him but get it out of your system either way."

The two of them looked like they'd been caught with their hands in the cookie jar. I wasn't sure if he had recognized her as that one girl who had idolized him for a summer or if they simply didn't like each other. He was in his early twenties and she couldn't even drive, so I knew it wasn't any actual romance from the past, but now they were semi-growed-up. Hormones changed things. I knew Yahn was...involved with the Reds, but that didn't mean Asha didn't feel a particular way at the moment. Regardless, they were going to be friends if I had to tie their hands together.

"It's not like that!" Yahn snapped. "I just didn't recognize her at first! I haven't seen her for years, and now she's..." he cut off abruptly and I could practically hear the steam blowing from his ears as he realized what he'd almost said. Something along the lines of, *and now she's all grown up and pretty*, if I had to guess.

"That must be why you were hiding from her in the cave," I said drily. "Because you definitely didn't recognize her." Yahn sputtered incoherently.

Grimm burst out laughing. "Plot twist! This is going to be a *long* ride, lovebirds." I looked over to see Asha glaring at me from atop Grimm's back. I flashed her a grin with a mildly apologetic shrug.

Rather than incriminate himself further, Yahn leapt to obey my order, jogging beside the unicorn to stay close to Asha. I heard them murmuring to each other back and forth, but it was stilted and stiff with awkwardness. I chuckled under my breath as Talon jogged at my side.

With no other plan, we ran after the lizard to find his creepy grand-mother's cottage in the haunted woods, fleeing a herd of spider deer and a gang of unicorns, because this was a fantasy adventure, and it seemed the author of my story had simply given up on me. Or he delighted in attempting to kill me with irony.

Either way, I doubted he had a happy ending in mind for me. He was a sadist.

20

As we jogged, I became very happy that I had Horseman armor bonded to me. Even though I wasn't wearing it, I found myself easily keeping pace with Talon and Carl and not feeling even a flicker of fatigue. In fact, it felt great. I was in pretty good shape, and all, but a jog like this should have hit me much harder by now, so it had to be the armor.

Or the magic of the Elder realm.

Regardless, I even had enough breath to tell Talon and Carl everything that had happened since our arrival. They listened attentively, keeping their gazes on our surroundings to make sure we weren't ambushed by... whatever they had been fighting while in the Elder realm. We reached a slight rise, and I risked a glance back over my shoulder, wondering if I would catch a glimpse of the arachno-deer.

I did and I didn't. I couldn't make anything specific out, but there was a huge swarm of darkness rolling over the land, headed towards the lake at the base of the waterfall. They were kicking up too much dust for me to see them clearly, but I could tell they were huge and there really were thousands of them.

We crested the hill and jogged down the other side, and I felt a wave of relief that we were no longer in their potential line of sight. Even still, the blackened forest we were running towards radiated a type of menace that made my insides squirm. We were still an hour away from it, if I had to guess, but it was much larger than I had estimated from atop the mountain. The trees were tall, scraggly, blackened things sporting leaves I hadn't noticed from above. I had asked Carl what kind of forest had black leaves and he'd told me they were actually a deep, deep red. I would see it for myself soon enough.

Tendrils of fog snaked through the tree trunks, casting the forest in an even spookier gloom.

After telling them about Anubis showing up to kidnap the Randulfs through a Gateway, Carl had stumbled, almost tripping over his own feet. He'd informed me about the dangers of Gateways and Shadow Walking in the Elder realm, confirming what Charon had told me. I'd then continued on about the Knightmare showing up and Asha's strange encounter with the helmet, followed up by me killing the Knightmare and healing the suit.

"My first couple of hours here was more insane than yours," I finally said. "I fought Anubis, Candy Skulls, saved a damsel in distress, and killed a Knightmare. What have you two errant knights been up to during that time?" I asked smugly.

Carl glanced back at Talon with a meaningful look. "Not it." Then he ran forward to put some distance between us as he led us towards his Grandmama's creepy ass forest.

I frowned. "What the hell was that all about?"

Talon grimaced and took a deep breath. The thing about Talon was that he always looked pissed off. His long fur emphasized his big glaring eyes, and pulled down at his cheeks, giving him a perpetual scowl. The fact that his fur had been braided into a viking-like mustache and beard only served to make him look more violent. But right now, he looked nervous.

"We have been here for seven days, Wylde," he finally said, using the name from when we'd first met.

I almost lost a step myself as I shot him a surprised look. I remembered Carl saying that it was nice I'd finally arrived, but I had dismissed it as a Carl-ism. "Seven days," I said flatly.

Talon nodded. "We were tracking Aiden and his five other Knightmares for almost a week when two of them broke off in different directions, circling around us to head back to the mountain. We were debating what to do—which of the three groups to follow—when Aiden and three of his Knightmares disappeared. We thought they had been killed, so we turned back to pursue the remaining two. That's when we sensed you arriving in the cavern, and then two days later three of *your* Knights disappeared. The Randulfs." I was relieved to hear that I wasn't the only one baffled by the illogical time distortions.

"We were in the cave for maybe an hour. We entered the Elder realm only a few minutes after you," I said.

Talon glanced at me and shrugged. "Seven days. And two more passed since we felt your knights arrive. Then they disappeared yesterday."

I frowned, doing some quick calculations in my head. "The cavern must be protected from the time difference or something. Either that or it gets more extreme the farther from the cave you get."

Talon curled his lip, baring his fangs. "Carl was not very talkative when I asked him questions about this place. I considered battling him to get answers, but I presumed you would be displeased by such a thing."

I let out a frustrated growl, glaring at Carl as he jogged ahead of us. "I'm not sure he's able to speak as freely as we want him to. The first time I saw this place, he had his mouth sewn shut with silver wire like he was being punished for something. I bet he's not able to talk to outsiders about the internal...politics."

Talon considered my words for a few moments and nodded. "That would actually explain many things."

I nodded. "Okay. We can't do anything about the past. Time moves differently here," I said, running over the facts we knew rather than focusing on those we didn't. I was actually somewhat relieved by this information, because it might grant Kára and the Randulfs more time in the Underworld. If seven days here meant one hour in the cave, what was the time difference in Hell?

I was hoping to all the gods that it was only seconds, but there was every possibility that it was the exact opposite. Maybe an hour here meant a year there. I shoved down the thought, knowing I could do nothing about it. Also, the Elder realm emphasized fear, so I could be getting in my own way by thinking too much.

"You came back to the mountain to chase down the Knightmare I fought, right?" He nodded. "Where is the second renegade Knightmare?"

Talon immediately shifted his attention to our left. "Maybe a day of hard running that way," he said, staring at a line that seemed to run parallel to the forest's perimeter. "They split up. We chose to pursue the one closest to you. It feels like he's heading back to where we last sensed Aiden," he said with a troubled frown. "Maybe reconnecting?"

I nodded. "Okay. Have you found any Elders? Maybe rallied them to stand up to the Knightmares?"

Talon grimaced and lowered his eyes to the ground. "We have seen many Elders. All murdered by Aiden's Knightmares. Whole villages."

"Goddamn it," I growled. "Did they try to fight back?"

Talon glanced at me, looking troubled. "It seemed like they were unprepared. Like they never fought him." His whiskers twitched irritably. "In one village, it seemed like they had welcomed him or were caught unprepared in the midst of a celebration. Carl believes they welcomed Aiden in and then he slaughtered them."

I shuddered at the thought, having a sinking suspicion. If they thought Aiden was a Temple, then they might have welcomed him in with open arms, believing him to be their savior. That was definitely something Aiden would do to them—just to hurt me.

I let out a frustrated sigh. "Okay. That means there is only one Knightmare left here. We can kill him and then get to this Reverie so we can escape this cursed place. If Aiden is gone, there is no more danger to the Elders."

Talon shrugged. "Carl never mentioned this Reverie. What is it?"

"I...actually don't know. I heard it was the heart of this place. The only way out," I said.

Talon glanced over at me. "You heard...from whom?" I did not answer his question. I don't know why, but it felt wrong to talk about Charon behind his back. He had wanted to tell me things but had been unable to do so, and his lips were sewn shut. I'd seen one other friend with his lips sewn shut.

Carl.

For whatever reason, it felt like I would be betraying Charon's trust by talking about him. On the other hand, he hadn't shown up when the Knightmare died, even though he had told me I could use a soul to go to the Underworld and save my friends.

In short, I didn't know what to make of my relationship with Charon. And I definitely didn't want to get him in trouble for what he knew. He might be my only ally in all of this mess. An ace in the hole.

"Reliable sources," I told Talon in a tone that brooked no further questions.

Talon grunted, knowing me well enough not to pry. He batted a paw at the embers and sparks dancing about on the breeze. "Carl said he has never seen a storm last so long without relenting." I arched an eyebrow at him and then glanced up at the sky with a frown. "Fireflakes," Talon explained, gesturing at the embers and sparks. "Like snow."

I narrowed my eyes. "Fireflakes," I muttered, risking a glance back at Asha. "He said that word?"

Talon grunted affirmatively.

They did look like fiery versions of snowflakes, so it wasn't necessarily suspicious that she had guessed the right term. Or was it?

"Hey, Yahn," I called out, motioning for him to join me and Talon. He flashed me a look of relief and hurried over. Asha watched us with an amused smile on her face. She waved at me and then said something to Grimm that made him laugh.

"I'm sorry about the spider-deer," Yahn blurted. "And for the confusion with Asha. I haven't seen her in years, and I thought I was losing my mind. She's a Regular, so I was completely thrown off to find her down in the cave. Then I thought I might be mistaken, but she's definitely the girl from my grandmother's church."

Talon chuckled darkly. "Is that all she is?"

I arched an eyebrow at Yahn, wanting to hear his answer.

Yahn grumbled unhappily. "There was never anything between us. Seriously. I hardly knew her, and she was just a little kid. I think we're both more confused than anything, and you mature adults are making it into something it's not. I saw her in the summer for a few years when Greta took me to church. She changed from a buck-toothed scarecrow to a... pretty young woman." He arched an eyebrow and leaned towards us conspiratorially. "I already have enough pretty young women in my life, and they would eat her alive," he said, referring to the Reds.

Two red-headed sisters who were shifter dragons.

Talon smirked. "And just what kind of relationship do you have with the Reds," he purred curiously.

Yahn smiled back, baring his teeth. "One that would make your tail twitch, pussycat."

Talon snarled and lunged for him, but Yahn had been expecting it. He immediately dipped his shoulder and twisted into Talon's advance as he wrapped his arm around the feline's waist. Before I knew what was happening, Yahn was hip-tossing Talon down onto the ground.

Talon hit with a surprised grunt and immediately leapt to his feet with a startled expression. Yahn was grinning proudly and holding his palms up in an innocent gesture. "I just needed you to see that I'm not wearing this armor because I'm a fucking pageboy. I'd appreciate it if you guys stopped treating me like one."

I burst out laughing and pointed at Talon's nose. "Oh, man. Your face!" I hooted. "You deserved that and then some, Talon. Give the man his flowers."

Talon shifted his glare from me to Yahn, and he finally flashed him an approving smile. "Welcome to the Knights of Camelot, Yahn." He leaned closer. "But if you ever try that shit again, I will make toothpaste from your bone marrow. Fair?"

Yahn dipped his chin and grinned. "But then I'd have to take a shit in your litter box to get even."

Talon's eyes bulged in shocked outrage.

"You will shit in his *what*?" Grimm roared, close enough to have heard Yahn's last comment. The unicorn started cackling madly as he trotted past us. Asha furrowed her brow, watching us like some bizarre science experiment. Finally, she turned her nose up at us, too dignified to reprimand our immaturity.

Yahn held out a hand towards Talon, inviting him to shake like gentlemen. Talon stared down at it for a few moments and finally smiled. He gripped Yahn's hand in his paw and shook it firmly. "I think I underestimated you, dragon."

Yahn shrugged. "Most usually do. Once."

Then he glanced at me and smiled. "I don't have a crush on Asha. Never did. She doesn't have a crush on me. Never did. Hope that doesn't break your heart or anything," he said with a shrug. "I have a job to do."

He waited a moment as we stared at him, unable to formulate an argument or rebuke. Then he dipped his chin and jogged back up to Grimm to stay by Asha's side. After a few moments, she glanced back at us with an amused grin. Then she stuck her tongue out at me and started chatting with Yahn again.

"Well," Talon finally said. "I think we *both* got what we deserved," he said with a grin. "The man has earned his flowers."

I found myself grinning as well. "We're getting too old for this shit, Tal." I patted my satchel with my palm, drawing his attention. "Any idea why the Knightmare thought his armor was broken?" I asked. "Or why it didn't bond with Asha?"

Talon grimaced unhappily. "Maybe it did not bond with her because it is broken. Maybe this place affects the suits somehow, not letting them bond to people?" He finally let out an annoyed growl from deep within his chest. "I do not know. She is not bonded to the suit, though," he confirmed. "I sense nothing from her."

Well, there went my conspiracy theory. I had no answers, but at least a suspicion had been alleviated. If she was an accidental Knight, Talon would have sensed it in her.

"Do you know what it means to be the Dark Horse?" he asked me, sounding troubled.

I frowned and shook my head. "No. Mac came up with the name and now she's gone. I'll tell you this, though. I'm starting to like the sound of it, Talon."

He nodded. "That is what concerns me, Wylde."

21

A short time later, Carl slowed down as the edge of the dark forest loomed ahead. He turned to wait for us, and he looked like he was going to give us a motivational speech before a battle. We came to a halt and waited anxiously.

"Here, you are children," Carl accused in a cold tone. "Spoiled, bratty, dangerous children. Here, you will heed my warnings, or we will all die," he said, shifting his attention to look directly at me. "Fear lives here. Breathe it in and cherish it because it means you are still alive."

I studied him warily, sensing the concern of my allies. "Are you talking about your Grandmama?" I asked, eyeing the gloomy, misty forest ahead. It looked like a forest fire had just been put out—five minutes before we arrived. Yet I still saw leaves in the canopy overhead and plenty of under-brush. The place just gave off an aura of scorched earth and death. It grew thicker and gnarlier deeper within.

Carl focused on me and shook his head. "No. I was speaking of the Elder realm at large. My Grandmama is much, much more dangerous."

"Then why are we going to visit her?" I argued. "How is she going to help us? I already know the river leads to the Reverie."

Carl studied me. "My Grandmama is a very powerful sorceress, and she might know a way to get into the Reverie without my people killing us all on sight." He pointed out towards the river. "I followed the river with Talon for days and we came across several villages where everyone had been slaughtered, even the children." Asha sucked in a horrified breath, and I heard Yahn speaking to her in soft tones to calm her down. Carl continued, "My guess is that the surviving Elders are not fond of humans right now. In their place, I would be hunting any humans or foreigners of any kind. I think my Grandmama is the best path to a solution," he said in a crisp tone as he pointed a claw towards the forest. He waited for any further argument. I gave him a grim nod. He turned to face the forest, not seeming to notice or care about the spike in anxiety he'd just given everyone. "Follow closely."

Then he walked into the forest, giving us no alternative but to comply.

I cast a hollow smile at Yahn and Asha, motioning for them to follow the robot velociraptor.

Hearing that his dear old Grandmama was a powerful sorceress had given me an idea about the hair I had found. I knew what I wanted to try but it was much more difficult than any spell I had attempted before. And since I only had one hair, I would only get one shot to use it. Having a sorceress who knew the Elder realm and the strange magic here could be very helpful. She might even be able to help or tell me if my plan was even possible.

If she didn't kill us and eat us, of course.

I leaned close to Talon as we entered the forest, studying Carl just ahead of us. "He seems different..."

Talon nodded. "You don't know the half of it. He is downright cheerful compared to when he sensed Mac disappearing. He practically lost his fucking mind and almost killed me for standing in his way."

I eyed Talon anxiously. "He's very protective of her," I said. "You sure you didn't just take it wrong? I mean, he wouldn't have *really* killed you."

Talon shot me a grim look. "It was like a switch flipped in his head. He turned into something...different. For the first time, I truly understood why everyone is so afraid of the Elders. Thankfully, I got out of his way in time and reassured him that we would find everyone. That seemed to pull him out of his primal mode, and he gave me a nod before racing back this way."

Talon sniffed the air as he glanced back over our shoulders. "It was kind of like our Wild Sides in Fae, but on a whole different level."

I nodded, having considered the same comparison. "Strange. He didn't once mention Mac's name when I was talking about them being taken to Hell."

Talon frowned pensively. Apparently, he hadn't recognized that fact. "That's...troubling," he finally said.

I glanced back at the distant mountain and waterfall, knowing the dark forest would soon block my view of the cavern. Was the place even open anymore? Had the explosion destroyed the exit and all the statues? Another thought hit me, and I frowned. "If you two were so close to the waterfall, chasing the Knightmare, how come we couldn't see you when we were looking down here?"

Talon shrugged absently. "Maybe the angle was off. Or we were in a ravine, blocked from your view. The place might seem fairly flat, but there are a lot of sand dunes and such."

I grimaced. "Bone dust, not sand."

Talon nodded. "Plenty of normal bones as well. Some even human," he said, almost like he was asking for an explanation. "Wasn't this place your ancestors' playground?"

I shrugged. "That's what I hear, but I knew nothing about it until recently." I frowned at the Elder realm in general. "It's not like I have enough ancestors to fill this whole place with bone dust. That's insane. It would take millions of bodies to blanket a whole realm in dust."

Talon pondered my words in silence for a few steps. "Maybe you had a lot more ancestors than you think," he suggested. "You just never got to hear about them because they died here."

The thought sent a chill down my spine, and I recalled Charon's claim that my ancestors' bone dust seemed to multiply and spread like some kind of disease. Surely, he'd been exaggerating. I shook off the thoughts. "Millions," I reminded Talon. Then I skidded to a halt and walked up to a pile of dust that had accumulated at the edge of a small cliff near a ravine on our left. I kicked at it and felt my toes connect with something solid as the entire cliff's edge sheered away. I jumped back a step, not wanting to fall down into the gap, and Talon snatched me by the bicep, pulling me clear. We watched as a boulder crashed down into the shallow gorge, sending a cloud of ivory grit puffing up into the air. The rock tumbled to a halt and my eyes almost popped out of my skull to realize that I was staring at a humanoid skull.

Except it looked as big as a golf cart. I could have fit my entire torso into one of the vacant eye sockets.

An orange snake slithered out of one of those eye sockets, hissed angrily at me for the disturbance, and then slipped back inside through one of the chipped nostrils. I stared in disbelief.

Grimm let out a horrendous sneeze from behind us, causing Talon to jump and hiss. "Hey!" the unicorn snapped angrily. "Watch it. I stopped snorting giant dust years ago!"

Talon met my eyes, glanced back at the giant's skull, and then stiffly resumed his walk deeper into the forest, looking much more motivated to pursue the Elder now. "Well," he said after a few moments, "at least we know it wasn't all formed by your ancestors' remains. And why there is so much of it."

I didn't comment as I swept my head left-to-right, idly counting the mounds of dust and patches of sand covering the rocky wasteland at the forest's entrance. What the hell were giants doing here, and what other creatures had died in this wasteland? I would have to ask Carl a lot more questions, I realized.

"Know anything about this forest?" I asked Talon as each step took us deeper into the dark, misty gloom. Unfortunately, the embers and sparks couldn't pierce the canopy above, so we were rapidly losing our ability to see clearly. The forest was dead silent as if nothing lived here. "Or why his grandmother lives in such an inhospitable place?"

Talon shook his head, the vertical slits of his eyes expanding to better see in the ensuing darkness. "No. He made us avoid the forest on our first trip out," he said meaningfully.

"Oh, goodie," I grumbled, checking to make sure my Horseman's Mask was readily accessible. "I really don't want to have to kill Carl's grandmama."

Talon chuckled, but it was clipped and forced. "How bad can one old lady be? He's probably just embarrassed."

"Maybe she eats goat," I said to Grimm over my shoulder.

Grimm snorted. "Maybe she eats vegans—"

"Lady unicorn bait," Asha reminded him in a warning tone. I glanced over my shoulder to flash her an approving grin. She beamed proudly. Yahn was grinning at her, but Grimm grumbled unhappily. He kept further anti-vegan talk to himself. I heard Asha pat his neck consolingly as I turned back around. "Good boy," she cooed.

22

C arl abruptly froze. "Stop!" he hissed, sniffing at the air. Tendrils of mist drifted between the trees like living tentacles. The forest smelled of smoke and char, like it really had been consumed by flames, yet the trees did not look burnt upon closer inspection. The earth was soft and loamy, almost feeling like foam beneath my boots. I kept my head on a swivel and Carl in my peripheral, wondering what he had sensed.

Out of the darkness, a squat little old lizard lady in a shawl shuffled through the undergrowth. She carried a worn basket on her arm as she squatted down to pluck up a mushroom from beneath the mist. She tucked it into her basket and continued on, coming straight for us but not acknowledging our presence.

Carl remained perfectly silent, watching her warily.

She walked directly up to Grimm and finally turned to stare into his eyes. Thankfully, he did not react. Then she deftly grabbed him by the horn and pulled his head lower with a warning hiss. Asha let out a nervous squawk, but Carl lifted his fist and shook his head adamantly for all of us to see, warning us to stand down. The little old lizard leaned closer to Grimm with a louder growl and sniffed him.

"Damned alicorns," she muttered in a wispy, thready voice, sounding like dried leaves rustling in the wind. Then she shoved his head away by the horn, dismissing him, and waddled directly up to me. I stood my ground, wondering why Carl hadn't said a single word to her. Were we supposed to remain silent? She stared up at me since she was significantly shorter, but she radiated power. It wasn't wizard magic, obviously, but I could tell Carl had not understated her ability to wield magic. She was a very powerful sorceress indeed.

Witches and sorceresses were known to be...very odd, hermit-like people, which explained why she lived out in the woods. It wasn't because they didn't like people; it was often because other people disappointed them. They grew bored of the mundane thoughts of their fellows and often sought out adventures and solving esoteric mysteries of their own choosing.

They were also highly volatile and unpredictable when it came to strangers entering their safe spaces. Their territory. They wanted solitude so they could focus exclusively on their unique hobbies and interests. And, since she was also an Elder, I upped the usual risk factors by an order of magnitude.

She had white scales like Carl, but hers were aged and spikier than his, reminding me more of a bearded dragon than a shiny snake. She also had striations of black and gray scales climbing up her snout, making me think of a serpentine zebra. Her eyes were hostile and penetrating, and I felt her probing me with her magic—not to harm me but to delve into me and assess my level of threat.

Her eyes narrowed dangerously from inches away. "You!" she hissed.

Well, she had spoken directly to me, so it would be rude not to answer her. I needed to intrigue her; show her I wasn't one of those boring, disappointing people, but I needed to do it subtly. Clever recognized clever, and a sorceress's pride was a deadly dragon to poke. I slowly lifted my hands to show her I meant no threat. "Me," I assured her, choosing my response very carefully.

She studied me with a suspicious gaze, sensing I was up to something. "You brought the black water back. You brought the dead river forth."

I nodded. "The waterfall did that," I said. "I brought the waterfall."

She sniffed at me again. "You also lit it on fire."

I smirked guiltily. "A Knightmare did that, but I killed him. I am now searching for a daydream."

Her eyes glittered with amusement, recognizing my play on words—the Reverie. Maybe Carl had been right to take us to her. She let out a breath and then clutched at her chest in a symbolic gesture. She might have almost smiled, but she masked it well. "Thank you for the dead river. The Reverie is more dangerous than the Knightmare."

I nodded. "It is the only way for me to kill the other Knightmares."

"You're probably going to die," she said in a matter-of-fact tone.

I took a deep breath, inhaling through my nose. "We all die someday. At least I had the honor of seeing a rose first," I said with a grin.

Her eyes widened in surprise, and she took a step back at my compliment. It looked...like she was blushing. At least, her nostrils were flaring wildly, and she held a claw to her chest. "I am a thorny old crone and I eat trespassers. How dare you mock my looks?"

Carl's eyes widened with horror, but I ignored him, keeping the smile on my face. "Every rose has thorns," I said easily. "Some roses have more thorns than others, but it makes the flower no less beautiful."

She narrowed her eyes suspiciously. "Clever words lead to quick deaths." She sniffed me curiously. "The Reverie is not all you seek, man-child. You have itchies in your britches," she said, pointing at my pants.

I grinned. "She told me she loved me. I was foolish enough to believe her. But that was a long time ago."

She folded her arms and studied me, smirking at my inappropriate quip. "Not that kind of itchy, although I could make you a potion for that," she suggested, arching a ridged eyebrow. I smiled and shook my head. "You have another request. A dangerous one. A magical one. A hairy secret," she said knowingly.

I nodded politely, wondering how the hell she knew about my tracker question, judging by her use of the word *hair*. "You are very perceptive. I might ask you about it." I swept my gaze across the forest, checking on my allies. They were all staring at me with varying degrees of panic at my reckless manner of conversation with the scary old sorceress. "Later. Maybe."

She narrowed her eyes dangerously. "Tell me."

I shrugged. "We will see."

Silence stretched between us, but I never broke eye contact with her. I kept my face neutral rather than confrontational. She studied me like I was a puzzle, and I knew I had chosen the correct conversation tactics. "When?" she finally asked.

I smiled politely. "After you promise not to kill or eat us."

She took a slow, hostile step closer, lowering her basket. "And if I do not agree to make that promise?"

I took a slow, hostile step towards her—perfectly mirroring her action as I stared into her eyes. "Then you will never learn the question, and that little puzzle will eat at your soul for years to come. All alone out here in the forest with nothing to think about but the fact that all the Elders were executed when the answer to my curious little question may have prevented it. The possibility of guilt would eat at you like...well, itchies in your britches. But you have a potion for that, as you said." I smiled and waited.

She studied me, chewing over my answer like it was a riddle. Her nostrils expanded and contracted but she did not blink. "You bluff with a dangerous sorceress, wizard."

I shrugged. "We have already discussed your thorns, sorceress. Maybe I'm bluffing, maybe I'm not. Call me on it if your pride is greater than your curiosity."

"Why take such a gamble over such a small thing?" she hissed, looking genuinely baffled.

"Because there is no reward without risk. And now that you are so interested in my question, imagine how much better the answer is going to be," I replied with a warm smile.

Her lips finally pulled back into a respectful smile. "You remind me of someone, wizard."

I wondered if she was referring to my father, but she hadn't mentioned my name yet. She hadn't even acknowledged Carl yet. "Impossible. No one is as impressive as me," I said with a haughty grin.

She flicked her tongue out at me and then chuckled. "Yes. You definitely remind me of him."

"Now, about that promise?" I pressed, waving a hand at my friends.

"Bah!" she complained with a violent slash of her claws. "Fine. I won't kill and eat any of you—"

"You won't kill *or* eat any of us," I corrected her. "That *or* part makes a big difference to the promise."

She burst out laughing, startling me with the unexpected display of emotion. Then she nodded her approval. "It was worth a try," she said with zero shame. "I swear that I won't kill *or* eat any of you. Satisfied?"

I dipped my chin at her. "Yes."

"Then quit dawdling and follow me," she snapped. Then she turned and started waddling back the way she'd come, deeper into the misty woods.

I saw Carl staring at me and I shrugged. "She seems nice."

Carl shook his head. "I have never seen a stranger make her laugh." Rather than looking proud of my small victory, he looked...troubled and confused. Sad? Then he was walking past me. Maybe he was upset she hadn't said anything to him. She was his grandmother after all, and he'd been completely ignored.

"Come on, Yahn!" I barked. "Stop making moon eyes at Asha and let's get a move on."

He flinched in surprise, opening his mouth to deny it, only to realize that denying it could possibly offend Asha. He shook his head and sighed. "Kára is going to love hearing about the friend who gave you itchy britchies," he said with a scowl.

I chuckled as he led Grimm past me. Asha scowled down at me from Grimm's back. "You know we don't like each other, so why do you keep teasing us about it?" she asked, looking genuinely curious. "Is it a boy thing?"

Grimm snickered. "Because each time he says it, you flinch and Yahn blushes," he said. "Nate will keep teasing you about it until you stop giving him a reaction. He's like a child. A very immature child who takes dangerous risks for no reason," he said, and he glared directly at me for the last bit, referring to my conversation with Grandmama Carl.

I scowled back at him. "Come on, man. It was necessary. You're supposed to be on my side."

Grimm snorted and swiveled his head away from me, flaunting his blue ribbon. "*You* never gave me a ribbon."

"*She's* a vegan!" I snapped, pointing at her.

"Recovering," Grimm argued, defending her because she held the key to his future romance. "Come on, Asha." Then he trotted past me. Yahn and Asha both turned to sneer at me as they horse-jacked my ride. I almost blurted out that Grimm was a virgin, but I chose to save it for a better opportunity.

Talon was waiting for me with an amused grin. "I hope you know what you're doing."

"Me, too," I admitted. "But we're not dead yet. That's something."

23

G randmama led us into a cozy little clearing with a small thatch-roofed wooden hut. The mist avoided the clearing, which wasn't creepy or foreboding at all. A fire pit with a single wooden chair stood off to the side of the house and I saw a black cauldron steaming above it, sending up a savory aroma. Knowing she ate trespassers, I lost any sense of my appetite after the first whiff. I spotted a trail leading away from the house in the opposite direction.

She gestured for me and Carl to follow her inside and then she waddled into the hut. I glanced at my crew and shrugged. "Hang out here and try not to die."

Yahn was sniffing the cauldron with a curious smile and Carl waggled a claw at him. "You do not want to eat that."

"What is it?" he asked with a disappointed sigh.

Carl turned to look at me. "Smells like unicorn." Rather than acknowledge Grimm's horrified gasp, he strode into the hut.

I looked at Grimm. "I thought you wanted to try some unicorn, Grimm?" I asked him with a smirk.

He stared at me with horrified look and shook his head. Asha patted his neck soothingly, consoling him.

I entered the sorceress's hut and found myself surprised with how...

normal it looked. Like any other little cabin, really. I'd expected mounted unicorn heads or deadly books of magic or green smoke. I saw a modest little bed, a rocking chair, a fireplace, and a large worktable overflowing with all manner of items.

Grandmama was hunched over the table, looking for something. Carl leaned against the back wall in silence, watching me. I arched a curious eyebrow and he shrugged.

I opened my mouth to ask her what she was doing.

"Not enough Temples for many, many years, and then too many at the same time," she complained to herself, batting aside a stack of glass vials that thankfully didn't break.

"Aiden?" I asked, glad that she had finally said my name. It felt like some kind of validation or approval. "Is he still here? Did he make it to the Reverie?"

She peered up at me and blinked a few times. Then she went back to rummaging through her ingredients, muttering and cursing under her breath. I watched as she plucked out specific items from the sprawling mess and put them into the basket that now sat on a short stool. "Do you have the scythe?" she asked absently.

I frowned, recalling Charon asking me the same question. I opened my satchel and lifted part of Cronus' scythe out to show her. She stared at it with zero expression for a moment. Then she cursed under her breath, scooped up a femur from the heap of items, and threw it at my head. I managed to catch it out of pure luck. I set it down on a side table and scratched my head with a confused frown.

Once again, I checked with Carl for his helpful advice. He just stared back at me and folded his arms across his chest. She had already resumed her search of the table, knocking aside artifacts, glass bottles, random sticks and dried flowers and mushrooms. It literally looked like someone had emptied a bag of refuse onto the table. There was absolutely no organization whatsoever.

I knew sorceresses were absentminded, often so focused on their own thoughts that they neglected many other things, but they also worked with very dangerous ingredients. Essentially, I had the sudden fear that I was hanging out with a clumsy, disorganized bombmaker.

I took a nervous step back and watched her tuck things into her basket.

I twitched every time she knocked over a glass vial, waiting for one of them to explode and turn us all into rabbits or something.

"I see you traded your muzzle for fancy new armor," Grandmama said in a frosty tone.

Carl faced her squarely but did not speak. She was talking about the last time I'd come here, when I'd found him stranded atop the mountain with his mouth sewn shut with silver wire. When he'd refused to look me in the eyes. I still had very little idea what that whole situation was about, but apparently it was very important to Grandmama.

"Actually, I took the wire from his mouth," I said, not wanting to get him in trouble. "It was barbaric."

She grew still. Then she slowly turned to look at me. "What did you just say?" She was clutching a very sharp butcher knife in one claw.

"You heard me," I said, meeting her eyes. "I'm not sure who did it to him, but I've thought long and hard about what I wanted to do in response."

She cocked her head like a snake about to strike. "Oh?"

I nodded.

"You felt sorry for him, so you took it off?" she asked in a dry hiss. "What do you have to say about this, Carl?" she asked, not breaking eye contact with me.

"I did not give him a choice," I growled, suddenly feeling defensive of my friend. "He did not say a word. He did not want me to do it. I told him he had no choice. I needed him to help me kill some gods."

"You needed his strength, so you let your dog off his leash and gave him a prize."

I took an aggressive step forward and waved a finger at her nose. "I needed my *friend*," I snarled. "And friends don't let friends wear braces."

Carl watched us very intently, not even seeming to breathe.

Grandmama narrowed her eyes, not appreciating my finger one bit. "You removed one leash and gave him another," she accused, gesturing at the armor with her knife.

My vision flashed red, and I swatted the blade from her claw. It slammed into the wall behind her. "He earned the armor all on his own. For valiant bravery, and ruthlessness, and a reckless disregard for his own safety, in too many fights to count. Your grandson is one crazy, scary, son of a bitch, and I will burn down this house to defend his name. He is now part of *my* family—a Temple. Because Temples are made, not born. No one calls my friend a coward. No one gets to muzzle my friend. No one disrespects a Temple. Or. They. Die."

I realized I had subconsciously donned my Horseman armor and I was about three millimeters from Grandmama's snout, snarling at her as my black blade and crackling white chain sizzled in my claws.

You could have heard a cockroach climax in the ensuing silence.

24

I saw a single tear roll out of the scary old sorceress's eyes. Then she let out a soft cry and wrapped her claws around me in a tight hug. My eyes widened in confusion as she whimpered joyfully into my neck.

I released my blade and my Horseman armor vanished. I patted her back awkwardly. "Um..."

She pulled away and then planted a fat lizardly smooch on my cheek. Then she turned to Carl and waddled over to him with a proud laugh, wrapping him up in a hug. I saw him let out a deep breath of relief as he hugged her back. He met my eyes over her shoulder, and I saw he was also crying a bit.

I ran a hand through my hair, confused as all hell.

They separated and she turned back to face me. "Thank you, Master Temple."

I pointed at Carl. "He earned his place. I just acknowledged it, Grandmama."

She beamed. "Call me Sugar, Master Temple." Then she freaking curtsied.

"Okay, Sugar," I said, struggling to keep up with the drastic change in attitudes. "Did you drug me with something, because I am very confused right now. You ignored him the whole way here."

She nodded. "Part of the test. To see what kind of Master Temple you truly were. I wanted to test Carl's claims about you. You did not let your fear of me stop you from defending Carl. You did not let your fear of failing in your quest—by angering me—stop you from defending Carl. You did not protect his weakness; you honored his strength. And," she said, turning to smile at Carl, "he did not break his silence to me, even though the wire was already removed."

Carl looked pleased but uncomfortable with the attention. "The wire was not necessary, but I would never dishonor myself by taking it off. I swore an oath."

"Which is why you came to me," Sugar said with a proud smile. "Because I swore no such oath, so I can blab to my heart's content."

Carl smirked and gave a guilty-as-shit shrug. "Yes. Master Temple has taught me to be very clever."

I smiled, but I was feeling rather frustrated, because Carl's honor had cost us precious time and a detour to his Grandmama's house. He could have saved us time by breaking his oath, but I knew I would never win that argument. Not after the intensity of the situation I'd just endured about the whole thing.

"How about you explain the wire to me? I still don't really understand why he had it or why he was sent up to the mountain. Or what we are doing here right now. Can you take us to the Reverie?"

Carl shook his head. "We do not have time to discuss—"

"Carl came back for the last annual festival," Sugar began, overriding his argument with a proud, grandmotherly gleam in her eyes. "He spoke very, very highly of you to the Bone Council—the eldest leaders of each tribe. Too highly, as it were. The Bone Council did not believe Carl when he tried to tell them about you. They thought he had been bewitched, so they had him muzzled," she said in a murderous tone. "I threatened to remove the wire and go execute the entire Bone Council, especially his parents," she added, wagging a protective claw, "but Carl made me promise not to do so. He said his honor was at stake and that you would prove the truth of his words." She smiled at me. "Which you just did. Thank you."

"Wait. His *parents* did that to him? They're on this Bone Council?"

Sugar glanced at Carl with a surprised frown. "They are the King and Queen. Carlos and Carla. My daughter and her husband. And I still wanted to slit their throats. Would have done it if Carl hadn't stopped me. Such a sweet boy."

Carl dipped his head respectfully. "They were pressured by all members of the Bone Council."

I felt like I was on a carousel, only catching glimpses of reality before being spun somewhere new. "Pause, please. Your parents did that to you, and they are the king and queen?" I asked Carl. He nodded, obviously not wanting to elaborate. I shifted my attention to Sugar. "And you're the queen's mother?" I sputtered. "And who the hell are the Bone Council? Your cousins? You're freaking royalty here and you didn't tell me?" I shouted, throwing my hands into the air. "What the hell, man?"

He grimaced. "I am not royalty. I renounced my titles long ago to become a warrior. Trained here with my Grandmama. She is a fine warrior and she taught me magic and songs."

No wonder they had such a close bond. It likely had something to do with how easily they had dismissed him when he spoke to the Bone Council. If his family was like other royals, they probably saw him as a threat.

"Okay. As fascinating as this all is, we desperately need to get to the Reverie. Your people are being slaughtered by a very bad man. And I have other friends who are also in danger unless I can get out of the Elder realm. Every second counts."

She nodded sadly. "A wounded survivor came into my forest. He told me about this Aiden Temple and three men in black armor riding into their villages, tricking Elders into bowing down to Master Aiden Temple only to execute them on the spot before they realized their mistake. It is why I pushed back against you so hard before," she told me. "Carl had never mentioned a sibling or relative. He said you were the last heir."

I grimaced at the blasphemy and horror of him using my name to commit genocide, but I had no way to disprove his claim yet. "I didn't know about Aiden until recently. His claim to my name and his presence here might be old news to you, but it's only been hours for me." I growled. "Why have the Elders not rallied to fight him? Carl and Talon say that they have seen numerous villages destroyed but no sign of battle. Are there no big cities here? No large standing armies? Couldn't this Bone Council help?"

She shrugged, but she looked just as angry as me. "I do not know why no one has rallied. We are nomadic warriors, so we prefer spreading out into tribes, not cities. I have heard nothing of the Bone Council going to war, but I am secluded in the forest. The only place you could call a city is the Citadel. The Reverie is within its walls, but the Citadel is a holy place only used for annual gatherings and celebrations. No one lives there. It is warded closed for the rest of the year."

I didn't like the sound of that. Warded closed. So, how had Aiden gotten through? "Warded?" I pressed.

She nodded. "The Reverie is also warded, but not to your bloodline. That must be how Aiden entered."

I clenched my jaw. Was that proof he was truly a Temple? It had to be. Charon's words echoed in my ears, and I felt myself growing even angrier. Bloodlines didn't matter in the scientific sense. Temples were made, not born.

I stared at her. "No one lives inside either the Reverie or the Citadel," I said in a dubious tone. "I was warned that it was incredibly dangerous, and you're saying I just have to walk inside an empty city and then an empty building?"

"You have to face what is inside the Reverie," Sugar said, holding up a claw.

I gestured impatiently with my hand. "Which is…"

She shook her head. "I do not know. That is why it is warded, and we only open the Citadel once a year. The Elders do not ever enter the Reverie's grounds. It is a sacred oath. We are simply to guard the place for the Temples."

"Please tell me that this once-a-year celebration is not right now," I said, feeling a migraine coming on. That would be the perfect opportunity for Aiden to kill everyone with one shot. "Or that it wasn't while he was here," I added, knowing he had been here for some time now.

She shook her head. "No. It is months away."

I let out a breath of relief. "Well, at least there is that."

"News of his conquest has to have spread by now. I do not understand how this man is so powerful and why no one has fought back," Sugar said, shaking her head. "The Bone Council has failed. My daughter and her husband have failed us."

I nodded angrily. "That is what I am trying to figure out. Everyone I've ever met is terrified of the Elders yet I have seen no show of their ferocity." Her face hardened with displeasure, but I held up my hands. "Do not get angry with me for pointing out the truth. I'm trying to help, but denying the facts does no one any favors. The sooner I get to the Reverie, the sooner I can track him down and confront him directly or bring enough forces back to squash him like a bug. I don't even know if he's still here. We can no longer track him through the armor he wears."

She shared a meaningful look with Carl, and he nodded.

"Are you certain he made it to the Reverie?" she asked me.

I shrugged. "He's left the Elder realm, and the only way out is blocked, so you tell me. All we know is that the bond through the armor he stole is no longer detectable. And I doubt we are lucky enough for him and his three friends to have suddenly died at the exact same time or taken a vacation to the Underworld."

She nodded. "Follow the river north and you will find the Citadel and the Reverie," she said.

I frowned. "We already knew that." I looked at Carl. "Tell me we didn't come here to be told something I already knew," I growled, growing frustrated. "Or for a history lesson."

Carl shook his head. "We need a key to get through the wards around the Citadel. I do not have this key, but she does," he said, turning to his Grandmama. "I relinquished my titles as prince."

They shared another strange look, and I cleared my throat. "Can you please give us the key, Sugar?" I asked, wondering if there was some kind of ritual over the damned magic house key.

Sugar nodded and then waddled over to her workbench, rummaging around again. "Ask me your hairy riddle, Master Temple."

"How about we deal with the key, first. I'm getting twitchy from your discreet looks at each other."

She smiled, not turning to look at me. "*I* am the key, Master Temple."

I frowned. "Oh. So, you're coming with us? Is that why you're packing your basket? Why didn't you just say so? We could have already left."

She chuckled. "Yes. I am coming with you. Now, stop hassling an old woman and tell me your riddle."

I sighed, recalling how slow she walked. I'd have to get her to ride

Grimm and make Asha walk or we'd never make it to the Citadel. "Fine. I found a hair back in the cavern atop the mountain on a friend's coat. She died, but I think it might belong to the person who trapped us here. I'm hoping that person is Aiden."

She paused her rummaging and slowly turned to face me with a devilish grin. "You want to send him a dark surprise. You have definitely come to the right place, Master Temple," she said, her murderous Grandmama eyes twinkling wickedly, like a normal grandmother who spied a fat grandchild and busted out her baking ingredients, finally having a reason to practice her favorite thing in the world.

Baking cookies, not the kid, of course. To sugar him up before returning him to the parents.

I held up a finger. "Kind of. But there's a kink in that plan." She waited and I could practically see her salivating. "Since we can't sense where Aiden is, I need my spell to be able to chase him across realms. I have no idea where he went, but he has a lot of strong allies in different pantheons, so it can't break down too quickly. I need this thing to hunt Aiden down but not kill him." She frowned. "Because it could be an innocent person's hair that just happened to get stuck on her coat, and I would hate to accidentally harm an innocent person."

"Or think that you killed Aiden and later walk into a trap," she said, tapping her snout with a long claw. "You need confirmation."

"Precisely. I need a hunter, like you said. Because I really want to kill Aiden myself. I want to watch him die with my own eyes for what he's done to everyone. It's like a game to me, and I intend to win," I said, recalling my last conversation with Aiden and his desire to play some grand game with his little brother. "And if he's working with a partner, I really want to find out who that is so I can slit their fucking throat."

She grinned. "I know just the thing, Master Temple. Come. Let's make some magic together."

25

I stepped out of the hut, leaving Sugar to prepare the last of her ingredients after I'd told her what I wanted. Talon and Yahn were sparring off to the side, and I knew it was to get Yahn familiar with Talon's long spear because we had no idea what weapons Aiden's Knightmares used, and the spear was an awkward weapon to suddenly have whipping at your face. Yahn used a sword and Talon was barking commands at him before lunging with the blade, teaching him the basic moves.

Since the Knightmares were wizards, I wasn't sure how helpful such training would be, but it kept them busy and boosted their confidence.

"That is a waste of their time," Carl murmured. "Yahn's strengths lie not in his ability to fight against a spear. He is a dragon who can blend into any background. His specialty is stealth, not open conflict."

I turned to look at Carl, who was leaning against the exterior of the hut with his arms folded and a distant look in his eyes, as if he were the only one present rather than part of a team. He also wasn't inside with his Grandmama. Something was on his mind.

I'd had no idea his familial bonds were so strong. He was always so aloof and strange, that I had never been entirely certain whether he liked me involving him in my shenanigans at Chateau Falco. If only he'd opened up more, I might have learned how to be a better friend.

I turned to watch Talon swatting Yahn on the head with the flat of his white spear and shrugged. "It builds his confidence. He might have to face a spear at some point, and the little he learns here could keep him alive longer. Confidence is a weapon, Carl."

He scoffed. "Overconfidence has killed more men than anything else in history. Well, besides big tits and loose lips, of course." I blinked, startled, but he continued on, making it more cringy. "And when I say loose lips, I'm not talking about spilled secrets, I'm talking about spread legs. Grand-mama taught me that."

I had questions. So many questions.

I was about to press him on it when Asha boldly walked up to him, brandishing a massive bone the size of her forearm. I had no idea what creature it had belonged to or where she had gotten it, but it looked old. "Could you make me a dagger, Elder Carl? I want one as strong as yours. Talon said you carve them from bones."

He looked startled by the small human, baffled by how she had ignored his obvious body language. He inspected the bone with a thoughtful frown. "Why? You are puny and pathetic and without power or potential."

She studied him for a few moments, and I was surprised she didn't run away crying at his harsh but honest criticism. "Maybe that is exactly why I want a blade," she said in a cool tone. "Because I'm scared and angry and determined not to die. And pissed off beats potential five times out of seven."

Carl stared at her curiously, as if he hadn't expected such a response. Then he glanced at me. "Is that true? Being pissed off beats potential that often?"

I managed not to laugh. "Oh, absolutely. Five out of seven statistics are absolutely guaranteed. They never lie. It's math."

Asha's cheeks flushed, sensing my sarcasm, but Carl remained aloof. "You will need training. I don't tolerate whining over broken bones and traumatic flesh wounds. Those are personal problems."

She glanced at me, but I gave her no reaction. Despite Carl trying to talk her out of it, she needed to be absolutely committed to her choice. No one could make it for her. Weak feelings and brittle resolve made for shoddy armor, no matter how noble or dignified they sounded. War was war. Crying about fairness and feelings was a distraction a would-be warrior could not afford.

Asha straightened her shoulders and nodded. "I've lost everyone I love. If this is to be my new family, I will pull my own weight. And if I have to defend myself, I want the enemy silently asking themselves where I acquired a weapon only an Elder dared carry. In their hesitation, I will have a moment to stab and run. Until you help me to address my lack of skill, that sliver of opportunity is better than waiting to die."

Carl actually raised an eyebrow, impressed by her response. "A weapon as fine as an Elder would carry," he murmured, inspecting the bone in her hand again.

She nodded, holding the bone out to him. "Please."

Carl snatched the bone and flung it over his shoulder without a word. It struck Grimm in the ass, and he belted out a shout of anger, but we ignored him. I saw Asha's face pale, fearing she had offended him in some way. Carl reached out and cupped his lethal claws over her shoulder as he squatted low to loom over her. Then...he squeezed it affectionately and nodded. "You shall have your blade tonight, Asha. Thank you for honoring me so. Until then, carry this," he said, and he drew one of his own bone daggers, pressing it into her palm. She accepted it with a startled look on her face. Then he released her and leaned back against the hut again. "We start training tomorrow. Practice swinging it to warm up your muscles. You may leave, disciple."

She grinned from ear-to-ear and then bowed awkwardly. Then she spun, clutching the bone dagger to her chest like a precious doll as she rushed over towards Yahn and Talon. I hadn't noticed, but they had stopped fighting to watch her exchange with Carl. Grimm trotted over, sniffing at her weapon as the group huddled close to inspect it and speak in low tones.

Talon glanced up at Carl over Asha's shoulder and gave him a nod of respect. Carl averted his gaze and resumed staring out at the forest with a pensive look. Well. I had no expectations of her being a great warrior anytime soon, but it was better than nothing. "Confidence is a weapon, Carl," I murmured absently. "Thank you for arming her."

He nodded faintly.

"At least she won't have to worry about falling prey to the big tits and loose lips of overconfidence," I added.

Carl burped up an unexpected laugh, looking startled by his own reaction. Then he smiled at me and nodded. "You were correct once again, Master Temple. My apologies. I am...distracted." Then he turned and walked away from me, seeking privacy.

I sighed. "Fucking Carl," I muttered. Then I clapped my hands together, drawing everyone's attention. "Listen up. Get some rest and eat some food. I'm going to go make some magic with Grandmama Sugar—" Grimm groaned, and Talon shook his head distastefully. "And then we're all going to head out of the forest."

"This should only take him thirty seconds," Grimm chimed in. Asha clapped a hand over her mouth, blushing, but everyone else chuckled. Laughter was good for morale, even at my expense.

I reached into my satchel, remembering a box of protein bars I'd shoved in there. I pulled out the box and tossed it to Yahn. "Pass them around. I'll see if I have anything better after...my thirty seconds of glory," I said dryly, narrowing my eyes at Grimm.

Yahn eyed the box with a judgmental grumble, his face clearly stating that he was disappointed in the flavor of free food I had pulled out of my magic satchel. I rolled my eyes.

"Did he at least get the peanut-butter ones?" Grimm called out in a whiny tone.

"No. Mint-chocolate chip," Yahn replied in a tone that implied he would rather eat rotten cabbage.

"Entitled little shits," I grumbled. "Go eat unicorn soup then!"

"Is it vegan?" I heard Asha ask Yahn in a polite tone.

"Well, it has mint," he murmured. "That's a plant."

Sugar wandered out of the hut, saving me from murdering my allies. She was already clutching a bundle of ingredients in the crook of one arm. "You ready?" she asked me. I nodded and she slipped a claw through my elbow so that I might escort her.

"Where are we going?" I asked. "The cauldron back there?"

She shook her head with a ghastly frown. "Oh, no. That's rule number one. Don't brew where you eat or sleep," she said, tugging me towards the other trail I had spotted earlier. The one that led deeper into the misty forest.

I chuckled, relieved to hear that she was more cautious than she had led me to believe with all her ingredients strewn about the workbench. Maybe she wasn't such a careless bombmaker.

Carl shadowed us as we walked up the narrow trail, surrounded by giant black trees and lurking mist. Wherever she was taking us for this spell, it was higher than the little valley she called home.

26

We stopped in a wide clearing surrounded by tall striated white and black trees, but the night sky opened up above us, the bulbous red moon shining down on a large fire pit surrounded by red stones the size of my head. A black cauldron hung over the cold fire pit, but it was already stocked with hunks of black wood.

An axe was buried into a nearby stump, and I saw more piles of chopped black wood piled around it. I arched an eyebrow. "You didn't tell me you had a muscular lumberjack neighbor, you naughty girl, Sugar."

She frowned up at me with a distracted look in her eyes. "I chop my own wood," she said without smiling at my joke. She pointed a claw at the pit as she resumed rifling through her basket with her other hand. "Start a big fire. Carl, fill the cauldron with water."

Carl walked up to the cauldron, and I realized he was carrying two medium-sized buckets. He didn't offer an explanation, so I assumed he'd carried them from the hut. He poured them into the cauldron as I got the fire started. I used magic because I didn't know how to do it the other way.

I stepped back beside Carl and assessed our work. The fire was roaring, the cauldron was starting to steam, and Sugar looked like she'd snorted some cocaine as she frantically pulled strange items from her basket and either tossed them into the cauldron or set them aside, muttering under her breath.

Embers and sparks fell down over the clearing, making it look like a million angry lightning bugs. Or that the surrounding forest was on fire, sending errant sparks dancing through the air. One of the two.

All in all, the scene was decidedly sinister and creepy, especially given my lizard companions.

Carl sat down in the grass, crossed his legs like he was preparing to meditate, and then silently watched the cauldron with a critical gaze, like he was at a college lecture given by one of his favorite science professors.

Unlike Carl, I was the kid who skipped most of those, preferring to go straight to lab class and see how quickly I could make an explosion of some kind with the unknown ingredients. There were many kinds of magic, and wizards often felt callings to specific areas of study. Witches and sorceresses loved this shit.

But this type of magic was not my forte. Too many numbers and measurements and ingredients to memorize. Too many damned rules.

I was more of a violent hippy wizard—I hated all forms of authority, right or wrong. I think it was their smugness—their lofty penchant for holding their pinkies out while they sipped tea and discussed magical theory. Their country club, academic approach to magic. To me, magic was a wild stallion, and I was a gritty handsome cowboy.

A free spirit. I liked to fly by the seat of my pants and react based on my instincts. I liked to swing my giant club of magic at Mr. Authority's nose just to see what happened.

I was well aware that my philosophy on magic caused me any number of problems, but those risks were worth the rewards. What good was magic if I only sat in dusty libraries and studied books? I'd rather be an accountant at a morgue.

All this to say that I almost shit my pants when the cauldron suddenly exploded with a cloud of pungent smoke and sent out dozens of wailing spirits into the night sky. They zipped up and out of sight, freed from their entrapment.

"What the fuck?" I demanded, feeling my heart thundering in my chest. Carl continued his calm study of the cauldron, and I realized that it hadn't actually exploded. It still hung above the fire—which was now white flames—and emitted steam—which was now green. The cauldron swung back and forth on its pole from the explosive burst of souls that Sugar had apparently tossed into her sorceress soup du jour.

Sugar had also ignored me in favor of tossing even more strange ingredients—sticks, a handful of purple mushrooms, a leather string, a handful of human-looking teeth, a gold coin, and a very impressive loogie that took her a few seconds of hacking to produce.

As she did these things, I saw her waiting between each added ingredient, sometimes longer, sometimes shorter. With each new item tossed into the pot, the thick steam above changed to almost every color of the rainbow in rapid succession. I leaned close enough to peer through the steam and noticed that the color of the stew inside did not ever match the steam, but it also changed colors just as rapidly.

It smelled like skittles and asparagus pee. At the same time.

I have no idea why, and I decided I didn't ever want to know.

I shook my head and stepped back, studying the white fire with curiosity. Had the wood done that by itself or had Sugar changed the fire somehow? "This is some crazy fucking magic, Carl. I never could have done a tracking spell like this."

"She is not finished," he said in an amused tone, not taking his eyes away from the cauldron. "This will be her masterpiece for the Master Temple." His nostalgic smile told me he was completely focused on watching his Grandmama's work, so I stopped bothering him. It would be pretty cool to see my parents do an epic spell again, after all these years. I found myself smiling at the thought.

If this all worked out well, maybe I would see them in the Underworld after I made a throw rug out of Anubis' hide—with his snarling head still attached, of course. Like those bear rugs of old. I had a few questions about my mother's misspent youth. One big criticism, really—how her opening her legs for the wrong man might have kicked off the Apocalypse. Who *was* Aiden's father, anyway?

Sugar interrupted my dark thoughts as she started speaking in a strange, foreign tongue. I didn't have to understand the words to know they were magic and highly dangerous. She was already singing a spell. I stared at her back as she worked, feeling myself sway on my feet at her hypnotic song, almost feeling as if I was falling into a trance. She started stirring the brew with a long bone spoon.

"Give me the tracker! I need a spell to track a spell!" Grandmama Sugar abruptly snapped, blindly extending a claw towards me as she stared down at the brew and took a deep sniff. I blinked in confusion, startled out of my hypnotic trance, not immediately comprehending what she'd meant about a spell to track a spell. Then it hit me. She was talking about Aiden's hair. The strand I'd found wrapped around Nadia's coat button. I carefully reached into my pocket and pulled it out. I pressed it into her hand, waiting until her fingers pinched it before I let go. I didn't want it flying away in the breeze, losing us our one chance. "Open yourself to the magic, Master Temple!" she screamed, making my ears ring because I was still standing precisely six inches away from her.

Then a column of dark light exploded out from the cauldron, shooting straight up into the sky with a beastly, deafening roar that had to be heard from miles away. I stared in awe even as my subconscious complied with her command. I didn't know what the hell she was trying to do—what kind of magic she was conjuring—but I wasn't about to screw it up. I opened myself to my magic and let out a shuddering sigh as the sights and sounds of the Elder realm hit me like an avalanche.

Calling upon my magic when I had no direct use for it was a humbling and inspiring experience.

When I called it up in the middle of a fight, all my awareness went towards casting an attack or a shield, letting the adrenaline take over my mind to respond instinctively—using my magic rather than observing it.

But when I simply embraced my magic and let it fill me—when I had no task or reason to actively use it—I felt like...

Well, like I was tripping balls. I saw things that were not usually there. You know, like a crazy person.

Sounds exploded in my mind, turning into tactile feedback that made my skin pebble. A leaf tumbling down from the trees gave me a sensation of the wind embracing and buffeting its fall, even as gravity pulled it down.

Smells took on taste, of course, but they also took on colors. I stared, transfixed, as streamers of different colored light drifted through the air all around the clearing, looking like someone had decorated the surrounding black and white trees with hundreds of colorful ribbons. I stared at them, engrossed to see the gloomy, spooky forest suddenly transformed into a dazzling celebration like I'd wandered into a woodland techno-music festival.

Colors became more vibrant, seeming to radiate drifting orbs of light in slowly flickering dances like I was looking at a forest of tiny suns, able to focus on each of the fiery tendrils without incinerating my retinas. It wasn't that they were bright, but they came to life.

Magic was...intoxicating. Many wizards had gone mad by sitting in empty rooms and holding their power for too long, letting it burn through their bodies, washing away all memories of how the real world looked.

I closed my eyes as I took in a deep breath, inhaling scents I hadn't noticed until now: the smell of the damp soil far beneath the bone dust permeating the Elder realm, the sharp scents of fresh cinnamon, lilac, oak, savory meat, and ripe berries. Things I had not seen in the surrounding forest, but now I knew they were here, somewhere.

Or...I was giving my magic too much credit, and Sugar's potion contained a fair bit of hallucinogenic mushrooms, LSD, and Elder ganja. What had those purple mushrooms been?

The column of black light shooting up from the sky was as wide as a thick tree trunk, too big for me to wrap my arms around, and it spun in a vortex like a tornado of liquid and smoke. In fact, it looked like braided rope twirling up into the sky as high as the eye could see.

Without warning, a fist suddenly seemed to grab onto my soul. My eyes shot open, and I gasped at the strange sensation. Then I saw ribbons of power flowing out of my chest and into Grandmama Sugar's outstretched claw. She twirled them around her scaly fingers and flung them down into the cauldron, chanting and dancing as she moved like a wild spirit. Those ribbons of power now connected me directly to the cauldron, unspooling out of me like a roll of thread. It felt like it was hollowing out my insides, but it also felt absolutely incredible.

The column of black light now spiraled with crackling red lightning that zapped up its surface and into the sky. Where the power hit the light clouds, they had evaporated, opening up a hole into the stratosphere. I watched as the crimson lightning raced up the column of swirling darkness, tore past the clouds, and then mushroomed out into an umbrella of crackling red light that illuminated the clouds all around. As I stared in awe, I saw the original clouds growing darker and more turbulent, roiling together as if pulled closer to the column of black and red lightning. Magnetized to the power. I could not breathe as I marveled at this stunning, overwhelming display of Elder magic.

Sugar's magic stick was far more impressive than mine. Maybe I needed to brush up on a few of my books.

This was unlike any tracking spell I had ever performed. In fact, my previous attempts now felt comparable to a kindergartener's hand drawn treasure map. In crayon.

"What do you want the hunter to look like, Master Temple?" Grandmama Sugar screamed, lost to the wild magic as she stood there with her claws held high above her head. I saw more living bolts of black lightning pouring out of her own arms, fueling the roaring inferno above the cauldron, making it darker and giving it a haunting, rumbling roar like some great monstrous beast. Her wrists were dripping with blood, and I watched it pour down her arms, dripping off her elbows and into the cauldron. Each drop sent a boom of thunder and red lightning screaming across the clouds like a heartbeat.

In that moment, I thought of Asha, all alone in a world gone mad and terrifying. Asking Carl to teach her how to defend herself because she was now her own savior.

I thought of Kára and my friends in the Underworld. My godchildren. Calvin's pubescent honking was going to attract all sorts of nasties in Hell.

I thought of Mac, specifically.

I felt a wicked smile pull at my lips, knowing the answer to Sugar's question.

"A DARK HORSE!" I bellowed loud enough for her to hear me clearly over the cacophony.

27

Maybe Mac had somehow known my Dark Horse would save her in the Underworld, and she'd given me the idea ahead of time. Could she see the future?

Sugar cackled like a lunatic. "Of course!" she shrieked, and then she flung her arms wider, opening her chest up to the power she was unleashing. Blood still rained down from her wrists to roll off her elbows, thumping into the cauldron like a drum and echoing across the sky with thunderous explosions. "May the Dark Horse chase down your prey, Master Temple, galloping across the sands of time, screaming across every realm imaginable!" I gasped as a figure of black smoke tore out of her chest, seemingly made of smoke and red fire, like it was one with the storm of black clouds above, complete with the flickers of crimson light within, birthed from Sugar's chest and nourished by the umbilical cord of black power rising up from the cauldron. The Dark Horse tore completely free of her chest, and I saw that she had added a hooded figure upon its back.

"Holy fucking shit!" Grimm screamed. "That's us!"

I wasn't even surprised to learn he had followed us. The ridiculous levels of power should have drawn everyone to come see if we were ending the world when we'd only told them we were doing a little magic. I couldn't pull my eyes away from the power to see if he was alone or joined by everyone.

"You're godsdamned right it is!" Grandmama Sugar screamed like a madwoman, sounding breathless at the exertion of responding to Grimm while so distracted.

I stared in awe, knowing I never would have been able to create something so terrifyingly beautiful.

"You have the scent, Dark Horse," Sugar shouted up at the apparition of me and Grimm. "Chase and terrorize your prey to the ends of the worlds. Locate and trap him so that your master, Nate Temple, can deliver justice!"

The specter looked at me with bright golden eyes and I saw a glowing green medallion hanging from his neck. He nodded and then galloped up the column of power like it was horizontal flatland. The Dark Horse screamed up into the sky, faster than even I would have thought possible, and then the sky exploded with crimson lightning and an eruption of growling thunder that echoed throughout the Elder realm, even making the trees in our forest rattle and shake.

I was getting very good at creating big bangs. Everyone in the Elder realm would have seen this.

Then the column of power winked out of existence and the clouds swiftly evaporated.

I fell to my knees as the cauldron simultaneously cracked in two and crashed down into the white fire, sending up a shower of sparks. I gasped, feeling utterly exhausted as I looked back near the cauldron, hoping to see Grandmama Sugar hadn't fallen into the flames.

Instead, I found her seated on her rump, looking gaunt and drawn, struggling to catch her breath. I scrambled over to her, reaching out a hand to help her, but another claw abruptly swatted my hand away. I looked up to see Carl shake his head at me—not angrily, but in firm seriousness— and then he scooped her up in his arms. She held out a hand as he took a step towards her hut. Her arms still bled freely, but I knew the wounds were not fatal. Carl paused and turned back to me, angling her in his arms so that she could see my face.

"Take care of my grandson, Master Temple. The boy needs his family," she rasped.

I nodded. "Of course, Sugar. I'll return him to you in no time, and I'll bring other friends with me."

She smiled sadly, shaking her head at the suggestion. "I don't have much time. You must listen."

Her words hit me hard, momentarily confusing me. Carl's somber demeanor over the past hour suddenly made a lot more sense. Why Carl had been so detached with everyone but so focused on his Grandmama.

Grandmama Carl had invested her life and the last of her magic into this spell for me. I never would have agreed to it had I known beforehand.

"Why?" I demanded, suddenly angry. "Why didn't you tell me the price?"

She reached out a trembling claw and gave me one of the warmest smiles I had ever seen as she squeezed my fingers. Her smile hit me like a physical hug—one of those hugs where the person wraps their entire body around yours, conforming to your shape as they bury their head in your neck and just radiate loving energy.

I felt my breath catch, wondering if it was her Elder magic or the power of us touching after such profound power had been expended—like aftershocks of magic. "Why?" I repeated sadly, staring at her smiling face.

"Carl told me you were his best friend," she whispered. "That Master Temple was his family. That was one reason they muzzled him," she whispered, flicking her tongue up under the chin of the grandson in question. He stared forward stoically, but I saw his nostrils flare and a tear roll down his scaly cheek. "Every boy deserves a best friend, Master Temple. A family who loves him for who he is, not what he can do for them."

I nodded, forcing a sad smile to my face. "It's Nate, Sugar. Hot grandmas who make wild, passionate magic with me get to call me Nate."

"Oh, dear!" she tittered like a teenaged girl and actually fanned her face at my flirtatious quip. Carl dipped his chin at me and closed his eyes for a very long moment—an acknowledgement of his gratitude to me that he did not want his Grandmama to see. "You are a rapscallion, Master... Nate." Her eyes shifted to my satchel and her smile grew inward at an unknown memory in her heart. "I always knew my husband would accomplish great things," she murmured fondly.

I blinked, caught entirely off guard. Carl looked just as startled. He stared at my satchel in stunned disbelief. "Grandfather?" he whispered, obviously taken aback.

The satchel was...made out of her husband's skin? Sweet, bearded Jesus. I rose to my feet and awkwardly held up the satchel, wondering if I should feel guilty or horrified or honored. Recalling how the Elders made bone blades of their fallen ancestors—and foes, to be fair—I realized there was no animosity in her comment. Callie had gotten me the satchel from Darling and Dear a long time ago. I'd heard it was very, very old, but I could not recall her ever mentioning the name of the particular Elder who had been...repurposed into my satchel. I held it up and she touched it with a gasp and a soft cry of pain—the kind only caused by the most joyous of things that dwell deep in one's heart. "Was his name Carl...something?" I asked, trying to cover the awkward silence.

They both frowned at me. "No. Charon."

I almost lost my footing and suddenly felt very dizzy. "Oh," I whispered, not knowing what to say. There was no way they were talking about...the Boatman.

Right? A secret like that would be impossible to keep. Carl had seen the Boatman and had never made the connection. Granted, Charon didn't look like the typical Elder. He looked very strange but more human than not. Then again...

If his skin had been used to make my satchel, he had probably needed to get *new* skin. And Elders had a penchant for muzzling deviants who knew dangerous truths. Charon's lips were sewn shut and Anubis had been terrified when he plucked out a few of the knots, threatening to finish the job. As that wonderfully visual thought danced across my frontal lobe, I felt an alarming squirming sensation in my stomach. There was simply no way they were talking about the Boatman.

Unfortunately, I didn't quite believe my own assurance. Everyone was scared of Charon. He knew a ton about the Elder realm. He'd said this was his home. He lived in my freaking cavern, brewing beer and carving statues of my ancestors. And his wife lived by the River Styx, as if sensing a connection to it.

But...she obviously didn't know the whole truth.

"I wish I could have met him," Carl whispered. "Everyone says he was a great warrior."

Grandmama Sugar nodded her agreement, and it became abundantly clear that neither of them had any suspicion that the Boatman was their long-lost Charon.

If it was the same man, he was one hell of an asshole to leave Sugar waiting for him. He must have had an exceptionally good reason.

Their private memory now shared, Grandmama Sugar took a deep breath to compose herself, and then she fixed me with a serious gaze. "If you wish, you can seek out the Dark Horse in your dreams. Focus on your desire and the spell we made together, especially the colors and the righteous fury you lent to me—that hatred for your enemy. Focus on that, and you will be able to check the status of your spirit hunter. Or you can wait for him to alert you on his own. He will return with a black sky that rumbles with blood lightning. Reach up to the sky when the storm comes, and he will grab your hand, pulling you to where he has cornered your prey. The rest is up to you, and then your hunter will dissipate."

I nodded. "Thank you, Sugar," I said, sensing that Carl was growing impatient. "We will wait outside," I told him. Then I gave him a nod and he carried her back down the path to the ramshackle hut.

I wasn't sure what kind of funeral processes Elders followed, but his body language told me that it was a private affair.

I turned to Grimm and saw that he stood alone, watching Carl walk past him with Sugar in his arms. He turned to me with a sober expression. "I sent the others back," he said. I nodded and mumbled a thanks. The clearing was strangely silent after the cacophony we had unleashed. "You okay, Nate?" I nodded absently and the silence stretched on. "You still going to let me bang that unicorn?"

I jolted at the bizarre change of topic. He really needed to be told the fact that the studs always got their heads bitten off after exchanging love juices. "Grimm. We actually really need to talk about that—"

"You're right," he said hurriedly. "Poor timing. We can chat later. I'll cover for you and tell everyone you're just...doing wizard stuff. I got you, boss."

Before I could argue, he trotted back down the path. I let out a sigh. I'd tell him about the fatal practices of unicorn husbandry later. It wasn't like we needed to worry about it for a while. When I saw the unicorn herd again, I would let him know.

I sat down in the grass and stared up at the blood red moon, wondering how long night lasted in the Elder realm. It had been night our entire trip so far, and I was dreading the arrival of the sun, despite Charon reassuring me Asha would be safe after her dip in the River Styx. Charon...

I felt my anger jumping to life at the thought of him abandoning his love, Sugar. I clenched my satchel tightly, recalling how he had looked uneasy when he stared at it. Or how he had not shown up after I'd killed the Knightmare. I forced down thoughts of the Boatman before they could take control.

Instead, I reached out for the Dark Horse spell as it ripped across the various pantheons. Unfortunately, all I felt from the specter was rage and fury. I couldn't tell where he was or what he was seeing.

I stared at the cracked cauldron and murmured a prayer for Sugar as embers and sparks continued to rain down around me.

28

W hen I walked back to the hut, it had been more than an hour since Grimm had left me in the clearing. The Dark Horse spell had found nothing but more of the same surrounding storm, even though the night sky here remained normal. He was in another realm, apparently. I had hoped for the storm to return, proof that he'd found my target. Anything to take me away from just sitting around, waiting, thinking of Sugar's death.

I saw that everyone had spread out to get some rest. The sense of sorrow hung heavy in the air. They all knew about Sugar's sacrifice by now.

Well, Yahn was snoring, sprawled out like a starfish beside the hut, but I knew he had a big heart and probably felt terrible about the situation. Talon was leaning against a stump, his eyes barely open, but the metallic sliver of reflection told me he was watching me. Catnapping. He rested with his pole arm across his lap, and his tail twitched at times, giving him away.

Carl was nowhere to be seen, so I assumed he was inside the hut with Sugar, judging by the candlelight glowing from beneath the front door. Asha was sitting on a big log beside the fire that had heated the cooking cauldron earlier. The chair sat empty, reminding me of Sugar's death. I averted my eyes quickly. Asha was working diligently at something in her lap. Thankfully, someone had removed the cauldron, so I didn't have to smell unicorn soup. Or think about Sugar's cracked magic cauldron. Asha was holding her new bone dagger, so I walked over to make sure she hadn't cut herself or something.

And sitting beside the fire sounded relaxing. Peaceful.

Grimm kept me and Asha in his peripheral vision as he scowled out into the dark forest near the perimeter of the clearing. His fiery eyes looked forebodingly into the gloomy woods. I smiled to myself. Grimm might act like a jerk, but he wouldn't let anything happen to her. He saw me watching and flicked his tail dismissively. I gave him a meaningful look and he nodded.

"Oh!" Asha said, startled by my sudden appearance. She made as if to rise up from her stump, but I waved her back down and took a seat next to her on the thick log. She hadn't hurt herself, so I shifted my attention to the fire, pretending I didn't notice Sugar's empty chair. "I didn't hear you coming back."

I nodded silently, just wanting to turn down the noise in my head.

I felt Asha watching me with a compassionate smile in my peripheral vision. She had seen entirely too much death lately. If I could figure this out and get us out of here, my goal was to make sure she was well taken care of. No more death to follow her, no more danger to plague her. She was a sweet kid. Fifteen was still a kid to my old, tired ass.

"You two made beautiful magic, Nate. I think she died doing what she loved. Don't feel sad," she said. "It was incredible. I've never seen anything like it." Grimm watched us from across the clearing, looking suspicious of her vegan machinations.

I waved a hand at him, urging him to leave us alone. He snorted and stamped a hoof for good measure.

I nodded. "Stronger than most magic I've ever seen," I admitted sadly, staring into the flames. "And now she's dead, or soon to be."

The fire crackled in front of us, and I stared into the flames, imagining Anubis' mangled face within the flames. Then Aiden's smirking grin as his flesh burned like parchment. Then Charon—

"Don't be angry at her, Nate," Asha whispered gently but passionately. "She died *for* something, not because something happened *to* her. It wasn't a failure on anyone's part, but her *choice*. To call it anything less cheapens her death and turns you into something worse than...the bad guys."

I stiffened as if I'd been slapped. I risked a glance at her, but her eyes were red-rimmed and lost, battling her own demons over her murdered family. The family I had unknowingly destroyed. "Is that what you did?" I asked honestly. "You can really sit there and think about the good, knowing that the bad triumphed?" I whispered, feeling lost and confused. I just wanted to hug Kára, goddamn it. To hear Mac laugh. To tease Calvin about his cracking voice. To mock Gunnar about his vision. To...respect Ashley Randulf wholeheartedly and not say anything that might earn me an ass whooping. Or, better yet, to say something abstract that immediately turned her ire on her husband, earning him an ass whooping.

I realized I was smiling. But it was a faint, whisper of a smile.

"Yes. That's all I *can* do," Asha whispered. "Anything else would destroy me. I must have hope."

"Hope," I muttered in a bitter tone. "What good is hope in this world?"

The fire crackled ominously, punctuating the silence. "Have you ever heard about the rat experiment?" Asha asked me. I frowned, glancing over at her and shaking my head. She turned to look into the fire, gathering her thoughts. "A scientist ran an experiment where he put a rat in a tub of water. It drowned after fifteen minutes. The rat gave up and drowned."

I arched an eyebrow, wanting to tell her that the scientist was a sick son of a—

"He took a second rat," she continued, "and ran the same experiment. This time, at the fifteen-minute mark, he pulled the rat out of the water. Dried him off with a towel and let him know he was okay." I realized I was leaning closer, drawn into the story. "Then the scientist dropped the rat back into the water."

I blinked. Her continuation only confirmed my earlier judgment. The scientist was a twisted bastard.

She said nothing, and the fire crackled.

"Ask me how long the second rat lasted." I looked over at her and saw that she was smiling distantly.

I shrugged. "I don't know. Sixteen minutes," I said, not understanding the point of the sick experiment.

She shook her head and finally turned to look at me. Her gaze was piercing. "Sixty...*hours.*"

My eyes widened in disbelief.

She nodded. "One little flicker of hope—the scientist saving him after fifteen minutes—gave him the belief that the scientist would save him before he died. That he could keep going and going and going, long after he thought he was too tired. Because the scientist wouldn't let him die. So, he kept right on paddling, believing nothing bad could happen to him. The scientist would save him when things got too hard. It had happened before. The fact that he was alive was proof that it had happened before and that it could happen again." She leaned closer, staring me in the eyes. "A taste of hope—of salvation—and that rat lasted two and a half *days* compared to a quarter of an *hour.*" With that mic drop, she turned back to the fire with a wistful...hopeful smile. "My father told me that story. Said it's why he named me Asha. It means *hope.*"

I had no words to respond. My anger and fear and frustration were still just beneath the surface, but I could not formulate a response to argue her point. She...was right.

The fact that he was alive was proof that it had happened before and that it could happen again.

"You're the Horseman of Hope. Grimm is very proud of that," she said, glancing over at me. "So, we are going to need you to pull your crap together and show us some of that hope before we all give up and stop paddling, Mr. Scientist." She wiped her eyes with her elbow, and I realized she was crying. "I'm scared we're all going to die," she whispered. "Everyone else gave up and died on me. Please help us. Tell me what you *need* from me," she croaked, clutching desperately at her lap.

29

I could feel her staring at me. Like a coward, I closed my eyes and took a calming breath. She was right, but I simply didn't have it in me. I was too angry at Sugar's sacrifice to help anyone else feel better. To lend out more of my already tattered faith. I was barely hanging onto it myself. Everyone lied to me, deceived me, betrayed me. I knew it wasn't fair for me to cry victim and hide behind that paper-thin armor, but my fragile feelings still tried to seduce me with temptation into that fraudulent reality. I clenched my jaw, trying to pull up *something* I could give her. A cliche. A quote. Something a friend had once said. Anything to get her to back off and give me one night of peace where I could just feel sorry for myself without judgment. I just wanted to sleep. And save Kára. And Gunnar. And kill Aiden. And kiss Mac's head. And—

Something touched my hand and I flinched in surprise, my eyes shooting open. I looked down to see that Asha was kneeling next to me and pressing something into my palm, wrapping my fingers around it with both of hers. I met her eyes, feeling confused. "You looked really sad," she said apologetically. "I wasn't trying to make you feel bad. I'm just scared of everything and I'm barely hanging on." I nodded stiffly. "Then you looked really angry. Presents always make me feel better...and I felt bad for not giving you a ribbon," she admitted with a playful grin. "I was going to surprise you later, but a laugh now is better than a gift tomorrow."

I continued to stare at her, confused. "What?"

She pointed at my hand and then leaned back with an eager, shameless, and expectant smile. "Look!" she urged, practically bubbling over with excitement, even though I could tell she was still scared. "Talon helped me find it in the clearing where you made the magic, but the decoration was all me. I used my new knife! You're going to laugh so hard, but that's okay!"

I saw speckles of Sugar's blood on my skin, but I ignored them. I opened my callused and scarred hand to see a flat wooden disc in my palm. It was as large as a silver dollar and made of the strange black and white striated wood from the trees in the clearing where we'd birthed our Dark Horse spell. The circular shape was far from symmetrical and even had a few pointed edges, but I could see she had tried to whittle it down into a near perfect circle like a coin. And Asha had carved a crude smile onto its face. The eyes were more like violent gouges that resembled mismatched X's. She'd even scratched a blocky tongue to hang from the lips.

It was horrifyingly poor quality to my eyes.

It was stunningly breathtaking to my heart.

My pocket felt like it was on fire.

"It's an emoji," she said into the silence. "A silly smiley face," she clarified, in case I was too old to know what an emoji was.

I continued to stare down at it, feeling the smoke from the fire burning my eyes.

"I didn't want to give you one of my hair ties and I wanted to practice using the blade while you made magic with Sugar. I know it's cheesy and not very good, but I wanted to make you something—"

I violently closed my fist over it and closed my eyes, my movement silencing Asha's explanation. The smoke was making my eyes water and my lungs hurt. Especially after Asha's reprimand.

"I still need to fix it," Asha said hurriedly, sounding embarrassed. "It kind of looks broken and unfinished. But I thought it might make you laugh. Cheer you up to show you the beta version. Remind you to smile when you feel sad—"

"It is perfect, Asha," I said, my voice hoarse. "I don't want you to fix it. I prefer broken things to perfect things."

"Oh..." she said, sounding torn between relief and confusion. "Are you sure? I can fix the eyes and smooth out the edges at least. You don't think it's ugly? I thought you would laugh at it."

I shook my head with a forced smile. "No. It is perfect the way it is, Asha. Thank you for the thoughtful gift. I have been rather grumpy lately. I've been told I need to get my crap together." She grinned guiltily. My pocket was only growing hotter, and I knew there would never be an ideal time to tell the truth. There never was. In fact, it was worse *because* I had waited.

I reached into my pocket and pulled out the small black and white picture Nadia had been carrying. There was a bloody fingerprint on the bottom. I took a deep breath and turned to Asha with a heartbroken look, feeling a tear rolling down my cheek. "Your mother was carrying this," I rasped, my voice sounding like dry gravel. "I know it is the opposite of a gift, but I would have wanted to know if I was in your place."

She reached out a hand and accepted the picture with trembling fingers, pinching it tightly as her eyes filled up with tears. She did not cry but she stared down at it with a horrible blank look on her face.

"I'm so sorry, Asha," I whispered. Then I climbed down off the log and knelt in front of her. I remained close enough for her to embrace but I didn't initiate anything. I rested my hands on my knees. One of them was tightly squeezed around the gift she had just carved for me—a bitter contradiction to the gift I had just given her.

I held it like a goddamned life preserver, wanting nothing more than to run away screaming that it wasn't my fault and I'm sorry and—

But it was my fault. Indirectly, but still my fault. My enemies had unknowingly targeted her.

That was on me. Period.

She stared down at the sonogram and I saw her lip tugging up at one corner in a haunted smile. "A brother," she whispered, tears rolling down her cheeks as she sniffled. "I...had hoped for a brother after Thomas died..."

I felt like the same knife that had torn into her mother and unborn brother's stomach was now twisting inside mine. An eye for an eye type payment of pain for keeping this from her. "Thomas was your brother?"

She nodded sadly. "Yes. He was the best."

"I should have told you sooner," I said. "I'm sorry, Asha. You deserved to know, but then we were attacked, and then..." I trailed off, hating my own self-justifications. "Excuses don't matter. I should have told you sooner. Immediately."

She slowly turned to look up at me and I almost flinched under the level of compassion in her green eyes. Strands of her black hair had come loose from her ponytail, flicking across her cheek in the gentle breeze. She reached up and wiped a tear from my eyes with her thumb. Then she cupped my cheek in a gentle squeeze and her face contorted in sorrow. "Oh, Nate. I already suspected it. My mom was always rubbing her belly with a distant smile, and she was wearing bulkier clothes to hide her weight. She was hiding it from me, even at the end, but I suspected." She smiled distantly, lowering her hand from my cheek. My skin felt suddenly cold without her touch. "Then you told the Knightmare she was pregnant. On the mountain."

I winced, feeling even more terrible. "Oh, damn. I didn't even think about that," I whispered. "So, this whole time," I said, gesturing at our journey so far. "You knew?"

She nodded. "I didn't know about the picture, but I distracted my thoughts by debating about whether the baby was a brother or a sister. It's one reason I wanted Carl to teach me to fight. To keep myself safe for *them*. Maybe one day I can save it from happening to someone else," she whispered in a haunted tone.

Goddamn.

What was this girl *made* of? She had shown no signs of depression or anything. I had feared the news might drive her to...hurting herself or giving up on life. But it seemed to have done the precise opposite. In fact, she had just schooled me on fortitude.

"I think it...*he* was going to be my mom's Christmas gift to me. Our Christmas gift to each other," she said. Then she sat back on her heels and hugged the tiny picture to her chest. "Thank you for the Christmas gift, Nate. Thank you for the hope," she said with a hollow smile.

I hung my head sadly, not knowing what to say. I definitely hadn't given her hope.

"Do you mind if I..." her words trailed off and I looked up to see her gesturing at the fire, "if I have some privacy?" she finally finished. "I just want to sit here for a while."

I scrambled to my feet, nodding hurriedly. "Of course, Asha. I'll be nearby if you need anything. I—"

She waved a hand at me and climbed to her feet. "It's okay. Really. I don't need anything," she said, sitting down on her stump from earlier. "Thank you."

I turned to leave, nodding awkwardly. "I understand—a"

"One last thing," Asha said, staring into the fire. "Could you be a Horseman for me?" My jaw trembled as I blinked away tears. "I think I really need a Horseman right now. I need some hope."

I nodded. "Okay," I vowed, squeezing the wooden disc in my palm, wanting to throw it into the fire. Not out of anger with her. I didn't deserve the coin after what I'd just done to her. But I knew she'd be horrified by such an outburst. It would be me lashing out because my feelings were hurt, burdened with guilt. Hurting Asha was the exact opposite of what I wanted. Instead, I promised to keep it close to my heart as a reminder of the heavy price of responsibility.

Of hope.

Sometimes, like now, it felt like a lead anchor pulling me down.

Other times, I could look at the goofy broken smile and remember the wins.

I had saved Asha.

I turned and walked away from the fire, needing to clear my head. Talon watched me from afar, his eyes shining in the moonlight as he leaned back against a stump like he'd been napping. He saw the look on my face and knew I wanted solitude.

I walked into the creepy forest, clutching the wooden disk with a murderous scowl.

"The Dark Horse will destroy everything you love, Aiden Maxon," I growled, refusing to grant him my last name. If Temples were made...

Then they could also be destroyed.

I wouldn't be able to get any sleep for quite some time now.

30

I woke up to Grimm breathing on my face from mere inches away. I punched him in the mouth on reflex and scooted back hurriedly. "Grimm! What the *hell*, man?" I demanded.

He shook his head and scowled at me. "Ow! You fell asleep in the woods, you fucking weirdo."

I sat up and looked around, surprised to find myself in the clearing where we'd summoned the Dark Horse spell. I scrambled to my feet, panicking. "Is everyone okay?"

"I'm not, you rat bastard!" Grimm snapped in a nasally complaint. "Who punches a unicorn?"

"We are all alive," Carl said from a few inches behind me, causing me to jump back with a shout. Did no one respect personal space here? I turned to find him staring at me with a familiar look. Like the night before hadn't happened. Like his Grandmama hadn't died. He pointedly rested his hand on a shiny new bone dagger and stared way too deeply into my eyes for me to feel comfortable after only being awake ten seconds. "Sugar is with us. We can enter the Citadel." Then he tapped his claw on the bone handle and I shuddered. He had removed her arm to carve a dagger from her bone. Talk about a loving grandson. On the bright side, we had our key to the Citadel.

"Does anyone have any coffee," I muttered, swiping my hair from my eyes.

I looked around to find everyone hanging out in the clearing. Talon was talking with Yahn in low tones and Asha was picking flowers in the field of dying grass.

"What is that?" Carl asked, pointing at my neck.

I reached up to touch my necklace and felt Asha's carving hanging there beside the coin that was my Horseman's Mask. I smiled, remembering using my magic to drill a hole through the top so I could wear it as a reminder to always have its namesake. "Hope," I told him. "Asha made it for me." I showed it to him with a lighthearted smile on my face. "She used your dagger."

He nodded thoughtfully and then walked away without a word. A few moments later, I heard him chastising Asha about the dagger, that it was an instrument to torture and maim, not to carve pretty things. She glanced at me over his shoulder. I held up the coin and shrugged, mouthing *sorry* to her. She bit back a smile and nodded obediently to Elder Carl, her new instructor in the arts of death.

I climbed to my feet and brushed off my pants. "We should get moving," I said, loud enough for everyone to hear. I glanced up at the dark sky. "How long is night here?" I muttered to myself, shaking my head. The moon was lower in the sky but still fully visible. Carl finished scolding Asha, and everyone gathered around me. "Lead the way to the Citadel, Carl," I told him.

He nodded and gestured for me to walk with him. Asha and Yahn walked up to Grimm and Asha climbed onto his back. Talon walked a few paces behind me as Carl pressed onward. I glanced over my shoulder at Talon. "Where is the last Knightmare?"

Every Knight turned to look in the same direction, silently answering my question. "The same direction Carl is going. He is not close," Talon said.

I nodded. "Of course." What I'd really wanted to make sure of was that he wasn't about to pop up in the forest and ambush us. If he wasn't close, we could travel easier. I gestured with my hand behind my back for Talon to hang back a bit. Then I turned to Carl. "I'm sorry about Sugar, Carl. She died too soon, in my opinion."

Carl continued looking ahead, leading us out of the clearing and back into the forest in the direction of the River Styx. "She lived a long and full life. Elder witches live thousands of years." I stared at him in stunned disbelief. I must have made a sound because he glanced back at me. He took one look at my face and patted the hilt of his brand-new dagger with his claw—the one made from Sugar's bone. "Do not feel guilty for her sacrifice, Master Temple. She lived longer than anyone I know. Bred lines of kings and queens for millennia. She chose her end, and that is honorable."

I nodded woodenly. "Okay, Carl." I was silent for a time, my mind racing. Thousands of years? Good lord. "You knew the whole time what she was planning," I said, recalling her telling me she was the key and that she would be coming with us. She had meant her bone not her person. He nodded to my question. "If she was grandmother to royalty, why did she live out in the woods in a crumbling hut?"

Carl smiled fondly. "She said she liked living near the dead river. She wanted to see it come back some day, saying that was all she ever needed in life."

I felt my heart breaking. Had she known that her husband worked on the River Styx? Or was it some kind of sick irony? Some instinctive pull towards the river that her heart had urged her to follow? From our conversation, she definitely hadn't seemed to know about the Boatman. Charon had determined that it was important not to tell her about his new job. He must have had a very good reason.

Charon had purposely refused to answer me when I had asked if he was an Elder. Had he been protecting Sugar because he was in love with her? It had to be love, because he had also chosen to remain close to her, brewing beer and carving statues in my cave.

And she had chosen—knowingly or coincidentally—to live close to him, waiting for the river of death to return to the Elder realm.

What if Charon had wanted me to come down here specifically because he knew Sugar would have to die? So he could be reunited with her. Maybe he had collected her soul when she died in her hut, and the two were boinking scalies down in Hell right now.

He had obviously chosen to leave me out of the reunion. Carl as well, or he would have been asking me very pointed questions right now, seeing as how he had just learned I was carrying his grandfather's skin as a satchel. It wasn't like my presence was required for Charon to pick up a soul. It was...a courtesy and appreciation he often granted me that he didn't grant others.

He chose when to let me see him by freezing time.

Which brought me back to thoughts of the Knightmare. He had not shown up and the body had turned to black dust. Had he intentionally taken the Knightmare's soul without making me aware? Or did the Knightmares not have souls? That seemed unlikely, because even bad guys had souls—obviously. There were plenty of detention centers for such assholes in the Underworld. It was kind of the primary purpose, actually.

I hadn't ever seen the VIP areas where the good souls went, which was probably intentional.

I didn't know the truth, but I had plenty of pointed questions for the Boatman when I saw him next. The level of my friendliness would depend entirely upon whether he showed up when I killed the second Knightmare, because I needed a soul to get to the Underworld. If he didn't show up for the second Knightmare's execution, the only souls left for me to steal would be one of my allies, and there was no way I could make myself do that.

Especially not Asha, after everything she had gone through.

I thumbed the wooden coin she had given me, smiling absently. She was a tough kid.

We walked through the dark forest in silence, on our way to the Citadel. "How far away is the Reverie?" I asked Carl.

He considered my question, his eyes calculating. "Maybe one week."

I clenched my jaw in frustration. "Let's make it faster," I growled. "Or at least find the Knightmare faster. Our friends in Hell don't have that long." Rather than argue with me, Carl started jogging through the woods. Everyone picked up their pace, looking grim and determined.

We might need to reassess the dangers of flying at some point. The risk might be necessary.

31

As we finally broke out of the forest, it had started growing considerably warmer. Carl had informed us that the sun would soon rise and that we should hydrate. We stood on a plateau overlooking the River Styx, but the area was full of rising hills, so Yahn and Grimm had gone ahead to do some scouting while we sat down and rested after jogging for a few hours. Asha walked awkwardly, sore from riding Grimm, but she didn't complain, knowing everyone else had been forced to run to keep up with Carl. I handed out water bottles from my satchel and then I sat down with a sigh. I leaned back against a small boulder and closed my eyes, relishing the break and the drink. Before long, I felt myself dozing off.

"I wish Grinder were here," Talon said, snapping me awake.

I had no idea how long I'd been out. Could have been three seconds or ten minutes. I smiled at Talon's comment, seeing him leaning against another boulder across from me. He was resting his spear across his lap, leaning his elbows over it, and his tail was twitching back and forth. "Aw. You miss Grinder? That's cute."

"No. I'm just hungry," Talon replied irritably, his eyes narrowing. "Grimm ate the whole goat leg all by himself because he's a selfish fat ass."

Grimm didn't respond, but only because he was probably still scouting our trail. We needed a way to get over the river and I preferred not to resort to flying until I knew we weren't surrounded by killer predators like the spider-deer or unicorns or whatever that porcupine wolf thing had been. The one the unicorn ripped in half with her horn.

I cocked my head curiously, something about Talon's comment nagging at me. Then it hit me. "Damn it. I don't think Grinder is going to be able to come back to us. I think both goats are going to wake up in the Underworld with Gunnar."

Talon snorted. "Well, they will both probably *love* that." I scowled at him, and he lifted his paws in a *what do you do* gesture. "We will know for sure when the sun comes up," Talon said. "Won't be long now."

I twitched nervously at the reminder, glancing up at the moon that had finally sunk to the level of the horizon. "Make sure Asha is in the shade when it comes out. I'd rather test out her River Styx SPF with a finger first, just to make sure."

Asha and Carl walked up to us, and she was beaming happily. "Carl showed me how to stab people!" she said, gripping the hilt of the dagger hanging from her waist. Carl had given her one of his many straps, cinching it tight to fit around her smaller frame. It looked preposterous with her military style boots, skinny jeans, and hoodie, but I smiled at her jubilant aura.

Carl nodded. "Next we will move to slashing and slicing. She stabs well for an incompetent tiny person."

Asha beamed as if it was a great compliment, and then sat down with us, turning my conversation with Talon into a semicircle. She grinned with pride to see her carving now hanging on my necklace.

"How long was I asleep?" I asked, wondering when Carl had found enough time to train Asha.

"Twenty minutes," Talon said with a dismissive shrug. "We're just waiting for Grimm and Yahn to return."

"Well," Asha said, "if we are going to be here for a few minutes without everyone running, can I ask a question?"

"Sure," I said, leaning back against the rock. "About what?"

She pursed her lips thoughtfully. "I'm confused about the Horsemen. In the Bible, the book of Revelations talks about the Apocalypse and the Four Horsemen," she said, scrunching up her nose. "Death, War, Famine, and...the plague guy," she said, her cheeks blushing lightly. "I can't remember his name."

I smiled and nodded. "Conquest. Or Pestilence, as some people call him," I said.

I felt a sudden buzzing in my ears, and I instinctively swatted at it. The noise immediately faded as the flying bug escaped my wrath. I shook my head and swiped my hair back just to be certain it hadn't landed on me or anything. I was relieved not to find a bug in my palm because I didn't want to discover that I'd accidentally sat down beside a nest of murder wasps or whatever the Elder realm had for flying insects.

Talon chuckled at my reaction, but his tall ears twitched instinctively as well, making the earrings jingle against each other. Hypocrite.

Asha snapped her finger at my answer. "Yes. Pestilence." Her eyebrows furrowed thoughtfully. "But you're the Horseman of Hope. That's not one of the four in the Bible."

I hesitated, wondering how much I should explain. She needed to know but I didn't want to terrify her. Talking about the Apocalypse always made people fidgety for some reason. "I kind of started a new band. The Dread Four."

Her eyes widened. "What about the other four? The originals? Are they dead?"

I waved a hand reassuringly. "No. They're fine. The Four Horsemen are related to the Bible, right? Christianity?" She nodded, leaning forward. "Well, I started a new group of Horsemen who will represent the other religions and beliefs."

She frowned. "That sounds like blasphemy, as Greta would say," she said with a playful smile.

I shrugged. "Not really. We're not replacing them or anything. The Dread Four are actually tasked with keeping the other pantheons—religions—of gods in line. We want to protect mankind from them. Very different than the Biblical Four Horsemen." I saw her frown and I smiled. "Clear as mud, right?"

Even Talon and Carl were leaning closer, listening intently. Much of this they probably took for granted, and they were interested to finally get an in-depth explanation of the Dread Four's purpose.

"The Dread Four doesn't sound very...friendly," she finally said. "No offense."

I chuckled. "The name is meant to scare our enemies, not people. We are actually allies with the Four Horsemen. Death is an old family friend of mine. We are not against each other or anything."

She nodded, looking relieved she wasn't hanging out with a man who wanted to kill a fraction of the population during the Apocalypse. Or a man who wanted to pick a fight with the Four Horsemen. That was fair. "But how did you *become* a Horseman? Did you just wake up one day and magic it or something?" she asked.

I shook my head. "It was actually my ancestor's fault. Matthias Temple. He made the original masks, but he neglected to tell anyone he'd made a spare set of four. He gave me one and almost started some very serious problems for the world. The Masks work in groups of four, you see. One by itself messes up the balance of power, so I had to find owners for the other three of my set," I said, wondering where Matthias—the Mad Hatter, as he was also known—was these days. The last thing I'd heard about him had been that he was traveling the world and keeping a low profile. He had met up with the Biblical Four Horsemen around the time when I'd adopted my own mask, because it had made the Biblical Horsemen sick for a time. Explaining all of that, though, would only confuse her, and it was all water under the bridge anyway.

The two teams of Horsemen no longer threatened each other and had achieved a balance of power that we could all live with.

"Your ancestor made the Masks?" she asked, her eyebrows lifting straight up. "That sounds like big magic. Like what you did last night."

I nodded. "He was a very powerful man." No need to melt her brain by telling her he was still alive on a beach somewhere. Or that he was certifiably insane. Actually, it was more accurate to say that he had a very, very dangerous perception of reality. He could make his own realities, after all. A Tiny God.

"I saw your armor on the mountain," she finally said. "Is it like theirs? Bonded to you?" she asked, pointing at Talon and Carl.

I nodded and pulled out my necklace. I focused on it, transforming it into my black Horseman's Mask. "This is the Mask of Hope. I can summon the paired armor just like these two can with their Knight armor."

She stared at it thoughtfully, nodding. "Who are the other Horsemen in the Dread Four?"

"You met Gunnar. Mac's dad. He's a werewolf, and he is also the Horseman of Justice. Callie Penrose, a powerful wizard in Kansas City is the Horsewoman of Despair, and my vampire friend, Alucard Morningstar, is the Horseman of Absolution." She had flinched at mention of the word vampire, but she trusted me well enough to realize that they might not be as frightening as she had once thought.

Unfortunately, that wasn't entirely true. I just picked one of the good ones.

"Hope and Despair are opposites, right?" she asked. "And depending on how you define Justice, it could be opposite of Absolution. Like, if Justice was a punishment. Or am I reaching?"

I chuckled. "Spot on. We balance each other."

"And you are the leader?" she pressed. I shrugged with a guilty smile. She glanced over my shoulder and waved with a big smile. "Yahn's back!"

I turned to look and saw Yahn jogging towards us. He wore a troubled frown, and he was breathing hard.

"Where is Grimm?" I asked, rising to my feet.

Yahn cringed. "Yeah. We have a problem," he said, motioning for us to hurry up and follow him. "Grimm found the herd of unicorns. He went to go talk to one of them." He met my eyes. "The white one he's been talking about so much."

"Well, it was nice knowing him," Carl said with a dismissive shrug.

I was already running, shoving Yahn ahead of me.

32

Yahn led us to a hill overlooking the River Styx. We all got down on our bellies and crawled up to the top, keeping a low profile as we peered out over the Elder realm. The River Styx bubbled in front of us, but a large herd of unicorns was grazing about two-hundred-yards away. They were various colors, but I saw none that were white like the one I'd seen atop the mountain with Grimm.

Fortunately, they were far away and hadn't noticed anything suspicious.

Unfortunately, I saw that the white unicorn Grimm had seen earlier—at least she looked the same—was grazing all by herself much closer to our viewing perch. Her back was facing us, so she didn't see Grimm stealthily sneaking from bush to bush, using them like a leapfrogging ninja to get closer to his non-consenting girlfriend.

"He's dead," Carl hissed. "That's the lead mare of the herd. He has exactly no chance."

Yahn and Talon nodded their agreement. I scowled at them and glanced behind us. Asha was standing in the shade of a broad tree at the base of the hill a few dozen yards away, because the sun was coming up soon and I was paranoid about her combusting into a pillar of flame. Charon was provably a liar, so I didn't want to risk her life on trusting his advice about the River Styx's water keeping her safe from the upcoming broiling sun. Maybe the water needed to be applied daily or something. We simply didn't know. But we didn't dare attempting to get any closer to the river to double-dip her in the water as insurance, because that would put us out in the open where the wild unicorns might spot us.

"It's kind of creepy to see so many unicorns," Yahn said. "I always thought Grimm was special. This is like Jurassic Park, but with unicorns."

"Almost everyone dies in Jurassic Park," I said, frowning at him.

"Then it is *almost* a good movie," Carl said.

Talon chuckled. "Carl's got jokes."

"How does this work?" Yahn asked. "Does he do a dance or something to get her attention?"

"Grimm said he needs to dominate her. He said that's how they do it. I'm not promoting it," I quickly added.

"The mares also bite the heads off their mates afterwards," Carl reminded me.

I grimaced. "Are you absolutely certain about that, Carl?" I asked.

He didn't even hesitate. "Certain. One-thousand-percentages."

"That's not how you say it," Talon muttered, his ears twitching with irritation.

"Keep your ears down," I told him. "Your bling could reflect light and let them know we're here."

He obeyed as best he could and hunkered lower to the ground, looking like a cat about to pounce. I watched as Grimm stalked through the glade, approaching the seemingly aloof mare like a thief in the night, using small trees and bushes and hedges and boulders as cover. It almost looked like he was playing a prank on her. Like me when I had cow tipped the Minotaur so long ago.

I came to the conclusion that I might have to actually save him. He might need protection for this late-night soiree. If they did the deed, I could summon my Horseman's armor for Grimm, protecting him from her decapitation kiss. Unfortunately, this meant I actually needed to stick around and observe their whole encounter. I'd initially hoped to stop him before he found his target, but that was no longer an option.

I hadn't wanted to *watch* it go down, but that was looking like the only option.

"Maybe we should kill her before Grimm can get to her," Yahn murmured. "The rest of the herd is far away from us, so we should still be able to escape."

I turned to look at him. "Your plan is to execute the lead mare of the herd. This is the first idea that came to your mind?" I asked in a monotone. "You are no longer allowed to come up with ideas for the team."

He winced and sighed. "So, we just wait and watch him die?"

The sun had finally started to rise but a small mountain on the opposite side of the unicorns blocked its direct light for the time being, buying us some time to be less noticeable from their view. I watched as the light hit other areas on the horizon, waiting for everything to erupt in steam or something. It was just like regular sunlight, to my eyes. It was ridiculously bright after the seemingly endless night, but it didn't seem as frightfully blinding as I had anticipated. I mean, it was a sun, of course, but I had built it up in my mind as some kind of nuclear bomb just on the horizon. Or a permanent flamethrower blasting the earth.

We watched, holding our breaths, as Grimm closed the distance. I had no idea how she hadn't sensed or heard him yet, but the breeze was blowing in his favor. Grimm peered his head out from the hedge, and I saw his nostrils flare. Then he leapt out behind her.

She definitely heard something, because she spun around and lowered her horn warningly, glaring at the strange male as her nostrils flared and she pulled her lips back in a vicious snarl.

Grimm spread his wings wide and reared up on his back hooves, kicking at the air with his front hooves. "I am Grimm!" I was surprised that we could actually hear him clearly. Maybe his voice carried over the water well. He was speaking forcefully, but not yelling. I held my breath, curious to hear his pickup line. "Woman, you have the thickest ass I have ever seen, and you will love me—"

Almost too quickly to notice, the unicorn charged forward, aiming her horn at Grimm's heart. He hopped back and twisted, batting her aside with his wings, and letting out a startled shout as her horn grazed his chest. He landed back on all fours and crouched warily, his blood dripping down his leg. It wasn't a serious wound, or I would have risked everything to kill her as quickly as possible, adopting Yahn's plan.

The other unicorn flared her wings out and snarled at him. "I am

Namea," she said by means of introduction. Grimm looked a little wild around the eyes, but he flared his wings out as well, mimicking her. Then the two began circling each other in an aggressive dance that held absolutely no romance.

"Maybe Grimm was right about how they handle these things," I murmured, barely able to breathe.

"What the fuck is wrong with you?" Grimm snapped.

The unicorn—Namea—lunged again, and Grimm almost tripped over his hooves as he jumped back. She laughed at him in a mocking tone. "Where did you come from, warrior?" Namea hissed.

"The mountain," he replied warily, still circling her. "I saw you hunting, and I decided I would have you—"

"You came a long way to die, Grimm," she interrupted, juking him again.

But Grimm didn't fall for it this time. He held his ground and lowered his horn. "We can do this the hard way or the harder way, Namea," Grimm growled, scraping his hoof across the ground.

"Give it to me the harder way, Loverboy," she teased. Then the tip of her horn started to glow with brilliant blue light, and she aimed it directly at Grimm's face. A blast of blue fire as thick as my waist screamed towards him, but Grimm unleashed his own beam of achromatic light at the last second.

The two forces met in the middle and the world exploded with blindingly bright light and a shockwave of force that ripped small trees and bushes entirely from the ground in a ring of rolling dust. It momentarily blinded my friends, judging by the strings of grunts and curses all around me. I squinted, blinking my eyes rapidly, to see the aftermath. Dust filled the air, but I saw the two unicorns about twenty feet apart, looking like they had also been blown backward by the explosion.

They both looked dazed and dizzy, tossing their manes back and forth as they stumbled on shaky legs.

In the distance, I saw that the herd of unicorns had turned around to locate the cause of the explosion. They saw their lead mare, Namea, confronting Grimm and slowly started ambling towards them. Shit, shit, shit. They obviously didn't fear for her safety, but they were wary about the blast of power.

Neither Grimm nor Namea seemed to notice their movement, too shaken by the result of their attacks clashing. I didn't know whether to root for him or to cry. If I tried to interfere, I would draw the attention of the whole herd, and there was no way we could take on that many unicorns. There were hundreds of them.

"What...was that?" Namea demanded, glaring at Grimm. "There was no *color*," she said with a bewildered shake of her mane.

"That was my painbow, Namea," Grimm said in a husky, smug tone. "I'm a rainbow hunter, woman. You wanted it the harder way."

"I...think I *liked* it," she said, dipping her head ever so slightly. She flicked her tail up and shuddered.

"This is kind of disgusting," Yahn whispered, pursing his lips. Talon and Carl both swatted his head, silencing him as they stared, transfixed by the sadist-unicorn-rom-com.

"Yeah, you did," Grimm said with a lewd chuckle, his wings flaring out wider like a peacock. "I've got something else you'll like—"

"Sisters!" Namea suddenly screamed, her voice booming across the empty space. "We have an invader!"

Grimm backed up a step, looking very confused as his wings went limp. "Wait. What?"

The herd of unicorns let out a terrible hunting cry, and then they were galloping at full speed, many of them taking flight with big sweeps of their wings. I sucked in a breath. Well, shit.

"Run, boy!" Namea snarled, laughing wickedly. "I want to see your thick rump wobble!" Then she tore after him, intending to obliterate him with her horn like I had seen her do to the spine-wolf.

Grimm, fully committed to dominating the supposed love of his life, faced his impending doom with steadfast fortitude and bravery for exactly one whole second.

Then he abruptly spun and started hauling ass away from Namea, cursing and shouting like a whipped dog. He zig-zagged back and forth, professing his confusion and his love over his shoulder in stammering one-liners. "You are my everything! Your eyes are sparkling windows to all the hells! Your horn is stained with the blood of your foes! The way the moon glows on your thick rump dizzies my brain!"

Namea laughed, her eyes glittering with excitement at the lavish praise as she doggedly pursued him in an effort to utterly obliterate her suitor.

"I love you!" Grimm screamed, angling her away from our location— kind of. Going across the river was really his only option for escape. Losing Namea and her herd in the forest.

"You fool!" Namea yelled, picking up on his plan to enter the forest. "You run from one death just to enter the witch's domain! She will eat you alive!"

"Don't talk trash about Sugar, my bloodthirsty love!" Grimm snapped defensively, leaping over a hedge and then immediately veering to the left and circling back around the white unicorn as she was forced to jump over the hedge as well. I watched his bloody blue ribbon fly off at the sharp maneuver and then slowly flutter to the ground. "Sugar's my friend!"

Namea skidded to a halt, looking startled by his comment, but also distracted by the falling blue ribbon. She bent low to sniff it, shook her her mane and sneezed, and then she resumed her chase.

"We need to get the hell out of here, guys," I said. "If one of those fliers sees us, we're fucked," I said.

The herd of unicorns was getting much closer, and I watched the sun finally rise over the distant mountain, bathing the landscape with light. No one burned or caught fire. I glanced back at Asha to see her standing in the sunlight without harm. I let out a sigh of relief, but I held up a finger, urging her to stay back.

"Talon," I said, swatting his shoulder. He blinked in surprise, so engrossed with the unicorn derby that he'd forgotten all about us. "Go guard Asha. I'm going to try something, and you might need to carry her into the woods at a dead run. I think the unicorns are scared of the forest. Of Sugar."

Carl nodded. "They do not come to the forest. Every unicorn feared my Grandmama."

I grinned. "And they don't know she's dead. If we can get Grimm to make it to the forest ahead of them, he might survive this reckless first date. They might let him escape."

Yahn was staring intently at the unicorns. "Do all unicorns hate rainbows?" he asked with a devilish grin and a mischievous twinkle in his eyes.

33

Carl scowled at him. "Master Temple told you to stop thinking out loud. He implied you are a moron with his tone of voice. He was very clear."

Yahn rolled his eyes. "Yeah, well, I've got a ballsy idea this time, and I'm not asking permission," he said, his grin turning wicked and determined. "Take care of the white one. I'll give the herd something to think about." His armor disappeared, and he climbed to his feet, standing in full view of everyone. Then, like it was the first time a girl told a boy they were ready to have...relations, Yahn burst into a blur of frantic movement, tugging his clothes off and flinging them to the ground as easily as if it was a tearaway jump suit. His pants were already down around his ankles by the time my brain processed what he was doing.

"What the hell?" I demanded, but then he pulled down his underwear and kicked off his shoes, standing on top of the hill like an idiot, wearing only calf-high socks—with the two red stripes, even.

Asha stared at his naked ass with eyes as big as saucers, her jaw hanging open. "What. The. *Fuck?*" she shouted up at us, so shocked that she had devolved to cursing.

Yahn hopped from one foot to the other with absolutely no shame, tearing off his socks, his precious bits bouncing and bobbing like a beggar shaking a cup of change. He met my bewildered gaze and winked. "It's disco ball time. Toe-tah-lee, yah?" He let out a loud laugh as if trying to draw every unicorn's attention.

Then the naked weredragon was running down the hill towards the River Styx. Grimm and Namea skidded to a halt to stare at the bizarre spectacle, like one does when one unexpectedly encounters a streaker in the wild. They were so startled, they completely forgot they were playing death-tag.

Before they could snap out of it, Yahn leapt up into the air, shifting into his glass dragon form and flying over the lovebirds. The herd of unicorns saw this new development—a glass dragon—and screamed at him, no longer interested in Grimm. Yahn flew directly into the sunlight and an explosion of rainbows showered down upon the ground, his glass scales acting like disco balls to project thousands of miniature rainbows in every direction.

Like a pack of cats at a laser light show, the scene turned to utter bedlam.

The herd of unicorns lost their fucking minds, every single one of them chasing down the flickers of light or leaping up into the air to take down the dragon. Yahn belched out fire and glass spears, raining it down upon the enraged unicorns as he flew past them, leading them away from the forest as fast as he could. The unicorns took off in hot pursuit, shooting beams of light at him and galloping across the earth to stab their horns into the reflections.

I gathered my magic and hurled a blast of power directly at Namea, throwing her senses into chaos—momentarily blinding her, muting all sounds from her ears, and plugging up her sense of smell.

Then I leapt to my feet. "Grimm!" I screamed, waving my arms back and forth. He spun to stare directly at me with a look of surprise, not realizing we'd been crashing his date. "Get your crazy horny ass over here before she shakes off my spell! I'll throw an illusion over you!" Then I hurled a semi-invisible screen over him, strengthening it between the white unicorn and Grimm.

He was already running towards me. I watched him leap over the river, unfurling his wings to cross the distance. I kept my eyes on Namea, who was manically shaking her head back and forth and bucking and kicking as she spun in a circle, looking like a rodeo bull. I felt my magic weakening under her power—which I hadn't known she had.

I kept my eyes on her as Grimm galloped up the rise and bolted past me, disappearing from her line of sight. Then I shoved everyone back down the hill towards the forest, hissing at them to remain silent as I dropped back down to the ground and discreetly peered over the rise to see if our plan had worked.

I slowly released my magic, letting the sense-distorting spell fade away. Namea abruptly stopped kicking and spinning. She snorted and stamped a hoof, slowly turning in a circle as she searched for her prey. I could no longer see Yahn in the sky, but the herd of unicorns looked like they were a good mile away now. They were blasting their horn-beams sporadically, so they were clearly still trying to kill Yahn. I hoped the crazy bastard's bond to his armor—since he wasn't actually wearing it—could protect him from that many pissed off unicorns.

Namea didn't run off after her sisters. Instead, the white unicorn flicked her tail up and trotted away, sniffing at the air as she searched for Grimm's trail, backtracking their earlier pursuit as if to find his scent. I watched her bend low to the ground and pierce the blue ribbon with her horn. She lifted her head, sniffing at the ends that hung before her nose. Her ears swiveled back and forth, but she didn't once focus on anything in our direction. I let out a sigh of relief and then scooted back down the hill to approach my friends.

"We did it," I told them. Talon let out a sigh of relief and nodded. Carl slowly shook his head as he stared at Grimm, impressed to see he had survived the encounter. Asha made as if to approach Grimm, and she had a big smile on her face. I waggled a finger at her and shook my head. "Not now, please, Asha. I need to talk to him in private."

Her shoulders wilted and she blushed. Then she turned around and took a few steps towards the forest, drawing her bone dagger. I watched her take a few practice swings and I nodded to myself. Carl did the same before turning to watch Grimm as if he was a bug in a box.

Then I rounded on Grimm. He was foaming at the mouth and grinning like an idiot. "Did you see her?" he whispered, his eyes glazing over. "I am in love with that hateful, murderous beast of a mare. My wildest dreams don't hold a candle to the reality of Namea's magnificent—"

I grabbed him by the horn and then slapped him on the top of the nose. "Dude." He snapped out of it and focused on me. I let go of his horn and shoved his head to the side. Then I took a step back and folded my arms, leveling him with a stern glare. "You *literally* almost ruined everything. Kára and the Randulfs are waiting in Hell for us to save them. We need you, Grimm. Asha needs you. She can't keep up without you."

He hung his head in shame and grumbled an apology.

I sighed, wanting to yell at him for a good five minutes. Then I felt a smile slowly tugging at my cheeks as I mentally rehearsed what I wanted to yell at him about. It was utterly ridiculous. My smile quickly morphed into a chuckle, and then an all-out cackle. "What the *hell*, man?" I laughed. "That was the craziest thing I've ever seen. That mare is a freaking lunatic!"

He preened and hopped from hoof-to-hoof in a little dance. "Right?" he hooted, clearly taking it as a compliment. "She definitely wants me."

"She called in reinforcements on you, Grimm. That's essentially a restraining order. Not very promising."

"She called me *warrior*," he whispered. Then he whinnied proudly, completely dismissing my comment. "And when we crossed beams—"

"When you almost blew each other up," I corrected, but he continued right over me.

"It was the most amazing sensation I have ever felt. It made my soul sing," he breathed.

Talon walked up to Grimm and shook his head. "You are the dumbest fucking horse I have ever met." Then he grinned, walked up to him, and patted him on the back. "Great job. She definitely wants you."

"Told you, Nate," Grimm chided me.

I shot Talon a warning glare, knowing he was just trying to get Grimm in more trouble. He shrugged innocently and took a few steps back to stand beside Carl. Both of them looked up at the sky, their gazes simultaneously shifting towards the ground like they were watching something fall.

Yahn appeared beside me out of thin air, naked as a jaybird, clutching his hands over his goods, and grinning like an idiot. "Did anyone grab my clothes?"

Asha dropped her dagger at the sound of his voice, and quickly turned to get an eyeful. To me, that brief look sounded like a dozen camera clicks, and then she calmly bent to pick up her dagger as if nothing had happened. I grinned, shaking my head. You didn't have to like someone to appreciate seeing them naked.

Talon frowned at him. "Summon up your armor and go get them yourself. Or you could have done it while you were still an invisible dragon."

Yahn blinked and then blushed. Apparently, he hadn't considered either idea before that moment. His armor whisked into place, and he took a few cautious steps, as if fearing the metal plates might pinch and chafe a very dangerous area if he wasn't careful. He let out a breath of relief. "I didn't want to bite a hole in my clothes or drool all over them." He glanced up at the sun with a smug grin as he walked past us. "Pretty warm here. You're welcome for saving your life, Grimm."

"You didn't stop her from stealing my heart," Grimm said dreamily.

Yahn chuckled as he ran to scoop up his clothes from the top of the crest. I waited, pacing back and forth anxiously. He rushed back over to me, breathing heavily. Rather than putting them on, he stared down at them for a moment. "You know. It's kind of freeing without my clothes on between the armor." He sashayed his hips to display his point.

"Boys," Asha muttered from behind us.

"Put your clothes on, Yahn. And that was very quick thinking," I told him, smiling. "Good job. Do we have anyone looking for us over here, or did they all leave?"

"Grimm's girlfriend is still trotting around out there, sniffing for his scent, but she looked like she was giving up. The rest of them are nowhere near us. Once I turned invisible, they had no idea where I was, so I flew away from them with ease." He frowned. "The white one has the ribbon Asha gave you, so I hope she's not good at tracking or anything."

I grimaced, having already considered the danger when I saw her pick it up. I stared into the distance in the direction of the Citadel. "If you can fly invisible, then you can scout ahead for us," I murmured, feeling a surge of excitement at the idea. The thought hadn't even crossed my mind, because I'd completely forgotten about his unique ability to camouflage himself to nigh invisibility after seeing him shift into a very visible glass dragon outside the mountain.

And it had fooled the unicorns.

Yahn's armor vanished, and he started tugging on his socks in an awkward naked dance.

A strange flicker of power danced across the back of my neck, and I thought I felt another bug buzzing in my ears. I swatted my hand with an annoyed gesture, but then I felt a sharp, strangely familiar flash of power behind me.

Horses neighed and Asha screamed.

I spun around, immediately shifting into my Horseman armor at the raw terror in her voice.

I was no longer the only Horseman in the Elder realm.

34

I stared at a smoldering hole through the actual air. It looked like shredded cloth, leading to...

Kansas City? I saw the arena downtown and the familiar night-time skyline of the city in the background.

But that was the last thing on my mind, and it wasn't why Asha had screamed. Two mounted Horsemen were silhouetted through the hole in the air, and I felt a flicker of excitement, wondering if it was Callie and Alucard.

That hope flickered away and died as War and Conquest trotted through the hole and into the Elder realm. War held his fiery sword, and it seemed like he had used it to make the hole in the air. I frowned, wondering why they looked so angry. Maybe they had expected the worst, knowing how dangerous the Elder realm was.

I couldn't fault them for that.

I understood why Asha had screamed. They looked absolutely terrifying, especially with their horses glaring at everyone. "It's okay," I told her. "They're friends."

With their support by my side, I suddenly felt a surge of excitement coursing through me. With two Horsemen backing us up, we *had* to be strong enough to take out Aiden. And War had just opened a Gateway of sorts with his sword! That was invaluable information for me to have. I smiled in surprise, waving at them.

"There you are, brother," War said with a broad smile. "Thank you for calling out our names or we never would have found you."

I frowned for a moment, and then remembered telling Asha about the Horsemen. I'd used their names a few times, and that was when I'd felt the first buzzing sound in my ears, like they had been trying to reach out to me. I shrugged, pointing at the Gateway as they led their horses through. "How did you do that? Gateways don't work here. Well, obviously they *do*, but I can't figure out how to do it."

War smiled intensely and I felt a flicker of uncertainty dance up my spine.

War lifted his sword. "The right kind of blade can make Gateways no matter what. We wouldn't be able to punish angels and demons if we couldn't get through their wards," he said with a smile.

I frowned thoughtfully. Interesting...

Did that mean my Feather could make a hole here? Get us out? The problem was, I didn't know how to do that; even if I did have the key, I didn't know how to find the lock.

"Well," I said, staring down at my blade. "I need to figure out that little trick. What can you show me?"

"Show you," War repeated in a cold tone. "He wants us to show him, Conquest."

The Horseman of Pestilence nodded very slowly. "Okay. I'll show him." Then he flung a smoking grenade at me—one of his metal nunchaku brazier things they used at exorcisms to ward away evil demons.

"Hey! What the *hell*!" I shouted as I batted it away, but he had thrown three more in the interim. I lashed out with my magic, wrapping the bombs in a cocoon of power before their poisonous smoke could hit anyone. I flung them far into the forest as my bone wings slammed into the ground behind me, hoisting me high into the air. "How *dare* you?" I roared, my voice booming into the clearing like thunder.

"How dare Callie Penrose!" War roared. His Mask of molten lava glared at me with raw hatred, and he pointed his flaming sword directly at me. "Death and Famine are *dead*, and you are about to be reunited!"

"And then we are going to murder all your weak little friends," Conquest snarled, glaring at my allies.

And then a crackling blast of red lightning whipped out of his fiery sword, slammed into me, and then wrapped around my chest like a net. I lifted my head to the sky and screamed as my very bones seemed to burn. I heard my allies shouting and yelling in the chaos, but I couldn't respond or understand them. War's lightning was going to cook me alive if I didn't do something. Immediately. I had only moments before it was too late.

Summon the Feather, my Mask purred in my ears. *Absorb the power and then disperse it.*

Without words, she showed me how.

I summoned my Feather and pointed the black blade up into the sky, using my magic to draw War's lightning into the crimson stone embedded in the blade like my Mask had shown me. The crackling electricity hissed as it danced up my body, condensing around the ruby, bathing the clearing in crackling red light as bright as a sun. I gasped at the sudden end to the pain that had been scorching my insides. The lightning had felt like a living thing.

It is like a hungry hound, my Mask purred. *Now kick the dog.* She laughed delightedly in my ears.

I lowered my gaze to see War and Conquest staring at me in disbelief. No. *Everyone* was staring at me with a look of awe and horror on their faces.

I smiled. "My turn."

My voice was a cold rasp like the opening of a cursed tomb.

I dropped the Feather, letting it hang by the ephemeral white chain clenched in my fist. Then I started swinging it over my head like a helicopter, and I sent War's lightning crackling around me in every direction, a dome of destruction. I knew—thanks to my Mask's voice—that the power would be absorbed if I tried hurling it at War or Conquest, although I didn't understand why. So, I sent the gathered energy away from everyone. The bolts of lightning screamed as they pulverized boulders and shattered the trunks of ancient trees, sending them crashing down to the ground with concussive thuds, already sizzling with crimson flames. The very air burned and hissed as I slowed my chain and lowered myself down to the ground.

Everyone was staring at me with fear, even my allies.

I pointed my Feather at War and then Conquest. "You treat loyalty like a condom, eagerly wearing it when convenient and then carelessly tossing it away when it is no longer useful."

"You dare lecture *us* on loyalty, Hope?" Conquest demanded, sputtering with an inner madness in his glowing green eyes. The insanely handsome man within was not visible. Just the plague doctor Mask of Pestilence. "After you authorized Callie to kill Death? There is no way she did that without your knowledge."

I studied them in silence.

They speak the truth, my Mask said. *Death is dead. Despair took his mask for herself. Famine was consumed by Absolution,* she added, referring to Alucard.

As impossible as their claim seemed, I could think of no other justification for them to come here and then instantly try to kill me. I was the leader of the Dread Four. They sat atop their nightmarish horses, committed to seeing justice served. Their brothers were dead, and they were here to avenge him or die trying. I wondered why they hadn't gone after Callie and Alucard instead. Maybe they had already killed them.

They had come here from Kansas City, after all.

But Conquest had threatened to murder my friends, and that was before I'd shrugged off War's attack. They hadn't come here to talk like gentlemen over a dispute—they had come here to execute us.

My allies stood in tense silence, looking ready for everything to go to hell in a handbasket.

A unicorn screamed in the near distance behind me, and everyone turned to look over my shoulder. I almost did the same, but that's when I saw Talon capitalize on the unexpected distraction.

Sir Talon lunged for War's neck with his poleaxe, but War batted it aside with his fiery sword and threw a blast of crimson lightning at his foe. The lightning struck Talon with a crackling hiss, sending him tumbling to the ground. War released his lightning with a dismissive growl. "Stand down, pussy. We'll get to you after."

Talon landed on all fours—heh—and jumped to his feet with a snarl. His fur was sticking straight up like a dandelion, and I could tell he was surprised to be alive. He'd taken a direct hit from a Horseman and his armor had withstood the damage. He crouched in an aggressive stance, looking like he was about to try again.

"Stand down!" War repeated. "Or I'll send another one that will really make your fur puff up," he laughed dismissively, but I could tell he was mildly concerned that Talon seemed none the worse for wear.

Talon's ears angled back in a dangerous manner, his earrings twinkling in the sunlight. "Who knows, Horseman. I might just *like* it. The bushier the fur, the friskier the kitty," he hissed. And then he launched himself at the Horseman again.

I had been so focused on Talon and War that I hadn't noticed Asha until I saw her standing directly behind Conquest with her bone dagger in her fist. She was biting her lower lip with fear, but her eyes were dead set on her target. My eyes widened in horror, and I hastily summoned my magic to throw a shield up between her and—

She leapt up and stabbed Conquest in the thigh, burying Carl's dagger to the hilt. The tip must have sunk deep enough to stab the horse, because the sickly-looking creature let out a scream of pain.

Conquest bellowed in surprise, staring down at the bone blade as he tried to control his horse. I flung my shield out, but the horse's frantic movements caused me to miss. "Fucking Carl! Elder scum!" Conquest screamed, as he blindly flung a smokey green blast of power at his attacker.

But it hadn't been the powerful Elder Carl. It had been a Regular teenaged girl defending her friend.

Talon.

"No!" Talon and I screamed as Asha flew back, tumbling and flipping like a rag doll.

35

A beam of arctic blue light slammed into Conquest's chest, interrupting his blast of green power and knocking him completely off his fucking horse. He flew across the clearing and slammed into a giant boulder, pinned in place by the beam of icy blue light through his gut, like a butterfly on a board.

Now I knew what had distracted everyone moments ago. Namea.

"My love!" Grimm screamed, squaring off against Conquest's horse, the tip of his horn now glowing with an upcoming painbow. "My girl is about to fuck you up."

I heard a murderous scream and galloping hooves as the beam of light winked out and Namea came charging into the fight. Conquest's horse started to turn away from Grimm to face the new threat, but he wasn't fast enough.

Namea hit him with another blast of blue light, instantly freezing him solid. But she didn't slow down. She slammed into him with her horn, and Conquest's sickly horse exploded into a hailstorm of diseased frozen horse bits. Her beam of light continued on, slamming back into Conquest's gut just as he had been recovering from the earlier attack, pinning him back to the boulder all over again. I watched as wicked, spiky hoarfrost started growing over his armor. He fought back against the spreading cold, drawing on his Horseman powers, but it quickly became a standstill. He could stop the frost, but he could not move to use his powers.

Because viruses didn't do well in cold temperatures.

Conquest screamed in horrified agony, his voice booming across the land like mountains crumbling.

I saw Asha slowly sit up, shaking her head woozily, and I almost let out an actual sob of relief. "Grimm!" I screamed. "Guard the vegan with your fucking life!"

He galloped to comply, and I heard him speaking to her in urgent tones. She blinked up at him, nodding dazedly, looking remarkably better than I had feared. I saw him bend his head low to touch her with his horn for some strange reason that I didn't have time to question.

"Hold that son of a bitch down, Namea!" I screamed, turning to glare at War, who sat atop his horse with a stupefied look on his face. "You make one more fucking move, and I will peel the very flesh from your brother's bones while I make you watch," I vowed, my bone wings flaring out above me.

War shifted his glare from Conquest's torment to his horse's slushpile and then finally to me. His eyes burned with fire, actually smoking. His fiery sword trembled in his fist. Conquest screamed again and he visibly flinched before pointing his sword directly at me. "Release him right now, or I swear to God—"

Yahn—who I had completely forgotten about until that moment— shimmered into view directly before War's horse in a strange crouch, like he had just landed an acrobatic feat. He wore his armor, and he sported forearm-length dragon claws from his fingers, and one of his arms was touching the ground like he was pointing at something interesting.

With a sickening *squelch*, the horse's head slid free of the neck and thumped to the ground right where his claw pointed.

Blood spurted out of the horse's neck like a fountain, spraying over Yahn's face and his white armor like a shower as he slowly rose from his crouch. He'd fucking decapitated War's horse.

Holy shit.

Yahn flashed War a devilish smile and then opened his mouth to catch some of the blood spraying from the headless horse's open neck. He gurgled it loudly and then spit it out with a dark laugh. The horse's front legs finally buckled, and he crashed to his knees, sending the Horseman of War tumbling down. War turned it into a roll and landed on his feet, staring at Yahn in stunned horror. The horse collapsed to its side, and I smiled as its legs kicked a few times.

"Headless horse, man!" Yahn said with a chuckle, still pointing at the severed horse's head, which was blinking in confusion.

I met War's manic eyes and pointed a thumb at Yahn. "He's so damned *sneaky*, right?"

War glared at Yahn, his face beet red with unrestrained fury. Unfortunately for the Horseman, I hadn't been referring to Yahn, because Talon had crept up directly behind him when he'd tumbled from his horse. Talon abruptly wrapped his arms around War's waist, picked him up high overhead, and then promptly body slammed War down to the ground hard enough to send up a cloud of dust.

"Frisky kitty takes shits tougher than you, bitch!" Talon snapped, turning his back on the fallen Horseman. Then he scratched his feet in the dirt, kicking bone dust into War's eyes like he'd just wrapped up a strenuous sesh in the litterbox.

War groaned and wiped at his eyes as he scrambled to his feet, turning to face Talon, but the feline was already walking away, and War found himself suddenly staring at Elder Carl, who promptly kicked him in the chest hard enough to crack ribs and send him flying into the forest where he slammed into a tree, splintering the trunk. Carl nodded satisfactorily and then casually turned to look at me. "Do we have permission to kill the Horseman, Master Temple? He threatened to kill us all, and the other one called me Elder scum before hurting Asha. I want to hear their screams echo across the Elder realm."

"Nate!" Grimm shouted. "You need to get over here. Right *now!*"

The frightened tone of his voice sent a chill down my spine. I spun to see that Asha was no longer sitting up, and Grimm was nudging her frantically, whining in a haunting sound I hadn't heard from him before.

I turned to Yahn with a desperate look. "Can you three handle him?"

His eyes darted to Asha, and he looked like he was about to vomit. The sickened look faded, replaced by unrelenting rage. Then he turned back to me with a cold look on his face and gave me a grim nod, his voice sounding like spilled gravel. "Little soy-boy like War? I *exist* to devour beta-males."

"Then have your fun, Sir Knights," I told them in a cold voice. "But do not underestimate him. Shout if you need back-up. I'm going to make sure Asha is okay and then I'll be back. Maybe she just bumped her head."

They nodded and turned to face War, who had already regained his feet and was storming towards them with his sword out. His head was bleeding and he looked to be having trouble breathing through the cracked ribs Carl had gifted him. The Knights' helmets slammed down into place and then Yahn disappeared with a malevolent laugh that boomed across the clearing. Talon's tail swished back and forth as he brandished his polearm, and Carl started circling to the side with his claws out, looking like a robotic velociraptor on the hunt.

"Fucking Carl wants to play, Horseman," Carl hissed. Yahn's disembodied laugh erupted again, from behind War, making him spin around, and then Talon yowled a horrible sound, making War spin back to face him, trying to keep his eyes on all three threats—two seen and one unseen.

I ran towards Asha and Grimm, my heart thundering in my chest. She had sat up after her fall. She had to be okay. Maybe she had a concussion. I skidded on my knees beside her, letting my armor disappear so I wouldn't terrify her. "Watch my back, Grimm," I said urgently, and then I looked down at Asha's pale face.

"My horn won't work," he whispered in a miserable cry.

Conquest laughed maniacally. "No horn will work!" There was no remorse in that laugh.

I had no idea what the fuck they were talking about, because I was frozen stiff as my eyes settled on Asha's hands. My breath caught.

"On second hand, Grimm," I whispered, turning to look my unicorn in the fiery eyes. "Conquest is never going to leave this clearing," I croaked. "Help Namea keep him there, but don't kill him. I will be getting my hands dirty soon. Indulge yourself, but don't kill him."

He snarled murderously, and then let out a sharp whinny as he took one last look at Asha. Then he was galloping away, screaming the foulest profanities I had ever heard.

Asha smiled up at me. "I got him," she said, smiling with those goddamned beautiful green eyes.

I ignored the dark veins spidering up from a few of her already black fingers on her left hand. "Yes, Asha," I said. "You sure did."

36

I stared into Asha's eyes, and I knew she was going to die. Conquest screamed in agony behind me, a soothing symphony to my inner anguish. But I had to be strong for Asha. I couldn't show her I was afraid. I loomed over her, embracing her, getting as close as I possibly could, letting her know she was loved.

It was all I could do.

I cupped her cheek with my hand. "How are you feeling? No. Don't try and sit up."

She smiled at me with an embarrassed look. "I just felt dizzy after I sat up, but I don't see any injuries," she said with a reassuring smile. "Grimm let me touch his horn, and then he cried on me," she said with a bewildered frown. Her eyes locked onto the carving hanging around my neck and she grinned. "Thank you for wearing my arts and crafts—"

She abruptly coughed with a startled look and my breath caught in my throat as I fought to keep my face devoid of fear. She lifted her right hand to her lips—thankfully not the one with blackened fingers—and wiped at her mouth. She pulled her hand away and stared at her bloody fingers, her eyes widening in confusion.

She looked up at me and winced in embarrassment. "Oh! I'm so sorry! I didn't mean to cough on you! I must have cut my lip or something."

I nodded, pretending I hadn't felt the blood hitting my face. "It's okay, Asha," I said, my mind racing. What the hell had Grimm been talking about with his horn? I needed to get her out of here, but I didn't know how, and there was absolutely no way War was going to teach me now. It was exactly like when her mother had died. Nadia's wound had also looked infected with some kind of poison, but she'd said the Knightmare did it to her before taking the armor.

Had she remembered incorrectly? Confused by the chaos? Fog of war, and all of that?

Had...*Conquest* been the one to stab Nadia? Or maybe he'd been the hooded stranger who lead them down here, poisoning the wound on the way as he pretended to befriend them, and then sealing the door to the Elder realm behind us all.

When had Callie killed Death? Anubis had seemed to already know about the Horseman's demise.

He'd said *Death is dead. Long live Death.* I hadn't understood him at the time, but now it made so much sense. Death was dead. Callie was the new Horseman of Death.

But they had also said Famine was dead. What the fuck was going on in Kansas City?

Yet...the Dark Horse spell hadn't tracked Conquest here. I could feel it still searching for the culprit in the depths of my mind.

Asha was staring up at my necklace as it swung back and forth. I looked down at it and saw the warped smiley face spattered with her blood. I closed my eyes, smothering my anguish over Asha's pain, not wanting it to show on my face. I gathered my resolve and opened my heart to the precious girl dying beneath me. It felt like an eternity, but I knew it lasted only a second. I opened my eyes and smiled down at her. "I've had girls spit worse in my face," I told her with a smile. "I could tell you stories."

Her eyes widened in surprise, and then she laughed, coughing up more blood again. I pretended not to notice, and I didn't dare wipe it away. "I... don't understand, Nate," she whispered, her voice starting to tremble. "It was just green smoke and I fell down and rolled. I didn't get cut or break anything. Other than cutting my lip, I guess."

I nodded, trying not to cry at the fear in her eyes. "I know, Asha," I croaked, ignoring the spreading tendrils of black veins climbing up her wrists. Both her hands had blackened fingers now, but she hadn't noticed that. She must have seen something in my eyes.

"But...Carl was going to teach me how to fight," she sobbed, her tears welling up as her lip trembled. "I was going to help Grimm b-bang the unicorn. I was going to fix your stupid coin," she stammered, crying as she reached up to swat at the bloody wooden disc. That's when she first noticed her blackened hands and her eyes widened in horror. "What's *happening* to me, Nate? I don't want to die!" She panted, beginning to panic. "I don't even hurt! I p-promise I'll get better. D-don't give up on me!" she begged me, stammering almost incoherently with fear. Her eyes were wild around the edges, and she tried to sit up, but I pressed her down and bent low to kiss her forehead. I kept my lips there, feeling tears pour down my cheeks and splash onto her alarmingly feverish forehead.

She wrapped her arms desperately around my neck and began to cry, whimpering desperately and frantically, begging me not to let go, not to let her die, not to leave her alone.

Over.

And over.

Again.

God.

Damn.

Everyone.

I wrapped my arms around her and hugged her back just as tightly as she clung to me, realizing I was kissing her forehead repeatedly like my lips were spiritual chest compressions to jumpstart her soul. "I'm not leaving you, Asha. I'm staying right here," I whispered between kisses, hating my lies but wishing they could be true. "You give better hugs than Kára," I told her, fighting back the anguish screaming through my insides.

She let out a moan and squeezed me tighter before letting go. I pulled away and saw that the black veins were now creeping up her throat. "I'm cold," she whispered. "Nate...I'm not feeling very good," she said, sounding concerned. "I'm s-scared. What is happening to me?"

I squeezed her blackened fingers. They were cold and stiff. Dead. She didn't respond to the pressure, all reflexive muscles abandoning her fingers as lost causes as the energy was redirected, fighting to keep the rest of her body alive. Her body was playing triage—a fatal game of Whac-A-Mole. "I'm right here, Asha."

Do something! I screamed at my Mask. *Please! I can't lose her too! She's just a fucking kid with the biggest goddamned heart I've ever seen!* I begged.

I...do not know how to heal her, the Mask purred back, sounding just as miserable as me. *All I can do is prevent the infection from spreading to you. That is taking up all my energy right now...And more would die if I attempted what you ask. The whole world needs you, Horseman.*

I hadn't even considered that. I hadn't cared. Asha looked to be enduring the Black Death. It would not be fast, and it would not be pretty. The bitterest irony I could have imagined after Conquest's brother had been killed by Callie. Allegedly.

Not allegedly, my Mask said sadly. Sympathetically.

Asha's eyes fluttered closed, and her head lolled to the side. My breath caught and I froze. Oh, god—

Then her head jerked back up and her eyes flashed open as she started panting frantically. "I'm not dead!" she screamed at the top of her lungs. "I'm still awake! I can see you, Nate! I promise! I'm still HEEEERE!" she shrieked, as if trying to convince me. "I CAN *SEE* YOU! I'M NOT DEAD!"

My heart shredded to pieces, and I nodded furiously, squeezing her cheeks and rubbing her tears away with my thumb. "I *know*, Asha. I know. You're not dead. You just fell asleep for a second! It's okay. You just took a quick nap," I assured her, hardly able to see through my tears as I sniffed my freely leaking nose.

"I...I saw an angel!" she whispered, her eyes growing distant. "I was in Heaven. I saw my brothers! *Both* of them! And daddy looked so handsome!" she whispered, blinking blindly, not seeming to see me at all.

Her head started to loll again, and her eyes fluttered like butterfly wings, but she jolted herself out of it with a gasp. She grasped at me with numb, dead hands.

I didn't know which one of us was more insane with horror at that moment.

Her eyes latched back onto me, momentarily able to see me again, and she cried out in relief. "I'm here. I'm still HERE!" she begged. "Don't leave me. PLEASE!" she sobbed, bawling desperately.

"I'm not leaving, Asha," I said, my throat raw with grief. I couldn't even think straight. The only reality was this moment, here, with Asha. I would not fucking leave her side if the entire world depended on me in that single moment. Fuck them all. I was not letting her die afraid on top of everything else she had suffered.

No.

Everything she had endured. She was a fighter. The strongest heart I had ever seen.

"I'm right here," I croaked, forcing a smile onto my face. "I am right here, and I am not going *anywhere*."

She nodded stiffly, seeming to be losing muscle control. "Hold my hand, please. I'm s-scared, and you're so handsome and brave and funny and caring and strong and-and-and all the best things *ever*," she whispered, her lip trembling with terror. "I l-love you. N-not l-like that, but because you m-make me feel s-safe, and I don't want you to let me go. K-keep me s-safe, Nate. I'm r-really scared. I tried *really* hard to help you. My hardest! But I'll t-try harder n-next time," she whispered in a miserable cry, as if she had failed me. "Hold my hand and keep them away! They are whispering to me! AND I DON'T LIKE IT! I DON'T TRUST THEM!"

I would have done anything to save her in that moment. *Anything*. To hear her laugh again one single time. To let her know that she hadn't failed me at all. Period. Never. Ever. I would have worshipped any god, sold my soul to any demon, bowed down to even the Masters to grant this child another opportunity at life.

But the world didn't work like that.

"You didn't f-fail me, Asha. You gave us our only chance. You carved me this shitty necklace, and you have to f-finish it," I told her. I was unable to clamp down my own sobbing now, but I squeezed her hand tightly, forcing myself not to look at the black veins trailing up her cheeks and touching her eyes. "I *am* holding your hand, Asha," I told her, knowing she could no longer feel my tight embrace. "I will *always* hold your hand," I lied, hating every single second of her torture but knowing I could never bear to look at myself in the mirror if I ended her pain with my blade.

Knowing I could never survive the last look of betrayal I would see in her eyes.

If there was one true God, he would save her any moment. I sent up a prayer. A last cry of hope for...Hope.

No one answered.

"I love you too, Asha," I said, masking the anger bubbling up in my soul as I used my shoulder to wipe the tears from my eyes so I could see every moment of this horrible, terrible experience. I started speaking, not even knowing what I was saying. I poured my heart out on this poor little girl, hating myself. "You're beautiful, and tall, and you have kick-ass boots, and your eyes look like glittering emeralds, and Calvin looked at you like you were the most beautiful girl he had ever seen. He couldn't even *speak* when he saw you, Asha. You'll see. When we pick him up, he'll be tripping over his own two feet, following you around like a lost puppy!"

She smiled and nodded, latching onto my words like a lifeline. "Okay. C-can we go see him n-now? I'm b-better," she assured me, coughing up more blood into my face, and not seeming to realize it. "I'm just d-dizzy. Y-you'll see," she stammered, panting wildly as her lungs started to shut down. "Just help me up and I'll c-carry my weight."

"Let's just rest a bit longer, Asha," I said with a faux laugh. "Then we will go see him. I promise," I lied.

"Can you g-give me a kiss?" she asked. "My m-mom always k-kissed my forehead when I was sick," she whispered faintly, her body trembling of its own accord as her eyes fluttered weaker than before.

"Of course, Asha," I croaked, bending low and planting the biggest, wettest kisses on her forehead. If she couldn't feel them, I wanted to make sure she heard them. Felt my love through sound, at least.

I leaned back and cupped her cheek again, ignoring the profound web of black veins covering most of her face, even though they were directly beneath my hand. I brushed her hair back and squeezed her cheek affectionately. "Better?" I asked her, knowing she was not better, and would never again be better.

She nodded dazedly, her head slowly falling to the side. "I...love you, Nate," she murmured, her words slurring. "Tell Yahn he's...handsome. Carl is...wonderful," she murmured, the stretches between words growing longer. She could no longer see anything, because the black veins were even in her eyes now. "Talon...is grouchy, but he let me...scratch his ears. He purred when I did it," she added, a weak giggle bubbling up from her wheezing lungs.

Blood also bubbled up with her laugh, rolling over her lips and down her chin, but she didn't notice.

"Did I...do good?" she whispered, and I had to lean close to hear her words. My tears fell down onto her cheeks, but she didn't notice that either.

"You did amazing, Asha," I whispered, staring at her beautiful face through a haze of tears.

She closed her eyes and used the last of her life force to give me the biggest smile she could manage, taking solace in my words, and then her head went completely slack in my hands.

Her chest did not rise again, and her heart did not beat. I pressed my palm against her chest and felt absolutely nothing. The breeze blew her beautiful dark hair over her smiling, peaceful face and I saw the blood-spattered wooden disc swinging from my neck.

Hope's last gift to me—the Horseman of Hope.

A blood-spattered, warped smiley face. With a trembling hand, I lifted the coin to my lips and kissed it. "Goodbye, Hope," I whispered, using the definition of Asha's name.

My Horseman armor rolled over me and the bone spines of my wings slammed down into the ground, forming a cage of rage around the innocent, sweet-hearted young girl—a final hug from her Horseman.

My heart thundered in my chest like the drums of war.

The scream that then tore out from my chest made my own ears pop.

"CONQUEST!"

37

I slowly turned to find my three Knights battered but still upright. War was staring at me warily, alerted by the sound of my scream. He'd definitely gotten the shit kicked out of him during the fight. He favored his right leg and one of his arms hung limp by his side.

Conquest was half frozen in icicles and still pinned to his boulder with crystalline ice through his gut, but Namea was no longer holding him with her beam of light. She didn't need to. I saw several bloody puncture wounds on his limbs and matched it to the blood dripping from Grimm's rainbow horn. Conquest already looked half dead and was in no shape to flee or fight.

Other than the echo of my shout a moment ago, the Elder realm was completely silent.

Grimm took one look at me and said, "Oh, shit."

His words may as well have been a shout, they were so clear.

War immediately lifted his sword and slashed it into the air with a strangely intent look on his face. I cocked my head curiously, watching him. The three Knights made as if to stop him, but I swept my hand to the side, knocking them all back on their asses with a gentle but forceful wave of air. They tumbled and rolled ten feet, cursing and grunting before they came to a bewildered halt. I held up my finger to them and shook it back and forth one time.

"My turn," I said in an icily calm growl as I started walking towards him, my bone spines slamming into the ground behind me in the slow drumbeat of a death march, heralding the Horseman of Hope as he approached his brother, War, on his last battlefield.

In my peripheral vision, Namea turned to look at Asha's body and snarled. The blood-spattered blue ribbon was clenched in her jaws for some strange reason. Then she galloped past me, skirting a safe distance to the side, and knelt down on her front hooves in a prayer-like pose.

I saw War working furiously at his hole in the air, but he mistakenly glanced back at the sound of my approach and fumbled his sword. It fell to the ground with a clanging sound, and the hole in the air instantly sealed. I clenched my jaw, still not sensing any understanding of what he'd been doing or how he had been doing it. How was he making the Gateway?

He frantically bent to pick up his sword, shouting something at me. It wasn't relevant. He was a dead man.

Can you figure out how he's doing that? I asked my Mask.

She hesitated, murmuring thoughtfully. It was almost like she was tapping a pencil against her teeth at a particularly frustrating math problem on a college prep test. *No. It is different than our power.*

Damn it.

Well, we probably shouldn't let him leave. He will miss the show, I told her.

Her laugh made me shudder with concern, even though she was on my team.

Dial back the evil villain soundtrack, I told her.

Fine, she said, sounding amused.

I walked up and kicked War in the tailbone as his sword started tearing another hole in the air. "Hey, fuckface," I said as he went tumbling to the ground, dropping his sword again. I hit him with a net of yellow lightning, pinning him to the ground. I picked up his sword and walked over to him as he struggled against my electrified web. Then I stabbed him through the thigh, pinning him to the ground with his own blade. He screamed in agony. "There! Now you will have matching scars with your brother, Conquest," I told him in a cheerful voice, talking over his screams. "I'm going to need you to just sit there and watch this. The price of having no...nobility." I made sure my power was secure, latching him down to the ground so he couldn't leave. If the Knights hadn't roughed him up, I wasn't sure I would have been strong enough to keep him there, but in his current state, he was as easy to handle as a baby.

I walked up to Conquest and smiled as he weakly battered his claws into the icicles boring through his stomach, fixing him to the boulder. Whatever Namea's power was, it was incredibly resilient. Then again, the Horseman was bleeding from close to a dozen of Grimm's horn-inflicted stab wounds. I glanced over my shoulder to see the three Knights standing a few paces behind me, wanting to support me but giving me a respectfully wide berth. I gestured at Namea. "What is she doing?"

The three Knights flinched, as if expecting me to attack them. Carl finally spoke up. "She says her horn can heal poison. Some of the more powerful mares have this ability, apparently."

I blinked at them, almost losing my freaking mind on the spot. If I had known that...

"Not *my* poison," Conquest said in a regretful wheeze, having lost some of his earlier confidence. I took a calming breath, relieved to hear that I hadn't unintentionally doomed Asha to death by not sending Namea over to her sooner. "I thought she was the Elder," he whispered. "I never would have—"

"If anyone is feeling squeamish, you should probably go take a walk," I told the Knights, cutting off Conquest's excuses. "There is nothing noble or virtuous or knightly about what is going to happen in the next few moments. What I'm about to do is going to be...*Biblical*," I said with a grim smile at my own irony.

They stared back at me with cold, determined nods.

I turned back to face Conquest. "Anything to say for yourself, Pestilence?" I asked, feeling my heart racing wildly as thoughts of Asha's last moments danced through my memory.

The plague doctor mask looked up at me, the green flames in his eyes flickering weakly. "Please," he whispered.

The Feather appeared in my fist, and I sliced off his right arm at the shoulder. The limb flopped to the ground, and he let out a scream of such agony that I just wanted to bottle it up and sell it. "Wrong answer," I said in a calm voice, even though I felt like a tornado of insanity inside.

His stump sprayed blood over the rocks, and the stone hissed in response, emitting a greenish vapor. War was screaming, begging for me to spare his brother's life. I flipped him off without looking. "You'll get your turn when I'm finished, War." He continued cursing and screaming. Conquest was staring at his twitching arm in agonized disbelief, and I recalled his origin story about being a doctor. "Oh, don't look so concerned, Conquest. I'll donate it to science," I assured him with a smile. "I will donate everything to science." Then I arched an eyebrow, waiting.

He panted frantically, his eyes dancing wildly. "You brought this on yourself, Hope! You never should have made Callie a Horseman. She executed Death! Women don't have the temperament—"

I sliced through his other arm, severing it in the exact same place. It flopped to the ground as well, grabbing at nothing like those arcade game claws were designed to do. "That was both sexist *and* not what I wanted to hear," I said with a disapproving frown. I let him scream for a few moments and then made a rolling motion with my blade, encouraging him to move the conversation along.

War's screams were incoherent roars of outrage and horror, but he was too weak to break free of my trap.

Conquest was gasping and choking, his twin stumps spraying poisonous blood over the rocks, eating away at the stone like acid. He looked absolutely ridiculous, kicking his feet like an idiot.

"Hey, Nate?" Grimm asked in a hesitant voice. I turned to look at him with a frown. He winked at me with the eye that Conquest couldn't currently see from his point of view. "Maybe you need to calm down for a minute."

I slumped my shoulders and hung my chin, nodding theatrically.

Grimm slowly walked up to Conquest. "You okay?" he asked in a gentle, compassionate tone, leaning closer to the armless Horseman. "I think I can talk him down," he whispered conspiratorially.

Conquest whimpered. "Oh, thank you! He's fucking gone mental—"

But Grimm had continued leaning forward, and I watched as his horn slowly pierced through Conquest's cheek, sliding over the top of his tongue and then slicing out through the other cheek. This, of course, cut off Conquest's commentary as efficiently as a mute button.

Then he started to scream again as Grimm slowly extracted his horn.

Blood gushed out of the gaping holes in his cheeks as he panted like a feral animal.

Someone threw up behind me, but I didn't want to embarrass them, so I didn't look to check who it was.

War had shifted from begging to threatening, but I could still sense he was in no position to escape. Grimm calmly wiped his bloody horn off on Conquest's chest and then backed up with a murderous grin. His fiery eyes burned hot and vengeful. Some of the blood dripped off his horn and spattered onto his nose, rolling down to his lips. He licked them and let out a groan of pleasure. "I just *love* appetizers," he said, staring into Conquest's eyes. "I lied. That was for Asha, you pathetic piece of filth." He turned his back on the armless Horseman and turned to me. "Feel better now?" he asked me in exactly the same compassionate tone he had used on Conquest. "Calmer?"

I nodded, taking a deep breath. "I do, actually. Thanks."

"Good. Let me know if you need anything else." Then he trotted a few paces away to watch.

Conquest stared into my eyes, now knowing he would find absolutely no mercy this day. "We did not start this, Hope. We came to avenge our brother—"

I sliced off his leg at the knee, careful not to hit both of them. He screamed, but the noises were growing less shocked and more whimpery. "You already tried that one," I told him in a patient tone. "You could phone a friend and let your brother answer for you, but that would require an awful lot of trust on your part."

He stared at me, harboring so much pain that his body was actually trembling. Blood painted the boulder, and he was surrounded by green vapor.

War stared back at me, not daring to speak. Or too angry to speak. Or waiting for Conquest's permission, which apparently wasn't coming. I shrugged, waiting. I was reminded of the Black Knight in the Monty Python flick, but it wasn't enough to make me smile. Part of me was screaming inside but I squashed it down, playing over my last few moments with Asha instead.

38

As much as Asha's death currently fueled my fire, I wasn't doing this strictly for her. I was doing it because they had come here perfectly willing to kill all my friends—and me—without giving me the courtesy of answering their questions.

The lack of honor.

The lack of loyalty.

They knew me and they had immediately jumped to the worst conclusion—that I would ever actually murder Death and then try to hide behind a cat's paw.

They knew me well enough to know, beyond a shadow of a doubt, that if I had wanted one of them dead, I would have shown up at their door with a six-pack, calmly warned them of their impending doom and why they'd earned it, and then handled it like a professional, scheduling a time in my calendar to deal with it like a gentleman.

Even if I'd killed Death in the heat of the moment, I would have immediately let the other brothers know exactly why I had done such a thing—because I would have wanted them to know that I took all responsibility, and if they had a problem with my decision, they could come handle it with me.

I didn't know if Callie had done what they had claimed—even though my Mask had confirmed it. If she had, I had no idea why she would have done such a thing, but I knew she would have immediately come to me to let me know precisely what she had done and why.

Callie Penrose was one scary, merciless, powerful, motherfucker of a wizard, but she had more honor than anyone I knew—omitting Gunnar, who had it to a fault.

But I had been trapped in the Elder realm. She probably had never gotten the chance to come to me. She would have tried, though. I knew that for a fact.

Because she was honorable.

These sons of bitches had come here to ambush me and my friends, never giving me the opportunity to talk like gentlemen. I understood their pain—if anyone killed one of my allies, I would have burned the world down to avenge them—but if the alleged killer was once an ally of mine, I would have given them the chance to explain themselves before I brutally murdered them.

I wouldn't have ambushed them and their *friends*.

I would have made my accusation, heard their case, and then made my decision, involving only the person accused of the murder.

I hadn't even begun to process the thought that Death was actually dead, or that Callie had been strong enough to kill him. What the fuck was going on in Kansas City?

So, Asha's death was just the spice on the sizzling steak of my rage right now. The steak was currently impaled on a boulder by a unicorn's icicle, whimpering and sobbing and groaning before me.

"You know what? I've got a question of my own," I said. "I'll skip the last leg if I believe your answer is truthful." I didn't bother giving him an option. "How long have you worked with Anubis?" He frowned, looking confused. "If Death dies, who better to go visit for help? You see, Anubis already knew Death had died. When he attacked me like a coward, he let it slip."

Conquest shook his head frantically, even glancing over at War. "I...I don't know what you are—"

I sliced off his last leg, cutting off his answer. I believed him, but I didn't want to leave my work unfinished. He would look preposterous with only one leg left. People would make fun of his corpse, and that was disrespectful. I was a gentleman, after all.

"I told you the truth!" he panted between screams.

I nodded. "Oh, I believe you," I assured him. "Have either of you two seen a Dark Horse recently? Big fiery, thundery son of a bitch in the sky?" I asked, checking on War. He stared at me with blind fury, completely speechless at what I had done to his brother. "No?" I asked, turning back to Conquest, who was too busy dealing with his own trauma to answer me. Well, he had no reason to lie about it now if it had been him, which only made me angrier. Who the fuck had trapped us here?

"I am *sorry*, Nate," Conquest finally whispered, barely able to hold his own head up.

I stepped closer and lifted his head to stare into his fiery green eyes. "I almost believe you, but I really need to be certain," I said, lifting the Feather to rest the blade under his throat.

He lifted his chin proudly. "I will see you in Hell someday, Nate Temple," he rasped.

I cocked my head, suddenly having an idea. Then I shook my head very, very slowly, feeling a smile stretching over my cheeks. "No, Conquest. Actually, you won't."

He narrowed his eyes. "What?"

"Say goodbye to War, Conquest," I said impatiently. "Your brother needs to hear it."

He opened his mouth to do so, and I severed his head before he had the chance to speak.

War bellowed in outrage. Conquest's Mask fell to the ground with a thud, and I let out a sigh, holding his head up by a clawful of hair. "I am the Dark Horse," I growled into his still-blinking eyes. Then, with a grunt, I lobbed it over my shoulder at Grimm. "Alley-oop!" I said.

He caught it in his mouth and immediately gobbled it down in loud, chomping sounds. Someone threw up again. I let them do it in peace, squatting down to inspect the Mask at my feet. I reached out and picked it up, and immediately fell down on my ass as an icy wave of power crashed over me.

My Mask let out a gasp of awe like she'd just climaxed in the middle of prayer at Sunday Mass—hit by both the power of the Holy Spirit and the power of the orgasmic trinity.

If you have to ask about that last bit, you don't deserve to know what it is.

I blinked dreamily at the afterglow of the bizarre sensation. *What the fuck was that?* I asked my Mask.

*Mmmmm...*was her response, unable to even formulate words for a few moments. *I need to study this. We are merging with it somehow.*

I felt a ripple of power to my left and I turned to see War leap through one of his strange Gateways before I could stop him. The fiery slash in the air winked out, leaving tendrils of smoke to curl up into the air. I scowled angrily, rising to my feet as I turned to glare at the three Knights. "Really?"

They shook their heads. "We were more concerned about whatever the hell just happened to you," Yahn answered. "I thought you were going to fall unconscious. He was gone before I even realized it." The others nodded their agreement. Grimm was still chewing on the head, licking his lips, completely unaware of what had happened as he moaned contentedly.

How the hell had War broken free of my power? He hadn't been able to move the entire time I was torturing his brother, and then he just ran away?

I started laughing, despite everything. "The Horseman of War," I said to the startled faces staring at me, "just fucking ran *away* from a *fight*." Then I doubled over, laughing even harder. I heard the Knights' voices fading away, apparently choosing to give me a few minutes to master my giggling fit.

After a while, I wiped at my eyes and straightened, still chuckling. I turned and saw that everyone was completely motionless, and I immediately sobered up. "What the fuck is this?" I growled, spinning in a slow circle to check my surroundings, wary of an ambush. Then I recognized it for what it was.

The Boatman was paying me a visit.

Namea was still bent down over Asha's corpse, which made me sad. Someone needed to tell her that even if Asha had still been in the throes of the poison, she wouldn't have been strong enough to cure the girl.

Grimm was frozen in the act of licking his lips, looking like a dog after eating peanut butter.

The three knights were running towards Namea, frozen in mid stride. Talon was actually midair, his ears tucked back, and his mouth open like he was shouting. Something must have motivated them, because they'd been behind me just moments ago and were now running.

Charon sat in his boat, which was hovering in the middle of the clearing, staring directly at me. I narrowed my eyes, knowing there was no way I was going to steal Asha's soul. I'd already made my choice. I slowly turned to look at Conquest's mutilated remains. Without hesitation, I lifted a claw and pointed.

"That motherfucker," I said.

Charon hung his head as if he'd feared my answer. But he finally gave me a nod. "So be it."

The world flickered oddly and then I was standing inside Charon's boat, feeling strangely hollow. I was no longer in my Horseman's armor, and I didn't have my satchel, but we were still in the Elder realm. Everything looked...wispy.

"Whoa," I said, feeling slightly queasy at the odd sensation.

Charon sat at the helm with his paddle across his knees, giving me a sad look. Then he silently handed me a beer from the plastic cooler at his feet. "You're going to want to drink this. Fast."

I accepted the beer and lifted it to him in a gesture of thanks. He did the same, drinking a beer of his own—because he wasn't concerned about drinking and boating—and then he dipped his paddle over the side of the canoe, even though we were hovering above solid ground.

There was a ripple of purple light where the tip of his paddle would have touched water if we were in a real boat, but he didn't do anything with it. He glanced at me and arched an eyebrow. "Any last words?"

I took a sip of my beer and glanced out at the clearing. Everyone was moving again, but they seemed to be doing so in slow motion. Grimm looked panicked, shifting his eyes back and forth in an attempt to find out where the fuck I had gone, but everyone else was running towards Namea. Her horn was glowing, and I saw that it was pressed directly into Asha's chest.

But all that faded from my mind as I saw Conquest staring directly up at me. "Holy shit!" I blurted, pointing at him. "Is that his soul?"

"Yes," Charon said.

Conquest's mouth moved but no sound came out. I leaned over the edge of the boat and lifted my beer to him. Then I flipped him off and took a healthy gulp of Charon's beer. "Fuck you and the horse you rode in on, Conquest. Enjoy eternity."

His face flashed with stunned horror and disbelief, finally understanding my earlier threat about not meeting him in Hell someday. He literally would never get that chance.

"Let's go to Hell, Charon. I have a hot date with a Valkyrie. Extra drachmae if you run the red lights."

He chuckled nervously, but he obliged.

39

We drifted through darkness, the boat rocking gently in unseen waters. I no longer felt hollow and wispy like before. That must have been because I had been in the Elder realm as a soul. Was my body sprawled out on the ground without my freaking soul? My friends would think I had died! I patted myself, growing alarmed.

"Man up," Charon muttered, rolling his eyes. "You're here in the flesh."

I scowled over at him. Purple lightning flashed in the very far distance, but it seemed to be happening both above and below us like we were flying in the clouds. It was very unsettling. "Man up," I mused. "Like letting your lover know you're still alive rather than watching her from a distance for a few thousand years?"

Charon stopped paddling and shot me a very cool warning glare. He absently reached up to touch the knotted cord through his lips, not seeming aware he was doing it. Like fondling a totem of a lost family loved one for nostalgia's sake. "Such a man probably had very good reasons," he said. Then he resumed his paddling, ending that line of inquiry.

"Whatever," I muttered. "Were you at least man enough to face her after all these years, or did you just call a taxi to pick her up—"

Charon rose to his feet and thumped the paddle blade down onto the floor of the boat, cutting me off with the lethality of his silence. The purple lightning in the distance abruptly cut off and I heard absolutely nothing. Not a single thing. The Underworld held its breath when this man rose to his feet.

I realized I had flinched and pulled back, gripped by terror.

The Boatman stared at me, not even trying to look dangerous. He just looked at me, seeing into the very depths of my soul as easily as a sociopath identifies an easy mark, or a lioness marks the weakest member of the herd.

It wasn't personal. It was the law of the jungle. Kill or be killed. Feelings didn't matter in the ideology of primal instinct.

I straightened my shoulders and rose to my feet, granting him the respect he deserved. If he wanted to shoot his shot, I would oblige. I had only spoken the truth. If this offended him, that was not my fault.

I waited, ready to throw down if necessary. This was not me being prideful. This was me holding Charon to the onerous guillotine of personal responsibility. If he wanted to take offense to the truth, he needed to commit fully to his plan of action.

Iron sharpens iron. Fire forges metal. So the world turns.

He appraised me with a look of respect—that I hadn't cowed from my flippant, truthful remark, but had instead risen to accept responsibility for my words.

"Sit down, you rutting stag," he finally muttered, ruining my moment of philosophical superiority. "Broken clocks," he said dismissively, but I caught a faint smirk as he sat back down and resumed paddling.

I sat down and stared out over the edge of the boat, thinking about recent events. Asha had died in the most horrible way, after surviving the most horrible losses that were indirectly caused by me. Furthering my guilt and rage, it had been the most emotionally heart-wrenching experience I had ever endured. Then I'd abandoned all of my personal restraints and moral checks in how I'd dealt with Conquest.

I had...crossed a few lines. I did not regret my choices, but I knew they had stained me. Much like a soldier in war must do things that will forever haunt him. The aftermath of battle was often worse than the battle that birthed it.

"What is a gentleman?" I asked out loud, more of a rhetorical question than expecting any kind of answer from the cab driver I'd just offended twice in a row.

"A dangerous, honorable man," Charon said without hesitation.

I arched an eyebrow at him. "Not a peaceful man?" I pressed.

He shook his head firmly. "Peace for the sake of peace is weakness. Weakness breeds cowardice. Cowardice breeds subconscious viciousness. Subconscious viciousness breeds hatred. Hatred breeds mobs. Mobs breed the chaos of no responsibility. No responsibility breeds mindless thugs fighting for scraps by any means necessary. Men who destroy mirrors because they fear their own reflections."

I nodded thoughtfully. "Thrasymachus. The ends justify the means. Might is right. Mob justice from men who are too scared to face and address their own flaws. They point a finger outwards rather than acknowledge the four pointing back at them."

Charon smirked, nodding. "This is the fruit born from the crop of weak men. Weak men make hard times. Hard times make strong men. Strong men make good times. Good times make weak men. Welcome to the carousel of life."

"And gentlemen?" I asked curiously.

"Gentle...men are *dangerous*. The gentleness of their nature is the sheath, but the man is the razor-sharp sword. One or the other can be corrupted, both together are a perfect complement."

I nodded thoughtfully, pondering his words.

Charon studied me in silence. "You're losing it, Nate."

I rested my elbows on my knees and raked my fingers into my hair, staring down at the rickety bottom of the boat. It looked bigger than last time. "Some stories don't have happy endings, Charon. Find a way to fucking deal with it. This is how I fucking deal with it," I growled, knowing this story didn't have a happy ending in line for me.

"Hmm," he said in a sympathetic tone.

"Just take me to Kára and Gunnar. I haven't finished my business in the Elder realm, and they are going to freak out when they find me suddenly missing." Another thought hit me. "How does time work between here and the Elder realm? What's the slippage?"

"It has been less than an hour since I last saw you. Don't worry."

I stared at him with bloodshot eyes. "Does it look like it's been an hour for me, Charon?"

He shook his head sadly. "It looks like you've endured a lifetime. Then again, you are very dramatic."

I didn't rise to the bait, knowing he was screwing with me intentionally, getting back at me for chastising his love life. "Why isn't Asha here with us?"

He glanced at me, and I saw a troubled, secretive look in his eyes. "She is the last person you need to worry about right now. I only share boat rides with family members, and only under the worst circumstances."

I cringed at the thought, knowing what he meant. An entire family killed at the same time could share a boat. But I knew there was nothing I could say or do to make him elaborate. When it came to keeping secrets, Charon was at the top of the list. He'd been doing it for thousands of years, after all.

"This boat is bigger," I said, actually taking the time to assess the vessel. "A lot bigger." Charon focused on his rowing, acting as if he hadn't heard me. "Why is the boat bigger, Charon?" I asked suspiciously.

He sighed and cracked open the red plastic cooler at his feet. Then he handed me one of his beers. "Drink. You are going to need it."

I took the beer and cracked it open. Then I lifted it to him in cheers. We clinked cans and took healthy drinks of the cold brew. "Just get me to my friends so I can kill Anubis and get out of this shit-hole. I've got work to do."

He nodded, staring out at our surroundings. "We're expecting company."

I shrugged dismissively on instinct, but then I frowned. "You said that only family members share," I said.

"Sure did," he said, not meeting my gaze.

"Well, then what the fuck do you mean when you say we're expecting company—"

He suddenly looked over my shoulder at something behind me. His eyes widened and he actually dropped his beer.

40

I leapt to my feet and turned around to see...

Well, a woman facing away from me. The second thing I noticed was that she was exceptionally good at being naked, and then all my rational thoughts jumped overboard from Charon's boat and into the abyss, without a life preserver, screaming YOLO!

Being a healthy adult male, my lizard brain swiftly took over the power vacuum and I instinctively appraised the situation from bottom to top. It was a brief but extremely thorough ass-ysis. I meant, analysis.

"What the hell is this?" a familiar voice demanded, and part of my surviving rational brain started to arm-wrestle with my lizard brain, trying to give me important information that might save my life, but it wasn't quite strong enough to prevail as the woman started turning around, already belting out threats. "I'll rip your throat out and feast on your soul, whoever the fuck you are—"

Her voice cut off the moment she saw my face. And that's when my lizard brain jerked my chin down to complete my visual inspection of the naked woman's front half, appreciating art on its most organic canvas:

Cans vs. ass.

The rational part of my brain finally won the arm-wrestling match in my mind, and I promptly whipped my gaze up to meet her face, blushing fiercely. It said something about my instincts that the last thing I noticed about her was that she had long white hair. And that was precisely when my lizard-brain handler ran away screaming, flipping switches and pressing buttons to leave me gaping like a moron, as he abandoned me to suffer the consequences of his influence.

"Nate?" Callie Penrose blurted, looking utterly bewildered. "Did you kidnap me? I was in the middle of a very hard negotiation, and then I was suddenly here!" She angrily planted her hands on her hips and glared.

This caused certain aesthetically pleasing parts of her body to bounce, which did not help my focus whatsoever. The *hard negotiation* comment almost sent me into a fit of adolescent giggles, and I realized she had no idea she was completely naked. I decided to avert my gaze entirely to focus on our dark surroundings, using my peripheral vision to address her. I gestured vaguely at her body. "Hard negotiations, eh?" I squeaked out a subconscious giggle before I could stop myself.

"What the hell are you laughing about—" She cut off abruptly. In my peripheral vision, I saw her face flush bright red. Then she immediately covered her breasts by wrapping one arm across them and gripping her upper ribcage. The other hand flew downwards to cover her forbidden fruit. "What is the meaning of this?" she demanded in an icy tone. "I've been looking everywhere for you! Where have you been?"

I pointed a thumb over my shoulder. "This is Charon. The Boatman. We're in Hell, Callie. No idea how you came here or why. Regardless, it's great to see you," I said before I fully considered how that might sound.

"Good evening," Charon said amicably, cracking open a new beer and extending it past me to hand to her. "You're going to want this, my dear. Trust me." I checked her in my peripheral vision, understanding the obvious—she had no hands available to accept the beer without giving us a show.

"Maybe you could summon your armor?" I suggested. "Cover up the dangerous bits. Protect us from at least *one* of the Seven Deadly Sins."

She sucked in a breath at the idea, not having considered it. Then I realized my innocent joke about Lust actually hit too close to home—literally—because she was actually battling the Seven Sins back home.

Between one moment and the next, she was suddenly clad in white quartz armor that emitted an eerie white vapor. Thankfully, her face remained normal rather than featuring the weeping, blindfolded woman's Mask of Despair. She took the beer with a violent gesture and took a big gulp, as if trying to wash away the last thirty seconds of history.

I did the same, thinking of Kára glaring at me from on high.

I let out a breath and turned back to face Callie, knowing I couldn't accidentally get into trouble again.

I flinched to see that she was now gripping a giant scythe in her fist—it had appeared with her armor. I stared at the familiar weapon, unable to speak. My Mask had told me the truth.

Callie had killed Death—my friend, Hemingway.

She noticed my reaction and glanced down at her hand, looking just as surprised as me to see Death's scythe in her fist. Then her face...broke. That was the only way I could think to describe it. It fractured into a rictus of sorrow and anguish and guilt and shame and...despair. Then, she took a calming breath and straightened her shoulders, facing me directly as she stared at me with watery eyes. "I did something terrible, and I need to tell you about it before you say anything else. No one else was involved, so if you are angry, take it out on me, Hope." She waited, expecting me to argue.

"Okay," I said in a soft whisper. "What did you do, Despair?" She needed to say it more than I needed to hear it. I already knew the truth, but I could tell it was weighing heavily on her conscience.

She took a deep breath, gathering her resolve. "I wanted to tell you, Nate," she whispered, and I saw that she was actually crying, reminding me of her Horseman's Mask. "But I couldn't *find* you."

I opened my mouth to respond but I couldn't formulate words. She had looked for me, but I wasn't home.

She extended the scythe to me with a determined look in her watery, blood-shot eyes. "Take it. I never wanted it. I can't bear to look at it anymore. It fecls...wrong in my hands, like it doesn't belong to me. I think he meant it for you, because I wanted to give it to you the moment I took it. I *tried* to give it to you, but I couldn't find you!" she said again, making it sound like an accusation. "He made me do it! I hate him for it," she hissed, and then her legs gave out and she dropped.

I lunged forward on instinct and caught her, pulling her close to me with a protective snarl. We stood there, pressed against each other, and I realized the embrace was decidedly inappropriate. "You okay?" I growled, unable to make my voice soft and compassionate.

She nodded and straightened, permitting me to let go of her. "Y-yes," she whispered. "Thank you for catching me. Moment of weakness, Hope. I'm sorry." The second after she'd said the words, she furrowed her brow, looking surprised she had said them. Then she regained her confidence and held the scythe between us like a shield. "Take it."

She was giving me no other alternative, so I accepted the weapon. I stared at it, feeling a shudder of unease roll over my shoulders. At the same time, the weapon purred in my hands, and I felt like Death was shaking my hand in a formal farewell. I suddenly realized that I was also wearing my own Horseman armor. Thankfully, my wings hadn't appeared to stab Charon in the throat or anything. I felt like the scythe was encouraging my armor to start picking fights with the nearest beating heart, and I forcefully squashed it, even though it left me trembling.

My Mask was purring at me again, intrigued by the new toy.

I noticed that Callie was now seated across from me, frowning with concern. "Nate?" she whispered. "Are you okay?"

I nodded stiffly and sat down. I propped the deadly weapon on the bench beside me, let go of it, took a calming breath as I released my Horseman armor, and then I looked up at Callie. I felt more in control of my thoughts without the blade in my hands and the armor shrouding me. "What happened?" I asked in a hoarse voice.

Callie took a deep breath to gather her thoughts, and then she told me everything. "I take full responsibility. Death kidnapped Ryuu. He strapped a bomb to his chest, demanding that I face him in battle, one-on-one, if I wanted to save him. He did it in front of a crowd of angels, demons, and his fellow Horsemen. I was so angry at him targeting Ryuu that I obliged him. But when we got close to each other in our first clash, his vitriol disappeared and he whispered to me in an entirely different tone, letting me know all was not as he'd made it seem," Callie said, her eyes distant at the memory. "He'd been putting on a show. He sounded sad and regretful but determined. He told me he knew this day would eventually come, and that no one could have any doubts about me defeating him, which was why he'd intentionally provoked me. He said I needed to *become* Death, to merge my Mask with his. I tried getting away, ending the fight, but he wouldn't let me. I couldn't back down in front of the audience or all chaos would have ensued. He said they couldn't know he was throwing the fight. He said the Four Horsemen had to die at the hands of the Dread Four or we would stand no chance in the Omega War."

I stared at her, stunned speechless. I hadn't known any of *that*.

"He had a message for you," Callie whispered, unable to meet my eyes.

"What?" I rasped, squeezing the scythe in my fist, even though I didn't remember grabbing it. I released it like it was a hot skillet, not giving myself the opportunity to assess my subconscious action.

She cleared her throat and wiped at her eyes. I was surprised to see that she was once again crying, and they were genuine tears. "*Tell Nate that I'm proud of him, and that I'm sorry*," she croaked. "He cried when he said it, Nate. I saw the tear fall from his eye, even though he was wearing his Mask. He...said *You are now Death, Callie Penrose. Memento Mori.*" She shuddered at the memory. "And then he gave me my opening. He *let* me kill him. He knew it was the only way to make his brothers turn on you. On us. I didn't murder him, Nate. I helped him commit suicide, and that is so much worse. I feel like my soul is stained."

And then she hung her head in her hands, sobbing miserably.

It instantly reminded me of Asha's dying cries, and I fell to my knees before her, wrapping her up in a comforting hug. She clutched me with a desperation that felt exactly like Asha's tiny arms, sobbing into my chest as I petted her hair soothingly. "It's okay," I murmured, fighting back my own inner pain as I rested my cheek on the top of her head. "Death is an asshole," I assured her, speaking to both her and Asha's spirit. "He was always scheming behind the scenes."

"I didn't want to do it," Callie whispered. "I mean, I did when I thought it was for *real*—when I thought he was actually threatening Ryuu. But then when he told me it was all a scam, I wanted no part in it. But...the look in his eyes was genuine. He meant it, Nate. I don't understand it, but he meant it with every fiber of his being. He truly believed that the Four Horsemen had to die. Was he right?"

I sighed. "I...have no idea, Callie. His plans usually worked out for the better over time. Like him saving Kára for me, even though he kept her rebirth as a Valkyrie secret from me for years."

Callie nodded, patting my back, and then she started detaching herself. I did the same and sat back on my seat, giving her time to regain her composure. I used the time to quench my rage over both Death's suicide and Asha's death.

41

Callie looked up at me after a few moments. "Do you understand the full scope of what he did? He set his brothers up. He murdered them by proxy, and we are the proxies. That's how dedicated he was to his cause. He planned his brothers' murders."

I grimaced, shaking my head. "That...is incredibly fucked up." I lifted my can and clinked it against hers. "This job isn't nine-to-five, Callie," I said with a sad smile. "Embrace the suck."

She smiled faintly and gestured at her body. "Obviously. You interrupted my...nocturnal proclivities. Quite literally, as a matter of fact. I'm sure Ryuu is panicking right now, wondering why the hell I'm no longer on top—" she cut off abruptly, looking more horrified than amused, although there was a little of both on her face.

Since I was not always a foolish man-child, I pretended I hadn't heard this admission. "What made you believe him?" I asked her. "Death."

She gave me a sad look. "When he spoke of *you*, Nate. The pain in his eyes was profound. Genuine. Heartfelt. He cared more about your feelings than he did for his brothers' actual lives. I don't know if that is alarming or heartwarming, but I made my choice and now I will stand by it. Scream at me. Hit me if you need to." Then she jutted her chin out at me in a challenging glare. "But I will hit back, because we *must* stand united for the Omega War, Hope. We will *win*. Together."

I somehow managed a grin. "Drink your beer, diva."

Her eyes widened, surprised that I wasn't blowing up on her, and I saw her shoulders relax as she leaned back, studying me pensively. "You have... changed," she said, as if speaking to herself. "You're not as hot-headed, but...I think you might actually be *more* dangerous than the last time I saw you."

I nodded. "A little girl died in my arms in the last hour," I said, staring down at my beer. "My perspectives have been...reforged."

"Oh, Nate," she whispered, sounding like her own heart was breaking. She reached out and squeezed my thigh, but I wasn't able to meet her compassionate gaze.

I shuddered at the terrible position Death had put her in. Good lord. I glanced at the scythe, still not trusting myself to touch it. "I'm sorry he put you in that position, Callie, but thank you for telling me."

She pulled her hand away and cocked her head, wiping at her eyes before she took a drink. "What else would I do? Of course I told you," she said, looking confused. "I've been searching everywhere for you. I *had* to be the one to tell you."

I smiled, nodding my agreement. I let my thoughts mull over Callie's story. I was proud of her. She had been trying to find me so she could tell me the full story. She hadn't hidden or tried to make excuses. Then, the moment she'd finally found me—even after being roused from an arousing tryst with her lover—she had immediately spilled the beans. She hadn't even hesitated. Hadn't made excuses. Hadn't tried to justify her actions. She'd started our reunion by claiming responsibility for killing my friend.

Callie was *exactly* as honorable as I had hoped she would be back when I had mentally contrasted her with how War and Conquest had reacted in the Elder realm. No. Callie was *more* honorable than I had assumed.

She'd brought me a grief gift.

Then again, Callie was sneaky and conniving. Maybe she'd shown up naked to sway my opinion...

I eyed her suspiciously. "Why did you show up naked? Was it to manipulate me?"

She arched an eyebrow and then doused me with her can of beer. Then she threw the empty can at my head. It bounced off and fell overboard. I burst out laughing, wiping the beer from my cheeks. "Okay! Mercy!" I begged, chuckling.

"Jerk," she muttered, but she was smiling. "Beer me, Charon!"

As if he'd been waiting for her request, he lobbed a can over my head. Callie caught it with the casual grace of a ninja and cracked open the beer. She took a long pull and then lowered the can, shaking her head at me with a resigned smirk. "I told you why I showed up naked, but I still don't know why I showed up in the first place," she said, arching her eyebrow at me.

"Nate killed Conquest," Charon said in a jovial tone. "Well, it was actually the most brutal torture—"

"Thank you, Charon," I interrupted, ignoring Callie's intense look. "I thought you, of all people, would know that loose lips sink ships. If we're spilling secrets, I can get started on yours at any moment," I said dryly.

The Boatman shut his mouth. Figuratively, of course.

I turned back to Callie. "He's right. More or less—"

"More," Charon clarified.

I glanced over my shoulder and scowled at him. "You done?" He nodded, smirking faintly. I turned back to Callie. "War and Conquest attacked me," I said, and then I told her the rest of the story, letting her know all about hunting Knightmares in the Elder realm, getting trapped there, and Asha dying. Callie listened with intense focus. I could have sworn she stiffened when I mentioned Aiden, but she didn't interrupt me. When I was finished speaking, I took a sip of my beer, wondering why the ride was taking so long and why Callie had appeared in the boat with me. I was about to ask Charon when Callie interrupted me.

"Grimm banged a unicorn?" she asked incredulously.

Charon burst out laughing.

I narrowed my eyes at her. "No, pervert. He failed miserably, and it probably saved his life, because women are dangerous, unruly beasts."

She grinned proudly, as if I had complimented her. Then her smile faded. "I was just trying to make you smile," she said. "You looked like you need it." She let out a sigh. "But I ran across a man named Aiden. I didn't speak to him or anything, but he seemed to have a lot of pull with the Conclave and the Shepherds…" I leaned forward, listening to everything she had to say, which wasn't very much. "Do you think it's the same man?"

I scratched at my chin thoughtfully. "I honestly don't know, but it's safest to assume it was him. He loves using other groups to do his dirty work. If you see him, let me know immediately. Do not approach him. He's got a suit of armor from Camelot—"

"Incoming number three," Charon murmured, already pulling out another beer.

Alucard was suddenly standing directly between me and Callie, wearing a sparkling blue mankini, an orange ascot, and retro sunglasses, leaving me to peer at the bulge of his junk from inches away and for Callie to get an up-close whiff of his ass. We both lurched back with twin shouts.

Alucard burst out laughing, and then he lifted his sunglasses a few inches, scanning his surroundings. Then the Horseman of Absolution's face lit up like Christmas morning. "I *love* boat rides!" he cheered. "Nate? Callie? Drinking?" he observed, noticing our drinks. "Where is the fucking captain of this booze cruise?"

Charon had already reached past me with a fresh can of beer, handing it to Alucard. "Drink it fast. Number four is coming much faster than the other two."

I frowned at him, but he had already turned away, content to completely ignore us as he continued paddling the boat through the darkness.

Alucard laughed and sat down beside Callie, grinning at us. Then he lifted his can to Charon. "Now, *that* is a fucking captain!" he cheered before taking a big drink. His whiskey-breath confirmed my suspicion. He was absolutely hammered. "Aye, aye, Captain!" he cheered, almost dropping his beer as he attempted to salute. "Remember, Nate? Everyone said that to you at your little magic shop."

"Bookstore," I growled, feeling my ears burning.

"It was so *stupid*!" he hooted, slapping his knee. "Man! That was such a long time ago. I used to work there, didn't I?" he asked, frowning dazedly. Callie looked torn between laughing hysterically and throwing him over-board out of embarrassment.

"You look like a drug dealer's girlfriend," I told him, eyeing his ridiculous ensemble. "Have some dignity."

"Well, this dick was on the prowl for some nitty gritty before you abducted me." Callie facepalmed with a loud groan, shaking her head. "Dick...nitty!" he hooted, cracking himself up. He leaned towards Callie, swaying crazily, "Did you tell him about my new horse?" he whispered loud enough to wake the dead.

"I'm cutting him off," Charon said, reaching out to snatch his beer.

"Mine!" Alucard blurted, swatting wildly at the Boatman's hand as he played drunken keep away with his beer. For Alucard to actually get drunk —vampires were amazing at holding their liquor—Alucard must have been devoted to his goal of getting smashed. "Bad captain! Shoo!"

I sighed, gently shoving Charon's hand away. "How about you tell me what they are doing here?" I asked him. Charon clammed up and resumed his paddling.

Callie stood and switched benches to sit next to me, leaving Alucard swaying on his own bench. "Have you two been here the whole time?" Alucard asked us, squinting in our general direction.

We glanced at each other. "For a few minutes," Callie said, sounding as if she doubted the meaning of his question. Perhaps he was so drunk he didn't remember if we had been here when he arrived on the booze cruise.

"Nate!" he switched topics with a bellowing shout. "Drink with me! I'm celebrating!"

I lifted my can with an amused smirk. "I am, Alucard. What are we celebrating?" I asked.

He leaned towards me and almost fell off the bench as he whispered a secret that could have been heard from Tartarus. "I killed Famine! The hangry one! Shhhhhh! It's a secret!" he slurred.

I turned to Callie with a surprised look, and she winced with a guilty nod. "That's why you started celebrating?" she asked Alucard, seeming to finally understand his drunken stupor.

Alucard noticed the look between us and narrowed his drunken eyes in her general direction. "Where have you been, little miss naughty?"

She frowned, struggling to keep up with his topic acrobatics. "What?"

Alucard nodded. "Ryuu was very upset. Said you disappeared in the middle of..." He grinned wolfishly. "Well, he said you disappeared, and his state of undress led me to assume that..." he trailed off under Callie's warning glare. He scowled. "You've been gone for two days—"

Callie leapt to her feet with a gasp. "What?" she shouted, panicking. "Two *days*?"

"Here comes number four," Charon announced. "Last guest." He made no move to grab another beer.

Before we could even open our mouths, the Horseman of War was suddenly seated next to Alucard. He actually looked more surprised than I felt.

Alucard cheered happily, leaning directly into his personal space. "Hello, brother!"

War snarled as he leaned away, unsheathed his fiery sword, and immediately took an expert swing at the drunken vampire's throat.

42

The blade whipped right through Alucard's face like smoke, doing no harm at all. He cursed, not looking remotely surprised. I let out a breath I hadn't known I'd been holding.

Alucard frowned at War. "Missed me, missed me, now you gotta kiss me," he sang, and then he planted a fat kiss on War's lips, giggling like a lunatic. War shoved him away with a snarl, spitting furiously.

I blinked, baffled at the exchange. He could shove him, but the sword did nothing?

Charon cursed. "That's it! The Four Horsemen Reunion Tour is over. Now that you're all here, I'm dropping you off."

The boat was suddenly going much faster. Although the scenery didn't change, I could feel it in my soul.

Alucard saw the confused look on my face and shrugged. "Yeah. We can't hurt each other because we're both baptized in that Biblical Horseman musk," he said, his New Orleans drawl becoming more pronounced.

War glared at us with pure hatred, and then sheathed his sword with an angry motion, confirming Alucard's claim. I suddenly understood why he had run away after I'd killed Conquest—why my magic had abruptly failed. War stared out the side of the boat, completely ignoring us. Callie eyed War for a moment and then nodded at me. "That seems to be true. I don't know why."

"It's because you are the Four Horsemen," Charon said. "You three killed the originals and took their crowns. War can no longer harm you. You cannot harm him."

Alucard chuckled like a lunatic. "Awkward," he said, drawing out the word like it was three syllables.

War leapt to his feet, his face turning red as he pointed his fiery sword at Charon. "Has he roped you into this coup? Are you one of Master Temple's numerous bitches now? Got you all primped and pretty, feeling like a valued member of his harem?"

Callie glared at his insinuation, but Alucard was gurgling his beer, swatting at Callie's shoulder to watch.

Charon sighed and rested his paddle on his knees. Then he leaned forward and stared directly at War. "Someone dear to me once had a saying. Have big balls before you swing a tiny dick," he said, lifting his paddle in one hand while smirking at War's flaming sword.

Alucard choked, spewing his beer up in a fountain that got all of the Horsemen. "What the *fuck*?" he blurted, choking and gasping to catch his breath. Callie bit back a grin, swatting him on the back to clear his airway.

War's face turned a remarkable shade of purple, but he was too busy sputtering to say any actual words. He did lower his sword.

Charon leaned back and drummed his fingers over his oar. "I'm far more frightening and powerful in this place. Be exceedingly careful who you disrespect, Tiny."

War re-sheathed his sword and sat down beside Alucard with a huff. Charon resumed his rowing.

Alucard wrapped his arm around War's shoulder in a commiserating gesture. "Hey, hey, hey," he whispered in an insistent request. "Lemme' tell you a secrets," he slurred, bending close to War's ear. Surprisingly, War allowed it, although with a suffering grimace. Alucard drew closer and closer, moving slower and slower as his eyes fluttered closed.

Then he passed out, mumbling incoherently as he cuddled the Horseman's shoulder.

War shrugged him back with a disgusted growl. Alucard fell and hit the floor of the boat on his back with a loud thud, his legs hanging out over the seat he'd occupied a moment before, highlighting his ridiculous sequined mankini. The fall did not wake him, even though his glasses had been knocked crooked and his beer was slowly spilling over his chest and ascot. He started snoring loudly, completely unconscious.

War glared at him and then us. "Christ. How much has he had to drink?" he demanded, biting back a grin.

Callie sighed, looking embarrassed. "I'll take care of him," she grumbled.

"Where are we going?" War asked absently.

"Conquest," the Boatman said, pointing at me, "is here to...save Gunnar and his friends. I'm the chauffeur." War stiffened and then slowly turned to look at me. Ironically, hope danced in his eyes for the first time during our trip. "The rest of you," Charon continued, "are free to leave at any time." As he said it, he watched War with a curious gleam in his eyes, daring him to do what we all knew he was here to do.

"I'm staying," War said, clenching his jaw. "I was already looking for Gunnar when you abducted me here," he said in a calm tone. "I want an end to this. I will not work with you three after what happened. I *cannot* work with you after all of this. I would never be able to trust you, and you would never be able to trust me. We could not be a team."

I nodded my agreement, as did Callie. Alucard's leg twitched his agreement.

Callie turned to look at me with a thoughtful expression, understanding the brevity of the situation. At the same time, there was nothing any of us could do against War. They could help with Anubis. Well, Callie could help me with Anubis. Alucard wasn't waking up for a good long while. He was actually a liability at the moment. Callie cleared her throat uneasily, but she did look me in the eyes as she spoke. "There is a lot going on in Kansas City—"

War snorted. "Understatement. You need to clean up that mess fast, Sister—" He cut off abruptly, stiffening. Then he pointedly turned to watch the nonexistent scenery, acting like he hadn't said anything.

We watched him for a few moments, and then Callie cast me a sympathetic frown, obviously wanting to extend an olive branch to him. I folded my arms and shook my head. He had made his bed. Callie sighed and finally nodded, banishing the guilt over her culpability. "If I've really been gone two days," she continued in a tone that she didn't even remotely trust Alucard's claim, "I need to get back."

I smiled, nodding. "Go. I can handle this. And I know you can handle your stuff," I assured her.

She smiled, looking surprisingly appreciative of my faith in her. She didn't need my approval, and she knew it, but hearing me say the words had a big impact on her—the professional respect.

"How do they leave?" I asked Charon.

The Boatman turned to us with a truly wicked grin. Then he pointed out the side of the boat, into the dark abyss. "You jump overboard. I've literally been swimming in wide circles this whole time," he said, chuckling. "Consider this the airport parking lot."

I stared at him in disbelief. "You've...been wasting our time while my friends are in danger?" I whispered, wanting to kill him. I'd felt him paddling faster, but that had just been him paddling in faster circles, apparently. We were stuck in traffic because our driver was a dick. Hell, right? Sucked a big one.

Charon leaned forward, and I sensed a menacing aura radiating from him. "You're the one who ordered the ride, Conquest," he said, emphasizing the name of the soul I had stolen. "Don't complain about the experiences in Hell. No one reads the reviews. I only have a one pentagram rating," he added dryly.

War burst out laughing.

I ignored him and waved Callie down, because she looked ready to take on the Boatman all by herself. Thankfully, she listened to me. I studied Charon pensively, squashing my anger and resorting to logic. Charon wouldn't do something to spite me for no reason. If he'd wanted to waste time, he could have just taken us on a joyride through Hell. This wasn't about wasting time.

I leaned over the side of the boat, frowning. Then I turned back to the Boatman. "You stayed here so they could hop overboard when they were ready. This is the only place where they still have the chance to change their minds. You wanted to get us in the same boat to give us a chance to talk and...work out our differences." I glanced at War, who was frowning thoughtfully. "Or not."

Charon leaned back with an impressed look. Then he gave me a slow nod. "Booze cruises are social events, and sometimes it's all about the journey, not the destination." Then he turned to Callie. "It would be my pleasure to toss him overboard for you."

She glanced at me, checking to see if she should trust him. I smiled. "Charon is an asshole, but he's an old family friend. I trust him."

Charon dipped his chin in gratitude. Then he rose to his feet, scooped up the limp, soggy vampire with no apparent strain, and flung him overboard with an amused laugh. Freefall woke Alucard up and he immediately screamed, "My beer!" His voice immediately cut out as if we had only imagined it.

Callie flashed me a smile. Then she extended a hand to War. "Horseman," she said.

He stared at the hand for a few moments, and then smiled sadly. He rose to his feet and shook her hand. "Horsewoman," he said. And he actually dipped his chin.

With that, Callie stepped up on the side of the boat, turned and waved, and then her armor abruptly vanished, leaving her stark naked. She leapt over the side, laughing for a few seconds, and then the sound cut off.

"Now can I have a beer?" War finally grumbled, shaking his head at the bizarre experience.

Charon nodded and kicked the cooler towards him. "Share," he said. And then he sat down and dipped his paddle back into the water. He poured the rest of his beer on his face and then flung the can into the abyss. "You two ready to go to Hell?" he asked with an eerie grin.

We simply nodded.

The scenery abruptly changed, revealing an impossibly large cavern of lava and flames. We cruised through the lava at an alarming clip, but I felt no wind, and no lava splashed onto us.

I stared at War, refusing to listen to my instinct to shy away and leave him alone. "Do I need to wave my finger in your face and recite 'I'm not touching you' until you acknowledge me?" I asked the side of his head.

Finally, he turned to glare at me. "You crossed a line, Hope," he growled, looking like he wanted to rip my face off with his bare hands.

I nodded. "Yes. Bring a sword to the warriors' table and die by the sword." War opened his mouth to challenge me, but I held up a finger.

"Bring dishonor to the warriors' table and die by dishonor. I didn't ask for the fight, but I did finish it. You should have known that about me."

War stared at me, clenching his jaw. After a few moments, he nodded very slowly, and then he let out a sigh that looked to deflate him by thirty pounds of mass. He looked...defeated. "Yes. I should have." He eyed the scythe next to me with a nostalgic frown. "He would have wanted you to have it," he said.

Very, very softly.

Part of me wanted to tell him that Death had orchestrated everything, but I wasn't sure if that would send him into a fit of denial. Having War in a peaceful attitude was beneficial to everyone.

Well...

It was beneficial to everyone *except* himself.

And that was fine by me.

I glanced at the scythe with a thoughtful frown. Something was nagging me about it. With a gasp, I looked up at Charon, understanding his question from the cave. *Do you have the scythe?* As if he'd been waiting for the question, he was already staring at me. Before I could say anything, he nodded. "Yes. That is what I was referring to in the brewery," he said with an amused grin. "Sugar as well."

Then he went back to his paddling, ignoring me. His body language told me there would be absolutely no elaboration on why he had asked the question, implying that it was very, very important for me to have it. And he had purposely chosen not to say the word *scythe* in front of War. He hadn't even let me ask the question. War frowned at each of us curiously, but he didn't look interested enough to press the issue for an explanation. He looked like a man walking to the gallows.

Again, fine by me.

43

Charon pulled up on the shore of a spit of black sand. "Get out," he said. "I've got stuff to do."

We climbed out of the boat and took a few steps to distance ourselves from the lava lake. Charon pushed off and turned his boat around without a word. Then he left without even waving or anything.

Ashley was prancing around with a pole held in her hands, spinning and singing as Calvin and Makayla cheered her on, also dancing and celebrating. On top of the pole was the severed head of Anubis.

And surrounding the fun family dance party had to be hundreds of dead Candy Skulls.

Gunnar stood off to the side in his human form, and he had his arms folded as he argued with Hades about something. Both men looked annoyed and frustrated.

I let out a breath of relief to see Snarler and Grinder both here as well. They stood near the bank of the lava lake and were taking turns dipping their hooves in the molten rock, screaming in pain, and then doing it all over again, urging the other to dip his hoof deeper.

All in all, it looked like a family picnic.

My anxiety ratcheted up, because I didn't see Kára anywhere, but I knew the rest of my friends wouldn't be celebrating if something had happened to her. I dismissed my fear and took a calming breath. I glanced at War and arched an eyebrow.

"I'm not changing my mind, Hope," he growled.

"Good." We walked towards the celebration. "And for what it's worth, I have no regrets about what happened earlier. Five minutes before you showed up, I would have risked anything to fight by your side, but then you two showed up and threatened my allies—who had nothing to do with anything—and you didn't even give me the chance to talk. I lost all respect for you at that moment."

War glanced over at me with a calm face. "Hell of a thing to say to a man walking towards the noose."

I grunted. "Hell of a thing to do to a man who respected you and trusted you."

War stopped and turned to face me. "You are right. We lost our heads when Death and then Famine died. You and Gunnar were the only ones left to confront, and I knew he answered to you, so we chose to come at you. It was poorly handled, but you can see how I got there. Why I felt the way I did."

I continued to stare at him, saying nothing.

He smirked and nodded approvingly. "I'm about to pay for my mistake, but for what it's worth, I'm sorry." He extended a hand towards me.

I didn't want to shake it.

I did it anyway.

If we didn't offer redemption to those who apologized for their crimes, the only people left in the world would be people with no desire to ever apologize for their crimes. There would be no reason to take responsibility for mistakes, and that would make for a very dangerous world.

"You're sounding awfully grim, War. You planning on throwing the fight? Committing seppuku?"

"I actually considered it," he said, turning to look at Gunnar in the distance. "But I don't think that one would grant it to me. He's not as invested as we are."

I nodded. "Yeah. Justice is funny like that," I said, eyeing Gunnar. "That dog won't fight just because you put him in the ring, but when you get him riled up, there's no taking the fight out of the dog."

"Honorable," War said.

"Stop making me like you, asshole."

He chuckled. "Okay. He looks like a real bitch."

I smiled. "Well, he is crippled, but I'd argue that it's only made him a stronger leader." I glanced at War thoughtfully. "As much as I want you to just keel over and die, he will know if you're faking it. He won't fall for any traps or anything, but he will know if you're phoning it in and he'll call it off."

War nodded, and then we started walking. "Oh, I plan to make him work for my Mask," he said. He pointed at Hades. "Ask him about the scythe. He can show you how to rip a hole in reality like I did with my sword—but better. Death showed me the trick, and Hades showed him." I frowned at him, and he shrugged. "Not sure how today is going to pan out for me, but I have hope," he said with a wink.

I nodded. "Okay, War," I said carefully, unable to hate him as much as I had a few moments ago. Bastard. I clapped him on the back. "Let's not get sappy about this. Executions are messy enough without that nonsense."

He grinned wolfishly. "Aye. No tears."

"No tears," I agreed, smiling sadly, feeling my eyes growing misty.

"Fucking Hell making my eyes water," War grumbled, staring down at the ground.

"This place sucks," I agreed, keeping my arm wrapped around his shoulder. He patted me on the back, and I thought I felt his shoulders tremble, but I didn't say anything. "It really sucks," I added, letting him hear the layers to my words.

He nodded stiffly, sniffling. "Damn allergies," he grumbled.

I wiped at my nose and blinked rapidly. "Damn allergies," I agreed.

Hades saw us approaching and instantly threw his hands into the air, waving at us. "Oh, hell no! Get the fuck out of here, you two. I've got enough shit to deal with, thanks to your other friends." Gunnar walked by his side as the anxious god stormed towards us, finally coming to a stop a few feet away. I felt Ashley and the twins watching us—not the goat twins, who looked to be psyching each other up for a cannonball contest, completely oblivious to our arrival.

Hades hesitated as his eyes settled on the scythe in my fist. He knew exactly what it was. His eyes immediately shifted to War in understanding, and he took a step to the side, looking frustrated.

Gunnar glanced at my scythe and then War, seeming to comprehend the relationship as well, but he didn't comment on it. "Thanks for coming, Nate, but we already resolved the situation. Ashley killed Anubis. Hades is pissed about it, because now he has to take back over the Underworld early."

I was relieved to hear it, even though I had a billion questions. "I had no doubts," I lied. That wasn't any shade on Gunnar and crew—it was my healthy respect for Anubis' scheming. I thought he would have had some insane plot that would have taken Gunnar's strengths into account, overwhelming them in some kind of impossible trap.

Hades scowled at Gunnar's brief summary, but he nodded his agreement. "I was enjoying my rotation off. I had another decade before I had to take my turn at the reins again. You bastards ruin everything good about being a god. Everything."

I grinned and took a dramatic bow, even though I had done absolutely nothing to annoy him. This time.

Gunnar rolled his eye and shook his head. "Hades doesn't know why Anubis made his move, but he promises to look into it and report back to me." His tone implied that it was not a request. Hades nodded, looking just as interested in the explanation. In fact, he looked angrier than Gunnar.

Gunnar saw me stretching out on my tiptoes to check behind him and he smiled. "Kára is fine. She's scouting," he assured me. I let out a sigh of relief, feeling like a weight had been lifted from my shoulders. Gunnar appraised my scythe for a few moments and then turned to War, who had been staring at him the entire duration of our conversation.

"Fucking Horsemen," Hades muttered, taking another step back.

War drew his sword and leveled it at Gunnar with such abruptness that his voice should have been dubbed and a samisen should have been plucking in the background. "I challenge you to a duel."

Gunnar grew very calm, appraising the flaming sword with one eye. He did not touch the hammer at his belt. He looked so unthreatened that his hammer didn't even let out a pop of static electricity. I grinned proudly. He wasn't even trying to be a dick, but he was nailing it. "Oh, really?" he finally asked, as if responding to a neighbor commenting on the weather tomorrow. War nodded. "And why would I want to do that?" he asked casually.

He sounded more curious than anything, but I did see his eye glance at my scythe.

"Because the winner takes the other's Mask. I either become Justice, or you become War."

Gunnar frowned. "You want to trade jobs?" he asked, sounding confused. Then he turned to me and pointed a thumb at War. "Is this some kind of prank?"

I took a step back and lifted my arm up, thumping my scythe down into the sand, pointing the blade away from them. "This is literally between you two," I said. "I've already played this game. So has Callie and Alucard."

Gunnar's eye narrowed warily but he didn't say anything.

"Winner takes all," War said. "This is not actually a request. It's a warning. I'm going to try to kill you, and those are the stakes."

Gunnar considered the situation for a few moments, as if checking his schedule. "Why?"

"Do you want a history lesson or can we skip that part and get straight to the only conclusion—the fight."

Gunnar stroked his beard pensively. "Nah. I want the history. I won't fight just to appease your ego. Life is too precious to squander on vanity or pride." Then he turned to me with a pointed look and cleared his throat.

War burst out laughing, lowering his sword. Then the bastard sheathed it.

"Hey!" I snapped. "That's some *bullshit*—"

"Language!" Ashley barked, pointing her pole with Anubis' head on it at me like it was a wooden spoon from my youth. Calvin and Mac grinned at me, waving.

War and Gunnar shook hands and dipped their chins at each other. Then they walked up to the edge of the lava lake, speaking in low tones. Like old pals.

I scowled, wishing Gunnar had just sucker punched him with Mjolnir while they were shaking hands. That would have been awesome for his legend. Then again, I was emotionally invested in this. I had been the victim of War's vengeful wrath, and that vicious cycle was now passed onto me, coursing through my veins.

My own earlier rebuke of War and Conquest's actions echoed through my mind, warning me against hypocrisy. I sighed, kicking at a rock on the ground.

Hades stormed over. "What the fuck is this, Nate? I've already got a pile of shit to deal with and you—"

I thumped Death's scythe between us and leaned on it as I met his eyes. He definitely recognized it, and he definitely thought about shitting his pants as he took a step back. "I've had a really shitty day, Hades. Fuck. Off."

He studied me for a few moments and then dipped his chin. "I know you think you're hot shit. It's justified, so calm down before you get all huffy." He leaned closer. "But you're not the only badass here, Temple. My job is to guard over people and...things that would make most gods' bowels turn to liquid fine enough to shit through a screen without hitting a wire."

I actually gagged at the visual and took a step back, horrified. "That is foul! You gave my *brain* a skid mark."

He puffed out his chest proudly and gave me a nod, glad that his point had resonated. "If you want respect, show some respect. We have both had shitty days. Gentlemen suck that shit up and deal with it."

I took a calming breath and sighed, leaning on the scythe with less hostility. "I apologize," I said, thinking back on my talk with Charon about being a gentleman. He waited a few seconds for me to add in a pithy remark. I thought about it. I really, really did.

Finally, he nodded. "So, I repeat...what the fuck is going on over there?"

I glanced over at Gunnar and War. They were taking turns skipping rocks in the lava river. What the fuck? "In a few moments, one of them will be dead, and the other will control both Horseman Masks," I told him in a hollow tone, only just now understanding that the outcome might not be in my favor. "They are discussing it." I watched them for a few moments. "I think they are discussing it. Or they're threatening each other..."

Hades eyed them dubiously. "You sure? Because to me, it looks like they are throwing rocks in my river, laughing like they're starring in a *Brokeback Mountain* reboot," Hades grumbled. "You know, where the underlying theme actually means 'happy'."

I cringed, pretending I hadn't heard his elaboration.

"Nah. This is what gentlemen are supposed to do before killing each other," I assured him, even though I didn't buy my own words. What were they doing? Skipping rocks and...

They were laughing. What the fuck?

Hades had noticed the same thing. I kept my face disinterested, not wanting to concern him. He glanced at me and muttered a curse, taking the look on my face as confirmation that I was right. "Maybe that's why I'm stuck down here. I never had the gift for that game," he admitted, letting out a frustrated sigh. "You? Your dad was one of that breed."

I managed not to flinch at his mention of my father. Instead, I shrugged. "Me? A gentleman?" I snorted.

Hades studied me and the scythe for a while, but I didn't meet his eyes. "Yeah," he said in a low growl. "I think it's in there somewhere. A dirtier, scruffier, alcoholic gentleman. One who *likes* getting his tuxedo bloody when an innocent life is on the line. The kind of gentleman who *waits* for such opportunities," he said, gauging my reaction.

I gave him nothing. "You say the sweetest things. Maybe I just like killing bastards."

Hades nodded. "Only the bastards, though. I can respect that. But it's a thin tight-rope, Nate. Be careful."

I glanced at him, and I saw the sincerity in his eyes. I gave him a slow nod. "I'm beginning to realize that," I admitted, finally dropping my defenses. "War told me you knew a worthwhile trick with this thing," I said casually, indicating Death's scythe.

Hades smirked and nodded. "If it gets you guys the fuck out of my house, I'll show you."

44

S eeing movement in my peripheral vision, I turned to see Ashley and the twins walking up to War. They said a few words and then shook his hand, taking turns. Then they backed away and took seats on nearby rocks to watch their father fight the Horseman of War, the last of the Biblical Four.

Instead, I saw War slowly lower to his knees before Gunnar. Then he sat back on his heels and Gunnar joined him, mirroring the position so the two were facing each other on their knees. Then I saw their lips moving as they spoke in words I couldn't hear.

Ashley and the kids watched the two men intensely.

Hades grunted, pulling my attention away. "You are a terrible student," he informed me.

I smiled. "Sorry." I focused on him, letting him know he had my full attention. He studied my scythe and finally held his hand out to me, silently asking me to hand it over. I hesitated, feeling possessive. I stared down at the Omegabet runes carved into the haft. I didn't have time to try and translate them. My friends were still stuck in the Elder realm, and I needed to get them out of there.

I handed the scythe to Hades.

He accepted it with a nod of thanks, and then he held the scythe up before him. "This can rip holes in reality, connecting you to and from the Underworld." I nodded, remembering Death once ripping open an entrance to Hell for me. Death had put on a very elaborate...act, almost a ritual. But when War had made such a rip, he had done no such thing.

"Just to and from the Underworld?" I frowned. "War made one from Kansas City to the Elder realm."

Hades shrugged. "Maybe each Horseman blade has this ability. Maybe it just takes practice, like with your magic." I nodded, thinking of the voice in my Mask, how she was always wanting to learn new things and show me new things. "All I know is that when I first saw this, I recognized it's relation to the land of the dead, and I told Death how to use it as a key to get in and out of the Underworld. That was a long time ago, so they've likely learned more uses for their weapons, and different ways of unlocking each world."

"Okay. What do I do?"

"It's very complicated," he said in a sobering tone. "Watch closely." I leaned forward, staring at the blade eagerly. He thumped me on the head with the back of the blade and then started chuckling. Before I could demand an explanation, he shoved the weapon into my chest. "Just think about where you want to go and then slash the air like you're attacking a particularly resilient curtain. A gang of offensive drapes."

I snatched the scythe away. "There has to be something more to it," I growled. "You're a shit teacher."

He grinned, but his humor faded after a few moments. "You need to be committed. It's not like hopping in a car. You need to consciously think about ripping, not just traveling to your destination—although you need to do that as well. You need to commit to *destruction*—a form of death." Then he held up his palms and shrugged. "Lesson over. I'm fresh out of certificates and gold stars."

I grunted, remembering when War had made one of the rips. He had looked very focused, and it had not been a quick slash. It had been a grueling tear that seemed to expend a lot of his energy. Was that because he hadn't been going to the Underworld? Or maybe each Horsman needed to embrace their namesake.

Death needed to commit to destruction because it was a form of death.

Maybe War had needed to commit to...battle or violence—a synonym for his Mask.

I studied my new scythe and thought of my Feather. If my theory was correct, I basically had to summon my care bear power of love and happy thoughts to use my blade to rip holes in reality.

This bit of knowledge would not add to my fearsome reputation, so I kept it to myself.

"Heard you spoke to Charon," Hades said in an overly casual tone.

I nodded. "Yeah."

"You're going to the Reverie," he said, and I could have sworn I saw him suppress a shudder.

"Yeah."

He let out a breath. "You take care of yourself out there, Nate. From what I hear, that place is about the stupidest place you could consider visiting. And the smartest." I looked over at him, but he was staring out at the lake, refusing to make eye contact. "Things are getting unstable out there. We are getting closer to the end. The Omega War."

I nodded calmly, gripping the scythe. "Bring it on."

Hades glanced at me sidelong, looking like he was assessing my resolve. "I've spoken to many of your ancestors about their visit to the Reverie and, no, I'm not permitted to share their experiences or failings or learnings," he quickly said when he saw my ears perk up. "But I can tell you this." I leaned closer, not wanting to miss a single word. "Most refuse to whisper a single word about it. Their souls shiver at whatever it is they faced. On my own, I have surmised that no two Temples face or learn or discover the same thing." He shrugged and brushed his hands together. "That's all I've got. Not sure if it helps, but there it is."

"Why did you say anything at all?" I asked.

He was silent for a time. "Well, I think we're going to need you very badly in this Omega War, and I fear what kind of man or beast Nate Temple might be by the time that horn of war first wails. I think the type of Nate Temple that enters that fight is possibly going to determine what kind of world we have *after*. You see, I don't think the Catalyst is guaranteed to win the war and then we all get to live happily ever after." He swallowed audibly and stared deep into my eyes, showing me his sincerity and his concern. "I fear there's a possible path where we win...but we wish we had not."

I stared at him, unable to blink.

"You mean that a victory with me might be worse than a loss to the Masters?" I whispered.

He nodded but held up a finger. "I *fear* it," he said, emphasizing the word. "I don't *know* it. The only one who can answer that question is you, and it seems the first step down the path to that answer, one way or another, is through the Reverie."

I nodded, not sure how to respond. A hollow promise of me being a good guy felt like it might cause more harm than good at the moment. That it would sound forced and fraudulent.

"Then it's time I start walking," I finally said. "Could you do me a favor? I need you to—"

"Nate!" Kára screamed excitedly from high above. I looked up to see the golden Valkyrie sweeping her metallic wings and grinning down at me with a relieved smile. "Armor up, because I'm not slowing down!" she warned, laughing, and then she dive-bombed me.

I grinned, noticing I had no time to argue or talk her out of it. I let my new scythe disappear and I summoned my armor just in the nick of time. My Valkyrie tackled me hard enough to send me slamming to the ground on my back, turning me into a toboggan that slid us across the black sand for a good thirty feet. She kissed and squeezed and nuzzled me the entire time.

We both let our armor wink out at the same moment, and then it was all groping hands, hot flesh, and wet lips as we kissed and cuddled. I laughed, feeling like I was being molested by an overzealous puppy after a long vacation.

After some time, she finally sat up and propped her hands on either side of my head, straddling my hips as she smiled down at me. Her dual-colored eyes felt like they were hypnotizing me. "Hey, Toots," I murmured.

"Heya' back, Mister," she purred, squeezing her thighs against me suggestively. "But *he* beat you to it," she said with a playful grin, pressing her ass into my lap to say hello to her stiffest and most ardent supporter. I grinned, knowing this wasn't the time or place, no matter what that guy said—

"We were in the middle of a conversation," Hades growled, having walked up to us. "Man stuff."

Kára flashed him a smile. "Well, I was about to show him some *woman* stuff, but you're free to watch. You're probably very lonely down here when Persephone is gone," she said, referring to his wife's dual citizenship with the Underworld and the one above. "Is that why you're so grumpy? Stopped up?"

Hades growled warningly and then squatted down beside her to stare into her eyes. "You about done? Because I was trying to show Nate how to go save his friends in the Elder realm. You know, the ones stranded there all alone who probably think he's dead. Time moves much faster there, after all."

Kára's face paled and she nodded stiffly. Then she got up and pulled me to my feet. "Of course," she murmured, looking as if she'd been slapped and felt she had earned it.

"Well, thanks, Hades," I grumbled, dusting off my pants. "You could have just traded an insult with her, not bludgeoned her with the guilt-trip club."

"Was I wrong?" he asked.

I sighed and met Kára's eyes. "He's not wrong. Only I can get them out." I summoned my scythe. "And this can help me get back to them. I'll explain all that later. A lot has happened."

She nodded in understanding, risking a glance at War and Gunnar's strange discussion. "I can see that." She let out a breath and put her hands on her hips, her green and blue eyes seeming to twinkle independently. "Okay. Then let's go. We can all join you." I gripped her shoulder and squeezed affectionately, shaking my head. The look she gave me was that of a cat tossed into a bathtub. "Oh, no you don't, Nate," she warned.

I squeezed harder. "Callie saw Aiden in Kansas City. I need all of you to get back to Chateau Falco as soon as possible and prepare for the worst. Hades can send you there. I don't know what Aiden is doing or planning, but there was a reason he trapped us in the Elder realm and then left. You all need to go back and rally the troops. Let everyone know to be on the lookout. Gunnar and Ashley can't do everything on their own. They can't fly or hop realms like you, Kára. You are my horn of war. Spread the message to my allies."

She pursed her lips, looking both sad and angry and honored at my faith in her. "Damn it," she hissed, pounding a fist into her thigh. "You better hurry up, Nate. I don't like the idea of you in there by yourself."

I shrugged. "It's just a rescue mission to get my friends out. I've discovered the way to get us out," I told her, thinking of the Reverie. "And Aiden is no longer there. Apparently, the Elder realm is some kind of playground for my ancestors. They all go on pilgrimage there at some point in their lives. Some rite of passage."

Hades nodded. "He speaks the truth, Valkyrie. I have heard it spoken by many of them."

She sighed, knowing I was right. There was a strange sound off to our left, and we turned towards Gunnar and War. My eyes widened to see War falling to his side with his sword sticking out from his chest. Gunnar knelt before him, looking like he was praying. Ashley and the twins stood vigil, watching their father, the new Horseman of War, pay his last respects.

War was dead. Long live War.

I let out a sigh of relief to see he had won, and then I turned to Kára. I didn't want to face the Randulfs, because then I would have to tell them about Asha, and I didn't have time to fall apart. I couldn't even make myself tell Kára, because the look of anguish I would see in her eyes would shatter my resolve.

"I need to go," I told her, and then I planted a kiss on her lips before she could argue.

"Not fair," she grumbled after I pulled away, but she was smiling stubbornly.

With a deep breath, I gripped the scythe in my fist, thinking of Carl in the Elder realm. I had no idea where they were, so I just focused on him, specifically, hoping for the best. Then I focused hard on the destruction and death I wanted to rain down upon the last Knightmare. Upon Aiden and his cronies.

Death was the kindest of the things I intended to do to him.

"I'll try anything twice," I muttered, and then I slashed the scythe through the air in front of me. I felt the scythe tear at something unseen, ripping through an invisible fabric with a screaming rasp. And I stared in fascination and horror as I tore open a hole in the air.

It was much more violent and destructive than my fiery Gateways.

This felt like I was damaging something, and I found myself wondering just how much I should trust Hades, the new Lord of the Underworld. The rip in the air was wide enough for me to walk through, and as I stared at the edges of the tear, I actually saw glowing purple fibers waving back and forth as if alive.

Well, in their death throes after I'd shredded through them.

It truly was like a fabric of sorts that the scythe's blade had ripped.

I stepped through into the Elder realm, hoping for the best, ready for the worst.

45

I stepped into the Elder realm, gripping my scythe in preparation to unleash my pent-up anger on anyone who looked at me sideways. It was night again, and the red moon hung high overhead, bathing the darkness with a crimson glow like fresh blood.

No one attacked, and the place felt entirely devoid of life. Sparks fell down from the sky, and I wondered where the hell I was. It didn't look like an area of the Elder realm I had already visited. It looked more hilly and I actually saw some greenery. Some.

Two white knights leapt out of the shadows from behind a boulder, lowering their weapons and gawking at me. "Nate?" Talon whispered in a hoarse voice. Carl stood beside him, looking exhausted but relieved to see me. He had my satchel over his shoulder, and he promptly handed it to me, as if eager to get his ancestor's flesh-bag off his person. I couldn't blame him.

I accepted it with a grateful smile and slipped it over my shoulder, feeling like it was protective armor. "Yeah. It's me," I said, relieved to see they were okay. I almost let out a cheer to learn that the scythe had brought me to Carl rather than somewhere else. So, I now knew it could track particular people down, which made sense, being Death's scythe—he would want to find specific people who were destined to die. "Where are we?" I looked around some more and then I did a little head count, feeling a frown stretch down over my lips. "Where are Yahn and Grimm?"

Carl was staring at the scythe in my hand with a thoughtful expression, but Talon just stared at me, looking somewhat feral. He had a scar on his cheek that looked healed over. It hadn't been there when I last saw him, which meant...

"How long have I been gone?" I whispered, suddenly horrified.

"Two weeks," Talon said, his eyes glittering. "We didn't know what else to do. Where else to go. We followed the last Knightmare and realized he was in the Citadel." He pointed over my shoulder, and I slowly turned to look. "Carl would not let us enter without you," he said unhappily.

A giant wall of sandstone blocks loomed behind me, stretching far in both directions, but angling in to suggest a circular shape around the area within. The Citadel. We stood before a giant opening in the wall, but the air was hazy, and it rippled like milky water. Staring at it, the hair on the back of my hands started to stand up as I became aware of the ward powering the opening, warning intruders away.

Through the haze, I could just make out a menacing black mansion on a hill, surrounded by a second stone wall in the center of the Citadel. It looked like the place had been abandoned after a war had bombed the hell out of it. The hair on the back of my arms stood straight up, and I felt an almost magnetic pull attracting me to the haunted gothic mansion, like a bug to a bug zapper.

"The Reverie," I whispered reverently, almost feeling an alcoholic buzz at the thought of entering through its door, even if it led to my doom.

Talon nodded and stepped up beside me. "Yes. We've been here for a few days, debating what to do. We sensed the Knightmare in there when we first arrived. Then...we no longer sensed him," he said with a puzzled frown, his ears hanging low and back as if facing a threat.

"He was *inside* the Citadel?" I asked, feeling protective of the place I had only just seen for the first time. Carl had been right. This was a holy place. An altar to greatness. I took a step back and shook my head violently, feeling its grip on me lessen significantly. I blinked nervously, wondering what the fuck was going on. Talon and Carl eyed me, looking nervous about my alternating personalities. "The Knightmare didn't come out through the entrance?" I asked, shaking off its siren song. I needed to guard my mind from this place.

But I knew I still needed to enter. This was a game of wills. It was testing me, somehow. I focused on the scythe, and it felt like a curtain slipped between me and the mansion—a very thin layer of protection.

Carl nodded. "Yes," he said, answering my question. "They must have found a member of the Bone Council and used them to get through the ward." He tapped the bone dagger on his hip, and I grimaced. Sugar's bone.

I nodded, understanding what he was suggesting. Aiden had gotten a key the same way we had.

"But no one has exited," Talon assured me. "We've kept watch." He turned to look at me with a wary frown. "Where did you go, Wylde?" he whispered, sounding hurt. "You just left us. We thought someone had taken you, and we didn't know what to do."

"So, we did our duty," Carl told Talon in a stern tone. "When one faces fear, they do their duty, no matter how frightening it may be. No matter how pointless it may seem. We did that. Have heart, pussycat."

Talon jolted at the moniker, even though Carl had not meant insult. He nodded stiffly, looking embarrassed at his momentary show of weakness. "You are correct, Sir Carl."

"I'm sorry," I told them. "Charon showed up to take me to the Underworld, and I had no time to warn you." I quickly caught them up on the particulars of my disappearance, reassuring them that everyone in the Underworld was safe and that Anubis was dead. That all the Four Horsemen were now dead.

They stared at me with grim countenances, finding no reason to mourn the Horsemen after what they'd suffered at the hands of Conquest and War. They eyed my scythe with approval.

"Now," I said in a stern tone, "where are Yahn and Grimm? Did Namea kill my unicorn?" I asked, feeling a ripple of lust at the thought of avenging him. I would kill every single unicorn in this place if she had—

"They are with Asha," Talon said carefully, gauging my reaction, "and the other unicorns."

I froze, my eyes widening. I grabbed him by the shoulders and shook him. "Asha is alive?" I whispered, my legs feeling weak at the news. "I saw her die! She had no pulse, Talon!" Was this why Charon had been so cagey about her when I'd asked where her soul was?

Talon winced uneasily. "She...is alive, in a manner of speaking," he said, not meeting my eyes. "Once you killed Conquest, she gasped and sat back up for a moment, somehow clutching back onto her last thread of life. Namea was able to keep her alive and remove the last of the poison, but Asha is not conscious. She just lays there, barely breathing. Her heart beats less than ten times per minute."

Carl nodded sadly. "She has a warrior's heart," he said. "But she is dead. It is cruel to keep her in limbo."

She was in a coma. That was what they were describing. Some kind of death-coma if her pulse was that low. She should have been dead. Maybe Namea was feeding enough power into her to get her muscles to twitch with a semblance of life, and they were believing it to be some kind of miracle.

"I think Carl is right," I said sadly. "If she's been like that for two weeks, she's already dead. Even if she did wake, the consequences of that weak of a pulse would probably destroy her brain."

Silence stretched between us, and they both nodded. "Namea won't let anyone near her. Grimm won't leave without her. Yahn won't leave without Grimm and...Asha's body. He said it was the command you gave him. To guard her with his life."

I hung my head and nodded. "I did say something like that to him," I admitted. "So, Asha is stuck in a coma; a dream from which she can never wake—"

My voice cut off abruptly and I felt my heart skip a beat as I heard my own words in my ears. Asha was stuck in a dream, and Charon had told me to go to the Reverie—another word for daydream. Had he known what would happen to her?

He'd known about Death's scythe. He'd also said this was *as good a place as any for a Horseman to die.*

He'd shrugged off the comment as merely a warning about this dangerous place.

Then I had killed Conquest—a Horseman—here.

Charon...had known *everything.*

46

It was not a stretch of the imagination to assume there was more to his advice for me to go to the Reverie. If he'd known about Conquest's death, maybe he had known Asha's fate and had been preemptively warning me to go to the Reverie to save her.

Or I was reading too much into things. Going to the Reverie couldn't bring Asha back. The simple act of me entering the place wouldn't be enough to heal her. Maybe I needed to bring *her* to the Reverie.

But that was a dangerous, poisonous hope to hold in my heart.

Yet...

The stranger who had lured her here had told her that the Dark Horse was her destiny.

I let out a grim sigh and turned back to the Citadel. "Let's get this over with, and then we can go collect them," I said, not wanting to give them a false hope that I might be able to heal Asha. I also didn't want to kill their hope for her future. If she was days away, we didn't have time to go collect her, and my scythe only ripped holes between me and Hell. It was a terrible, necessary line to straddle, and I was reminded of my talk with Hades. He had warned me against what kind of man I could eventually become.

A savior or a destroyer.

I turned to Carl and pointed at his bone blade. "Open the Citadel, Sir Carl."

He bowed formally. "Yes, Master Temple. Welcome home. It has been too long since your blood vacationed here at your summer estate," he said in a formal recital, averting his eyes.

Talon shot me an inquisitive look and I shrugged like a hero. He smirked, nodding, and looked strangely relieved to find I was just as confused as him. Carl walked up to the entrance and stabbed Sugar's dagger into the empty air. The milky haze exploded with the sound of a thousand screams, and then evaporated with the sound of a nest of rattlesnakes.

"That's a fucked-up doorbell," Talon murmured, curling his lips up to reveal his teeth.

Carl held his claw out towards the Citadel, inviting us inside. We entered the holy, cursed, consecrated Temple grounds, and it took everything in my power to fight back the magnetic pull towards the Reverie. Gripping Death's scythe helped, and it grew warm in my palms. I reached up to grip Asha's wooden coin on my necklace, and that helped me even more. I couldn't afford to lose myself here. I had to save Asha after all this.

Either by granting her peace or waking her from her nightmare.

I strode through the opening in the massive wall, anticipating a tingling warning sensation, but it felt like any large opening—oppressive and humbling, but just a doorway.

Carl took a deep breath through his nostrils, looking at peace to be back in the holy Citadel that was usually only open once per year. "The fear smells so delicious," he murmured to himself, and then he was leading us onward. He seemed distracted and focused at the same time. I knew asking him questions about our surroundings would be pointless.

"Keep an eye on him," I breathed to Talon. He nodded, gripping his white spear warily. We followed Carl through an empty...fairgrounds, of sorts. It wasn't a village, although there were several buildings lining the roadway leading to the Reverie. Along the way, there were also several open amphitheaters for watching performances or fights. I saw numerous cooking areas with large fire pits and empty covered cauldrons that hadn't been used in some time. Near the cooking areas were dozens of wooden tables and benches, looking like the world's largest collection of picnic tables. It seemed the Elders feasted here during their celebrations. As we progressed through the Citadel, I saw more closed buildings, possibly to hold beds for resting during the celebrations. Or maybe to provide a little privacy after the Elders had a few too many drinks and found a new best friend they wanted to kiss and cuddle.

But I only gave these things cursory glances. My attention was focused solely on our ultimate destination because it was a constant struggle not to simply sprint ahead of Carl and kick down the door and let my doom consume me.

My grip on the scythe and Asha's coin helped center me, but I was still breathing heavily.

Finally, we came around the last bend in the road before we reached the Reverie, and we stopped dead in our tracks. The Reverie loomed just beyond an ancient wall of black stone that glistened like it was polished or soaked in oil.

Massive double gates made of thick, black metal bars were too narrow for any of us to squeeze through. A large black shield of the Temple Family Crest decorated the center of the gates, which would split down the middle when opening. A single word adorned the top of the gate in an elegant yet threatening font.

Reverie.

The black mansion loomed beyond, seeming to darken even the air around it, cloaking the fortress in gloom. I cocked my head at the mansion, gripping my scythe for the mental protection. Something about the place seemed...familiar. It didn't look like Chateau Falco...yet, it kind of *did*.

Kind of like how a certain car model could share a name but be produced decades apart. They weren't the same, but the similarities were just there. It was a different version of the car you knew, but definitely related.

That thought made me remember Aiden, and I felt my anger flare, so I closed my eyes and took a calming breath. Then I focused on what had actually drawn our attention in the first place—it hadn't been the Reverie.

A newly constructed crucifix had been hammered into the center of the road a dozen paces away from the gate to the Reverie. It was ten-feet-tall at the peak, and the wood was freshly cut and sawed.

A man was pinned to the top.

The man I had killed outside the cavern. The Knightmare I'd used as a lava paintbrush. The man who had stabbed Asha's mother.

Further proof of this fact was that he did not wear any armor. He was completely naked, and he had not died well. But...I had seen him crumble to black dust. I absently checked my satchel and confirmed it still held his armor. "I killed this man outside the mountain. I have his armor right here," I said, patting my satchel. A gentle breeze whispered across the black wall surrounding the Reverie, seeming to laugh at my confusion.

"You're sure it's the same man?" Talon asked. "Could he be his brother?"

I studied him, noting the cleft chin, the stringy hair, and the familiar facial structure. "That is him." I frowned. "Unless it is his *twin* brother," I admitted. I turned to the Knights. "Is this the Knightmare you sensed here?" I pressed.

They studied the man and then shrugged uncertainly. "I sense nothing from him. I sense nothing anywhere, but this seems like where he would have been."

Talon nodded his agreement, glancing back at the entrance to the Citadel as if to triangulate our position. "But if we sensed him earlier, then he had his own armor. This cannot be the Knightmare you killed, or we would not have sensed him in the first place," Talon said, frowning suspiciously.

I nodded my agreement. Which meant that this man was a twin to the Knightmare I had killed. And if that was the case, maybe I hadn't executed Nadia's murderer. Maybe this man had been the murderer.

"What I want to know, is where this man's armor wandered off to," I growled. "You guys can't sense it anywhere?"

They shook their heads.

I pursed my lips and strolled up to the gates without a word. I sliced my palm with Death's scythe and slapped it on the center of my family's crest. The gate puffed out in a cloud of smoke, completely disappearing with an audible sigh that made my heart flutter. I didn't think cutting myself had been necessary to open the gate, but it had felt proper.

Carl looked at me pensively.

I stepped past the imaginary line separating the Reverie from the Citadel and held my breath. Carl leapt to stick by my side, but Talon hung back to watch our backs. As soon as I stepped over the threshold, I gasped, noticing an epic thunderstorm overhead. Black clouds roiled and shifted, and red lightning crackled across the sky, but the storm didn't seem to be impacting us on the ground as it should. No wind or rain.

It was not natural—

Carl skidded to an abrupt halt and struck me with an arm across the chest, halting me. "Stop!" he hissed in terror. "Danger!"

47

I obeyed Carl's tone, even though the forceful blow to my chest had instantly made my anger flare up. Carl was glaring up at the Reverie, as tense as a coiled spring. He was not staring at the storm overhead.

"Four Knightmares," he whispered, flicking his tongue out to taste the air.

"I can no longer sense your armor, Sir Carl," Talon said in a dangerous purr. I turned to see that Talon had instinctively obeyed Carl's warning and had frozen in mid-step, just beyond the space where the gate had been. His head was cocked, and he was blinking at Carl with a stunned look on his face, as if not believing what he was seeing. "I can see it, but I cannot sense it," he said, sounding very frightened.

"I can sense you," Carl said, still glaring at the Reverie, ready for an ambush.

Talon leapt over the line where the gates had stood and started to let out a breath of relief, obviously sensing Carl again, but then his eyes bulged in horror. "Four Knightmares," he hissed, his ears flattening as he glared at the Reverie. He lowered his glaive and stepped up to my other side as if anticipating an ambush.

He hadn't seemed to care about the storm above either. They noticed it in brief glances, but they saw the mansion as the true danger—the four

Knightmares within, to be specific. Aiden and the three who had disappeared from their senses so long ago.

I risked a quick glance at where the gates had been and felt a wave of fear roll over my shoulders. "The ward blocks the armor bond," I growled, suddenly feeling very, very nervous about entering the Reverie. "That's why you could sense Talon outside, but he couldn't sense you. It's a one-way block."

The only four Knightmares left were the four who had supposedly disappeared almost as soon as we'd arrived in the Elder realm—Aiden and three of his cronies. I closed my eyes for a moment, squeezing the scythe's haft hard enough to make my bones ache.

"Aiden has been here the whole *time*," I growled, ignoring a crimson bolt of lightning that illuminated the Reverie in a sinister glow. Thunder boomed ominously, as if responding to my rage. "That motherfucking son of a bitch! We couldn't sense him because he slipped inside the Reverie. He knew we would hunt the last straggler Knightmare. All he had to do was wait for us to show up."

The mansion was made of shiny black stone like the wall, but on closer inspection it looked like polished obsidian. The storm only made it look more ominous, and the rumbling thunder made it sound like the mansion was breathing and growling, then shifting and moving in the flashes of crimson lightning.

As I studied the seemingly sentient monster of a building, I realized that the layout was exactly the same as Chateau Falco. The stone facade of the building was different, with taller windows and more gothic fixtures, looking more like a castle, but...

Damn. This was Chateau Falco.

"You notice it as well," Talon murmured uneasily, glancing up at the building.

I nodded. "Took me a while, but yeah. The more I look at it, the more I see the similarities."

The Reverie was like a sketch drawn from a dark memory of seeing Falco one time. On a stormy night. In the rain. While running for your life from a pack of monsters.

"There's no place like home," I growled as another peal of crimson lightning lit the roiling black sky. If I'd needed proof that Aiden was here, the malevolent storm was it. I had sent the Dark Horse spell after a strand of Aiden's hair, hunting and tracking him across the realms. Yet...I hadn't seen this storm until I entered the Reverie's property. I hadn't seen it from outside the gate. Was this some kind of pocket realm or something?

Was that why I hadn't sensed anything from my Dark Horse hunter yet?

Seeing the red lightning, I lifted my hand into the air, recalling Sugar's directions on how to capture my prey once the storm located him. Nothing happened, and I slowly lowered my hand, frowning up at the sky.

The storm seemed wilder than the one I had created, believe it or not. Had it taken on a life of its own? I could not sense my magic inside it. Had Aiden altered it in some way? Taken charge of it?

"Keep an eye on the storm," I warned the Knights. "It is not natural."

"Like the one you sent after Aiden?" Talon asked. "Is this your Dark Horse spell?"

Carl shook his head firmly. "This is not Master Temple's storm. This is the balmy, comforting embrace of the Reverie, the holiest of places." He stared up at the storm with a wondrous glaze in his eyes. "I have never felt so aroused."

Talon took a step away from him. "Never say that word again, Carl."

I nodded my agreement. "What are the Knightmares doing?" I asked. "Where are they?"

"Three are inside, but they have not moved," Carl murmured, shifting his attention towards the front door.

"One is around back," Talon said, pointing towards the side of the building. "Making that awful, terrible noise," he murmured, sounding afraid. His tail swished back and forth wildly.

I strained my ears and noticed that I did hear something. Faintly. As we listened in transfixed curiosity, it started growing louder and louder, like someone was slowly turning up the volume on a speaker, overpowering the storm, or perhaps harmonizing with it.

A haunting, straining whine danced on the spooky night air, and it took me a few moments to realize it wasn't a monster or anything insidious. It was a violin. A perversely off-key violin that sounded like it had been intentionally tuned to make the hair on the back of my neck stand on end.

Well, it looked like we were expected. I remembered how those within the perimeter of the Reverie had no problem sensing the fellow Knights beyond the gate. Talon tapped my shoulder, almost making me jump. He pointed towards the violin. "Aiden," he whispered confidently. "That one is Aiden. He doesn't appear to be approaching. The music hasn't changed locations. Just around the side of the house. I sense three more deep inside the Reverie," he said with a scowl for the mansion. "They do not approach."

I clenched my jaw and nodded. "Looks like it's time to dance, boys."

"This is definitely a trap," Talon sighed.

"Let's spring it," Carl said, extending metallic claws from his armor. The crimson lightning flashed above, making their murderous eyes twinkle like devilish stars. Then their helmets slammed down over their faces.

I summoned my Horseman armor, making sure I was ready for anything. It felt different after murdering Conquest. I felt stronger and more alert, but not necessarily double the strength. Just...more versatile. It felt like I'd upgraded my armor with better material and honed my weapons a little sharper. I noticed veins of green light through the black quartz. Yuck. Germs were gross.

Now I was going to look like a black, crusty booger. The Horseman of Snot.

Maybe I should have killed War instead.

You ready? I asked the voice attached to my Mask. *Any cool new tricks I should know about?*

She purred delightedly. *I'm still merging with Conquest's Mask, but I think you will appreciate the upgrade.*

Am I now the Horseman of Conquest as well? I asked her.

She hesitated for a few moments, considering the question. *No...and yes. He is no more. You are still Hope, but with some of his abilities. I think. It is all so very strange...*

Well, that wasn't very reassuring to hear. I'd hoped she would know exactly what the hell was going on.

But I was glad to hear that I wasn't a nasty plague doctor Horseman.

I gripped Death's scythe and felt a nostalgic smile cross my cheeks. *No problem if I use this, right? My armor isn't going to wink out of existence or anything?*

She laughed. *Oh, no, my host. The scythe feels like it was born to fit our hands. Death and Conquest now ride on Hope's shoulders...*

I shuddered at the thought, though it felt...right.

Maybe that was what Mac had meant about me being the Dark Horse. It sure hadn't helped Asha.

I squared my shoulders and pressed on towards the haunting violin. "Together," I growled.

Talon and Carl nodded eagerly.

And it almost felt like Conquest and Death nodded just as eagerly.

48

We stalked around the corner of the Reverie and spotted Aiden. He was surrounded by a ring of wooden poles like tiki torches, but the top of each pole was ornamented with a severed head. He had his eyes closed and he was playing a violin—the source of the horrible, eerie tune.

Aiden continued his lamenting dirge as we approached, pretending like he was lost in his own song and hadn't noticed our presence. He had definitely known the moment we arrived, due to the armor bond. He wore a robe and slippers, looking like we'd caught him fresh out of bed, but that obviously wasn't the case. His ankles were crossed, and he was reclining on a throne with a wistful smile on his face.

It was all carefully crafted theater, designed to break our spirit.

His throne was a heaping pile of Elder corpses that he had carefully arranged for this exact moment.

Carl's shoulders slumped and he stared at the bodies like his heart had just been torn from his chest.

Aiden opened his eyes, pretending like he'd finally noticed our arrival. He remained in a lounging position and rested the dark violin on his knee. He flashed me a roguish grin. "Brother! It's been too long!" He lazily waved the black bow at me from head-to-toe. "Love the new look. I like the green veins of bloodthirsty Conquest pulsing beneath all that Hope," he said, amused by his cleverness. "I wonder which controls you," he mused.

"You are one sick fuck, Aiden," I growled, staring at the viscera and gore dripping down the throne of corpses. The stench was atrocious. "You have no idea what you've done. The rest of the Elders will not let this offense go unpunished. I'm tempted to let them have their way with you instead of grinding my own claws into your chest cavity."

Aiden frowned, feigning hurt and confusion. "Oh, this?" he asked, gesturing with the bow at his throne. "They were very unaccommodating to weary travelers. We brought them gifts and everything, but they refused to be hospitable." He picked at a piece of intestine sticking to his leg and pursed his lips before flinging it to the side. Then he held up the bow before him, showing it off. "Do you have any idea how difficult it is to string Elder gut into a new bow? The bone part was simple enough, but stringing and drying the gut? Pfft. Even with magic, it was particularly tedious," he complained, waving the bow back and forth. He pointed the bow at the body of an Elder draped across the front of the throne. He was using that Elder's head to support his crossed ankles, so I couldn't see the face. The stomach had been torn open and disemboweled, showing us where he'd gotten the guts for his bow. I felt bile rise up in the back of my throat at the thought. Violin strings were historically made with catgut.

Aiden...had turned one of these poor bastard's guts into a bow string, all so that he could torment Carl.

I frowned. "You do know that the *strings* of the violin used to be made from catgut, not the hair of the bow."

Aiden burst out laughing. "No wonder it didn't work! Well," he said, turning to smile at Carl. "I tried very hard. So hard..."

Carl's helmet disappeared. "You will die, Aiden Temple," he rasped, still staring at the dead bodies.

Aiden frowned unhappily. "You didn't like my song," he said, lowering his gaze to the violin. It immediately exploded into kindling and then flared away in a white fire that was so hot it didn't even leave smoke in the air. He slowly lifted his eyes to Carl, and they looked horribly offended. "You know, Elder Carl, this is *exactly* the kind of inhospitality your family showed me and my friends when we asked if we could rest our feet in the

Citadel." He gestured absently at the bodies. "I gave them a piece of my mind, as you can see."

Carl took a step closer, but I gripped him by the shoulder and shook him. "He's *trying* to rile you up, Carl," I breathed. "Don't let rage rule your reason. We are missing something here. Focus. This is all a game to him."

Carl's eyes were wide around the edges as they locked onto mine. "My mother and father are on that pile of corpses," he breathed, looking frantic and furious and about a millisecond away from losing his sanity.

My heart skipped a beat as I stared into my friend's eyes. "Oh, Carl," I breathed.

Aiden cleared his throat and we spun to look back at him. "Oh, Carl," he mocked in the exact same tone I had used. He was staring directly at the Elder, grinning like a wolf. "It's not just your mother and father. I wanted to show you proper respect, after all..." He uncrossed his ankles and set them to the side, revealing the head of the Elder he'd been using as a footrest.

A female Elder stared at us with terror in her dead features.

Carl crashed to his knees and let out a terrible, agonized howl.

Aiden leaned forward and took a deep breath through his nose, looking as if he wanted to breathe in every drop of pain he was giving Carl. "Did you like your sister's song, Carl? I know I did. Especially the screams before I turned her into a proper instrument of my desire," he said, spinning the bow over the back of his knuckles. Finally, he tossed it at Carl's knees with a merciless chuckle. "Memento from the altar of the dead. It's clever because it's like our family crest, Nate. Memento Mori. But it's a memento because I tortured and killed her to make Carl a gift!" he hooted, slapping at his knee delightedly.

"You are a fucking psychopath," Talon said in a flat, emotionless tone, as if he was literally trying to define the psyche of the person before him.

Aiden frowned at Talon. "No. My parents abandoned me, so I did my best to get their attention. I'm just looking for love, you see. It never had to be this way."

Talon shook his head and thumped his spear into the grass. "Well, maybe I should take a closer look at your heart just to be sure. Maybe I can put some love in there for you."

Aiden grinned, leaning forward. "Oh, please do, Talon. When I tire of playing with you, I can tell you all about how I murdered your entire race so many years ago in Fae."

Talon abruptly stiffened and took a step back. "That...is not possible. You aren't old enough," he said, sounding deeply troubled.

Aiden rolled his eyes. "I'm older than my brother," he said, pointing at me. "You think he's the only one who learned how to gain some extra years in Fae?" He waved a hand and winked at me. "We were neighbors, brother, and you never knew it." He turned back to Talon, and I didn't know who was more hurt or furious: me or my two allies. "Now, my magic was a little wild and unpredictable back then. You'd be surprised what the Wild Side can do to an angry orphan with too much magic. I'm much more refined now, but I'm afraid I made quite the mess when I killed all your people, Talon," he said, leaning back and looking up at the broiling storm as if retrieving the memory. "That city of glass was something to behold," he told Talon with a fond smile, still staring up at the clouds. "The way all their blood spattered on the glass walls and floors and ceilings. Everything was going fine until that fucking goat-god showed up," he muttered, his smile slipping. "I knew I wasn't ready to go up against one like him. Not back then. I hadn't learned any control yet. I was a dog off his leash," he admitted with a guilty smirk. He eyed Talon with a hopeful smile. "I'm truly glad I didn't kill you that day. The irony of you becoming besties with my brother is truly priceless. Think about how fun it will be when I kill his pet dog and his pet cat! Talk about a beautiful game! I wonder what his next move will be after I skin you both alive," he said, glancing at me with an arched eyebrow. "Oh, not right now, of course. I've done quite enough for this round. I want to save *some* surprises, otherwise you will just feel numb to it all."

I wanted to rip his face off, but I knew something was very, very wrong about the situation.

His smile widened as he stared into my eyes with an approving look. "You *see* it, brother. I knew I was right to let you live. To play this game together. You know I'm being mischievous."

I nodded. "Not gonna lie. I'm having bad thoughts about you right now, wondering if I should ignore my gut feeling," I said, fighting back my desire to unleash my rage. Charon had warned me against that. This was the land of fear. The Reverie had destroyed countless Temples for some reason and, judging by how familiar Aiden was with so many dangerous magics and histories, I was betting he knew all about that. In fact, I was almost completely certain he was trying to push me into a certain action right now. He had arranged our confrontation to happen here at the Reverie for some very specific reason—to make us lose control.

He'd said repeatedly that this was some kind of grand game to him. He wasn't here to fight me. He was here to utterly destroy every single thing I knew and loved. He didn't need to make me any angrier to fight him. This was something else entirely.

49

Aiden let out a sigh and bowed his head respectfully. "Well, as much as I hate losing a particular battle, I am so incredibly proud of you for passing my little test." He smirked at Carl and Talon. "Now you are probably going to have to fight them to keep them from coming after me and setting off the little trap you know I've set for you." He rubbed his hands together excitedly. "This is delicious. I thought for sure this would be the end for you. Well played, frater."

"I am not your brother, Aiden," I growled. "Why lure us here? Why use your own Knightmare as bait? You had to know I was coming here anyway."

Aiden waved dismissively. "I didn't need the twins, but I knew that you seeing the face of the wizard you had already killed at the waterfall would rattle you. I didn't have anything else to do with him," he said with a shrug, "so I put him to use."

He hadn't said a single word about Asha.

If not Aiden, who had brought her down here and locked us inside? And how did he seem to know everything we had done while we were here? He knew about Conquest and how I'd killed the Knightmare at the waterfall, even though he'd been nowhere near either event. I knew this, too, was part of his game.

He closed his eyes and took an exaggerated deep breath, forcing himself to calm down. It was all a show. He was doing everything in his power to get a rise out of all of us. He wanted us to think he was batshit crazy, but I knew he wasn't unstable. He was meticulous.

So, what was his plan? What was I missing?

"Well, this has been grand, Nate, but I really must be off." He rose to his feet and then hopped down from the throne, throwing his hands wide as if he'd just stuck a landing after an impressive gymnastic feat. Then he bowed dramatically to Carl and Talon individually. "Oh, I almost forgot, Nate," he said, abruptly striding towards me. Talon and Carl lunged simultaneously to rip him to shreds from either side. Aiden didn't look or even break stride as his Knightmare armor whispered into place and he punched them both in the face, sending them flying. He stared into my eyes the entire time, smirking. Then he reached into his pocket and pulled out a folded piece of paper. He held it out to me, waving it in my face with a growing frown.

"Nate," he chided, sounding hurt, "you're being rude."

I continued staring into his eyes, trying to see what kind of madness had created such a broken wretch of a man. "What is your purpose?" I asked with a quizzical frown. "I can tell you don't want to hurt me. Yet."

He nodded adamantly. "Oh, absolutely not. I definitely don't want to hurt you, brother. I'm going to make you hurt yourself. If you and I threw down right now, it would be the best thirty seconds of my life. I would likely win, but you would have a minor chance of defeating me. But then... what the hell would I do with the rest of my life? There is no darkness without light, no love without pain, no joy without sorrow," he explained, looking genuinely saddened. "You are my purpose, brother. Once I'm finished with you, I don't think I'll even have a reason to live anymore," he admitted with a sad frown.

"You're telling the truth," I said, staring into his eyes. "You believe that absolutely."

He furrowed a brow and nodded. "Of course!" Then he drew a dagger and brought it crashing down towards my face. I stared into his fiery eyes without blinking, knowing this was another of his tests. His blade stopped an inch from my eyeball, crackling with power. It winked out of existence, and he grinned. "Brothers, man!" he hooted. "It's like we can read each other's minds!"

I felt like a part of *me* was going insane. I knew if I tried anything to harm him right now, it wouldn't work. Much like our last encounter outside the cemetery. It wasn't the same kind of thing as that dome of power but there was something up his sleeve that would prevent us from killing each other...

Because that was truly the last thing he wanted.

His game was not finished.

He wouldn't let us kill each other until we progressed through his madhouse of insanity.

"Where the fuck did you become so...mad?" I whispered, deciding that crazy didn't quite cut it. "I'm truly sorry for whatever it is you went through, Aiden, to make you this way."

Aiden grinned mischievously, obviously finding my confusion hilarious. Then he waved the card in my face again until it became apparent he was going to shove it in my mouth if I didn't snatch it from his hands. I grabbed it and lowered it to my side. It was a small envelope with something hard inside. I feared opening it, knowing his penchant for horrifying gifts. Like a psychopathic crow giving his lovers random shinies he stole from his travels, Aiden gave out random nightmares he'd collected on his flight through madness.

"It's an invitation to a party!" he whispered excitedly. "I want you to meet my brothers officially."

"Two of your...brothers are already dead," I told him, knowing he had sacrificed one on the crucifix and I had killed the other outside the waterfall—the twins.

Aiden scoffed and swatted my shoulder with the back of his hand in a playful, brotherly manner. "Those two were just useful idiots," he said. "I never even learned their names. I only needed three, you see."

I narrowed my eyes suspiciously, knowing this was some kind of hint for the next round of our game.

"I'm not going to your party unless you tell me why you came here to kill Elders. They were obviously not as much of a threat as everyone seemed to fear."

Aiden grinned and then bopped me on the nose with one finger.

"Fear," he mused, "is everywhere here. I wanted to see if you were strong enough to overcome it. To set down the rage or pick it up and wield it. Or if it would drive you mad like it has so many of our ancestors." He stepped back and appraised me up and down with a playful scowl. "I must admit, when I saw what you did to Conquest, I thought our little game was finally over. I was so very, very sad," he said with a dramatic pout. "I was ready to end our game when I saw you coming around the corner. The song, you see, was for your funeral, not just Carl's family." He stepped closer and peered into my eyes eagerly. "But then I saw your eyes, and I knew our game had only just begun," he whispered, sounding drunk with excitement.

"You could not have seen what I did to Conquest. You were here or we would have sensed your armor," I said, frowning.

Aiden grinned. "Ah, yes. You haven't gone inside yet," he said, gesturing at the Reverie. "The Black Chateau Falco," he said with feigned spookiness, even waggling his fingers. "You should definitely go in there before you leave. It's our summer home, apparently. The building itself is underwhelming, in a way. I think the whole noble quest thing everyone talks about is really just the journey to get here. If you will succumb to the fear. Wasn't a problem for me or my men, so I'm not sure what the big deal was. Probably one of those old traditions that loses value over time. Old families, am I right?" I stared at him, waiting. "Oh, the Reverie," he said, my blank look reminding him of the topic. "That's also part of my game, you see. You will find revelations in the Reverie. Answers you so desperately seek. Breadcrumbs as a reward for your victorious battle today! A memento for you, dear brother."

I kept my face calm and collected, knowing he was fishing for a reaction. "When I find time, Aiden," I said dismissively. "How am I supposed to play our game if I can't leave the Elder realm? You trapped me here, remember?"

Aiden frowned for the first time, looking genuinely surprised. "What?"

I felt a cold shiver run down my spine. If Aiden hadn't trapped me here, who the fuck had sealed the entrance? For some reason, I knew Aiden was not bluffing. He would have reveled in my confusion if he had been responsible. "Asha and Nadia," I said, studying him for a reaction. "The mother and daughter."

Aiden arched an eyebrow. "The human girl you had with you? I was going to ask you about her. Thought she might be some kind of secret weapon, but then Conquest killed her so easily." He shrugged. "I thought she was just a stray you brought along with you."

My heart was racing wildly. There was a third party to this insanity and even Aiden didn't know who it was. It hadn't been Anubis, because I could still sense my spell hunting in the back of my mind.

Aiden saw the confusion in my eyes and an eager smile slowly stretched across his face. "Ah. It seems we have a mystery to solve together, brother. Like Sherlock Holmes and Watson!" He frowned thoughtfully. "We should do this adventure together before we try to kill each other. Before we finish our game."

I snorted. "I'm not going on an adventure with you, Aiden," I said drily.

"Oh, boo," he complained. "Fine. Have it your way. The girl is dead anyway." He inspected the scythe in my fist with a curious look. As I watched his eyes, I saw the act he was putting on fade away to be replaced by supreme, rational, calculating intelligence. As crazy as Aiden was, he was certifiably a genius. He was powerful. He saw things most overlooked. He reached out and tapped the scythe with a fingernail. "Huh. It's a key."

I frowned at him and then glanced at Death's scythe. "A key to what?"

Aiden wasn't looking at me. He was lost in thoughts only he could follow. "Hell, obviously," he murmured, slowly reaching out to tap it again with a fingernail. It let out a faint chiming sound and he grunted. "Well, well, well. It opens doors to all *sorts* of dangerous places. Realms. Treasures. Paradises. Catacombs…" he waved a hand and then nodded satisfactorily; his curiosity sated. "You should keep it. It can get you out of here since you don't know the other way yet."

"What is the other way?" I asked.

He smirked, shaking his head. "No way, brother. That would be cheating. I won't show you my hand yet! You have to go into the Reverie to find out." He glanced up at the sky again, humming as he studied the storm. "Wicked weather here," he commented. "Your doing? Is this the giant explosion you did in the woods?"

I studied him with a blank expression, wondering how he had seen any of the things he'd seen during our travels. Aiden knew of the Dark Horse spell and assumed this was it, even though he didn't look troubled by it. I shook my head. "Nope."

"Well. Until next time," he said before patting me on the arm. Then he strode past me, humming to himself as he walked. He paused to speak over his shoulder. I turned to look at him, but he wasn't facing me. He held up a finger as he turned his head to look at me sidelong. "Don't forget to go inside. Answers reside in the Reverie. Daydreams are often the origins of nightmares," he said with an amused smirk.

Then he continued on, humming happily. Between one moment and the next, he winked out of existence.

50

The moment Aiden left, Talon and Carl let out furious snarls and leapt to their feet, as if they'd been pinned down since Aiden hit them. They were wild around the eyes, looking in every direction for the man they wanted to kill more than any other.

My brother.

"Easy, guys," I told them. "Easy. Aiden knows how to get in your heads, so we need to learn how to use ours to outsmart him. He will die for what he's done, but we won't beat him with anger or vengeance. That's exactly what he wants you to do—lose control."

Talon took a calming breath, closing his eyes. Then he took several more until he was back in control. Then he opened his eyes with a frown. "I can no longer sense any of the Knightmares," he said, frowning.

Carl nodded his agreement, but his eyes were flat and lifeless. "They are gone." Then he turned to look at the pile of dead bodies. His family. "Could you give me a few minutes to say goodbye?" he asked in that frightening empty tone, staring down at the violin bow Aiden had made for him.

I glanced at Talon, silently asking if he thought that was a good idea. He nodded hesitantly.

"Of course, Carl. I'm going to go check out the Reverie with Talon. Just a look. I want to see if there is a way out of here. We'll meet you out front in five minutes."

Carl, so lost in his sorrow, didn't even argue with me for saying I was going to enter the Reverie. I thought that would snap him out of his grief, wanting to come and protect me.

"You sure that's a good idea, Nate?" Talon asked me, shuddering at the memory of Aiden's schemes. I didn't know if Aiden had truly killed all of Talon's people, but he'd definitely known enough details to bluff his way through it just to break Talon's stoicism. Just because it was possible didn't mean Aiden had been telling the truth.

On the other hand, I would not put it past him. It was a coin flip.

"You said the Knightmares were inside earlier and they were fine. They've been living here for weeks with no problem. I think I can risk a careful peek without killing myself."

Talon sighed but nodded.

We made our way to the front door and found it unlocked. I took a deep breath, held it, and then shoved it open, gripping Death's scythe over my shoulder to swing at even the faintest movement. The door opened on silent hinges into a dark hallway of black marble, black walls, black paint, black vases...

Everything was black, as weird as that sounded. And I began to get a very strange feeling in my gut. A whisper of a memory. The entryway was exactly the same size and layout as the one in Chateau Falco, it was just completely black. The side table. The bouquet of black roses sticking out of the black vase. The walls. The floors. The few paintings.

Talon hissed and shoved me behind him, leveling his white spear at a bloody man leaning against the wall.

He was in no shape to harm anyone. He only had a short time left on this earth. What confused me was that he wasn't a Knightmare. I couldn't see him clearly in the dark interior, so I summoned a ball of flame, illuminating the foyer.

I took one look at the man and gasped in sudden recognition.

"Matthias!" I shouted. "What the fuck are *you* doing here?"

Talon almost dropped his spear in surprise. Then he lifted it back up and started sweeping the perimeter of the room, searching for traps or more hidden bodies.

"Oh, thank god," Matthias sobbed upon seeing me. I rushed over and knelt down beside my ancient ancestor. I grabbed his arm gently, searching for a part that didn't look beaten, broken, bruised, or slashed. One of his eyes was swollen and he was bleeding from numerous serious wounds. Most of his fingers had been broken and his legs had been beaten to battered pulp, preventing him from escaping on foot. He looked up at me with his functioning eye and began to cry. "Please let me die, Nate," he whispered, drooling. "I don't want Aiden to hurt me any more!"

Good god. This was the *gift* Aiden had left me. A broken shell of a once-great mind. It hadn't been enough to let a madman live out his days in peace with his broken mind. Aiden had given him a broken body to match.

"Nate," Talon said, drawing my attention. I looked up quickly to see him pointing at a wall-to-wall black mirror on the opposite side of the foyer. Though it shined, it did not cast a reflection of Talon, who was standing right in front of it. He slowly lifted his spear to point at an adjacent wall. At a message written in blood. *EXIT!* the crimson letters said, with a smiley face and a giant arrow pointing at the glossy, non-reflective mirror. Talon extended the tip of his spear towards it and the end disappeared within the mirror.

My eyes widened in surprise. Talon pulled it back out and checked the end of his spear. He met my eyes and shrugged, letting me know it was fine. Some kind of portal? But to where? Was that the way out Charon had hinted at? The only way out is through. To face your fear.

To walk into the abyss.

The bloody love note on the wall was obviously from Aiden, and I knew he didn't want me to die by falling down into the abyss. He wanted to destroy me. It was probably legit.

I turned back to Matthias. He would know. "What are you doing here, Old One?" I whispered gently.

Matthias stared ahead at nothing, looking lost in his own nightmare, his non-swollen eye dancing with madness. He had been known as the Mad Hatter, after all. And Aiden had told me that many of our ancestors had been driven mad by the Elder realm. Charon had hinted at it as well. Was...that what had happened to Matthias? What sowed the seeds of his eventual madness?

"Matthias?" I pressed. He flinched and looked up at me, so I repeated my question.

He trembled with fear, but he finally responded in a haunted whisper. I quickly realized he was missing some of his teeth, judging by his slurring. "I came here after I traveled the world for a time," he whispered. "I wanted solitude. To get away from it all after..." he trailed off and let out a miserable sob, unable to say his son, Ichabod's name. I swallowed guiltily, hoping he didn't recall the particulars of his son's demise. "But the world was too loud, so I came back to our Summer home, the Reverie." He smiled nostalgically, remembering childhood memories. "No one knew I was here because the Elders remember not to step foot inside. This is a sacred, holy place, after all," he said with a wink. Then he laughed harshly, like it was a long-standing inside joke with our family. It was, but I did not know the joke. "Then *he* came," Matthias whispered, and his eyes danced with fear as his body tensed. "Aiden was such a sweet boy, at first," Matthias whispered, coughing on his own blood. "I gave him the last set of masks, hoping it would make him happy," he said, his eyes growing distant. "It did *not* make him happy, Nate. He said they were worthless to him unless the Four Horsemen died." I felt my heart drop into my stomach.

Oh, no. Matthias had given Aiden a new set of Horseman Masks. What the living fuck? Aiden had wanted the Four Horsemen dead. Had he orchestrated their deaths? Callie had seen him in Kansas City, and that was where the first Horseman—Death—had been killed. But...how could he have set something like that up?

"Nate?" Matthias wheezed, his body starting to slump and his eye fluttering closed. "I...was wrong. Aiden will never be happy, because he is... well, he's quite *mad*." He let out a laugh, coughing up some blood. "But this is the Reverie," he whispered, smiling woozily, "we're all mad here."

"How do we *leave*, Matthias?" I asked, brushing some hair back from his eyes, knowing I only had seconds.

He weakly jerked his chin to the strange black mirror. "That goes back to Chateau Falco. This place is her echo, although the Reverie has no Beast. She is a drafty, lonely, shell of her former self. She needs a Beast, but they don't grow on trees, do they?" he said, laughing at his own joke.

I flinched, thinking of Ruin living inside...the tree at Chateau Falco. In a way, he did grow on a tree. Or squatted in one, at least. And since he was Falco's son, I might have a place for him here.

With a final, bubbling wheeze, Matthias Temple died.

"OHHHHH BROTHER!" Aiden's voice boomed from the front lawn.

Talon and I ran for the door.

Aiden and three strangers stood near the gate to the Reverie, far enough away to prevent me from immediately murdering them. I skidded to a halt and slapped a hand against Talon's chest as I saw four suits of armor lying on the ground between me and Aiden's crew. They were not black or white. They were gray and rusted, dented and mangled, and they looked completely unusable. Ever. They were even steaming.

Aiden had told me he *only needed four*, leading me to think he'd been referring to the suits of armor.

He had been talking about the Horseman Masks he'd tortured Matthias into giving him.

"Why did they take their armor off," Talon asked warily.

I was too late to stop it, so I just pointed. "That's why, Talon. They don't need the armor anymore."

Aiden and his three wizards pressed their brand-new Horseman Masks to their faces, and a deafening bell tolled across the Elder realm, sending a wave of dust to pepper us. I wiped at my eyes and looked back up at the gate. Four new Horsemen stared back at me, but I had eyes only for one.

Aiden's Mask was a grinning clown face with squinting eyes. "The suits of armor were my fishing lures to get you here," Aiden said with a laugh. "Bait. But you can have the Reverie and all its deadly treasures. You've got time before our next round. Now, let the *real* games begin, Brother. Horsemen versus Horsemen. Oh, and don't forget the dinner party invitation," he reminded me, tapping his chest to indicate the card he had given me.

Then the four of them latched hands, connecting to Aiden, before they winked out of existence, leaving only Aiden's victorious, echoing laughter in their place. And the four ruined suits of armor.

Carl came running from around the corner, looking ready to unleash hell. He scanned us for injuries and then pointed towards the Citadel. "Yahn is coming!" he hissed. "And he is not alone."

"Good," I growled, pounding my fist into my palm. "We can send them through the portal in the Reverie. Get them back to Chateau Falco so I can figure out how the hell to stop my brother," I snarled, gritting my teeth.

Then I started pacing anxiously, struggling to process the insanity of Aiden's machinations. "There can't be three sets of Horsemen," I muttered under my breath.

The Biblical Four are all dead, Hope, my Mask whispered in my mind, sounding shaken. *The Dread Four consumed them, making them count as only one set of Horsemen in the world. There was a power vacuum that needed to be filled...*

51

Talon grabbed me by the shoulder, snapping me out of my thoughts. "You need to see this," he said urgently, turning me to face the Citadel. I heard galloping. A lot of galloping. I walked back to the entrance to the Reverie where the gate had once been and blinked to see hundreds of unicorns racing up the roadway of the deserted festival grounds.

Yahn rode on Grimm, and another Knight in white armor with their helmet on rode atop a familiar white unicorn. "Namea?" I asked, frowning. "What the hell is going on?" I demanded as the herd of horses skidded to a halt just outside the wall. They glanced up at the crucifix but dismissed it before turning to stare at us.

All of them. Hundreds of murderous, hungry unicorns stared at us like a hive mind.

Carl frowned guiltily. "I forgot to lock the door to the Citadel. Sorry, Master Temple."

"No," I said, shaking my head. "Who the hell is that?" I demanded, pointing at the second Knight.

"I think you know," Talon said with a hollow smile. "If Namea is here..."

Yahn waved at us. "We tracked you through the armor bond, but you disappeared a short while ago, so we just kept going in this direction. We flew," he clarified.

Grimm locked eyes with me and then pointed his head sideways at Namea with a shit-eating grin, silently bragging about his girlfriend. Despite the horrors we'd recently endured, I smiled at him and rolled my eyes.

Then I turned to glare at the new Knight. "I told you I was unicorn bait," Asha's voice said, and then her helmet whispered away. She shook out her hair and grinned at me.

A flashback of my last few moments with her hit me like a truck and my legs gave out. Talon caught me, chuckling. "Easy, Wylde. Easy."

"How...did you know?" I whispered, staring at Asha like she was a figment of my imagination.

"Just a guess after I saw Namea," Talon said. "I told you she refused to leave the girl's side. And I felt a new suit of armor approaching us with Yahn."

Asha had hopped down off her unicorn and was running towards me with a guilty frown on her face. "I'm so sorry! Are you hurt?" And then she saw the wooden medallion hanging around my neck. The creepy smile she'd carved for me. "You kept it!" she shrieked excitedly. And then she wrapped her arms around me and gave me a tight hug.

"Of course I kept it, Asha," I whispered, blinking through tears. Then I took a deep breath and closed my eyes. "I'm so happy you're alive," I whispered, hugging her back.

She pulled away and grinned at me, wiping her eyes with her hands as she awkwardly rose up on her toes and then thumped back down on her heels. She beamed at my necklace one more time and gave me a pleased nod. "I don't know what happened. I remember you kissing my forehead and then...I woke up like this," she said. "Maybe I really did bond with the armor by the waterfall, but I was just doing it wrong the whole time. I don't know. I'm just a freaking kid!"

I shook my head and pointed up at the man on the crucifix, finally understanding where his armor had vanished to. "That's the man who... hurt your mom, Asha. He had a twin brother, apparently." Her eyes widened in surprise, and then I saw her trying to figure out the rest of the mystery. She gasped. "Oh! When I cut my finger on the helmet! It was his!"

I shrugged. "He refuses to answer my questions," I said, scowling up at him. "That's my guess, though. I think you accidentally bonded—or partially bonded—his armor before he grabbed it, and it gave him all sorts of problems. That's why Aiden killed him, and that decision finally broke the shared bond, sending the second set of armor to you." I shook my head in wonder. "I think that partial bond is what kept you alive for so long when everyone thought you were dead."

Asha shuddered at the memory. "I don't remember *that*. I just remember...a lot of bad dreams," she whispered. "Then I woke up wearing this."

Grimm cleared his throat. "To elaborate, she woke up out of a coma with no warning, glowing and floating above the table like a damned hovercraft. Scared the living shit out of us."

Namea studied us in silence. Her intelligent eyes darted from face-to-face, focusing on us when we spoke, but she didn't say anything.

But if Grimm was here, that meant he hadn't tried to bang her. "Hey, Grimm. I really need to talk to you about something."

He nudged the white unicorn with his rump, and she snarled back at him. "This is Namea. The one I told you about by the waterfall. You haven't been formally introduced."

"I admired your work on Conquest, Dark Horse," Namea told me, her voice ringing like bells. "The screams you drew out of him made my heart quiver. It was music to my ears. Honor to the Dark Horse!"

The entire herd of unicorns repeated the cheer and then stamped a hoof in perfect unison, making me jump. I glanced at Asha sidelong. "Did you tell them that nickname?"

She shook her head. "She seemed to already know it," she breathed. "I'm pretty sure everyone saw your spell. That or Grimm was boasting about it."

Grimm was pointedly not meeting my gaze, scraping his hoof on the ground like he'd found a particularly remarkable pebble for the vitally important rock collection he'd started that very second.

I turned to smile at Namea and dipped my chin in gratitude. "Thank you, Namea. I admire how you almost whipped the hell out of my unicorn, Grimm. It was very entertaining to watch him run away from you."

She shook her mane proudly. "Any time."

"But I'm most grateful for you healing and caring for my friend, Asha," I said, wrapping an arm around her shoulders. "She is very special to me."

Namea smiled adoringly at Asha and turned her head to show off the bloody blue ribbon tied in her mane. It looked better on her than it had on Grimm. "She is a special girl," Namea agreed. "I saw how you wept over her and then the raw chaos you inflicted upon her attacker. You will always be a friend to the unicorns, Dark Horse."

The unicorns did their salute stomp again, and I smiled awkwardly. This next part was going to ruin our friendship. "So, Namea. You should know that Grimm isn't aware of your...mating habits," I finally said, blushing as I felt everyone staring at me. "And I really need him not to be decapitated. I'm a Horseman and well, he is my horse."

"Wait. What?" Grimm asked, cocking his head as he forgot all about his rock collecting hobby. "Who the hell said anything about decapitation?"

Namea narrowed her eyes and lowered her horn towards me, displeased that I had ruined her surprise. Asha stepped in front of me and waggled a finger at Namea. "You put your horn back up right now, missy! I'll have none of that. Grimm is my friend. He saved my life."

"What the hell?" Grimm demanded, turning to face Namea in a more defensive stance.

Namea stamped a hoof and let out a frustrated neigh. "Fine," she said irritably, but her voice was hauntingly sweet and gentle at the same time, so she sounded like an angry princess. "I will not decapitate him after we mate."

Grimm stared at her in stunned disbelief. "Hold on a second. Is that why you made me wait?"

She shook her mane. "I was tired," she said in her honey-sweet voice. "From healing Asha."

"And the decapitation bit?" Grimm demanded. "Asha's been awake for days now. You've been tired for days?"

Namea shook her mane again. "I wanted to meet the Dark Horse before I made any hasty decisions. And you called my rump thick. I...liked that," she admitted, sounding mildly embarrassed. "If I decapitated you, I'd have no one else to tell me my rump is thick. That is all."

Asha scowled at her. "You told me it was because the first thing he did in the fight was to go check on me after I got hurt. And then he went to help you punish my attacker. You said, and I quote, *he looked so cute when he was stabbing Conquest.*"

Namea snorted and stamped a hoof. "Did I? Can't recall," she said absently. "Anyway, thanks to the Dark Horse and Grimm, we can now enter the forest again. This is a great gift. Better hunting in the forest."

She was referring to Sugar being dead. I risked a glance at Carl, but he seemed lost in his own thoughts, probably thinking of all his other dead family members. I sighed, nodding.

I turned to Asha. "Are you sure you want the armor? Earlier, you said you didn't want it. Even for protection," I reminded her.

She nodded. "That was before...everything," she said, squaring her shoulders. "And there are different ways to fight. I am not defenseless. Carl taught me how to use this," she said, pulling out her bone dagger.

I grunted. "A few days of stabbing practice won't help against—"

She flung her hands out and seven blinding blades of light struck the crucified man high above us, hitting both wrists, ankles, throat, and then one in each nipple. Carl let out a startled laugh. My eyes bulged and I licked my lips. "I guess you learn fast?"

She smiled and my heart skipped a beat. There was something... angelic about her, like a good spirit in the flesh. Her bright nature had always been there, but something about the armor was highlighting it. Polishing it. She was gaining confidence.

"When I was dreaming, the armor seemed to speak to me, teaching me things. Guiding me. Of course, I didn't know it was the armor until I had woken up," she admitted. She lifted her gauntlet up to her face and slowly twisted her wrist, rolling her fingers like she'd just taken a double-dose of mushrooms. "I do not think you truly realize what these suits are for. What they can do. They are not just protection and power. They are knowledge. Wisdom. Life. Heartache. Pain. Love." Her eyes focused back on me. "I think the other knights left impressions in them. I think I've been speaking to one of the original Knights—"

52

The storm abruptly exploded across the sky, silencing all conversation as it grew by an order of magnitude. Then that new, enhanced storm condensed directly above me, sucking inwards to a tight knot of black clouds and crackling red lightning. I could feel it. The Dark Horse spell had found its prey.

I sensed everyone staring at me, nervously. I cleared my throat and turned to face Talon. "Gather everyone here on the steps of my summer home," I said.

And then I motioned Carl to follow me. I walked into the dark mansion. Carl noticed the dead body of Matthias, and I was surprised to see him bow his head in a respectful gesture.

The storm raged outside, and I knew it was almost time for me to leave. To see what the Dark Horse spell had discovered. My mind was a storm of worries, mirroring the chaos outside.

The Biblical Four Horsemen were gone, and Aiden had a new band of Horsemen of his own; an evil parody of a brother stealing his brother's toys.

I didn't know who Anubis had been working for. Himself? Aiden? Whomever my Dark Horse spell had located? And now he was dead, which was likely going to cause all sorts of unintended consequences for me.

And Aiden had destroyed four sets of armor. I wasn't sure if they were salvageable, but they hadn't looked like they were. Would Alex be upset?

Matthias was dead.

But I now had the sinister Reverie to explore. A black mansion of strange power that was the exact opposite of the white mansion Matthias had once built for himself in Fae. My new summer home, even though I could sense it was incredibly dangerous.

But there was one happy ending in all the chaos. My friends had survived Hell, and Asha was a brand-new Knight. I hadn't saved her. She had saved herself. All my friends had saved themselves. That burden I always carried on my shoulders, fearing for them...

Was growing lighter.

And then there was the card Aiden had given me. The invitation. I shuddered at the thought as another rumble shook the walls of the Reverie, telling me to hurry. I cleared my mind and I walked up to the black mirror that was not a mirror. I stared at the shiny black surface and saw absolutely no reflection.

I glanced back at Carl. "They say when you stare into the abyss, the abyss stares back."

He studied me for a few moments. "Who is 'they'?" he asked, genuinely curious.

"I have no idea, Carl," I said. "Let me go see what the abyss has to say," and then I stepped into the darkness. The inky blackness touched my skin, and I waited to feel something...icky. Instead, I found myself suddenly standing in my mansion back in St. Louis. Falco purred in welcome, and I felt a sense of relief from the sentient mansion.

I let out a sigh of relief. "Falco, you minx!" I hooted. "God damn, I've missed you!"

The house shuddered approvingly, agreeing with the sentiment. It was almost like she'd been holding her breath, and she was finally letting it out, relieved to have me inside of her again...

Okay. Not like that—whatever.

"How do you feel about a bunch of homicidal unicorns taking over our lawn care?" I asked her, shaking off the awkward thought.

Falco purred agreeably.

I smiled. "Okay. Expect company and keep the grounds on high alert. I'll be back soon."

I slipped back through the portal and promptly found myself back in Reverie. Carl grinned in relief. "What did the abyss have to say?"

I smiled at him. "It said welcome home. Get everyone through the portal and tell them to hunker down. The unicorns can come, too," I told him, motioning for him to follow me outside. I would come back to this place later.

The front steps were crowded as everyone anxiously stared up at the sky. The dark clouds had condensed into a spinning ring of black smoke, striated with continuous crimson lightning, looking like some maniacal science experiment. I saw the Dark Horse galloping around and around the ring of clouds, making them spin faster and faster, the lightning brighter and brighter, his hooves ringing with great booms of thunder.

It was time. My hunter had found my prey. I grinned eagerly.

"Follow Carl!" I shouted at everyone.

"What about you?" Namea shouted over the booming, definitely unnatural storm as Carl, Talon, and Yahn started ushering the herd of unicorns through the front door of the mansion.

I checked my pocket, feeling the card Aiden had given me. I hadn't opened it yet, and I wanted to make sure it was secure. I met Namea's eyes and lifted my hand into the air. "The Dark Horse is hungry. I'm going hunting, Namea. Take care of them while I'm gone."

Grimm stormed over and nudged me unhappily. "While *we* are gone… cock-block," he muttered, eyeing Namea's thick rump with regret.

I laughed and climbed onto his back.

Namea smiled and dipped her horn at me in a bow of respect. She winked at Grimm, turned, and then flicked up her tail as she glanced back over her shoulder. It was the equivalent of her flashing Grimm—gross— because Grimm went wild, rearing up on two feet and letting out a scream that harmonized with the raging storm above.

A bolt of crimson lightning flashed down from the sky and struck my outstretched hand. Rather than incinerating me, the lightning wrapped around my hand like a snake, and I squeezed my fist closed, gripping it tightly.

"Let's go get 'em, boss!" Grimm yelled. The lightning yanked us up into the sky, hurling us both into the pitch-black clouds. I gasped as we merged with the storm, galloping across the clouds and leaping through realms as swift as lightning bolts.

Before I knew it, we were struck back down to the ground with a peal of crimson lightning that hit the ground like an angry god's hammer, barely missing a colossal tree looming nearby. We stood before the entrance of an earthen cavern. Grimm turned in a slow circle as the storm above rapidly dissipated, searching for danger.

"Yggdrasil," I said, frowning, recognizing the giant tree we'd almost hit. It didn't seem like the Dark Horse had found anyone.

"I think your spell is broken, Nate," Grimm said.

I hopped off his back and summoned Death's scythe. I felt a strange tugging sensation urging me towards the cave. The spell must have trapped my prey inside. I complied, ready to summon my armor if things got hairy. "Wait here, Grimm. Watch for a trap."

"What are the odds you're dumb enough to get trapped in a cave twice in the same adventure?" Grimm asked me.

I chuckled and held up the scythe. "At least I can use the scythe to rip a hole to Hell if this is a trap. I don't yet know how to use it to rip holes to other places. I'll use Hell as a layover and then beg Hades to send me back home."

"While I sit here like an idiot, waiting for you," he replied.

"Look on the bright side," I told him, speaking over my shoulder as I walked into the cave. "At least you're not banging Namea."

He shouted a curse at me, but I kept walking into the dark cave. I sensed no danger, but I did start to feel a lot of power just ahead of me.

I hadn't wanted to frighten Grimm, so I hadn't told him what the cave was. Well, what I suspected.

Mimir's well. The same place Odin had traded his eye to learn all the magic and runes in existence. Odin was also known in stories to appear as a hooded wanderer. Had he been the one to trap me in the Elder realm? And was that a sign he was on the wrong side or was it his way of saving me from something much, much worse down the road?

The hooded stranger had warned Asha that the Dark Horse would be her destiny, and, in a way, it had. But that also meant he'd known about the

Dark Horse spell I would use. He'd known from the very beginning when he led her into the cave.

Which meant he knew I was here.

Or...insert crazy plot-twist number three: I'd been led here on purpose...by Aiden Temple.

I finally rounded a corner and came upon a large glowing well.

A hooded figure had his arms propped on the wall of the well and was leaning over it, looking down into the glowing liquid. They looked too tall to be Odin. Too tall to be Aiden. Unless his plot-twist was to wear lifts in his shoes and really mess with my head.

If Aiden had come down here to obtain the power of Mimir's well, the Horseman ability he'd picked up would be the least of my worries. The least of the world's worries.

"Turn around or I'll kill you right now," I warned, "whoever the hell you are."

The figure slowly turned to face me, and it looked like they were in great pain. With the glow behind them, I could not make out their face. I summoned up a ball of light in my free hand, gripping Death's scythe with the other.

My magic illuminated the last face I had expected to see here.

And apparently Team Temple needed to adopt a vision plan on our corporate insurance, because where the person's eye should have been was a bloody empty socket.

"Talk about a confusing cliffhanger," I said, staring at Quinn MacKenna.

Despite the blood oozing down her face, she gave me a very weak smile, looking like she was on her last legs. "Well, if it isn't the Dark Horse, himself," she whispered. "What took ye so long? Actually, nevermind. I don't care."

I stared at her in stunned disbelief. "What are *you*—"

"Isn't it obvious?" Quinn gestured to her gaping eye wound. "Anyway, what are the chances ye have a flask on ye? Because I could *really* use a drink."

Nate Temple will return in 2022...

*Turn the page to read a sample of <u>UNCHAINED</u> - Feathers and Fire Series Book 1, or **BUY ONLINE (FREE with Kindle Unlimited subscription)**. Callie Penrose is a wizard in Kansas City, MO who hunts monsters for the Vatican. She meets Nate Temple, and things devolve from there...*

(Note: Callie appears in the TempleVerse after Nate's book 6, TINY GODS...Full chronology of all books in the TempleVerse shown on the 'Books by Shayne Silvers' page)

TRY: UNCHAINED (FEATHERS AND FIRE #1)

The rain pelted my hair, plastering loose strands of it to my forehead as I panted, eyes darting from tree to tree, terrified of each shifting branch, splash of water, and whistle of wind slipping through the nightscape around us. But...I was somewhat *excited*, too.

Somewhat.

"Easy, girl. All will be well," the big man creeping just ahead of me, murmured.

"You said we were going to get ice cream!" I hissed at him, failing to compose myself, but careful to keep my voice low and my eyes alert. "I'm not ready for this!" I had been trained to fight, with my hands, with weapons, and with my magic. But I had never taken an active role in a hunt before. I'd always been the getaway driver for my mentor.

The man grunted, grey eyes scanning the trees as he slipped through the tall grass. "And did we not get ice cream before coming here? Because I think I see some in your hair."

"You know what I mean, Roland. You tricked me." I checked the tips of my loose hair, saw nothing, and scowled at his back.

"The Lord does not give us a greater burden than we can shoulder."

I muttered dark things under my breath, wiping the water from my eyes. Again. My new shirt was going to be ruined. Silk never fared well in the rain. My choice of shoes wasn't much better. Boots, yes, but distressed, *fashionable* boots. Not work boots designed for the rain and mud. Definitely not monster hunting boots for our evening excursion through one of Kansas City's wooded parks. I realized I was forcibly distracting myself, keeping my mind busy with mundane thoughts to avoid my very real anxiety. Because whenever I grew nervous, an imagined nightmare always—

A church looming before me. Rain pouring down. Night sky and a glowing moon overhead. I was all alone. Crying on the cold, stone steps, an infant in a cardboard box—

I forced the nightmare away, breathing heavily. "You know I hate it when you talk like that," I whispered to him, trying to regain my composure. I wasn't angry with him, but was growing increasingly uncomfortable with our situation after my brief flashback of fear.

"Doesn't mean it shouldn't be said," he said kindly. "I think we're close. Be alert. Remember your training. Banish your fears. I am here. And the Lord is here. He always is."

So, he had noticed my sudden anxiety. "Maybe I should just go back to the car. I know I've trained, but I really don't think—"

A shape of fur, fangs, and claws launched from the shadows towards me, cutting off my words as it snarled, thirsty for my blood.

And my nightmare slipped back into my thoughts like a veiled assassin, a wraith hoping to hold me still for the monster to eat. I froze, unable to move. Twin sticks of power abruptly erupted into being in my clenched fists, but my fear swamped me with that stupid nightmare, the sticks held at my side, useless to save me.

Right before the beast's claws reached me, it grunted as something batted it from the air, sending it flying sideways. It struck a tree with another grunt and an angry whine of pain.

I fell to my knees right into a puddle, arms shaking, breathing fast.

My sticks crackled in the rain like live cattle prods, except their entire length was the electrical section — at least to anyone other than me. I could hold them without pain.

Magic was a part of me, coursing through my veins whether I wanted it or not, and Roland had spent many years teaching me how to master it. But I had never been able to fully master the nightmare inside me, and in moments of fear, it always won, overriding my training.

The fact that I had resorted to weapons — like the ones he had trained me with — rather than a burst of flame, was startling. It was good in the fact that my body's reflexes knew enough to call up a defense even without my direct command, but bad in the fact that it was the worst form of defense for the situation presented. I could have very easily done as Roland did, and hurt it from a distance. But I hadn't. Because of my stupid block.

Roland placed a calloused palm on my shoulder, and I flinched. "Easy, see? I am here." But he did frown at my choice of weapons, the reprimand silent but loud in my mind. I let out a shaky breath, forcing my fear back down. It was all in my head, but still, it wasn't easy. Fear could be like that.

I focused on Roland's implied lesson. Close combat weapons — even magically-powered ones — were for last resorts. I averted my eyes in very real shame. I knew these things. He didn't even need to tell me them. But when that damned nightmare caught hold of me, all my training went out the window. It haunted me like a shadow, waiting for moments just like this, as if trying to kill me. A form of psychological suicide? But it was why I constantly refused to join Roland on his hunts. He knew about it. And although he was trying to help me overcome that fear, he never pressed too hard.

Rain continued to sizzle as it struck my batons. I didn't let them go, using them as a totem to build my confidence back up. I slowly lifted my eyes to nod at him as I climbed back to my feet.

That's when I saw the second set of eyes in the shadows, right before they flew out of the darkness towards Roland's back. I threw one of my batons and missed, but that pretty much let Roland know that an unfriendly was behind him. Either that or I had just failed to murder my mentor at point-blank range. He whirled to confront the monster, expecting another aerial assault as he unleashed a ball of fire that splashed over the tree at chest height, washing the trunk in blue flames. But this monster was tricky. It hadn't planned on tackling Roland, but had merely jumped out of the darkness to get closer, no doubt learning from its fallen comrade, who still lay unmoving against the tree behind me.

His coat shone like midnight clouds with hints of lightning flashing in the depths of thick, wiry fur. The coat of dew dotting his fur reflected the moonlight, giving him a faint sheen as if covered in fresh oil. He was tall, easily hip height at the shoulder, and barrel chested, his rump much leaner than the rest of his body. He — I assumed male from the long, thick mane around his neck — had a very long snout, much longer and wider than any werewolf I had ever seen. Amazingly, and beyond my control, I realized he was beautiful.

But most of the natural world's lethal hunters were beautiful.

He landed in a wet puddle a pace in front of Roland, juked to the right, and then to the left, racing past the big man, biting into his hamstrings on his way by.

A wash of anger rolled over me at seeing my mentor injured, dousing my fear, and I swung my baton down as hard as I could. It struck the beast in the rump as it tried to dart back to cover — a typical wolf tactic. My blow singed his hair and shattered bone. The creature collapsed into a puddle of mud with a yelp, instinctively snapping his jaws over his shoulder to bite whatever had hit him.

I let him. But mostly out of dumb luck as I heard Roland hiss in pain, falling to the ground.

The monster's jaws clamped around my baton, and there was an immediate explosion of teeth and blood that sent him flying several feet away into the tall brush, yipping, screaming, and staggering. Before he slipped out of sight, I noticed that his lower jaw was simply *gone*, from the contact of his saliva on my electrified magical batons. Then he managed to limp into the woods with more pitiful yowls, but I had no mind to chase him. Roland — that titan of a man, my mentor — was hurt. I could smell copper in the air, and knew we had to get out of here. Fast. Because we had anticipated only one of the monsters. But there had been two of them, and they hadn't been the run-of-the-mill werewolves we had been warned about. If there were two, perhaps there were more. And they were evidently the prehistoric cousin of any werewolf I had ever seen or read about.

Roland hissed again as he stared down at his leg, growling with both pain and anger. My eyes darted back to the first monster, wary of another attack. It *almost* looked like a werewolf, but bigger. Much bigger. He didn't move, but I saw he was breathing. He had a notch in his right ear and a jagged scar on his long snout. Part of me wanted to go over to him and torture him. Slowly. Use his pain to finally drown my nightmare, my fear. The fear that had caused Roland's injury. My lack of inner-strength had not only put me in danger, but had hurt my mentor, my friend.

I shivered, forcing the thought away. That was *cold*. Not me. Sure, I was no stranger to fighting, but that had always been in a ring. Practicing. Sparring. Never life or death.

But I suddenly realized something very dark about myself in the chill, rainy night. Although I was terrified, I felt a deep ocean of anger manifest inside me, wanting only to dispense justice as I saw fit. To use that rage to battle my own demons. As if feeding one would starve the other, reminding me of the Cherokee Indian Legend Roland had once told me.

An old Cherokee man was teaching his grandson about life. "A fight is going on inside me," he told the boy. "It is a terrible fight between two wolves. One is evil — he is anger, envy, sorrow, regret, greed, arrogance, self-pity, guilt, resentment, inferiority, lies, false pride, superiority, and ego." After a few moments to make sure he had the boy's undivided attention, he continued.

"The other wolf is good — he is joy, peace, love, hope, serenity, humility, kindness, benevolence, empathy, generosity, truth, compassion, and faith. The same fight is going on inside of you, boy, and inside of every other person, too."

The grandson thought about this for a few minutes before replying. "Which wolf will win?"

The old Cherokee man simply said, "The one you feed, boy. The one you feed..."

And I felt like feeding one of my wolves today, by killing this one...

Get the full book ONLINE! http://www.shaynesilvers.com/l/38952

Turn the page to read a sample of **WHISKEY GINGER** *- Phantom Queen Diaries Book 1, or* **BUY ONLINE.** *Quinn MacKenna is a black magic arms dealer from Boston, and her bark is almost as bad as her bite.*

TRY: WHISKEY GINGER (PHANTOM QUEEN DIARIES # 1)

The pasty guitarist hunched forward, thrust a rolled-up wad of paper deep into one nostril, and snorted a line of blood crystals —frozen hemoglobin that I'd smuggled over in a refrigerated canister—with the uncanny grace of a drug addict. He sat back, fangs gleaming, and pawed at his nose. "That's some bodacious shit. Hey, bros," he said, glancing at his fellow band members, "come hit this shit before it melts."

He fetched one of the backstage passes hanging nearby, pried the plastic badge from its lanyard, and used it to split up the crystals, murmuring something in an accent that reminded me of California. Not *the* California, but you know, Cali-foh-nia—the land of beaches, babes, and bros. I retrieved a toothpick from my pocket and punched it through its thin wrapper. "So," I asked no one in particular, "now that ye have the product, who's payin'?"

Another band member stepped out of the shadows to my left, and I don't mean that figuratively, either—the fucker literally stepped out of the shadows. I scowled at him, but hid my surprise, nonchalantly rolling the toothpick from one side of my mouth to the other.

The rest of the band gathered around the dressing room table, following the guitarist's lead by preparing their own snorting utensils—tattered magazine covers, mostly. Typically, you'd do this sort of thing with a dollar-bill, maybe even a Benjamin if you were flush. But fangers like this lot couldn't touch cash directly—in God We Trust and all that. Of course, I didn't really understand why sucking blood the old-fashioned way had suddenly gone out of style. More of a rush, maybe?

"It lasts longer," the vampire next to me explained, catching my mildly curious expression. "It's especially good for shows and stuff. Makes us look, like, less—"

"Creepy?" I offered, my Irish brogue lilting just enough to make it a question.

"Pale," he finished, frowning.

I shrugged. "Listen, I've got places to be," I said, holding out my hand.

"I'm sure you do," he replied, smiling. "Tell you what, why don't you, like, hang around for a bit? Once that wears off," he dipped his head toward the bloody powder smeared across the table's surface, "we may need a pick-me-up." He rested his hand on my arm and our gazes locked.

I blinked, realized what he was trying to pull, and rolled my eyes. His widened in surprise, then shock as I yanked out my toothpick and shoved it through his hand.

"Motherfuck—"

"I want what we agreed on," I declared. "Now. No tricks."

The rest of the band saw what happened and rose faster than I could blink. They circled me, their grins feral...they might have even seemed intimidating if it weren't for the fact that they each had a case of the sniffles —I had to work extra hard not to think about what it felt like to have someone else's blood dripping down my nasal cavity.

I held up a hand.

"Can I ask ye gentlemen a question before we get started?" I asked. "Do ye even *have* what I asked for?"

Two of the band members exchanged looks and shrugged. The guitarist, however, glanced back towards the dressing room, where a brown paper bag sat next to a case full of makeup. He caught me looking and bared his teeth, his fangs stretching until it looked like it would be uncomfortable for him to close his mouth without piercing his own lip.

"Follow-up question," I said, eyeing the vampire I'd stabbed as he gingerly withdrew the toothpick from his hand and flung it across the room with a snarl. "Do ye do each other's make-up? Since, ye know, ye can't use mirrors?"

I was genuinely curious.

The guitarist grunted. "Mike, we have to go on soon."

"Wait a minute. Mike?" I turned to the snarling vampire with a frown. "What happened to *The Vampire Prospero*?" I glanced at the numerous fliers in the dressing room, most of which depicted the band members wading through blood, with Mike in the lead, each one titled *The Vampire Prospero* in *Rocky Horror Picture Show* font. Come to think of it...Mike did look a little like Tim Curry in all that leather and lace.

I was about to comment on the resemblance when Mike spoke up, "Alright, change of plans, bros. We're gonna drain this bitch before the show. We'll look totally—"

"Creepy?" I offered, again.

"Kill her."

Get the full book ONLINE! http://www.shaynesilvers.com/l/206897

(Note: Full chronology of all books in the TempleVerse shown on the 'BOOKS BY SHAYNE SILVERS' page.)

MAKE A DIFFERENCE

Reviews are the most powerful tools in my arsenal when it comes to getting attention for my books. Much as I'd like to, I don't have the financial muscle of a New York publisher.

But I do have something much more powerful and effective than that, and it's something that those publishers would kill to get their hands on.

A committed and loyal bunch of readers.

Honest reviews of my books help bring them to the attention of other readers.

If you've enjoyed this book, I would be very grateful if you could spend just five minutes leaving a review on my book's Amazon page.

Thank you very much in advance.

ACKNOWLEDGMENTS

Team Temple and the Den of Freaks on Facebook have become family to me. I couldn't do it without die-hard readers like them.

I would also like to thank you, the reader. I hope you enjoyed reading *DARK HORSE* as much as I enjoyed writing it. Be sure to check out the two crossover series in the Temple Verse: The **Feathers and Fire Series** and the **Phantom Queen Diaries**.

And last, but definitely not least, I thank my wife, Lexy. Without your support, none of this would have been possible.

ABOUT SHAYNE SILVERS

Shayne is a man of mystery and power, whose power is exceeded only by his mystery...

He currently writes the Amazon Bestselling **Nate Temple** Series, which features a foul-mouthed wizard from St. Louis. He rides a bloodthirsty unicorn, drinks with Achilles, and is pals with the Four Horsemen.

He also writes the Amazon Bestselling **Feathers and Fire** Series—a second series in the TempleVerse. The story follows a rookie spell-slinger named Callie Penrose who works for the Vatican in Kansas City. Her problem? Hell seems to know more about her past than she does.

He coauthors **The Phantom Queen Diaries**—a third series set in The TempleVerse—with Cameron O'Connell. The story follows Quinn MacKenna, a mouthy black magic arms dealer in Boston. All she wants? A round-trip ticket to the Fae realm...and maybe a drink on the house.

He also writes the **Shade of Devil Series**, which tells the story of Sorin Ambrogio—the world's FIRST vampire. He was put into a magical slumber by a Native American Medicine Man when the Americas were first discovered by Europeans. Sorin wakes up after five-hundred years to learn that his protégé, Dracula, stole his reputation and that no one has ever even heard of Sorin Ambrogio. The streets of New York City will run with blood as Sorin reclaims his legend.

Shayne holds two high-ranking black belts, and can be found writing in a coffee shop, cackling madly into his computer screen while pounding shots of espresso. He's hard at work on the newest books in the TempleVerse—You can find updates on new releases or chronological reading order on the next page, his website, or any of his social media accounts. **Follow him online for all sorts of groovy goodies, giveaways, and new release updates:**

Get Down with Shayne Online
www.shaynesilvers.com
info@shaynesilvers.com

facebook.com/shaynesilversfanpage
amazon.com/author/shaynesilvers
bookbub.com/profile/shayne-silvers
instagram.com/shaynesilversofficial
twitter.com/shaynesilvers
goodreads.com/ShayneSilvers

BOOKS BY SHAYNE SILVERS

CHRONOLOGY: All stories in the TempleVerse are shown in chronological order on the following page

NATE TEMPLE SERIES

(Main series in the TempleVerse)

by Shayne Silvers

FAIRY TALE - FREE prequel novella #0 for my subscribers

OBSIDIAN SON

BLOOD DEBTS

GRIMM

SILVER TONGUE

BEAST MASTER

BEERLYMPIAN (Novella #5.5 in the 'LAST CALL' anthology)

TINY GODS

DADDY DUTY (Novella #6.5)

WILD SIDE

WAR HAMMER

NINE SOULS

HORSEMAN

LEGEND

KNIGHTMARE

ASCENSION

CARNAGE

SAVAGE

DARK HORSE

FEATHERS AND FIRE SERIES

(Also set in the TempleVerse)

by Shayne Silvers

UNCHAINED

RAGE

WHISPERS

ANGEL'S ROAR

MOTHERLUCKER (Novella #4.5 in the 'LAST CALL' anthology)

SINNER

BLACK SHEEP

GODLESS

ANGHELLIC

TRINITY

HALO BREAKER

ANGEL DUST

PHANTOM QUEEN DIARIES

(Also set in the TempleVerse)

by Cameron O'Connell & Shayne Silvers

COLLINS (Prequel novella #0 in the 'LAST CALL' anthology)

WHISKEY GINGER

COSMOPOLITAN

OLD FASHIONED

MOTHERLUCKER (Novella #2.5 in the 'LAST CALL' anthology)

DARK AND STORMY

MOSCOW MULE

WITCHES BREW

SALTY DOG

SEA BREEZE

HURRICANE

BRIMSTONE KISS

MOONSHINE

YULETIDE PUNCH

CHRONOLOGICAL ORDER: TEMPLE VERSE

FAIRY TALE (TEMPLE PREQUEL)

OBSIDIAN SON (TEMPLE 1)

BLOOD DEBTS (TEMPLE 2)

GRIMM (TEMPLE 3)

SILVER TONGUE (TEMPLE 4)

BEAST MASTER (TEMPLE 5)

BEERLYMPIAN (TEMPLE 5.5)

TINY GODS (TEMPLE 6)

DADDY DUTY (TEMPLE NOVELLA 6.5)

UNCHAINED (FEATHERS...1)

RAGE (FEATHERS...2)

WILD SIDE (TEMPLE 7)

WAR HAMMER (TEMPLE 8)

WHISPERS (FEATHERS...3)

COLLINS (PHANTOM 0)

WHISKEY GINGER (PHANTOM...1)

NINE SOULS (TEMPLE 9)

COSMOPOLITAN (PHANTOM...2)

ANGEL'S ROAR (FEATHERS...4)

MOTHERLUCKER (FEATHERS 4.5, PHANTOM 3.5)

OLD FASHIONED (PHANTOM...3)

HORSEMAN (TEMPLE 10)

DARK AND STORMY (PHANTOM...4)

MOSCOW MULE (PHANTOM...5)

SINNER (FEATHERS...5)

WITCHES BREW (PHANTOM...6)

LEGEND (TEMPLE...11)

SALTY DOG (PHANTOM...7)

BLACK SHEEP (FEATHERS...6)

GODLESS (FEATHERS...7)

KNIGHTMARE (TEMPLE 12)

ASCENSION (TEMPLE 13)

SEA BREEZE (PHANTOM...8)

HURRICANE (PHANTOM...9)

BRIMSTONE KISS (PHANTOM...10)

ANGHELLIC (FEATHERS...8)

CARNAGE (TEMPLE 14)

MOONSHINE (PHANTOM...11)

TRINITY (FEATHERS...9)

SAVAGE (TEMPLE...15)

HALO BREAKER (FEATHERS...10)

ANGEL DUST (FEATHERS...11)

DARK HORSE (TEMPLE...16)

YULETIDE PUNCH (PHANTOM...12)

SHADE OF DEVIL SERIES

(Not part of the TempleVerse)

by Shayne Silvers

DEVIL'S DREAM

DEVIL'S CRY

DEVIL'S BLOOD

DEVIL'S DUE (coming 2022...)

Printed in Great Britain
by Amazon

76973726R00199